D0485259

VIKING CRITICAL LIBRARY

DEATH OF A SALESMAN

Text and Criticism

ARTHUR MILLER was born in New York City in 1915 and studied at the University of Michigan. His plays include *All My Sons* (1947), *Death of a Salesman* (1949), *The Crucible* (1953), *A View from the Bridge* and *A Memory of Two Mondays* (1955), *After the Fall* (1964), *Incident at Vichy* (1965), *The Price* (1968), *The Creation of the World and Other Business* (1972), and *The American Clock* (1980). He has also written two novels, *Focus* (1945) and *The Misfits*, which was filmed in 1960, and the text for *In Russia* (1969), *In the Country* (1977), and *Chinese Encounters* (1979), three books of photographs by Inge Morath. His most recent works include a memoir, *Timebends* (1987), the plays *The Ride Down Mt. Morgan* (1991), *The Last Yankee* (1993), *Broken Glass* (1994), and *Mr. Peters' Connections* (1999), *Echoes Down the Corridor: Collected Essays, 1944–2000,* and *On Politics and the Art of Acting* (2001). He has twice won the New York Drama Critics Circle Award, and in 1949 he was awarded the Pulitzer Prize. He was the recipient of the National Book Foundation 2001 Medal for Distinguished Contribution to American Letters, he was awarded with the prize Prince of Asturias of Letters in 2002, and most recently in 2003 was awarded the Jerusalem Prize.

GERALD WEALES is Emeritus Professor of English at the University of Pennsylvania. He is the author of *Religion in Modern English Drama, American Drama Since World War II, The Play and Its Parts, Tennessee Williams, The Jumping-Off-Place, Clifford Odets,* and *Canned Goods as Caviar: American Film Comedy of the 1930s.* Mr. Weales is the editor of *Edwardian Plays, The Complete Plays of William Wycherley,* and The Viking Critical Library edition of Arthur Miller's *The Crucible.* He has written a novel, *Tales for the Bluebird,* and two books for children. Mr. Weales won the Goerge Jean Nathan Award for Drama Criticism in 1965.

The Viking Critical Library

THE VIKING CRITICAL LIBRARY

ARTHUR MILLER

Death of a Salesman

TEXT AND CRITICISM

EDITED BY

Gerald Weales

PENGUIN BOOKS

PENGUIN BOOKS
Published by the Penguin Group
Penguin Group (USA) Inc., 375 Hudson Street, New York, New York 10014, U.S.A.
Penguin Group (Canada), 90 Eglinton Avenue East, Suite 700, Toronto,
Ontario, Canada M4P 2Y3 (a division of Pearson Penguin Canada Inc.)
Penguin Books Ltd, 80 Strand, London WC2R 0RL, England
Penguin Ireland, 25 St Stephen's Green, Dublin 2, Ireland (a division of Penguin Books Ltd)
Penguin Group (Australia), 250 Camberwell Road, Camberwell,
Victoria 3124, Australia (a division of Pearson Australia Group Pty Ltd)
Penguin Books India Pvt Ltd, 11 Community Centre, Panchsheel Park, New Delhi – 110 017, India
Penguin Group (NZ), cnr Airborne and Rosedale Roads,
Albany, Auckland 1310, New Zealand (a division of Pearson New Zealand Ltd)
Penguin Books (South Africa) (Pty) Ltd, 24 Sturdee Avenue,
Rosebank, Johannesburg 2196, South Africa

Penguin Books Ltd, Registered Offices: 80 Strand, London WC2R 0RL, England

Death of a Salesman first published in the United States of America
by The Viking Press 1949
The Viking Critical Library *Death of a Salesman* first published
in the United States of America by The Viking Press 1967
Published in Penguin Books 1977
This edition published in Penguin Books 1996

20 19 18

Copyright Arthur Miller, 1949
Copyright © renewed Arthur Miller, 1977
Copyright © The Viking Press, Inc., 1967
All rights reserved

LIBRARY OF CONGRESS CATALOGING IN PUBLICATION DATA
Weales, Gerald Clifford, 1925– comp.
Arthur Miller: Death of a salesman, text and criticism.
Reprint of the 1967 ed. published by The Viking Press, New York,
in series: The Viking critical library.
1. Miller, Arthur, 1915– Death of a salesman.
I. Miller, Arthur, 1915– Death of a salesman. 1977.
[PS3525.15156D438 1977] 812'.5'2 76–51779
ISBN 0 14 02.4773 4

Printed in the United States of America
Set in Linotype Electra

Contents

Introduction

I

This introduction is not even going to pretend to have the last word on *Death of a Salesman*. There have already been a great many words written about Arthur Miller's play—far more than anyone could want to read—words written by the playwright himself, by reviewers in newspapers and magazines, by critics in literary quarterlies and scholarly journals, by textbook editors in introductions, by academic hacks in trots called "Notes," by graduate students in dissertations, by undergraduate students in term papers, by high school students in daily themes. As long as the play is dramatically alive—and the television broadcast on May 8, 1966, reconfirmed its vitality—and as long as that life can be seen, however imperfectly, on the page and in the classroom, the flow of words will not stop. This volume includes, besides the play itself (which may well be the last word on *Death of a Salesman*), a tiny sampling of the words that have been spoken over the grave of Willy Loman—a corpse who happily refuses to stay dead, who ever since he first died the death of a salesman on the stage of the Morosco Theatre on February 10, 1949, has come back to elicit sympathy, evoke pity, provoke anger, stir up controversy, ask for judicial appraisal.

It might be assumed that an editor putting together a collection of essays always chooses those he admires, but that is the case only if he is editing a bedside reader, a catchall containing, as Maria sang in *The Sound of Music*, "a few of my favorite things." This collection has quite another job to do. It is an attempt to present a wide variety of opinions about and inter-

pretations of *Death of a Salesman* in the hope that the reader
will be forced to defend or to modify his own view of the
play from the attacks or the seductions of critics who cannot
see it that way at all. There are essays here that I like very
much and others that I cannot stand at all. There are critics
here whom I admire for their liveliness and their wit, but whose
opinions seem to me dead wrong (that is, they disagree with
me) and others whose ideas are beyond reproach but whose style
sends me running for cover. It amuses me that the most anti-
"Salesman" essay in the volume is written by a man whose reading of the play is almost identical with mine, but who sees vices
where I see virtues. I have no intention of using this introduction to praise or blame essays by name or number; in this context, my opinion is of limited use to the reader. There is an essay
of my own included, but, like its neighbors, it is elbowing its
way through the crowd, trying to catch the reader's eye. *Look,
look,* each of the selections is saying, *from here—from where I
stand—you get a perfect view of* Death of a Salesman. The
play that can be pinned down, labeled accurately, seen clearly
from one view is a dead one, and "Salesman" is certainly not
that. Although each of the contributors has *the* answer, the
collection as a whole is designed not to provide answers, but
questions.

The selections are divided into a number of categories, based
on what they are rather than on what they say. First of all, there
are the author's own remarks. What an author thinks he did in
a work or what he tried to do may be illuminating to the reader,
but once a work is finished, the author, looking back at it, is not
much more trustworthy than any other reader. Bertrand Russell
is supposed to have said of *Principia Mathematica*, which he
wrote with Alfred North Whitehead, "When we were working
on it, only God, Whitehead, and I knew what it meant. Now
Whitehead is dead and I have forgotten." The story is probably
apocryphal, but it is a cautionary tale worth keeping in mind
as you approach what Arthur Miller says about *Death of a Salesman.* The selections here include essays written when the play
was new and second thoughts written or spoken (there is a

radio interview) almost ten years later. The system of love, which Miller assigns to Biff in the Introduction to *Collected Plays*, is never mentioned in his early comments on "Salesman." A playwright, like any other man, grows and changes over the years, and it is not surprising that he comes to see an early work, if he is still attracted to it, in terms which fit the present cast of his mind. At about the time he wrote the Introduction, he was working on *The Misfits*, the "cinema-novel" in which this concept of love figured centrally. Just recently, in an interview with Olga Carlisle and Rose Styron,[1] he said that "Salesman" is about power and who should wield it. I assume the remark grew out of his present intellectual concerns, but the immediate impetus for any comment and its distance in time from the act of creation does not make it less valid, less perceptive than what he wrote then. Besides, back in 1949, A. Howard Fuller had already described the play as a power struggle, although I am quite sure that Miller was not recalling Fuller's article as he developed his ideas about power for the interviewers.

Following the selections from Miller is a long excerpt from Jo Mielziner's account of the production of "Salesman" from the designer's viewpoint. Aside from what it may teach about the play itself, Mielziner's diary—along with the paragraphs on auditions and rehearsals excerpted from the Miller article "The American Theater"—helps to remind the reader that *Death of a Salesman* is a play, something to be put on a stage. Much of the commentary on "Salesman" gives too little attention to that fact. As the reader makes his way through these essays and finds himself involved in general questions of theme and genre and social significance, he should keep Mielziner somewhere in the back of his mind, remembering that Willy Loman is not a concept but a character who has to be given flesh by an actor.

Of the essays on the play, there are three different kinds. First, the reviews. For the most part, they were written after the immediate experience of the play on stage; in most cases, the writer had no occasion to examine the printed play, to

[1] For works mentioned in this introduction which are not included in the volume itself, see the bibliography, pp. 422–426.

reconfirm his first impressions. Newspaper reviewers, working against a demanding deadline, have to decide what they think and to get those thoughts on paper, often in less than an hour. For that reason, Robert Garland and William Hawkins can hardly be expected to turn out carefully styled essays; at best, they can offer a mixture of opinion and reporting, held together by their personal journalistic mannerisms. For instance, the Garland review, despite its briefness, is marked by repetition and his trying habit of calling the audience the "congregation," but he does give a reasonably clear idea of what the play is about as well as a useful account of audience reaction. Reviewers writing for weeklies, monthlies, or quarterlies presumably have more time to ponder what they have seen and more time to turn the proper phrases to communicate it. Occasionally, as in T. C. Worsley's seemingly endless dinner metaphor, one has the impression that a handle into the play has been grasped and held too tightly because a magazine deadline has to be met. For all their differences in style, all the reviewers, from Garland in the *Journal-American* to Eleanor Clark in *Partisan Review*, have one thing in common, the job of bringing to their readers a reaction which is less an attempt to penetrate the play than to convince the reader that he should or should not see it. That the review is primarily an instrument of persuasion does not mean, however, that it cannot provide an analysis of a play that will withstand the later, more leisurely examinations of critics whose trade does not force them to be in a hurry.

Technically, the Ivor Brown article, "As London Sees Willy Loman," might be called a review, since he is presumably writing only after having seen the London production. I have placed it with the essays on "Salesman," however, for Brown is not so much reporting on as interpreting the play by an examination of English reactions to it. The essays in this group are primarily analyses of the play, usually from carefully defined points of view. Brown clearly writes as an Englishman. Fuller as a businessman. Daniel E. Schneider as a psychoanalyst. Joseph A. Hynes as a self-confessed hatchet man. John Gassner as a dramatic critic, working comfortably within the frame of the history of drama. However idiosyncratic an approach to the play may be—say George Ross's report on the Yiddish "Salesman"— it may illuminate aspects of the play which the reader has failed to notice.

The third group of essays are attempts to see Miller's work as a whole, usually through a thematic device which, by a little stretching, can be made to fit all his plays. Such essays have a place in this volume because they put "Salesman" into the larger context of the playwright's work. I almost said "total work," but that would have been inaccurate. My own essay, which is the most recent one in that group, carries Miller only through *The Misfits*; most of the essays are built on the five *Collected Plays*. Some studies of Miller—Sheila Huftel's book, Robert Hogan's pamphlet, Jean Gould's essay—take in *After the Fall* and *Incident at Vichy*, but none of them do so in a way that adds anything to an understanding of "Salesman."[2] The reason, I think, is that the hiatus between the London production of the revised *A View from the Bridge* (1956) and the New York production of *After the Fall* (1964) marked a change in Miller which carried him a great distance from *Death of a Salesman*. Technical and even thematic likenesses can be found between "Salesman" and the later plays, particularly "Fall," but their dissimilarities are much more obvious. For that reason, I have limited the general essays on Miller to those which deal with his work of the 1940s and 1950s.

The final section of the book, the works which I have labeled "Analogues," has a double function—critical and charitable. Critics often find it useful in discussing a work to compare it to another which is in some way analogous, as William Wiegand does in his essay when he compares Biff, as ex-football hero,

---

[2] I include in this summary dismissal my own recent essay, "Arthur Miller's Shifting Image of Man." Since it was designed as a United States Information Agency lecture on Miller's work, it contains much discussion of "Salesman" but, except for a brief comparison between "Salesman" and "Fall," it adds nothing to the assumptions about "Salesman" that inform the essay included in this volume. The new essay is really more concerned with examining the recent plays in the light of the ideas put forward in the earlier one than it is in re-examining the early plays, including "Salesman," in the face of "Fall" and "Vichy."

to Ben in Clifford Odets' *Paradise Lost*. There are studies of *Death of a Salesman* which attempt with minimal success to get to the play through *Babbitt* and *King Lear*.[3] There is hardly space here for a second full-length play, be it "Lear" or "Lost," or for a novel. I have, however, included the deaths of two other salesmen—Eudora Welty's short story "Death of a Traveling Salesman," which Eleanor Clark used to beat Miller in her review of "Salesman," and Tennessee Williams's one-act play "The Last of My Solid Gold Watches"—and a story about another "lost" athletic hero—Irwin Shaw's "The Eighty-Yard Run." There is also a how-not-to chapter from a how-to book on selling, first published in 1909, about the time that Willy, had he existed in fact rather than in Miller's and our fancy, would have made his decision to become a salesman. The charitable function of these selections derives from the suspicion that a reader, faced with essay after essay discussing the author and his play, however good or odd those essays may be, will want to climb the walls after the twentieth repetition of the words "tragedy," "society," "identity." At that point, a story or another play might seem as welcome as an oasis in a desert movie.

I I

This book, as I suggested earlier, is to provide questions, not answers, about *Death of a Salesman*. I could invent questions—and I may suggest a few before I get out of this introduction[4]—but the primary intention was to use existing reviews and essays to present those questions that have grown up, naturally or unnaturally, as criticism of the play developed. The initial reception of the play—the newspaper reviews and those in popular magazines—was extremely favorable. "Salesman" became "the play of the moment," which, in the context of Broadway, means that it was given extensive attention—comment, interviews,

---

[3] See the entries for George W. Couchman and Paul N. Siegel in the bibliography.

[4] Also see "Topics for Discussion and Papers," pp. 415–421.

pictures—in all the popular media. Perhaps as a reaction to this, the reviewers in the more intellectual weeklies and in the monthlies and quarterlies turned doubting eyes on it, declared for it with reservations, or against it with enthusiasm. In time, as is the case with most plays (they are either accepted as a part of a country's repertory or are forgotten), *Death of a Salesman* became more a fact, less a bone of contention. At least, the grounds of the dispute shifted. Critics worried less about whether or not "Salesman," like a kitten, should be encouraged to thrive or drowned at birth. It was obviously a lively animal, capable of looking after itself, so critics began to quarrel about what it is. On occasion (see Joseph A. Hynes's essay) that quarrel could stir up some heat, but for the most part the obvious merits of "Salesman" and its increasing acceptance as one of the most important American plays made it a subject of discussion, explication, and analysis. Value judgments were still made—and must be made by every reader or playgoer who meets "Salesman"—but more and more the emphasis has been on questions about the play which must precede any judgment. Those questions, as this collection shows, have been with us since the play opened, but in the first reactions to the play the need to say *yes* or *no* to it had precedence over the kind of questioning that concerns us here. Anyone reading through the essays in this volume will see at once that certain problems keep recurring—about the genre of the play, its style, its subject matter, its characters. I want to take a few paragraphs to point out the most obvious of these, confident that the careful reader will find more of his own and—more important—find the ones for which he thinks he has the answers.

First of all, the problem of tragedy. With seventeen years of "Salesman" criticism piled up in front of me, I cannot avoid the obvious fact that the question most often asked about the play is: is it or isn't it a tragedy? It is a question that interests me not at all, but in a volume like this it cannot be escaped. When I undertook to edit this book, I told the publishers that I planned to keep out of it all considerations of "Salesman" as tragedy. It was a small *hubris* of my own. Whatever essay I turned to, whatever comment I read, the tragic question came roaring down on me, directly, obliquely, implicitly—often out of Miller's own mouth. In fact, it is almost certainly Miller who is responsible for the avalanche of genre-defining criticism. In the Introduction to *Collected Plays*, Miller pretends surprise at "the academy's charge that Willy lacked the 'stature' for the tragic hero," just as though he had not provoked the academy into charging. Certainly William Hawkins' calling it a "classical tragedy" in the pages of the *World-Telegram* or A. Howard Fuller's casual acceptance of the tragic label in *Fortune* was not likely to stir any academic dovecotes. Two weeks after "Salesman" opened, Miller's essay "Tragedy and the Common Man" appeared in *The New York Times*. There was no mention of "Salesman" in the article, but there was no mention of Joseph Wood Krutch or Aristotle either and their thoughts on tragedy were obviously being put in their place. The primness of the piece, the assumption that it was too nice to mention the name of the play it was defending, annoyed many readers, a number of whom took to their typewriters to straighten out the straightener-out. That much reprinted essay (it is in this volume, too) has echoed down the years, pulling a host of is-it-or-isn't-it analyses in its wake.

Juliet, musing on her balcony, says, "So Romeo would, were he not Romeo call'd,/Retain that dear perfection which he owes/Without that title." So "Salesman" would, were it not tragedy called, retain. . . . Yet, remembering what happened to those two Veronese kids when they forgot the importance of labels, I am willing to consider the argument of those who think it important to hang the exact generic definition on Miller's play. Their case is most succinctly stated by Joseph A. Hynes, for whom the play is not a tragedy according to the definition he uses:

. . . attempts to assign a name arise not merely from some pointless academania for labels, but from a desire to *know* and name differences. Thus if one wishes to call Mr. Miller's play a tragedy, one must assign a new name to *Hamlet*.

It is my perverse preoccupation with each play as an individual work that makes me suspect that they can best be differentiated if we call them by the names they have been given, that we can come closer to the essential plays if we call one *Death of a Salesman* and the other *Hamlet* than if we call one *tragedy* and the other *non-tragedy*. Besides, I suspect that there is less innocence in the label search than Hynes's words suggest. For many critics (and, alas, for Miller, too), the word "tragedy" is a value judgment; it gives the play it is attached to the kind of importance Willy found in the punching bag that carried Gene Tunney's signature. Since aestheticians and critics have spent the last 2500 years trying and failing to agree on a definition of tragedy, it then becomes possible for any critic who wants to praise "Salesman" because he likes it or damn it because he does not to set forth his definition and then show that "Salesman" does or does not conform to it. A number of the reviews and essays in this collection do just that. For this reason, it is best to approach the critic with "tragedy" in his mouth warily, suspicious of what he is up to. Not that all such essays are *parti pris*. Sometimes the critic is playing the defining game for its own sweet sake, as George de Schweinitz seems to be doing in his essay. Sometimes, generic definition is used as a critical tool, a way of getting at the author's work, as in William B. Dillingham's essay, in which he uses Hegel's definition of tragedy as an approach to thematic recurrence in Miller.

Essays that deal with theme, like Dillingham's, which is concerned with "loss of conscience," or Wiegand's examination of the "the man who knows" or my own preoccupation with the "image of man," are attempts to see Miller's plays (including "Salesman") in terms other than "tragic" and "nontragic." Such attempts are certain to run up against another major question about "Salesman." To what extent is it social criticism? An attack on capitalism? Certain critical attitudes toward American society, as Miller's own remarks indicate, lay at the center of the play, but it cannot—as Harold Clurman and John Gassner indicate in their discussions of its social implications—be reduced to an old-fashioned propaganda play. Even Eleanor Clark, who sometimes seems to assume that such a play was what Miller wanted to write, has to struggle with the apparent contradictions in it. Raymond Williams, who of all the critics in this volume is most involved with the social utility of literature, sees "Salesman" as a treatment of alienation, in the classical Marxist rather than the existential sense, and sees in Miller the beginnings of a new social drama. On the other hand, Fuller, from his executive's desk, sees the play as one man's failure and not as an indictment of the system. You pays your commitment and you takes your choice.

The tragic question (is it or isn't it?) and the social question (does it or doesn't it?) can only be answered by deciding what happens in the play. Decision there depends on how one interprets the characters and there has been plenty of difference of opinion about Willy and his family. Is Willy, for instance, a born loser, or is he a game little fighter who, having been sold a bill of goods about the American Dream, keeps slugging it out against unequal odds? Does he have the wrong dream? Is there a right one for him? Is he the "loud-mouthed dolt and emotional babe-in-the-woods" that John Gassner calls him and, if so, does his love for Biff, as Gassner suggests, somehow let him transcend that characterization? Ivor Brown calls him a "poor, flashy, self-deceiving little man," but both Schneider, who points out that his name is "low-man," and Eleanor Clark, who assumes he is "common man," turn that reading into a kind of abstraction. Wiegand calls him a victim, and Raymond Williams seems to agree since he finds him a social-martyrdom image. Hynes says he is a schizophrenic. Clurman is interested in him as a salesman, but Fuller, who has an understandable interest in salesmen, prefers him as Everyman. Bierman, Hart, and Johnson, performing as a trio, find a basic conflict between the salesman and the man in him. It should be clear from this cacophonous chorus of opinion that Willy Loman is a complex character, able to slither away from the single pin that hopes to fix him to a particular label in a particular display case. It is possible that he is all these things at once and that one reason why it is so difficult to find an overriding theme in *Death of a*

Salesman is that it is a play about the last terrible day of a man and about the flood of facts and lies, of reality and fantasy, of the actual and the potential that made him and killed him. Surely, the fascinating thing about Willy is not that he can be reduced to a representative man in some illustrative drama or other, but that he takes to the stage (takes flesh) as a man who just cannot keep his mouth shut and who never understands when he is condemning and when he is defending himself.

When I first saw "Salesman" and first read it, I assumed that Willy was the play's protagonist. I still do, although I am less complacent about my assumption than I was then. Not long after "Salesman" opened, I went to Georgia Tech—my first teaching job—ready to spread *the* word about Miller's play to that band of incipient engineers. I still remember the day the play came up for discussion. We were meeting on the lawn —it was spring—and I stood, *my* truth in my hand, the class a semicircle in front of me. As first one student and then another began to speak, the circle seemed to close; I found myself surrounded by a ring of potentially hostile strangers. They had apparently read some other play altogether and they were not prepared to talk about an elderly salesman and his petty problems. It is Biff's story, they insisted; it is a play about a son's troubles with his father. And so it is—in part, at least—and an Oedipal ritual as well if we believe Schneider. At the time, I supposed that the reaction of my class was simply a matter of easy identification, the natural response of a pack of sons. Now, I recognize—and several of the essays in this book illustrate— that there are solid dramatic reasons for assuming that Biff is the character in "Salesman" with whom an audience identifies. Since plays customarily deal with some kind of discovery and since Willy's recognition of Biff's love does not alter his basic self-delusion about success, the audience's attention, sympathy, concern turn to Biff who—if we are to believe, among others, Clurman and Gassner—finds his "true self," finds understanding. Hynes agrees with this reading of Biff and assumes that the shift in audience attention breaks the structure of the play, pushes Willy out of the spotlight. There are a number of questions one might ask about Biff—such as, what are the implications of his self-discovery in relation to Willy? to the play? to American society? to the accepted idea of success? The basic question, however, is whether or not Biff makes a discovery. Miller seems to believe that he does, as he indicates in the *Times* article that celebrated "Salesman's" first birthday and in his consideration in the Introduction to *Collected Plays* of what Biff's new knowledge means. Still, I think I hear the voice of Tennessee Williams explaining why he never really liked the Broadway third act to *Cat on a Hot Tin Roof*: "I don't believe that a conversation, however revelatory, ever effects so immediate a change in the heart or even the conduct of a person in Brick's state of spiritual disrepair." Read Biff for Brick and it is a siren song I want to hear. For me, the Requiem of the play is ironic, the gathering of a group of people who never understood Willy at all, and how much more effective it would be if Biff's "I know who I am, kid," were taken as still another sample of Loman self-delusion, the true legacy (the insurance being the false) of Willy.

The neat ironic ending that I so admire in *Salesman* poses problems of its own. It is not a solution to the main question about Biff; it is questionable in its own right. The Requiem has been attacked for its sentimentality, for what Hynes calls its "Hallmark-Card flourish." Certainly, productions usually go for easy tears when they stage it. The questions to be asked of the Requiem are: Is it tearful? If so, did Miller or the audience put the tears there? If Miller, what does that imply about the play as a whole? If the audience, what does that imply about the way a society deals with potential irritants?

Interpreting the character of Linda may be one way of answering the question about the tears in the Requiem. Any actress worth her Equity card can milk Linda's words at Willy's grave and bring out handkerchiefs all over the audience. I doubt that that was Miller's intention, but a great many critics—see Eleanor Clark's complaint about Mildred Dunnock's "high-pitched nobility" in the role—assume that it was. The important question about Linda does not concern her ability to make us cry. What

one must decide about her is whether she is Willy's constant
mainstay ("the perfect wife," to use T. C. Worsley's words) or
whether, as Dillingham says, she is a contributing force in his
fatal commitment to the wrong dream. The majority of the
critics from the beginning have voted for Linda as the character
the audience should admire. John Mason Brown saw her as the
"marriage vow . . . made flesh." Robert Garland assumed that
she was the one character in the play who could see clearly
what was going to happen. William Beyer went so far as to
decide that the play is "the mother's tragedy." Before you join
the wife-and-mother bandwagon, however, you might do well
to look closely at Linda in operation, particularly in the scenes
with Ben and in the scene in which Willy comes back from
New England lying and then slowly admitting the truth about
the smallness of his sales. There is no doubt that Linda is a
good wife, but there is doubt about what that means in the
context of the play. It is not necessary to decide, as all those
ladies who wrote to Miller did (he mentions them in the Introduction to *Collected Plays*), that Linda is the central character
in "Salesman," but it is important to decide just what her
function is in the play.

Nor should the lesser characters be ignored. In his article,
Schneider recaps the plot of the play as though he were Hap
telling a dream that he had. He does so because it is important
to him that both Willy and Hap are younger sons, indications
that the basic "and hidden" motivation is "the guilt of the
younger son for his hatred of his older brother." No one need
buy Schneider's reading of the play, but the question of what
Hap is doing in it needs to be answered. And what of Charley?
Is Hynes correct when he assumes that he fails as a functional
character? And what of Bernard? of Howard? of Ben? Are these
acceptable characters or stereotypes? The answers to these questions involve the whole problem of the play's style. If the play
belongs, as Gassner says it does, in the tradition of American
realism, then those characters may stand out as unreal, stock.
If, however, Miller's borrowing of expressionistic techniques
allows him to use a type character when he needs one to make

a point, they may be functioning legitimately within a particular scene.

In this brief hit-and-run trip through the Miller criticism, I have touched on most of the questions that have worried critics confronted with the play. As the essays in the volume indicate, there are no easy answers. Most of the questions are still open, waiting for a definitive answer (which will not be found), and the newcomer approaching "Salesman" for the first time—particularly if he has made his way through the conflicting voices of the commentators—may come on a fresh way of seeing—if only in self-defense. If he does, it will probably be because he has made an attempt to answer some of the questions mentioned here or some of the other questions—touched on in the essays in this volume, or listed in "Topics for Discussion"—that will lead to a fuller understanding of "Salesman." Questions, for instance, about Miller's prescribed use of music; about light changes indicated in the stage directions; about the ways in which he uses and departs from ordinary language; about the comic lines and how they are to be read; about the order in which the scenes come, how a particular scene from the past is triggered by a word or phrase in the present; about . . . about . . . about . . . about . . . but any reader with a mind of his own and a little imagination will already have had my questions and those of the other critics up to here (you can write the stage direction to suit your own visual image). He will want to invent questions of his own, but not until he has read the play and responded to it and begun to wonder why and how the response came.

G. W.

November 1 9 6 6

Chronology

1915   Arthur Miller born in New York City.

1936   *Honors at Dawn*, first play, produced at the University of Michigan. Wins university's Avery Hopwood Award.

1937   *No Villain* produced at university.

1938   *No Villain*, revised and entitled *They Too Arise*, produced at the university. Wins another Hopwood Award and a prize of the Theater Guild Bureau of New Plays. Graduates from the University of Michigan. Joins the Federal Theater Project.

1944   During war, writes radio plays. *The Man Who Had All the Luck* produced in New York. Miller gathers material in Army camps, which becomes basis for screenplay of *The Story of G.I. Joe* and for a book of reportage, *Situation Normal*.

1945   *Focus*, a novel, published.

1947   *All My Sons* produced. Wins New York Drama Critics' Circle Award and Donaldson Award.

1948   Film version of *All My Sons* produced.

1949   *Death of a Salesman* produced and published. Wins Pulitzer prize, New York Drama Critics' Circle Award, Antoinette Perry Award, American Newspaper Guild Award, Theater Club Award, and Donaldson Award.

1950   *An Enemy of the People*, Miller's adaption of Ibsen's play, produced and published.

1951   Film version of *Death of a Salesman* produced.

1953   *The Crucible* produced and published. Wins Antoinette Perry Award.

1955   *A Memory of Two Mondays* and *A View from the Bridge* produced and published. Wins New York Drama Critics' Circle Award for "View."

1 9 5 6   Miller appears before House Un-American Activities Committee; refuses to inform on others. *A View from the Bridge,* revised, produced in London. Miller receives honorary degree from University of Michigan.

1 9 5 7   Prosecution and conviction for contempt of Congress. *Collected Plays* published.

1 9 5 8   Contempt conviction reversed by higher court. Miller elected to The National Institute of Arts and Letters. Film version of *The Crucible* produced in France.

1 9 5 9   Miller wins Gold Medal for Drama from The National Institute of Arts and Letters.

1 9 6 1   *The Misfits,* a movie, produced and screenplay published.

1 9 6 2   Film version of *A View from the Bridge* produced.

1 9 6 4   *After the Fall,* commissioned as the first production of the Lincoln Center Repertory Company, produced at the ANTA–Washington Square Theater. *After the Fall* published. *Incident at Vichy* produced in December.

1 9 6 5   *Incident at Vichy* published. Miller elected International President of P.E.N. (Poets, Essayists, and Novelists).

1 9 6 6   Television production of *Death of a Salesman.*

1 9 6 7   *I Don't Need You Any More,* a collection of short stories, published.

THE TEXT

The reproductions on the following pages are from a typescript of *Death of a Salesman* which Arthur Miller was working on about a month before the first rehearsal. The revisions are in his handwriting.

Linda

His blue suit. He's so handsome in that suit. He could be a...
anything in that suit! ~~I think the whole situation is in for a~~
~~change now, Willy, I really mean it.~~

Willy

There's no question, no question at all. *(Gee,)* ~~I'll~~ On the way home tonight
~~I'll~~ *(I'm gonna)* ~~I'll~~ buy some seeds.

Linda

That's ~~a~~ *(a be)* wonderful. ~~idea. Get carrots and beets and—~~
Bit not enough sun gets back there. Nothing'll grow anymore.

Willy

~~Sure, because after all, we do get three hours of sun in~~
~~the backyard.~~ *I know. I just feel like a little diggin'.*

~~Linda~~

~~(Leans over to him, kisses him)~~
~~Willy, when the garden comes to your mind I know you're feeling~~
~~right again.~~

Willy

(You wait,) ~~Linda,~~ kid, before it's all over we're gonna get a little place
out in the country, and I'll raise some vegetables, a couple of
chickens...

Linda

Peacefulness comes into your eyes as soon as you talk about it.

Willy

It's really ~~what~~ *(all)* I ~~always~~ *(ever)* wanted. And maybe they'd get married,
and come for a weekend. I'd build a little guesthouse...cause
in the country there's so much room. And a little playhouse for
the children, and a seesaw, and a nice red swing... A thing like
that would put new life into me. Cause I got so many fine tools,
all I'd need would be a little lumber and peace of mind.

Linda

(Joyfully)
You'll do it yet, dear! *(Opening his jacket) I sewed the lining...*

Willy

What time is he seeing ~~Jonas?~~ *(Oliver)*

Linda

I don't know; he went in bright and early to get an appointment.
Imagine both of them working together in sporting goods! All
their training would come into use.

Willy

(Nods)
I could build two guesthouses, so when they come they'd both have
privacy. What enjoyment! - specially with a couple of kids around.
Did he decide how much he's going to ask Jonas for?

                    Linda
He didn't mention it, but I imagine ten or fifteen thousand.

                    Willy
          (Nods)
I'd build both guesthouses alike. Wouldn't that be something?--
our house in the middle, and two little guesthouses on each side.

                    Linda
You going to talk to Howard today?

                    Willy
Yeah, I'm going right now.
          (He gets up)
He gets in about ten thirty. I'll put it to him straight and
simple: *WE'LL JUST HAVE TO TAKE ME OFF THE ROAD.*

                    Linda *(HELPING HIM ON WITH HIS JACKET)*
Because they must have some kind of work in New York for a man
like you.

                    Willy
Beyond the shadow of a doubt. After all, a man can't drive a
car till he drops. There's a limit after all.

                    Linda *(HELPING HIM ON WITH HIS JACKET)*
And, Willy, don't forget to ask him for a little advance, because
we've got the insurance premium! ~~on the first.~~ *IT'S THE GRACE PERIOD NOW.*

                    Willy
That's a hundred..?

                    Linda
A hundred-and-eight, sixty-eight. ~~Because we're in the grace
period right now.~~

                    ~~Willy~~
~~Oh, he'll let me have it; I'll talk to him...~~

                    ~~Linda~~
Because we're a little short again and...

                    Willy
          (Irked)
Why are we short?

                    Linda
          (Apologizing)
Well, you had the motor job on the car...

                    Willy
That goddam Studebaker, what else is there?

Linda

Well you got one more payment on the refrigerator...

Willy

But it just broke again...

Linda
(Fearing his arousal)
Well, it's old, dear...

Willy

I told you we should ~~buy~~ WE BOUGHT a well-advertised machine...

~~Linda~~

~~But in those days it was well-advertised.~~

~~Willy~~

~~(He is angry at her)~~
~~Not as well-advertised as General Electric.~~ Charley bought a
General Electric and it's twenty years old and it's still good!

Linda (ANSWERING) (ALMOST BURSTING OUT)

~~well, funny something myself.~~
BUT WOULD YOU PAY FOR A GENERAL ELECTRIC?!

Willy WILLY (CONTINUING)

You're always finding bargains! Once in my life I would like to
own something outright before it's broken! I'm always in a race
with the junkyard! I just finished paying for the car and it's
on its last legs. The refrigerator consumes belts like a goddam
maniac. They time those things...they time them so when you finally paid for them, they're used up. ~~The next time we buy some-~~
~~thing it's for cash, and I don't want any bargains—only well-~~
~~advertised brands!~~

A
I NOT TO
IN YOU, THAT'S

Linda

~~Say that~~ refrigerator was a very good...

Willy

Very good! Who the hell ever bought a Hastings refrigerator but
you?

Linda—— (HOW COMELY)

~~(She goes up to him gomelinly)~~
All right dear, don't argue any more.

Willy

So how much does it all come to?

Linda

All told, about two hundred dollars would carry us. But that
includes the last payment on the mortgage. After this payment,
Willy, the house belongs to us.

Death of a Salesman

Certain private conversations
in two acts and a requiem

BY ARTHUR MILLER

STAGED BY ELIA KAZAN

Original Cast

IN ORDER OF APPEARANCE

WILLY LOMAN	Lee J. Cobb
LINDA	Mildred Dunnock
BIFF	Arthur Kennedy
HAPPY	Cameron Mitchell
BERNARD	Don Keefer
THE WOMAN	Winnifred Cushing
CHARLEY	Howard Smith
UNCLE BEN	Thomas Chalmers
HOWARD WAGNER	Alan Hewitt
JENNY	Ann Driscoll
STANLEY	Tom Pedi
MISS FORSYTHE	Constance Ford
LETTA	Hope Cameron

The setting and lighting were designed by JO MIELZINER.
The incidental music was composed by ALEX NORTH.
The costumes were designed by JULIA SZE.
Presented by Kermit Bloomgarden and Walter Fried at the
Morosco Theatre in New York on February 10, 1949.

The action takes place in Willy Loman's house and yard and in various places he visits in the New York and Boston of today.

Throughout the play, in the stage directions, left and right mean stage left and stage right.

Act One

A melody is heard, played upon a flute. It is small and fine, telling of grass and trees and the horizon. The curtain rises.

Before us is the Salesman's house. We are aware of towering, angular shapes behind it, surrounding it on all sides. Only the blue light of the sky falls upon the house and forestage; the surrounding area shows an angry glow of orange. As more light appears, we see a solid vault of apartment houses around the small, fragile-seeming home. An air of the dream clings to the place, a dream rising out of reality. The kitchen at center seems actual enough, for there is a kitchen table with three chairs, and a refrigerator. But no other fixtures are seen. At the back of the kitchen there is a draped entrance, which leads to the living-room. To the right of the kitchen, on a level raised two feet, is a bedroom furnished only with a brass bedstead and a straight chair. On a shelf over the bed a silver athletic trophy stands. A window opens onto the apartment house at the side.

Behind the kitchen, on a level raised six and a half feet, is the boys' bedroom, at present barely visible. Two beds are dimly seen, and at the back of the room a dormer window. (This bedroom is above the unseen living-room.) At the left a stairway curves up to it from the kitchen.

The entire setting is wholly or, in some places, partially transparent. The roof-line of the house is one-dimensional; under and over it we see the apartment buildings. Before the house lies an apron, curving beyond the forestage into the orchestra. This forward area serves as the back yard as well as the locale of all Willy's imaginings and of his city scenes. Whenever the action is in the present the actors observe the imaginary wall-lines, entering the house only through its door at the left. But in the scenes of the past these boundaries are broken, and characters enter or leave a room by stepping "through" a wall onto the forestage.

From the right, Willy Loman, the Salesman, enters, carrying two large sample cases. The flute plays on. He hears but is not aware of it. He is past sixty years of age, dressed quietly. Even as he crosses the stage to the doorway of the house, his exhaustion is apparent. He unlocks the door, comes into the kitchen, and thankfully lets his burden down, feeling the soreness of his palms. A word-sigh escapes his lips—it might be "Oh, boy, oh, boy." He closes the door, then carries his cases out into the living-room, through the draped kitchen doorway.

Linda, his wife, has stirred in her bed at the right. She gets out and puts on a robe, listening. Most often jovial, she has developed an iron repression of her exceptions to Willy's behavior—she more than loves him, she admires him, as though his mercurial nature, his temper, his massive dreams and little cruelties, served her only as sharp reminders of the turbulent longings within him, longings which she shares but lacks the temperament to utter and follow to their end.

LINDA, *hearing Willy outside the bedroom, calls with some trepidation:* Willy!

WILLY: It's all right. I came back.

LINDA: Why? What happened? *Slight pause.* Did something happen, Willy?

WILLY: No, nothing happened.

LINDA: You didn't smash the car, did you?

WILLY, *with casual irritation:* I said nothing happened. Didn't you hear me?

LINDA: Don't you feel well?

WILLY: I'm tired to the death. *The flute has faded away. He sits on the bed beside her, a little numb.* I couldn't make it. I just couldn't make it, Linda.

LINDA, *very carefully, delicately:* Where were you all day? You look terrible.

WILLY: I got as far as a little above Yonkers. I stopped for a cup of coffee. Maybe it was the coffee.

LINDA: What?

WILLY, *after a pause:* I suddenly couldn't drive any more. The car kept going off onto the shoulder, y'know?

LINDA, *helpfully:* Oh. Maybe it was the steering again. I don't think Angelo knows the Studebaker.

WILLY: No, it's me, it's me. Suddenly I realize I'm goin' sixty miles an hour and I don't remember the last five minutes. I'm—I can't seem to—keep my mind to it.

LINDA: Maybe it's your glasses. You never went for your new glasses.

WILLY: No, I see everything. I came back ten miles an hour. It took me nearly four hours from Yonkers.

LINDA, *resigned:* Well, you'll just have to take a rest, Willy, you can't continue this way.

WILLY: I just got back from Florida.

LINDA: But you didn't rest your mind. Your mind is overactive, and the mind is what counts, dear.

WILLY: I'll start out in the morning. Maybe I'll feel better in the morning. *She is taking off his shoes.* These goddam arch supports are killing me.

LINDA: Take an aspirin. Should I get you an aspirin? It'll soothe you.

WILLY, *with wonder:* I was driving along, you understand? And I was fine. I was even observing the scenery. You can imagine, me looking at scenery, on the road every week of my life. But it's so beautiful up there, Linda, the trees are so thick, and the sun is warm. I opened the windshield and just let the warm air bathe over me. And then all of a·sudden I'm goin' off the road! I'm tellin' ya, I absolutely forgot I was driving. If I'd've gone the other way over the white line I might've killed somebody. So I went on again—and five minutes later I'm dreamin' again, and I nearly— *He presses two fingers against his eyes.* I have such thoughts, I have such strange thoughts.

LINDA: Willy, dear. Talk to them again. There's no reason why you can't work in New York.

WILLY: They don't need me in New York. I'm the New England man. I'm vital in New England.

LINDA: But you're sixty years old. They can't expect you to keep traveling every week.

WILLY: I'll have to send a wire to Portland. I'm supposed to see Brown and Morrison tomorrow morning at ten o'clock to show the line. Goddammit, I could sell them! *He starts putting on his jacket.*

LINDA, *taking the jacket from him:* Why don't you go down to the place tomorrow and tell Howard you've simply got to work in New York? You're too accommodating, dear.

WILLY: If old man Wagner was alive I'd a been in charge of New York now! That man was a prince, he was a masterful man. But that boy of his, that Howard, he don't appreciate.

When I went north the first time, the Wagner Company didn't know where New England was!

LINDA: Why don't you tell those things to Howard, dear?

WILLY, *encouraged:* I will, I definitely will. Is there any cheese?

LINDA: I'll make you a sandwich.

WILLY: No, go to sleep. I'll take some milk. I'll be up right away. The boys in?

LINDA: They're sleeping. Happy took Biff on a date tonight.

WILLY, *interested:* That so?

LINDA: It was so nice to see them shaving together, one behind the other, in the bathroom. And going out together. You notice? The whole house smells of shaving lotion.

WILLY: Figure it out. Work a lifetime to pay off a house. You finally own it, and there's nobody to live in it.

LINDA: Well, dear, life is a casting off. It's always that way.

WILLY: No, no, some people—some people accomplish something. Did Biff say anything after I went this morning?

LINDA: You shouldn't have criticized him, Willy, especially after he just got off the train. You mustn't lose your temper with him.

WILLY: When the hell did I lose my temper? I simply asked him if he was making any money. Is that a criticism?

LINDA: But, dear, how could he make any money?

WILLY, *worried and angered:* There's such an undercurrent in him. He became a moody man. Did he apologize when I left this morning?

LINDA: He was crestfallen, Willy. You know how he admires

you. I think if he finds himself, then you'll both be happier and not fight any more.

WILLY: How can he find himself on a farm? Is that a life? A farmhand? In the beginning, when he was young, I thought, well, a young man, it's good for him to tramp around, take a lot of different jobs. But it's more than ten years now and he has yet to make thirty-five dollars a week!

LINDA: He's finding himself, Willy.

WILLY: Not finding yourself at the age of thirty-four is a disgrace!

LINDA: Shh!

WILLY: The trouble is he's lazy, goddammit!

LINDA: Willy, please!

WILLY: Biff is a lazy bum!

LINDA: They're sleeping. Get something to eat. Go on down.

WILLY: Why did he come home? I would like to know what brought him home.

LINDA: I don't know. I think he's still lost, Willy. I think he's very lost.

WILLY: Biff Loman is lost. In the greatest country in the world a young man with such—personal attractiveness, gets lost. And such a hard worker. There's one thing about Biff—he's not lazy.

LINDA: Never.

WILLY, *with pity and resolve:* I'll see him in the morning; I'll have a nice talk with him. I'll get him a job selling. He could be big in no time. My God! Remember how they used to follow him around in high school? When he smiled at one of them their faces lit up. When he walked down the street . . . *He loses himself in reminiscences.*

LINDA, *trying to bring him out of it:* Willy, dear, I got a new kind of American-type cheese today. It's whipped.

WILLY: Why do you get American when I like Swiss?

LINDA: I just thought you'd like a change—

WILLY: I don't want a change! I want Swiss cheese. Why am I always being contradicted?

LINDA, *with a covering laugh:* I thought it would be a surprise.

WILLY: Why don't you open a window in here, for God's sake?

LINDA, *with infinite patience:* They're all open, dear.

WILLY: The way they boxed us in here. Bricks and windows, windows and bricks.

LINDA: We should've bought the land next door.

WILLY: The street is lined with cars. There's not a breath of fresh air in the neighborhood. The grass don't grow any more, you can't raise a carrot in the back yard. They should've had a law against apartment houses. Remember those two beautiful elm trees out there? When I and Biff hung the swing between them?

LINDA: Yeah, like being a million miles from the city.

WILLY: They should've arrested the builder for cutting those down. They massacred the neighborhood. *Lost:* More and more I think of those days, Linda. This time of year it was lilac and wisteria. And then the peonies would come out, and the daffodils. What fragrance in this room!

LINDA: Well, after all, people had to move somewhere.

WILLY: No, there's more people now.

LINDA: I don't think there's more people. I think—

WILLY: There's more people! That's what's ruining this country! Population is getting out of control. The competition is maddening! Smell the stink from that apartment house! And another one on the other side . . . How can they whip cheese?

On Willy's last line, Biff and Happy raise themselves up in their beds, listening.

LINDA: Go down, try it. And be quiet.

WILLY, *turning to Linda, guiltily:* You're not worried about me, are you, sweetheart?

BIFF: What's the matter?

HAPPY: Listen!

LINDA: You've got too much on the ball to worry about.

WILLY: You're my foundation and my support, Linda.

LINDA: Just try to relax, dear. You make mountains out of molehills.

WILLY: I won't fight with him any more. If he wants to go back to Texas, let him go.

LINDA: He'll find his way.

WILLY: Sure. Certain men just don't get started till later in life. Like Thomas Edison, I think. Or B. F. Goodrich. One of them was deaf. *He starts for the bedroom doorway.* I'll put my money on Biff.

LINDA: And Willy—if it's warm Sunday we'll drive in the country. And we'll open the windshield, and take lunch.

WILLY: No, the windshields don't open on the new cars.

LINDA: But you opened it today.

WILLY: Me? I didn't. *He stops.* Now isn't that peculiar! Isn't that a remarkable— *He breaks off in amazement and fright as the flute is heard distantly.*

LINDA: What, darling?

WILLY: That is the most remarkable thing.

LINDA: What, dear?

WILLY: I was thinking of the Chevvy. *Slight pause.* Nineteen twenty-eight . . . when I had that red Chevvy— *Breaks off.* That funny? I coulda sworn I was driving that Chevvy today.

LINDA: Well, that's nothing. Something must've reminded you.

WILLY: Remarkable. Ts. Remember those days? The way Biff used to simonize that car? The dealer refused to believe there was eighty thousand miles on it. *He shakes his head. Heh!* *To Linda:* Close your eyes, I'll be right up. *He walks out of the bedroom.*

HAPPY, *to Biff:* Jesus, maybe he smashed up the car again!

LINDA, *calling after Willy:* Be careful on the stairs, dear! The cheese is on the middle shelf! *She turns, goes over to the bed, takes his jacket, and goes out of the bedroom.*

Light has risen on the boys' room. Unseen, Willy is heard talking to himself, "Eighty thousand miles," and a little laugh. Biff gets out of bed, comes downstage a bit, and stands attentively. Biff is two years older than his brother Happy, well built, but in these days bears a worn air and seems less self-assured. He has succeeded less, and his dreams are stronger and less acceptable than Happy's. Happy is tall, powerfully made. Sexuality is like a visible color on him, or a scent that many women have discovered. He, like his brother, is lost, but in a different way, for he has never allowed himself to turn his face toward defeat and is thus more confused and hard-skinned, although seemingly more content.

HAPPY, *getting out of bed:* He's going to get his license taken away if he keeps that up. I'm getting nervous about him, y'know, Biff?

BIFF: His eyes are going.

HAPPY: No, I've driven with him. He sees all right. He just doesn't keep his mind on it. I drove into the city with him last week. He stops at a green light and then it turns red and he goes. *He laughs.*

BIFF: Maybe he's color-blind.

HAPPY: Pop? Why he's got the finest eye for color in the business. You know that.

BIFF, *sitting down on his bed:* I'm going to sleep.

HAPPY: You're not still sour on Dad, are you, Biff?

BIFF: He's all right, I guess.

WILLY, *underneath them, in the living-room:* Yes, sir, eighty thousand miles—eighty-two thousand!

BIFF: You smoking?

HAPPY, *holding out a pack of cigarettes:* Want one?

BIFF, *taking a cigarette:* I can never sleep when I smell it.

WILLY: What a simonizing job, heh!

HAPPY, *with deep sentiment:* Funny, Biff, y'know? Us sleeping in here again? The old beds. *He pats his bed affectionately.* All the talk that went across those two beds, huh? Our whole lives.

BIFF: Yeah. Lotta dreams and plans.

HAPPY, *with a deep and masculine laugh:* About five hundred women would like to know what was said in this room.

They share a soft laugh.

BIFF: Remember that big Betsy something—what the hell was her name—over on Bushwick Avenue?

HAPPY, *combing his hair:* With the collie dog!

BIFF: That's the one. I got you in there, remember?

HAPPY: Yeah, that was my first time—I think. Boy, there was a pig! *They laugh, almost crudely.* You taught me everything I know about women. Don't forget that.

BIFF: I bet you forgot how bashful you used to be. Especially with girls.

HAPPY: Oh, I still am, Biff.

BIFF: Oh, go on.

HAPPY: I just control it, that's all. I think I got less bashful and you got more so. What happened, Biff? Where's the old humor, the old confidence? *He shakes Biff's knee. Biff gets up and moves restlessly about the room.* What's the matter?

BIFF: Why does Dad mock me all the time?

HAPPY: He's not mocking you, he—

BIFF: Everything I say there's a twist of mockery on his face. I can't get near him.

HAPPY: He just wants you to make good, that's all. I wanted to talk to you about Dad for a long time, Biff. Something's—happening to him. He—talks to himself.

BIFF: I noticed that this morning. But he always mumbled.

HAPPY: But not so noticeable. It got so embarrassing I sent him to Florida. And you know something? Most of the time he's talking to you.

BIFF: What's he say about me?

HAPPY: I can't make it out.

BIFF: What's he say about me?

HAPPY: I think the fact that you're not settled, that you're still kind of up in the air . . .

BIFF: There's one or two other things depressing him, Happy.

HAPPY: What do you mean?

BIFF: Never mind. Just don't lay it all to me.

HAPPY: But I think if you just got started—I mean—is there any future for you out there?

BIFF: I tell ya, Hap, I don't know what the future is. I don't know—what I'm supposed to want.

HAPPY: What do you mean?

BIFF: Well, I spent six or seven years after high school trying to work myself up. Shipping clerk, salesman, business of one kind or another. And it's a measly manner of existence. To get on that subway on the hot mornings in summer. To devote your whole life to keeping stock, or making phone calls, or selling or buying. To suffer fifty weeks of the year for the sake of a two-week vacation, when all you really desire is to be outdoors, with your shirt off. And always to have to get ahead of the next fella. And still—that's how you build a future.

HAPPY: Well, you really enjoy it on a farm? Are you content out there?

BIFF, *with rising agitation:* Hap, I've had twenty or thirty different kinds of jobs since I left home before the war, and it always turns out the same. I just realized it lately. In Nebraska when I herded cattle, and the Dakotas, and Arizona, and now in Texas. It's why I came home now, I guess, because I realized it. This farm I work on, it's spring there now, see? And they've got about fifteen new colts. There's nothing more inspiring or—beautiful than the sight of a mare and a new colt. And it's cool there now, see? Texas is cool now, and it's spring. And whenever spring comes to where I am, I suddenly get the feeling, my God, I'm not gettin' anywhere! What the hell am I doing, playing around with horses, twenty-eight dollars a week! I'm thirty-four years old, I oughta be makin' my future. That's when I come running home. And now, I get here, and I don't know what to do with myself. *After a pause:* I've always made a point of not wasting my life, and everytime I come back here I know that all I've done is to waste my life.

HAPPY: You're a poet, you know that, Biff? You're a—you're an idealist!

BIFF: No, I'm mixed up very bad. Maybe I oughta get married. Maybe I oughta get stuck into something. Maybe that's my trouble. I'm like a boy. I'm not married, I'm not in business, I just—I'm like a boy. Are you content, Hap? You're a success, aren't you? Are you content?

HAPPY: Hell, no!

BIFF: Why? You're making money, aren't you?

HAPPY, *moving about with energy, expressiveness:* All I can do now is wait for the merchandise manager to die. And suppose I get to be merchandise manager? He's a good friend of mine, and he just built a terrific estate on Long Island. And he lived there about two months and sold it, and now he's building another one. He can't enjoy it once it's finished. And I know that's just what I would do. I don't know what the hell I'm workin' for. Sometimes I sit in my apartment—all alone. And I think of the rent I'm paying. And it's crazy. But then, it's what I always wanted. My own apartment, a car, and plenty of women. And still, goddammit, I'm lonely.

BIFF, *with enthusiasm:* Listen, why don't you come out West with me?

HAPPY: You and I, heh?

BIFF: Sure, maybe we could buy a ranch. Raise cattle, use our muscles. Men built like we are should be working out in the open.

HAPPY, *avidly:* The Loman Brothers, heh?

BIFF, *with vast affection:* Sure, we'd be known all over the counties!

HAPPY, *enthralled:* That's what I dream about, Biff. Sometimes I want to just rip my clothes off in the middle of the store and outbox that goddam merchandise manager. I mean I can outbox, outrun, and outlift anybody in that store, and I have to take orders from those common, petty sons-of-bitches till I can't stand it any more.

BIFF: I'm tellin' you, kid, if you were with me I'd be happy out there.

HAPPY, *enthused:* See, Biff, everybody around me is so false that I'm constantly lowering my ideals . . .

BIFF: Baby, together we'd stand up for one another, we'd have someone to trust.

HAPPY: If I were around you—

BIFF: Hap, the trouble is we weren't brought up to grub for money. I don't know how to do it.

HAPPY: Neither can I!

BIFF: Then let's go!

HAPPY: The only thing is—what can you make out there?

BIFF: But look at your friend. Builds an estate and then hasn't the peace of mind to live in it.

HAPPY: Yeah, but when he walks into the store the waves part in front of him. That's fifty-two thousand dollars a year coming through the revolving door, and I got more in my pinky finger than he's got in his head.

BIFF: Yeah, but you just said—

HAPPY: I gotta show some of those pompous, self-important executives over there that Hap Loman can make the grade. I want to walk into the store the way he walks in. Then I'll go with you, Biff. We'll be together yet, I swear. But take those two we had tonight. Now weren't they gorgeous creatures?

BIFF: Yeah, yeah, most gorgeous I've had in years.

HAPPY: I get that any time I want, Biff. Whenever I feel disgusted. The only trouble is, it gets like bowling or something. I just keep knockin' them over and it doesn't mean anything. You still run around a lot?

BIFF: Naa. I'd like to find a girl—steady, somebody with substance.

HAPPY: That's what I long for.

BIFF: Go on! You'd never come home.

HAPPY: I would! Somebody with character, with resistance! Like Mom, y'know? You're gonna call me a bastard when I tell you this. That girl Charlotte I was with tonight is engaged to be married in five weeks. *He tries on his new hat.*

BIFF: No kiddin'!

HAPPY: Sure, the guy's in line for the vice-presidency of the store. I don't know what gets into me, maybe I just have an overdeveloped sense of competition or something, but I went and ruined her, and furthermore I can't get rid of her. And he's the third executive I've done that to. Isn't that a crummy characteristic? And to top it all, I go to their weddings! *Indignantly, but laughing:* Like I'm not supposed to take bribes. Manufacturers offer me a hundred-dollar bill now and then to throw an order their way. You know how honest I am, but it's like this girl, see. I hate myself for it. Because I don't want the girl, and, still, I take it and—I love it!

BIFF: Let's go to sleep.

HAPPY: I guess we didn't settle anything, heh?

BIFF: I just got one idea that I think I'm going to try.

HAPPY: What's that?

BIFF: Remember Bill Oliver?

HAPPY: Sure, Oliver is very big now. You want to work for him again?

BIFF: No, but when I quit he said something to me. He put his arm on my shoulder, and he said, "Biff, if you ever need anything, come to me."

HAPPY: I remember that. That sounds good.

BIFF: I think I'll go to see him. If I could get ten thousand or even seven or eight thousand dollars I could buy a beautiful ranch.

HAPPY: I bet he'd back you. 'Cause he thought highly of you, Biff. I mean, they all do. You're well liked, Biff. That's why I say to come back here, and we both have the apartment. And I'm tellin' you, Biff, any babe you want . . .

BIFF: No, with a ranch I could do the work I like and still be something. I just wonder though. I wonder if Oliver still thinks I stole that carton of basketballs.

HAPPY: Oh, he probably forgot that long ago. It's almost ten years. You're too sensitive. Anyway, he didn't really fire you.

BIFF: Well, I think he was going to. I think that's why I quit. I was never sure whether he knew or not. I know he thought the world of me, though. I was the only one he'd let lock up the place.

WILLY, *below:* You gonna wash the engine, Biff?

HAPPY: Shh!

Biff looks at Happy, who is gazing down, listening. Willy is mumbling in the parlor.

HAPPY: You hear that?

They listen. Willy laughs warmly.

BIFF, *growing angry:* Doesn't he know Mom can hear that?

WILLY: Don't get your sweater dirty, Biff!

A look of pain crosses Biff's face.

HAPPY: Isn't that terrible? Don't leave again, will you? You'll find a job here. You gotta stick around. I don't know what to do about him, it's getting embarrassing.

WILLY: What a simonizing job!

BIFF: Mom's hearing that!

WILLY: No kiddin', Biff, you got a date? Wonderful!

HAPPY: Go on to sleep. But talk to him in the morning, will you?

BIFF, *reluctantly getting into bed:* With her in the house. Brother!

HAPPY, *getting into bed:* I wish you'd have a good talk with him.

The light on their room begins to fade.

BIFF, *to himself in bed:* That selfish, stupid . . .

HAPPY: Sh . . . Sleep, Biff.

Their light is out. Well before they have finished speaking, Willy's form is dimly seen below in the darkened kitchen. He opens the refrigerator, searches in there, and takes out a bottle of milk. The apartment houses are fading out, and the entire house and surroundings become covered with leaves. Music insinuates itself as the leaves appear.

WILLY: Just wanna be careful with those girls, Biff, that's all. Don't make any promises. No promises of any kind. Because a girl, y'know, they always believe what you tell 'em, and you're very young, Biff, you're too young to be talking seriously to girls.

Light rises on the kitchen. Willy, talking, shuts the refrigerator door and comes downstage to the kitchen table. He pours milk into a glass. He is totally immersed in himself, smiling faintly.

WILLY: Too young entirely, Biff. You want to watch your schooling first. Then when you're all set, there'll be plenty of girls for a boy like you. *He smiles broadly at a kitchen chair.* That so? The girls pay for you? *He laughs.* Boy, you must really be makin' a hit.

Willy is gradually addressing—physically—a point offstage, speaking through the wall of the kitchen, and his voice has been rising in volume to that of a normal conversation.

WILLY: I been wondering why you polish the car so careful. Ha! Don't leave the hubcaps, boys. Get the chamois to the hubcaps. Happy, use newspaper on the windows, it's the easiest thing. Show him how to do it, Biff! You see, Happy? Pad it up, use it like a pad. That's it, that's it, good work. You're doin' all right, Hap. *He pauses, then nods in approbation for a few seconds, then looks upward.* Biff, first thing we gotta do when we get time is clip that big branch over the house. Afraid it's gonna fall in a storm and hit the roof. Tell you what. We get a rope and sling her around, and then we climb up there with a couple of saws and take her down. Soon as you finish the car, boys, I wanna see ya. I got a surprise for you, boys.

BIFF, *offstage:* Whatta ya got, Dad?

WILLY: No, you finish first. Never leave a job till you're finished—remember that. *Looking toward the "big trees":* Biff, up in Albany I saw a beautiful hammock. I think I'll buy it next trip, and we'll hang it right between those two elms. Wouldn't that be something? Just swingin' there under those branches. Boy, that would be . . .

Young Biff and Young Happy appear from the direction Willy was addressing. Happy carries rags and a pail of water. Biff, wearing a sweater with a block "S," carries a football.

BIFF, *pointing in the direction of the car offstage:* How's that, Pop, professional?

WILLY: Terrific. Terrific job, boys. Good work, Biff.

HAPPY: Where's the surprise, Pop?

WILLY: In the back seat of the car.

HAPPY: Boy! *He runs off.*

BIFF: What is it, Dad? Tell me, what'd you buy?

WILLY, *laughing, cuffs him:* Never mind, something I want you to have.

BIFF, *turns and starts off:* What is it, Hap?

HAPPY, *offstage:* It's a punching bag!

BIFF: Oh, Pop!

WILLY: It's got Gene Tunney's signature on it!

Happy runs onstage with a punching bag.

BIFF: Gee, how'd you know we wanted a punching bag?

WILLY: Well, it's the finest thing for the timing.

HAPPY, *lies down on his back and pedals with his feet:* I'm losing weight, you notice, Pop?

WILLY, *to Happy:* Jumping rope is good too.

BIFF: Did you see the new football I got?

WILLY, *examining the ball:* Where'd you get a new ball?

BIFF: The coach told me to practice my passing.

WILLY: That so? And he gave you the ball, heh?

BIFF: Well, I borrowed it from the locker room. *He laughs confidentially.*

WILLY, *laughing with him at the theft:* I want you to return that.

HAPPY: I told you he wouldn't like it!

BIFF, *angrily:* Well, I'm bringing it back!

WILLY, *stopping the incipient argument, to Happy:* Sure, he's gotta practice with a regulation ball, doesn't he? *To Biff:* Coach'll probably congratulate you on your initiative!

BIFF: Oh, he keeps congratulating my initiative all the time, Pop.

WILLY: That's because he likes you. If somebody else took that ball there'd be an uproar. So what's the report, boys, what's the report?

BIFF: Where'd you go this time, Dad? Gee we were lonesome for you.

WILLY, *pleased, puts an arm around each boy and they come down to the apron:* Lonesome, heh?

BIFF: Missed you every minute.

WILLY: Don't say? Tell you a secret, boys. Don't breathe it to a soul. Someday I'll have my own business, and I'll never have to leave home any more.

HAPPY: Like Uncle Charley, heh?

WILLY: Bigger than Uncle Charley! Because Charley is not—liked. He's liked, but he's not—well liked.

BIFF: Where'd you go this time, Dad?

WILLY: Well, I got on the road, and I went north to Providence. Met the Mayor.

BIFF: The Mayor of Providence!

WILLY: He was sitting in the hotel lobby.

BIFF: What'd he say?

WILLY: He said, "Morning!" And I said, "You got a fine city here, Mayor." And then he had coffee with me. And then I went to Waterbury. Waterbury is a fine city. Big clock city, the famous Waterbury clock. Sold a nice bill there. And then Boston—Boston is the cradle of the Revolution. A fine city. And a couple of other towns in Mass., and on to Portland and Bangor and straight home!

BIFF: Gee, I'd love to go with you sometime, Dad.

WILLY: Soon as summer comes.

HAPPY: Promise?

WILLY: You and Hap and I, and I'll show you all the towns. America is full of beautiful towns and fine, upstanding people. And they know me, boys, they know me up and down New England. The finest people. And when I bring you fellas up, there'll be open sesame for all of us, 'cause one thing, boys: I have friends. I can park my car in any street in New England, and the cops protect it like their own. This summer, heh?

BIFF and HAPPY, *together:* Yeah! You bet!

WILLY: We'll take our bathing suits.

HAPPY: We'll carry your bags, Pop!

WILLY: Oh, won't that be something! Me comin' into the Boston stores with you boys carryin' my bags. What a sensation!

Biff is prancing around, practicing passing the ball.

WILLY: You nervous, Biff, about the game?

BIFF: Not if you're gonna be there.

WILLY: What do they say about you in school, now that they made you captain?

HAPPY: There's a crowd of girls behind him every time the classes change.

BIFF, *taking Willy's hand:* This Saturday, Pop, this Saturday— just for you, I'm going to break through for a touchdown.

HAPPY: You're supposed to pass.

BIFF: I'm takin' one play for Pop. You watch me, Pop, and when I take off my helmet, that means I'm breakin' out. Then you watch me crash through that line!

WILLY, *kisses Biff:* Oh, wait'll I tell this in Boston!

Bernard enters in knickers. He is younger than Biff, earnest and loyal, a worried boy.

BERNARD: Biff, where are you? You're supposed to study with me today.

WILLY: Hey, looka Bernard. What're you lookin' so anemic about, Bernard?

BERNARD: He's gotta study, Uncle Willy. He's got Regents next week.

HAPPY, *tauntingly, spinning Bernard around:* Let's box, Bernard!

BERNARD: Biff! *He gets away from Happy.* Listen, Biff, I heard Mr. Birnbaum say that if you don't start studyin' math he's gonna flunk you, and you won't graduate. I heard him!

WILLY: You better study with him, Biff. Go ahead now.

BERNARD: I heard him!

BIFF: Oh, Pop, you didn't see my sneakers! *He holds up a foot for Willy to look at.*

WILLY: Hey, that's a beautiful job of printing!

BERNARD, *wiping his glasses:* Just because he printed University of Virginia on his sneakers doesn't mean they've got to graduate him, Uncle Willy!

WILLY, *angrily:* What're you talking about? With scholarships to three universities they're gonna flunk him?

BERNARD: But I heard Mr. Birnbaum say—

WILLY: Don't be a pest, Bernard! *To his boys:* What an anemic!

BERNARD: Okay, I'm waiting for you in my house, Biff.

Bernard goes off. The Lomans laugh.

WILLY: Bernard is not well liked, is he?

BIFF: He's liked, but he's not well liked.

HAPPY: That's right, Pop.

WILLY: That's just what I mean. Bernard can get the best marks in school, y'understand, but when he gets out in the business world, y'understand, you are going to be five times ahead of him. That's why I thank Almighty God you're both built like Adonises. Because the man who makes an appearance in the business world, the man who creates personal interest, is the man who gets ahead. Be liked and you will never want. You take me, for instance. I never have to wait in line to see a buyer. "Willy Loman is here!" That's all they have to know, and I go right through.

BIFF: Did you knock them dead, Pop?

WILLY: Knocked 'em cold in Providence, slaughtered 'em in Boston.

HAPPY, *on his back, pedaling again:* I'm losing weight, you notice, Pop?

Linda enters, as of old, a ribbon in her hair, carrying a basket of washing.

LINDA, *with youthful energy:* Hello, dear!

WILLY: Sweetheart!

LINDA: How'd the Chevvy run?

WILLY: Chevrolet, Linda, is the greatest car ever built. *To the boys:* Since when do you let your mother carry wash up the stairs?

BIFF: Grab hold there, boy!

HAPPY: Where to, Mom?

LINDA: Hang them up on the line. And you better go down to your friends, Biff. The cellar is full of boys. They don't know what to do with themselves.

BIFF: Ah, when Pop comes home they can wait!

WILLY, *laughs appreciatively:* You better go down and tell them what to do, Biff.

BIFF: I think I'll have them sweep out the furnace room.

WILLY: Good work, Biff.

BIFF, *goes through wall-line of kitchen to doorway at back and calls down:* Fellas! Everybody sweep out the furnace room! I'll be right down!

VOICES: All right! Okay, Biff.

BIFF: George and Sam and Frank, come out back! We're hangin' up the wash! Come on, Hap, on the double! *He and Happy carry out the basket.*

LINDA: The way they obey him!

WILLY: Well, that's training, the training. I'm tellin' you, I was sellin' thousands and thousands, but I had to come home.

LINDA: Oh, the whole block'll be at that game. Did you sell anything?

WILLY: I did five hundred gross in Providence and seven hundred gross in Boston.

LINDA: No! Wait a minute, I've got a pencil. *She pulls pencil and paper out of her apron pocket.* That makes your commission . . . Two hundred—my God! Two hundred and twelve dollars!

WILLY: Well, I didn't figure it yet, but . . .

LINDA: How much did you do?

WILLY: Well, I—I did—about a hundred and eighty gross in Providence. Well, no—it came to—roughly two hundred gross on the whole trip.

LINDA, *without hesitation:* Two hundred gross. That's . . . *She figures.*

WILLY: The trouble was that three of the stores were half closed for inventory in Boston. Otherwise I woulda broke records.

LINDA: Well, it makes seventy dollars and some pennies. That's very good.

WILLY: What do we owe?

LINDA: Well, on the first there's sixteen dollars on the refrigerator—

WILLY: Why sixteen?

LINDA: Well, the fan belt broke, so it was a dollar eighty.

WILLY: But it's brand new.

LINDA: Well, the man said that's the way it is. Till they work themselves in, y'know.

They move through the wall-line into the kitchen.

WILLY: I hope we didn't get stuck on that machine.

LINDA: They got the biggest ads of any of them!

WILLY: I know, it's a fine machine. What else?

LINDA: Well, there's nine-sixty for the washing machine. And for the vacuum cleaner there's three and a half due on the fifteenth. Then the roof, you got twenty-one dollars remaining.

WILLY: It don't leak, does it?

LINDA: No, they did a wonderful job. Then you owe Frank for the carburetor.

WILLY: I'm not going to pay that man! That goddam Chevrolet, they ought to prohibit the manufacture of that car!

LINDA: Well, you owe him three and a half. And odds and ends, comes to around a hundred and twenty dollars by the fifteenth.

WILLY: A hundred and twenty dollars! My God, if business don't pick up I don't know what I'm gonna do!

LINDA: Well, next week you'll do better.

WILLY: Oh, I'll knock 'em dead next week. I'll go to Hartford. I'm very well liked in Hartford. You know, the trouble is, Linda, people don't seem to take to me.

They move onto the forestage.

LINDA: Oh, don't be foolish.

WILLY: I know it when I walk in. They seem to laugh at me.

LINDA: Why? Why would they laugh at you? Don't talk that way, Willy.

Willy moves to the edge of the stage. Linda goes into the kitchen and starts to darn stockings.

WILLY: I don't know the reason for it, but they just pass me by. I'm not noticed.

LINDA: But you're doing wonderful, dear. You're making seventy to a hundred dollars a week.

WILLY: But I gotta be at it ten, twelve hours a day. Other men—I don't know—they do it easier. I don't know why—I can't stop myself—I talk too much. A man oughta come in with a few words. One thing about Charley. He's a man of few words, and they respect him.

LINDA: You don't talk too much, you're just lively.

WILLY, *smiling:* Well, I figure, what the hell, life is short, a couple of jokes. *To himself:* I joke too much! *The smile goes.*

LINDA: Why? You're—

WILLY: I'm fat. I'm very—foolish to look at, Linda. I didn't tell you, but Christmas time I happened to be calling on F. H. Stewarts, and a salesman I know, as I was going in to see the buyer I heard him say something about—walrus. And I—I cracked him right across the face. I won't take that. I simply will not take that. But they do laugh at me. I know that.

LINDA: Darling . . .

WILLY: I gotta overcome it. I know I gotta overcome it. I'm not dressing to advantage, maybe.

LINDA: Willy, darling, you're the handsomest man in the world—

WILLY: Oh, no, Linda.

LINDA: To me you are. *Slight pause.* The handsomest.

From the darkness is heard the laughter of a woman. Willy doesn't turn to it, but it continues through Linda's lines.

LINDA: And the boys, Willy. Few men are idolized by their children the way you are.

Music is heard as behind a scrim, to the left of the house, The Woman, dimly seen, is dressing.

WILLY, *with great feeling:* You're the best there is, Linda, you're a pal, you know that? On the road—on the road I want to grab you sometimes and just kiss the life outa you.

The laughter is loud now, and he moves into a brightening area at the left, where The Woman has come from behind the scrim and is standing, putting on her hat, looking into a "mirror" and laughing.

WILLY: 'Cause I get so lonely—especially when business is bad and there's nobody to talk to. I get the feeling that I'll never sell anything again, that I won't make a living for you, or a business, a business for the boys. *He talks through The Woman's subsiding laughter; The Woman primps at the "mirror."* There's so much I want to make for—

THE WOMAN: Me? You didn't make me, Willy. I picked you.

WILLY, *pleased:* You picked me?

THE WOMAN, *who is quite proper-looking, Willy's age:* I did. I've been sitting at that desk watching all the salesmen go by, day in, day out. But you've got such a sense of humor, and we do have such a good time together, don't we?

WILLY: Sure, sure. *He takes her in his arms.* Why do you have to go now?

THE WOMAN: It's two o'clock . . .

WILLY: No, come on in! *He pulls her.*

THE WOMAN: . . . my sisters'll be scandalized. When'll you be back?

WILLY: Oh, two weeks about. Will you come up again?

THE WOMAN: Sure thing. You do make me laugh. It's good for me. *She squeezes his arm, kisses him.* And I think you're a wonderful man.

WILLY: You picked me, heh?

THE WOMAN: Sure. Because you're so sweet. And such a kidder.

WILLY: Well, I'll see you next time I'm in Boston.

THE WOMAN: I'll put you right through to the buyers.

WILLY, *slapping her bottom:* Right. Well, bottoms up!

THE WOMAN, *slaps him gently and laughs:* You just kill me, Willy. *He suddenly grabs her and kisses her roughly.* You kill me. And thanks for the stockings. I love a lot of stockings. Well, good night.

WILLY: Good night. And keep your pores open!

THE WOMAN: Oh, Willy!

The Woman bursts out laughing, and Linda's laughter blends in. The Woman disappears into the dark. Now the area at the kitchen table brightens. Linda is sitting where she was at the kitchen table, but now is mending a pair of her silk stockings.

LINDA: You are, Willy. The handsomest man. You've got no reason to feel that—

WILLY, *coming out of The Woman's dimming area and going over to Linda:* I'll make it all up to you, Linda, I'll—

LINDA: There's nothing to make up, dear. You're doing fine, better than—

WILLY, *noticing her mending:* What's that?

LINDA: Just mending my stockings. They're so expensive—

WILLY, *angrily, taking them from her:* I won't have you mending stockings in this house! Now throw them out!

Linda puts the stockings in her pocket.

BERNARD, *entering on the run:* Where is he? If he doesn't study!

WILLY, *moving to the forestage, with great agitation:* You'll give him the answers!

BERNARD: I do, but I can't on a Regents! That's a state exam! They're liable to arrest me!

WILLY: Where is he? I'll whip him, I'll whip him!

LINDA: And he'd better give back that football, Willy, it's not nice.

WILLY: Biff! Where is he? Why is he taking everything?

LINDA: He's too rough with the girls, Willy. All the mothers are afraid of him!

WILLY: I'll whip him!

BERNARD: He's driving the car without a license!

The Woman's laugh is heard.

WILLY: Shut up!

LINDA: All the mothers—

WILLY: Shut up!

BERNARD, *backing quietly away and out:* Mr. Birnbaum says he's stuck up.

WILLY: Get outa here!

BERNARD: If he doesn't buckle down he'll flunk math! *He goes off.*

LINDA: He's right, Willy, you've gotta—

WILLY, *exploding at her:* There's nothing the matter with him! You want him to be a worm like Bernard? He's got spirit, personality . . .

As he speaks, Linda, almost in tears, exits into the living-room. Willy is alone in the kitchen, wilting and staring. The leaves are gone. It is night again, and the apartment houses look down from behind.

WILLY: Loaded with it. Loaded! What is he stealing? He's giving it back, isn't he? Why is he stealing? What did I tell him? I never in my life told him anything but decent things.

Happy in pajamas has come down the stairs; Willy suddenly becomes aware of Happy's presence.

HAPPY: Let's go now, come on.

WILLY, *sitting down at the kitchen table:* Huh! Why did she have to wax the floors herself? Everytime she waxes the floors she keels over. She knows that!

HAPPY: Shh! Take it easy. What brought you back tonight?

WILLY: I got an awful scare. Nearly hit a kid in Yonkers. God! Why didn't I go to Alaska with my brother Ben that time! Ben! That man was a genius, that man was success incarnate! What a mistake! He begged me to go.

HAPPY: Well, there's no use in—

WILLY: You guys! There was a man started with the clothes on his back and ended up with diamond mines!

HAPPY: Boy, someday I'd like to know how he did it.

WILLY: What's the mystery? The man knew what he wanted and went out and got it! Walked into a jungle, and comes out, the age of twenty-one, and he's rich! The world is an oyster, but you don't crack it open on a mattress!

HAPPY: Pop, I told you I'm gonna retire you for life.

WILLY: You'll retire me for life on seventy goddam dollars a week? And your women and your car and your apartment, and you'll retire me for life! Christ's sake, I couldn't get past Yonkers today! Where are you guys, where are you? The woods are burning! I can't drive a car!

Charley has appeared in the doorway. He is a large man, slow of speech, laconic, immovable. In all he says, despite what he says, there is pity, and, now, trepidation. He has a robe over pajamas, slippers on his feet. He enters the kitchen.

CHARLEY: Everything all right?

HAPPY: Yeah, Charley, everything's . . .

WILLY: What's the matter?

CHARLEY: I heard some noise. I thought something happened. Can't we do something about the walls? You sneeze in here, and in my house hats blow off.

HAPPY: Let's go to bed, Dad. Come on.

Charley signals to Happy to go.

WILLY: You go ahead, I'm not tired at the moment.

HAPPY, *to Willy:* Take it easy, huh? *He exits.*

WILLY: What're you doin' up?

CHARLEY, *sitting down at the kitchen table opposite Willy:* Couldn't sleep good. I had a heartburn.

WILLY: Well, you don't know how to eat.

CHARLEY: I eat with my mouth.

WILLY: No, you're ignorant. You gotta know about vitamins and things like that.

CHARLEY: Come on, let's shoot. Tire you out a little.

WILLY, *hesitantly:* All right. You got cards?

CHARLEY, *taking a deck from his pocket:* Yeah, I got them. Someplace. What is it with those vitamins?

WILLY, *dealing:* They build up your bones. Chemistry.

CHARLEY: Yeah, but there's no bones in a heartburn.

WILLY: What are you talkin' about? Do you know the first thing about it?

CHARLEY: Don't get insulted.

WILLY: Don't talk about something you don't know anything about.

They are playing. Pause.

CHARLEY: What're you doin' home?

WILLY: A little trouble with the car.

CHARLEY: Oh. *Pause.* I'd like to take a trip to California.

WILLY: Don't say.

CHARLEY: You want a job?

WILLY: I got a job, I told you that. *After a slight pause:* What the hell are you offering me a job for?

CHARLEY: Don't get insulted.

WILLY: Don't insult me.

CHARLEY: I don't see no sense in it. You don't have to go on this way.

WILLY: I got a good job. *Slight pause.* What do you keep comin' in here for?

CHARLEY: You want me to go?

WILLY, *after a pause, withering:* I can't understand it. He's going back to Texas again. What the hell is that?

CHARLEY: Let him go.

WILLY: I got nothin' to give him, Charley, I'm clean, I'm clean.

CHARLEY: He won't starve. None a them starve. Forget about him.

WILLY: Then what have I got to remember?

CHARLEY: You take it too hard. To hell with it. When a deposit bottle is broken you don't get your nickel back.

WILLY: That's easy enough for you to say.

CHARLEY: That ain't easy for me to say.

WILLY: Did you see the ceiling I put up in the living-room?

CHARLEY: Yeah, that's a piece of work. To put up a ceiling is a mystery to me. How do you do it?

WILLY: What's the difference?

CHARLEY: Well, talk about it.

WILLY: You gonna put up a ceiling?

CHARLEY: How could I put up a ceiling?

WILLY: Then what the hell are you bothering me for?

CHARLEY: You're insulted again.

WILLY: A man who can't handle tools is not a man. You're disgusting.

CHARLEY: Don't call me disgusting, Willy.

Uncle Ben, carrying a valise and an umbrella, enters the fore-stage from around the right corner of the house. He is a stolid man, in his sixties, with a mustache and an authoritative air. He is utterly certain of his destiny, and there is an aura of far places about him. He enters exactly as Willy speaks.

WILLY: I'm getting awfully tired, Ben.

Ben's music is heard. Ben looks around at everything.

CHARLEY: Good, keep playing; you'll sleep better. Did you call me Ben?

Ben looks at his watch.

WILLY: That's funny. For a second there you reminded me of my brother Ben.

BEN: I only have a few minutes. *He strolls, inspecting the place. Willy and Charley continue playing.*

CHARLEY: You never heard from him again, heh? Since that time?

WILLY: Didn't Linda tell you? Couple of weeks ago we got a letter from his wife in Africa. He died.

CHARLEY: That so.

BEN, *chuckling:* So this is Brooklyn, eh?

CHARLEY: Maybe you're in for some of his money.

WILLY: Naa, he had seven sons. There's just one opportunity I had with that man . . .

BEN: I must make a train, William. There are several properties I'm looking at in Alaska.

WILLY: Sure, sure! If I'd gone with him to Alaska that time, everything would've been totally different.

CHARLEY: Go on, you'd froze to death up there.

WILLY: What're you talking about?

BEN: Opportunity is tremendous in Alaska, William. Surprised you're not up there.

WILLY: Sure, tremendous.

CHARLEY: Heh?

WILLY: There was the only man I ever met who knew the answers.

CHARLEY: Who?

BEN: How are you all?

WILLY, *taking a pot, smiling:* Fine, fine.

CHARLEY: Pretty sharp tonight.

BEN: Is Mother living with you?

WILLY: No, she died a long time ago.

CHARLEY: Who?

BEN: That's too bad. Fine specimen of a lady, Mother.

WILLY, *to Charley:* Heh?

BEN: I'd hoped to see the old girl.

CHARLEY: Who died?

BEN: Heard anything from Father, have you?

WILLY, *unnerved:* What do you mean, who died?

CHARLEY, *taking a pot:* What're you talkin' about?

BEN, *looking at his watch:* William, it's half-past eight!

WILLY, *as though to dispel his confusion he angrily stops Charley's hand:* That's my build!

CHARLEY: I put the ace—

WILLY: If you don't know how to play the game I'm not gonna throw my money away on you!

CHARLEY, *rising:* It was my ace, for God's sake!

WILLY: I'm through, I'm through!

BEN: When did Mother die?

WILLY: Long ago. Since the beginning you never knew how to play cards.

CHARLEY, *picks up the cards and goes to the door:* All right! Next time I'll bring a deck with five aces.

WILLY: I don't play that kind of game!

CHARLEY, *turning to him:* You ought to be ashamed of yourself!

WILLY: Yeah?

CHARLEY: Yeah! *He goes out.*

WILLY, *slamming the door after him:* Ignoramus!

BEN, *as Willy comes toward him through the wall-line of the kitchen:* So you're William.

WILLY, *shaking Ben's hand:* Ben! I've been waiting for you so long! What's the answer? How did you do it?

BEN: Oh, there's a story in that.

Linda enters the forestage, as of old, carrying the wash basket.

LINDA: Is this Ben?

BEN, *gallantly:* How do you do, my dear.

LINDA: Where've you been all these years? Willy's always wondered why you—

WILLY, *pulling Ben away from her impatiently:* Where is Dad? Didn't you follow him? How did you get started?

BEN: Well, I don't know how much you remember.

WILLY: Well, I was just a baby, of course, only three or four years old—

BEN: Three years and eleven months.

WILLY: What a memory, Ben!

BEN: I have many enterprises, William, and I have never kept books.

WILLY: I remember I was sitting under the wagon in—was it Nebraska?

BEN: It was South Dakota, and I gave you a bunch of wild flowers.

WILLY: I remember you walking away down some open road.

BEN, *laughing:* I was going to find Father in Alaska.

WILLY: Where is he?

BEN: At that age I had a very faulty view of geography, William. I discovered after a few days that I was heading due south, so instead of Alaska, I ended up in Africa.

LINDA: Africa!

WILLY: The Gold Coast!

BEN: Principally diamond mines.

LINDA: Diamond mines!

BEN: Yes, my dear. But I've only a few minutes—

WILLY: No! Boys! Boys! *Young Biff and Happy appear.* Listen to this. This is your Uncle Ben, a great man! Tell my boys, Ben!

BEN: Why, boys, when I was seventeen I walked into the jungle, and when I was twenty-one I walked out. *He laughs.* And by God I was rich.

WILLY, *to the boys:* You see what I been talking about? The greatest things can happen!

BEN, *glancing at his watch:* I have an appointment in Ketchikan Tuesday week.

WILLY: No, Ben! Please tell about Dad. I want my boys to hear. I want them to know the kind of stock they spring from. All I remember is a man with a big beard, and I was in Mamma's lap, sitting around a fire, and some kind of high music.

BEN: His flute. He played the flute.

WILLY: Sure, the flute, that's right!

New music is heard, a high, rollicking tune.

BEN: Father was a very great and a very wild-hearted man. We would start in Boston, and he'd toss the whole family into the wagon, and then he'd drive the team right across the country; through Ohio, and Indiana, Michigan, Illinois, and all the Western states. And we'd stop in the towns and sell the flutes that he'd made on the way. Great inventor, Father. With one gadget he made more in a week than a man like you could make in a lifetime.

WILLY: That's just the way I'm bringing them up, Ben—rugged, well liked, all-around.

BEN:. Yeah? *To Biff:* Hit that, boy—hard as you can. *He pounds his stomach.*

BIFF: Oh, no, sir!

BEN, *taking boxing stance:* Come on, get to me! *He laughs.*

WILLY: Go to it, Biff! Go ahead, show him!

BIFF: Okay! *He cocks his fists and starts in.*

LINDA, *to Willy:* Why must he fight, dear?

BEN, *sparring with Biff:* Good boy! Good boy!

WILLY: How's that, Ben, heh?

HAPPY: Give him the left, Biff!

LINDA: Why are you fighting?

BEN: Good boy! *Suddenly comes in, trips Biff, and stands over him, the point of his umbrella poised over Biff's eye.*

LINDA: Look out, Biff!

BIFF: Gee!

BEN, *patting Biff's knee:* Never fight fair with a stranger, boy. You'll never get out of the jungle that way. *Taking Linda's hand and bowing:* It was an honor and a pleasure to meet you, Linda.

LINDA, *withdrawing her hand coldly, frightened:* Have a nice —trip.

BEN, *to Willy:* And good luck with your—what do you do?

WILLY: Selling.

BEN: Yes. Well . . . *He raises his hand in farewell to all.*

WILLY: No, Ben, I don't want you to think . . . *He takes Ben's arm to show him.* It's Brooklyn, I know, but we hunt too.

BEN: Really, now.

WILLY: Oh, sure, there's snakes and rabbits and—that's why I moved out here. Why, Biff can fell any one of these trees in no time! Boys! Go right over to where they're building the apartment house and get some sand. We're gonna rebuild the entire front stoop right now! Watch this, Ben!

BIFF: Yes, sir! On the double, Hap!

HAPPY, *as he and Biff run off:* I lost weight, Pop, you notice?

Charley enters in knickers, even before the boys are gone.

CHARLEY: Listen, if they steal any more from that building the watchman'll put the cops on them!

LINDA, *to Willy:* Don't let Biff . . .

Ben laughs lustily.

WILLY: You shoulda seen the lumber they brought home last week. At least a dozen six-by-tens worth all kinds a money.

CHARLEY: Listen, if that watchman—

WILLY: I gave them hell, understand. But I got a couple of fearless characters there.

CHARLEY: Willy, the jails are full of fearless characters.

BEN, *clapping Willy on the back, with a laugh at Charley:* And the stock exchange, friend!

WILLY, *joining in Ben's laughter:* Where are the rest of your pants?

CHARLEY: My wife bought them.

WILLY: Now all you need is a golf club and you can go upstairs and go to sleep. *To Ben:* Great athlete! Between him and his son Bernard they can't hammer a nail!

BERNARD, *rushing in:* The watchman's chasing Biff!

WILLY, *angrily:* Shut up! He's not stealing anything!

LINDA, *alarmed, hurrying off left:* Where is he? Biff, dear! *She exits.*

WILLY, *moving toward the left, away from Ben:* There's nothing wrong. What's the matter with you?

BEN: Nervy boy. Good!

WILLY, *laughing:* Oh, nerves of iron, that Biff!

CHARLEY: Don't know what it is. My New England man comes back and he's bleedin', they murdered him up there.

WILLY: It's contacts, Charley, I got important contacts!

CHARLEY, *sarcastically:* Glad to hear it, Willy. Come in later, we'll shoot a little casino. I'll take some of your Portland money. *He laughs at Willy and exits.*

WILLY, *turning to Ben:* Business is bad, it's murderous. But not for me, of course.

BEN: I'll stop by on my way back to Africa.

WILLY, *longingly:* Can't you stay a few days? You're just what I need, Ben, because I—I have a fine position here, but I—well, Dad left when I was such a baby and I never had a chance to talk to him and I still feel—kind of temporary about myself.

BEN: I'll be late for my train.

They are at opposite ends of the stage.

WILLY: Ben, my boys—can't we talk? They'd go into the jaws of hell for me, see, but I—

BEN: William, you're being first-rate with your boys. Outstanding, manly chaps!

WILLY, *hanging on to his words:* Oh, Ben, that's good to hear! Because sometimes I'm afraid that I'm not teaching them the right kind of— Ben, how should I teach them?

BEN, *giving great weight to each word, and with a certain vicious audacity:* William, when I walked into the jungle, I was seventeen. When I walked out I was twenty-one. And, by God, I was rich! *He goes off into darkness around the right corner of the house.*

WILLY: . . . was rich! That's just the spirit I want to imbue them with! To walk into a jungle! I was right! I was right! I was right!

Ben is gone, but Willy is still speaking to him as Linda, in nightgown and robe, enters the kitchen, glances around for Willy, then goes to the door of the house, looks out and sees him. Comes down to his left. He looks at her.

LINDA: Willy, dear? Willy?

WILLY: I was right!

LINDA: Did you have some cheese? *He can't answer.* It's very late, darling. Come to bed, heh?

WILLY, *looking straight up:* Gotta break your neck to see a star in this yard.

LINDA: You coming in?

WILLY: Whatever happened to that diamond watch fob? Remember? When Ben came from Africa that time? Didn't he give me a watch fob with a diamond in it?

LINDA: You pawned it, dear. Twelve, thirteen years ago. For Biff's radio correspondence course.

WILLY: Gee, that was a beautiful thing. I'll take a walk.

LINDA: But you're in your slippers.

WILLY, *starting to go around the house at the left:* I was right! I was! *Half to Linda, as he goes, shaking his head:* What a man! There was a man worth talking to. I was right!

LINDA, *calling after Willy:* But in your slippers, Willy!

Willy is almost gone when Biff, in his pajamas, comes down the stairs and enters the kitchen.

BIFF: What is he doing out there?

LINDA: Sh!

BIFF: God Almighty, Mom, how long has he been doing this?

LINDA: Don't, he'll hear you.

BIFF: What the hell is the matter with him?

LINDA: It'll pass by morning.

BIFF: Shouldn't we do anything?

LINDA: Oh, my dear, you should do a lot of things, but there's nothing to do, so go to sleep.

Happy comes down the stair and sits on the steps.

HAPPY: I never heard him so loud, Mom.

LINDA: Well, come around more often; you'll hear him. *She sits down at the table and mends the lining of Willy's jacket.*

BIFF: Why didn't you ever write me about this, Mom?

LINDA: How would I write to you? For over three months you had no address.

BIFF: I was on the move. But you know I thought of you all the time. You know that, don't you, pal?

LINDA: I know, dear, I know. But he likes to have a letter. Just to know that there's still a possibility for better things.

BIFF: He's not like this all the time, is he?

LINDA: It's when you come home he's always the worst.

BIFF: When I come home?

LINDA: When you write you're coming, he's all smiles, and talks about the future, and—he's just wonderful. And then the closer you seem to come, the more shaky he gets, and then, by the time you get here, he's arguing, and he seems angry at you. I think it's just that maybe he can't bring himself to—to open up to you. Why are you so hateful to each other? Why is that?

BIFF, *evasively:* I'm not hateful, Mom.

LINDA: But you no sooner come in the door than you're fighting!

BIFF: I don't know why. I mean to change. I'm tryin', Mom, you understand?

LINDA: Are you home to stay now?

BIFF: I don't know. I want to look around, see what's doin'.

LINDA: Biff, you can't look around all your life, can you?

BIFF: I just can't take hold, Mom. I can't take hold of some kind of a life.

LINDA: Biff, a man is not a bird, to come and go with the springtime.

BIFF: Your hair . . . *He touches her hair.* Your hair got so gray.

LINDA: Oh, it's been gray since you were in high school. I just stopped dyeing it, that's all.

BIFF: Dye it again, will ya? I don't want my pal looking old. *He smiles.*

LINDA: You're such a boy! You think you can go away for a year and . . . You've got to get it into your head now that one day you'll knock on this door and there'll be strange people here—

BIFF: What are you talking about? You're not even sixty, Mom.

LINDA: But what about your father?

BIFF, *lamely:* Well, I meant him too.

HAPPY: He admires Pop.

LINDA: Biff, dear, if you don't have any feeling for him, then you can't have any feeling for me.

BIFF: Sure I can, Mom.

LINDA: No. You can't just come to see me, because I love him. *With a threat, but only a threat, of tears:* He's the dearest man in the world to me, and I won't have anyone making him feel unwanted and low and blue. You've got to make up your mind now, darling, there's no leeway any more. Either he's your father and you pay him that respect, or else you're not to come here. I know he's not easy to get along with—nobody knows that better than me—but . . .

WILLY, *from the left, with a laugh:* Hey, hey, Biffo!

BIFF, *starting to go out after Willy:* What the hell is the matter with him? *Happy stops him.*

LINDA: Don't—don't go near him!

BIFF: Stop making excuses for him! He always, always wiped the floor with you. Never had an ounce of respect for you.

HAPPY: He's always had respect for—

BIFF: What the hell do you know about it?

HAPPY, *surlily:* Just don't call him crazy!

BIFF: He's got no character— Charley wouldn't do this. Not in his own house—spewing out that vomit from his mind.

HAPPY: Charley never had to cope with what he's got to.

BIFF: People are worse off than Willy Loman. Believe me, I've seen them!

LINDA: Then make Charley your father, Biff. You can't do that, can you? I don't say he's a great man. Willy Loman never made a lot of money. His name was never in the paper. He's not the finest character that ever lived. But he's a human being, and a terrible thing is happening to him. So attention must be paid. He's not to be allowed to fall into his grave like an old dog. Attention, attention must be finally paid to such a person. You called him crazy—

BIFF: I didn't mean—

LINDA: No, a lot of people think he's lost his—balance. But you don't have to be very smart to know what his trouble is. The man is exhausted.

HAPPY: Sure!

LINDA: A small man can be just as exhausted as a great man. He works for a company thirty-six years this March, opens up unheard-of territories to their trademark, and now in his old age they take his salary away.

HAPPY, *indignantly:* I didn't know that, Mom.

LINDA: You never asked, my dear! Now that you get your spending money someplace else you don't trouble your mind with him.

HAPPY: But I gave you money last—

LINDA: Christmas time, fifty dollars! To fix the hot water it cost ninety-seven fifty! For five weeks he's been on straight commission, like a beginner, an unknown!

BIFF: Those ungrateful bastards!

LINDA: Are they any worse than his sons? When he brought them business, when he was young, they were glad to see him. But now his old friends, the old buyers that loved him so and always found some order to hand him in a pinch—they're all dead, retired. He used to be able to make six, seven calls a day in Boston. Now he takes his valises out of the car and puts them back and takes them out again and he's exhausted. Instead of walking he talks now. He drives seven hundred miles, and when he gets there no one knows him any more, no one welcomes him. And what goes through a man's mind, driving seven hundred miles home without having earned a cent? Why shouldn't he talk to himself? Why? When he has to go to Charley and borrow fifty dollars a week and pretend to me that it's his pay? How long can that go on? How long? You see what I'm sitting here and waiting for? And you tell me he has no character? The man who never worked a day but for your benefit? When does he get the medal for that? Is this his reward—to turn around at the age of sixty-three and find his sons, who he loved better than his life, one a philandering bum—

HAPPY: Mom!

LINDA: That's all you are, my baby! *To Biff:* And you! What happened to the love you had for him? You were such pals! How you used to talk to him on the phone every night! How lonely he was till he could come home to you!

BIFF: All right, Mom. I'll live here in my room, and I'll get a job. I'll keep away from him, that's all.

LINDA: No, Biff. You can't stay here and fight all the time.

BIFF: He threw me out of this house, remember that.

LINDA: Why did he do that? I never knew why.

BIFF: Because I know he's a fake and he doesn't like anybody around who knows!

LINDA: Why a fake? In what way? What do you mean?

BIFF: Just don't lay it all at my feet. It's between me and him—that's all I have to say. I'll chip in from now on. He'll settle for half my pay check. He'll be all right. I'm going to bed. *He starts for the stairs.*

LINDA: He won't be all right.

BIFF, *turning on the stairs, furiously:* I hate this city and I'll stay here. Now what do you want?

LINDA: He's dying, Biff.

Happy turns quickly to her, shocked.

BIFF, *after a pause:* Why is he dying?

LINDA: He's been trying to kill himself.

BIFF, *with great horror:* How?

LINDA: I live from day to day.

BIFF: What're you talking about?

LINDA: Remember I wrote you that he smashed up the car again? In February?

BIFF: Well?

LINDA: The insurance inspector came. He said that they have evidence. That all these accidents in the last year—weren't—weren't—accidents.

HAPPY: How can they tell that? That's a lie.

LINDA: It seems there's a woman . . . *She takes a breath as*

BIFF, *sharply but contained:* What woman?

LINDA, *simultaneously:* . . . and this woman . . .

LINDA: What?

BIFF: Nothing. Go ahead.

LINDA: What did you say?

BIFF: Nothing. I just said what woman?

HAPPY: What about her?

LINDA: Well, it seems she was walking down the road and saw his car. She says that he wasn't driving fast at all, and that he didn't skid. She says he came to that little bridge, and then deliberately smashed into the railing, and it was only the shallowness of the water that saved him.

BIFF: Oh, no, he probably just fell asleep again.

LINDA: I don't think he fell asleep.

BIFF: Why not?

LINDA: Last month . . . *With great difficulty:* Oh, boys, it's so hard to say a thing like this! He's just a big stupid man to you, but I tell you there's more good in him than in many other people. *She chokes, wipes her eyes.* I was looking for a fuse. The lights blew out, and I went down the cellar. And behind the fuse box—it happened to fall out—was a length of rubber pipe—just short.

HAPPY: No kidding?

LINDA: There's a little attachment on the end of it. I knew right away. And sure enough, on the bottom of the water heater there's a new little nipple on the gas pipe.

HAPPY, *angrily:* That—jerk.

BIFF: Did you have it taken off?

LINDA: I'm—I'm ashamed to. How can I mention it to him? Every day I go down and take away that little rubber pipe. But, when he comes home, I put it back where it was. How can I insult him that way? I don't know what to do. I live from day to day, boys. I tell you, I know every thought in his mind. It sounds so old-fashioned and silly, but I tell you he put his whole life into you and you've turned your backs on him. *She is bent over in the chair, weeping, her face in her hands.* Biff, I swear to God! Biff, his life is in your hands!

HAPPY, *to Biff:* How do you like that damned fool!

BIFF, *kissing her:* All right, pal, all right. It's all settled now. I've been remiss. I know that, Mom. But now I'll stay, and I swear to you, I'll apply myself. *Kneeling in front of her, in a fever of self-reproach:* It's just—you see, Mom, I don't fit in business. Not that I won't try. I'll try, and I'll make good.

HAPPY: Sure you will. The trouble with you in business was you never tried to please people.

BIFF: I know, I—

HAPPY: Like when you worked for Harrison's. Bob Harrison said you were tops, and then you go and do some damn fool thing like whistling whole songs in the elevator like a comedian.

BIFF, *against Happy:* So what? I like to whistle sometimes.

HAPPY: You don't raise a guy to a responsible job who whistles in the elevator!

LINDA: Well, don't argue about it now.

HAPPY: Like when you'd go off and swim in the middle of the day instead of taking the line around.

BIFF, *his resentment rising:* Well, don't you run off? You take off sometimes, don't you? On a nice summer day?

HAPPY: Yeah, but I cover myself!

LINDA: Boys!

HAPPY: If I'm going to take a fade the boss can call any number where I'm supposed to be and they'll swear to him that I just left. I'll tell you something that I hate to say, Biff, but in the business world some of them think you're crazy.

BIFF, *angered:* Screw the business world!

HAPPY: All right, screw it! Great, but cover yourself!

LINDA: Hap, Hap!

BIFF: I don't care what they think! They've laughed at Dad for years, and you know why? Because we don't belong in this nuthouse of a city! We should be mixing cement on some open plain, or—or carpenters. A carpenter is allowed to whistle!

Willy walks in from the entrance of the house, at left.

WILLY: Even your grandfather was better than a carpenter. *Pause. They watch him.* You never grew up. Bernard does not whistle in the elevator, I assure you.

BIFF, *as though to laugh Willy out of it:* Yeah, but you do, Pop.

WILLY: I never in my life whistled in an elevator! And who in the business world thinks I'm crazy?

BIFF: I didn't mean it like that, Pop. Now don't make a whole thing out of it, will ya?

WILLY: Go back to the West! Be a carpenter, a cowboy, enjoy yourself!

LINDA: Willy, he was just saying—

WILLY: I heard what he said!

HAPPY, *trying to quiet Willy:* Hey, Pop, come on now . . .

WILLY, *continuing over Happy's line:* They laugh at me, heh?

Go to Filene's, go to the Hub, go to Slattery's, Boston. Call out the name Willy Loman and see what happens! Big shot!

BIFF: All right, Pop.

WILLY: Big!

BIFF: All right!

WILLY: Why do you always insult me?

BIFF: I didn't say a word. *To Linda:* Did I say a word?

LINDA: He didn't say anything, Willy.

WILLY, *going to the doorway of the living-room:* All right, good night, good night.

LINDA: Willy, dear, he just decided . . .

WILLY, *to Biff:* If you get tired hanging around tomorrow, paint the ceiling I put up in the living-room.

BIFF: I'm leaving early tomorrow.

HAPPY: He's going to see Bill Oliver, Pop.

WILLY, *interestedly:* Oliver? For what?

BIFF, *with reserve, but trying, trying:* He always said he'd stake me. I'd like to go into business, so maybe I can take him up on it.

LINDA: Isn't that wonderful?

WILLY: Don't interrupt. What's wonderful about it? There's fifty men in the City of New York who'd stake him. *To Biff:* Sporting goods?

BIFF: I guess so. I know something about it and—

WILLY: He knows something about it! You know sporting goods better than Spalding, for God's sake! How much is he giving you?

BIFF: I don't know, I didn't even see him yet, but—

WILLY: Then what're you talkin' about?

BIFF, *getting angry:* Well, all I said was I'm gonna see him, that's all!

WILLY, *turning away:* Ah, you're counting your chickens again.

BIFF, *starting left for the stairs:* Oh, Jesus, I'm going to sleep!

WILLY, *calling after him:* Don't curse in this house!

BIFF, *turning:* Since when did you get so clean?

HAPPY, *trying to stop them:* Wait a . . .

WILLY: Don't use that language to me! I won't have it!

HAPPY, *grabbing Biff, shouts:* Wait a minute! I got an idea. I got a feasible idea. Come here, Biff, let's talk this over now, let's talk some sense here. When I was down in Florida last time, I thought of a great idea to sell sporting goods. It just came back to me. You and I, Biff—we have a line, the Loman Line. We train a couple of weeks, and put on a couple of exhibitions, see?

WILLY: That's an idea!

HAPPY: Wait! We form two basketball teams, see? Two water-polo teams. We play each other. It's a million dollars' worth of publicity. Two brothers, see? The Loman Brothers. Displays in the Royal Palms—all the hotels. And banners over the ring and the basketball court: "Loman Brothers." Baby, we could sell sporting goods!

WILLY: That is a one-million-dollar idea!

LINDA: Marvelous!

BIFF: I'm in great shape as far as that's concerned.

HAPPY: And the beauty of it is, Biff, it wouldn't be like a business. We'd be out playin' ball again . . .

BIFF, *enthused:* Yeah, that's . . .

WILLY: Million-dollar . . .

HAPPY: And you wouldn't get fed up with it, Biff. It'd be the family again. There'd be the old honor, and comradeship, and if you wanted to go off for a swim or somethin'—well, you'd do it! Without some smart cooky gettin' up ahead of you!

WILLY: Lick the world! You guys together could absolutely lick the civilized world.

BIFF: I'll see Oliver tomorrow. Hap, if we could work that out . . .

LINDA: Maybe things are beginning to—

WILLY, *wildly enthused, to Linda:* Stop interrupting! *To Biff:* But don't wear sport jacket and slacks when you see Oliver.

BIFF: No, I'll—

WILLY: A business suit, and talk as little as possible, and don't crack any jokes.

BIFF: He did like me. Always liked me.

LINDA: He loved you!

WILLY, *to Linda:* Will you stop! *To Biff:* Walk in very serious. You are not applying for a boy's job. Money is to pass. Be quiet, fine, and serious. Everybody likes a kidder, but nobody lends him money.

HAPPY: I'll try to get some myself, Biff. I'm sure I can.

WILLY: I see great things for you kids, I think your troubles are over. But remember, start big and you'll end big. Ask for fifteen. How much you gonna ask for?

BIFF: Gee, I don't know—

WILLY: And don't say "Gee." "Gee" is a boy's word. A man walking in for fifteen thousand dollars does not say "Gee!"

BIFF: Ten, I think, would be top though.

WILLY: Don't be so modest. You always started too low. Walk in with a big laugh. Don't look worried. Start off with a couple of your good stories to lighten things up. It's not what you say, it's how you say it—because personality always wins the day.

LINDA: Oliver always thought the highest of him—

WILLY: Will you let me talk?

BIFF: Don't yell at her, Pop, will ya?

WILLY, *angrily:* I was talking, wasn't I?

BIFF: I don't like you yelling at her all the time, and I'm tellin' you, that's all.

WILLY: What're you, takin' over this house?

LINDA: Willy—

WILLY, *turning on her:* Don't take his side all the time, god-dammit!

BIFF, *furiously:* Stop yelling at her!

WILLY, *suddenly pulling on his cheek, beaten down, guilt ridden:* Give my best to Bill Oliver—he may remember me. *He exits through the living-room doorway.*

LINDA, *her voice subdued:* What'd you have to start that for? *Biff turns away.* You see how sweet he was as soon as you talked hopefully? *She goes over to Biff.* Come up and say good night to him. Don't let him go to bed that way.

HAPPY: Come on, Biff, let's buck him up.

LINDA: Please, dear. Just say good night. It takes so little to make him happy. Come. *She goes through the living-room doorway, calling upstairs from within the living-room:* Your pajamas are hanging in the bathroom, Willy!

HAPPY, *looking toward where Linda went out:* What a woman! They broke the mold when they made her. You know that, Biff?

BIFF: He's off salary. My God, working on commission!

HAPPY: Well, let's face it: he's no hot-shot selling man. Except that sometimes, you have to admit, he's a sweet personality.

BIFF, *deciding:* Lend me ten bucks, will ya? I want to buy some new ties.

HAPPY: I'll take you to a place I know. Beautiful stuff. Wear one of my striped shirts tomorrow.

BIFF: She got gray. Mom got awful old. Gee, I'm gonna go in to Oliver tomorrow and knock him for a—

HAPPY: Come on up. Tell that to Dad. Let's give him a whirl. Come on.

BIFF, *steamed up:* You know, with ten thousand bucks, boy!

HAPPY, *as they go into the living-room:* That's the talk, Biff, that's the first time I've heard the old confidence out of you! *From within the living-room, fading off:* You're gonna live with me, kid, and any babe you want just say the word . . . *The last lines are hardly heard. They are mounting the stairs to their parents' bedroom.*

LINDA, *entering her bedroom and addressing Willy, who is in the bathroom. She is straightening the bed for him:* Can you do anything about the shower? It drips.

WILLY, *from the bathroom:* All of a sudden everything falls to pieces! Goddam plumbing, oughta be sued, those people. I hardly finished putting it in and the thing . . . *His words rumble off.*

LINDA: I'm just wondering if Oliver will remember him. You think he might?

WILLY, *coming out of the bathroom in his pajamas:* Remember him? What's the matter with you, you crazy? If he'd've stayed with Oliver he'd be on top by now! Wait'll Oliver gets a look at him. You don't know the average caliber any more. The average young man today—*he is getting into bed*—is got a caliber of zero. Greatest thing in the world for him was to bum around.

Biff and Happy enter the bedroom. Slight pause.

WILLY, *stops short, looking at Biff:* Glad to hear it, boy.

HAPPY: He wanted to say good night to you, sport.

WILLY, *to Biff:* Yeah. Knock him dead, boy. What'd you want to tell me?

BIFF: Just take it easy, Pop. Good night. *He turns to go.*

WILLY, *unable to resist:* And if anything falls off the desk while you're talking to him—like a package or something—don't you pick it up. They have office boys for that.

LINDA: I'll make a big breakfast—

WILLY: Will you let me finish? *To Biff:* Tell him you were in the business in the West. Not farm work.

BIFF: All right, Dad.

LINDA: I think everything—

WILLY, *going right through her speech:* And don't undersell yourself. No less than fifteen thousand dollars.

BIFF, *unable to bear him:* Okay. Good night, Mom. *He starts moving.*

WILLY: Because you got a greatness in you, Biff, remember that. You got all kinds a greatness . . . *He lies back, exhausted. Biff walks out.*

LINDA, *calling after Biff:* Sleep well, darling!

HAPPY: I'm gonna get married, Mom. I wanted to tell you.

LINDA: Go to sleep, dear.

HAPPY, *going:* I just wanted to tell you.

WILLY: Keep up the good work. *Happy exits.* God . . . remember that Ebbets Field game? The championship of the city?

LINDA: Just rest. Should I sing to you?

WILLY: Yeah. Sing to me. *Linda hums a soft lullaby.* When that team came out—he was the tallest, remember?

LINDA: Oh, yes. And in gold.

Biff enters the darkened kitchen, takes a cigarette, and leaves the house. He comes downstage into a golden pool of light. He smokes, staring at the night.

WILLY: Like a young god. Hercules—something like that. And the sun, the sun all around him. Remember how he waved to me? Right up from the field, with the representatives of three colleges standing by? And the buyers I brought, and the cheers when he came out—Loman, Loman, Loman! God Almighty, he'll be great yet. A star like that, magnificent, can never really fade away!

The light on Willy is fading. The gas heater begins to glow through the kitchen wall, near the stairs, a blue flame beneath red coils.

LINDA, *timidly:* Willy dear, what has he got against you?

WILLY: I'm so tired. Don't talk any more.

Biff slowly returns to the kitchen. He stops, stares toward the heater.

LINDA: Will you ask Howard to let you work in New York?

WILLY: First thing in the morning. Everything'll be all right.

Biff reaches behind the heater and draws out a length of rubber tubing. He is horrified and turns his head toward Willy's room, still dimly lit, from which the strains of Linda's desperate but monotonous humming rise.

WILLY, *staring through the window into the moonlight:* Gee, look at the moon moving between the buildings!

Biff wraps the tubing around his hand and quickly goes up the stairs.

Curtain

Act Two

Music is heard, gay and bright. The curtain rises as the music fades away. Willy, in shirt sleeves, is sitting at the kitchen table, sipping coffee, his hat in his lap. Linda is filling his cup when she can.

WILLY: Wonderful coffee. Meal in itself.

LINDA: Can I make you some eggs?

WILLY: No. Take a breath.

LINDA: You look so rested, dear.

WILLY: I slept like a dead one. First time in months. Imagine, sleeping till ten on a Tuesday morning. Boys left nice and early, heh?

LINDA: They were out of here by eight o'clock.

WILLY: Good work!

LINDA: It was so thrilling to see them leaving together. I can't get over the shaving lotion in this house!

WILLY, *smiling:* Mmm—

LINDA: Biff was very changed this morning. His whole attitude seemed to be hopeful. He couldn't wait to get downtown to see Oliver.

WILLY: He's heading for a change. There's no question, there simply are certain men that take longer to get—solidified. How did he dress?

LINDA: His blue suit. He's so handsome in that suit. He could be a—anything in that suit!

Willy gets up from the table. Linda holds his jacket for him.

WILLY: There's no question, no question at all. Gee, on the way home tonight I'd like to buy some seeds.

LINDA, *laughing:* That'd be wonderful. But not enough sun gets back there. Nothing'll grow any more.

WILLY: You wait, kid, before it's all over we're gonna get a little place out in the country, and I'll raise some vegetables, a couple of chickens . . .

LINDA: You'll do it yet, dear.

Willy walks out of his jacket. Linda follows him.

WILLY: And they'll get married, and come for a weekend. I'd build a little guest house. 'Cause I got so many fine tools, all I'd need would be a little lumber and some peace of mind.

LINDA, *joyfully:* I sewed the lining . . .

WILLY: I could build two guest houses, so they'd both come. Did he decide how much he's going to ask Oliver for?

LINDA, *getting him into the jacket:* He didn't mention it, but I imagine ten or fifteen thousand. You going to talk to Howard today?

WILLY: Yeah. I'll put it to him straight and simple. He'll just have to take me off the road.

LINDA: And Willy, don't forget to ask for a little advance, because we've got the insurance premium. It's the grace period now.

WILLY: That's a hundred . . . ?

LINDA: A hundred and eight, sixty-eight. Because we're a little short again.

WILLY: Why are we short?

LINDA: Well, you had the motor job on the car . . .

WILLY: That goddam Studebaker!

LINDA: And you got one more payment on the refrigerator . . .

WILLY: But it just broke again!

LINDA: Well, it's old, dear.

WILLY: I told you we should've bought a well-advertised machine. Charley bought a General Electric and it's twenty years old and it's still good, that son-of-a-bitch.

LINDA: But, Willy—

WILLY: Whoever heard of a Hastings refrigerator? Once in my life I would like to own something outright before it's broken! I'm always in a race with the junkyard! I just finished paying for the car and it's on its last legs. The refrigerator consumes belts like a goddam maniac. They time those things. They time them so when you finally paid for them, they're used up.

LINDA, *buttoning up his jacket as he unbuttons it:* All told, about two hundred dollars would carry us, dear. But that includes the last payment on the mortgage. After this payment, Willy, the house belongs to us.

WILLY: It's twenty-five years!

LINDA: Biff was nine years old when we bought it.

WILLY: Well, that's a great thing. To weather a twenty-five year mortgage is—

LINDA: It's an accomplishment.

WILLY: All the cement, the lumber, the reconstruction I put in this house! There ain't a crack to be found in it any more.

LINDA: Well, it served its purpose.

WILLY: What purpose? Some stranger'll come along, move in, and that's that. If only Biff would take this house, and raise a family . . . *He starts to go.* Good-by, I'm late.

LINDA, *suddenly remembering:* Oh, I forgot! You're supposed to meet them for dinner.

WILLY: Me?

LINDA: At Frank's Chop House on Forty-eighth near Sixth Avenue.

WILLY: Is that so! How about you?

LINDA: No, just the three of you. They're gonna blow you to a big meal!

WILLY: Don't say! Who thought of that?

LINDA: Biff came to me this morning, Willy, and he said, "Tell Dad, we want to blow him to a big meal." Be there six o'clock. You and your two boys are going to have dinner.

WILLY: Gee whiz! That's really somethin'. I'm gonna knock Howard for a loop, kid. I'll get an advance, and I'll come home with a New York job. Goddammit, now I'm gonna do it!

LINDA: Oh, that's the spirit, Willy!

WILLY: I will never get behind a wheel the rest of my life!

LINDA: It's changing, Willy, I can feel it changing!

WILLY: Beyond a question. G'by, I'm late. *He starts to go again.*

LINDA, *calling after him as she runs to the kitchen table for a handkerchief:* You got your glasses?

WILLY, *feels for them, then comes back in:* Yeah, yeah, got my glasses.

LINDA, *giving him the handkerchief:* And a handkerchief.

WILLY: Yeah, handkerchief.

LINDA: And your saccharine?

WILLY: Yeah, my saccharine.

LINDA: Be careful on the subway stairs.

She kisses him, and a silk stocking is seen hanging from her hand. Willy notices it.

WILLY: Will you stop mending stockings? At least while I'm in the house. It gets me nervous. I can't tell you. Please.

Linda hides the stocking in her hand as she follows Willy across the forestage in front of the house.

LINDA: Remember, Frank's Chop House.

WILLY, *passing the apron:* Maybe beets would grow out there.

LINDA, *laughing:* But you tried so many times.

WILLY: Yeah. Well, don't work hard today. *He disappears around the right corner of the house.*

LINDA: Be careful!

As Willy vanishes, Linda waves to him. Suddenly the phone rings. She runs across the stage and into the kitchen and lifts it.

LINDA: Hello? Oh, Biff! I'm so glad you called, I just . . . Yes, sure, I just told him. Yes, he'll be there for dinner at six o'clock, I didn't forget. Listen, I was just dying to tell you. You know that little rubber pipe I told you about? That he connected to the gas heater? I finally decided to go down the cellar this morning and take it away and destroy it. But it's gone! Imagine? He took it away himself, it isn't there! *She listens.* When? Oh, then you took it. Oh—nothing, it's just that

I'd hoped he'd taken it away himself. Oh, I'm not worried, darling, because this morning he left in such high spirits, it was like the old days! I'm not afraid any more. Did Mr. Oliver see you? . . . Well, you wait there then. And make a nice impression on him, darling. Just don't perspire too much before you see him. And have a nice time with Dad. He may have big news too! . . . That's right, a New York job. And be sweet to him tonight, dear. Be loving to him. Because he's only a little boat looking for a harbor. *She is trembling with sorrow and joy.* Oh, that's wonderful, Biff, you'll save his life. Thanks, darling. Just put your arm around him when he comes into the restaurant. Give him a smile. That's the boy . . . Good-by, dear. . . . You got your comb? . . . That's fine. Good-by, Biff dear.

In the middle of her speech, Howard Wagner, thirty-six, wheels on a small typewriter table on which is a wire-recording machine and proceeds to plug it in. This is on the left forestage. Light slowly fades on Linda as it rises on Howard. Howard is intent on threading the machine and only glances over his shoulder as Willy appears.

WILLY: Pst! Pst!

HOWARD: Hello, Willy, come in.

WILLY: Like to have a little talk with you, Howard.

HOWARD: Sorry to keep you waiting. I'll be with you in a minute.

WILLY: What's that, Howard?

HOWARD: Didn't you ever see one of these? Wire recorder.

WILLY: Oh. Can we talk a minute?

HOWARD: Records things. Just got delivery yesterday. Been driving me crazy, the most terrific machine I ever saw in my life. I was up all night with it.

WILLY: What do you do with it?

HOWARD: I bought it for dictation, but you can do anything with it. Listen to this. I had it home last night. Listen to what I picked up. The first one is my daughter. Get this. *He flicks the switch and "Roll out the Barrel" is heard being whistled.* Listen to that kid whistle.

WILLY: That is lifelike, isn't it?

HOWARD: Seven years old. Get that tone.

WILLY: Ts, ts. Like to ask a little favor if you . . .

The whistling breaks off, and the voice of Howard's daughter is heard.

HIS DAUGHTER: "Now you, Daddy."

HOWARD: She's crazy for me! *Again the same song is whistled. That's me! Ha! He winks.*

WILLY: You're very good!

The whistling breaks off again. The machine runs silent for a moment.

HOWARD: Sh! Get this now, this is my son.

HIS SON: "The capital of Alabama is Montgomery; the capital of Arizona is Phoenix; the capital of Arkansas is Little Rock; the capital of California is Sacramento . . ." *and on, and on.*

HOWARD, *holding up five fingers:* Five years old, Willy!

WILLY: He'll make an announcer some day!

HIS SON, *continuing:* "The capital . . ."

HOWARD: Get that—alphabetical order! *The machine breaks off suddenly.* Wait a minute. The maid kicked the plug out.

WILLY: It certainly is a—

HOWARD: Sh, for God's sake!

HIS SON: "It's nine o'clock, Bulova watch time. So I have to go to sleep."

WILLY: That really is—

HOWARD: Wait a minute! The next is my wife.

They wait.

HOWARD'S VOICE: "Go on, say something." *Pause.* "Well, you gonna talk?"

HIS WIFE: "I can't think of anything."

HOWARD'S VOICE: "Well, talk—it's turning."

HIS WIFE, *shyly, beaten:* "Hello." *Silence.* "Oh, Howard, I can't talk into this . . ."

HOWARD, *snapping the machine off:* That was my wife.

WILLY: That is a wonderful machine. Can we—

HOWARD: I tell you, Willy, I'm gonna take my camera, and my bandsaw, and all my hobbies, and out they go. This is the most fascinating relaxation I ever found.

WILLY: I think I'll get one myself.

HOWARD: Sure, they're only a hundred and a half. You can't do without it. Supposing you wanna hear Jack Benny, see? But you can't be at home at that hour. So you tell the maid to turn the radio on when Jack Benny comes on, and this automatically goes on with the radio . . .

WILLY: And when you come home you . . .

HOWARD: You can come home twelve o'clock, one o'clock, any time you like, and you get yourself a Coke and sit yourself down, throw the switch, and there's Jack Benny's program in the middle of the night!

WILLY: I'm definitely going to get one. Because lots of time

I'm on the road, and I think to myself, what I must be missing on the radio!

HOWARD: Don't you have a radio in the car?

WILLY: Well, yeah, but who ever thinks of turning it on?

HOWARD: Say, aren't you supposed to be in Boston?

WILLY: That's what I want to talk to you about, Howard. You got a minute? *He draws a chair in from the wing.*

HOWARD: What happened? What're you doing here?

WILLY: Well . . .

HOWARD: You didn't crack up again, did you?

WILLY: Oh, no. No . . .

HOWARD: Geez, you had me worried there for a minute. What's the trouble?

WILLY: Well, tell you the truth, Howard. I've come to the decision that I'd rather not travel any more.

HOWARD: Not travel! Well, what'll you do?

WILLY: Remember, Christmas time, when you had the party here? You said you'd try to think of some spot for me here in town.

HOWARD: With us?

WILLY: Well, sure.

HOWARD: Oh, yeah, yeah. I remember. Well, I couldn't think of anything for you, Willy.

WILLY: I tell ya, Howard. The kids are all grown up, y'know. I don't need much any more. If I could take home—well, sixty-five dollars a week, I could swing it.

HOWARD: Yeah, but Willy, see I—

WILLY: I tell ya why, Howard. Speaking frankly and between the two of us, y'know—I'm just a little tired.

HOWARD: Oh, I could understand that, Willy. But you're a road man, Willy, and we do a road business. We've only got a half-dozen salesmen on the floor here.

WILLY: God knows, Howard, I never asked a favor of any man. But I was with the firm when your father used to carry you in here in his arms.

HOWARD: I know that, Willy, but—

WILLY: Your father came to me the day you were born and asked me what I thought of the name of Howard, may he rest in peace.

HOWARD: I appreciate that, Willy, but there just is no spot here for you. If I had a spot I'd slam you right in, but I just don't have a single solitary spot.

He looks for his lighter. Willy has picked it up and gives it to him. Pause.

WILLY, *with increasing anger:* Howard, all I need to set my table is fifty dollars a week.

HOWARD: But where am I going to put you, kid?

WILLY: Look, it isn't a question of whether I can sell merchandise, is it?

HOWARD: No, but it's a business, kid, and everybody's gotta pull his own weight.

WILLY, *desperately:* Just let me tell you a story, Howard—

HOWARD: 'Cause you gotta admit, business is business.

WILLY, *angrily:* Business is definitely business, but just listen for a minute. You don't understand this. When I was a boy—eighteen, nineteen—I was already on the road. And there was a question in my mind as to whether selling had a future for me. Because in those days I had a yearning to go to Alaska. See, there were three gold strikes in one month in Alaska, and I felt like going out. Just for the ride, you might say.

HOWARD, *barely interested:* Don't say.

WILLY: Oh, yeah, my father lived many years in Alaska. He was an adventurous man. We've got quite a little streak of self-reliance in our family. I thought I'd go out with my older brother and try to locate him, and maybe settle in the North with the old man. And I was almost decided to go, when I met a salesman in the Parker House. His name was Dave Single-man. And he was eighty-four years old, and he'd drummed merchandise in thirty-one states. And old Dave, he'd go up to his room, y'understand, put on his green velvet slippers—I'll never forget—and pick up his phone and call the buyers, and without ever leaving his room, at the age of eighty-four, he made his living. And when I saw that, I realized that selling was the greatest career a man could want. 'Cause what could be more satisfying than to be able to go, at the age of eighty-four, into twenty or thirty different cities, and pick up a phone, and be remembered and loved and helped by so many different people? Do you know? when he died—and by the way he died the death of a salesman, in his green velvet slippers in the smoker of the New York, New Haven and Hartford, going into Boston—when he died, hundreds of salesmen and buyers were at his funeral. Things were sad on a lotta trains for months after that. *He stands up. Howard has not looked at him.* In those days there was personality in it, Howard. There was respect, and comradeship, and gratitude in it. Today, it's all cut and dried, and there's no chance for bringing friendship to bear—or personality. You see what I mean? They don't know me any more.

HOWARD, *moving away, to the right:* That's just the thing, Willy.

WILLY: If I had forty dollars a week—that's all I'd need. Forty dollars, Howard.

HOWARD: Kid, I can't take blood from a stone, I—

WILLY, *desperation is on him now:* Howard, the year Al Smith was nominated, your father came to me and—

HOWARD, *starting to go off:* I've got to see some people, kid.

WILLY, *stopping him:* I'm talking about your father! There were promises made across this desk! You mustn't tell me you've got people to see—I put thirty-four years into this firm, Howard, and now I can't pay my insurance! You can't eat the orange and throw the peel away—a man is not a piece of fruit! *After a pause:* Now pay attention. Your father—in 1928 I had a big year. I averaged a hundred and seventy dollars a week in commissions.

HOWARD, *impatiently:* Now, Willy, you never averaged—

WILLY, *banging his hand on the desk:* I averaged a hundred and seventy dollars a week in the year of 1928! And your father came to me—or rather, I was in the office here—it was right over this desk—and he put his hand on my shoulder—

HOWARD, *getting up:* You'll have to excuse me, Willy, I gotta see some people. Pull yourself together. *Going out:* I'll be back in a little while.

On Howard's exit, the light on his chair grows very bright and strange.

WILLY: Pull myself together! What the hell did I say to him? My God, I was yelling at him! How could I! *Willy breaks off, staring at the light, which occupies the chair, animating it. He approaches this chair, standing across the desk from it.* Frank, Frank, don't you remember what you told me that time? How you put your hand on my shoulder, and Frank . . . *He leans on the desk and as he speaks the dead man's name he accidentally switches on the recorder, and instantly*

HOWARD'S SON: ". . . of New York is Albany. The capital of Ohio is Cincinnati, the capital of Rhode Island is . . ." *The recitation continues.*

WILLY, *leaping away with fright, shouting:* Ha! Howard! Howard! Howard!

HOWARD, *rushing in:* What happened?

WILLY, *pointing at the machine, which continues nasally, childishly, with the capital cities:* Shut it off! Shut it off!

HOWARD, *pulling the plug out:* Look, Willy . . .

WILLY, *pressing his hands to his eyes:* I gotta get myself some coffee. I'll get some coffee . . .

Willy starts to walk out. Howard stops him.

HOWARD, *rolling up the cord:* Willy, look . . .

WILLY: I'll go to Boston.

HOWARD: Willy, you can't go to Boston for us.

WILLY: Why can't I go?

HOWARD: I don't want you to represent us. I've been meaning to tell you for a long time now.

WILLY: Howard, are you firing me?

HOWARD: I think you need a good long rest, Willy.

WILLY: Howard—

HOWARD: And when you feel better, come back, and we'll see if we can work something out.

WILLY: But I gotta earn money, Howard. I'm in no position to—

HOWARD: Where are your sons? Why don't your sons give you a hand?

WILLY: They're working on a very big deal.

HOWARD: This is no time for false pride, Willy. You go to your sons and you tell them that you're tired. You've got two great boys, haven't you?

WILLY: Oh, no question, no question, but in the meantime . . .

HOWARD: Then that's that, heh?

WILLY: All right, I'll go to Boston tomorrow.

HOWARD: No, no.

WILLY: I can't throw myself on my sons. I'm not a cripple!

HOWARD: Look, kid, I'm busy this morning.

WILLY, *grasping Howard's arm:* Howard, you've got to let me go to Boston!

HOWARD, *hard, keeping himself under control:* I've got a line of people to see this morning. Sit down, take five minutes, and pull yourself together, and then go home, will ya? I need the office, Willy. *He starts to go, turns, remembering the recorder, starts to push off the table holding the recorder.* Oh, yeah. Whenever you can this week, stop by and drop off the samples. You'll feel better, Willy, and then come back and we'll talk. Pull yourself together, kid, there's people outside.

Howard exits, pushing the table off left. Willy stares into space, exhausted. Now the music is heard—Ben's music—first distantly, then closer, closer. As Willy speaks, Ben enters from the right. He carries valise and umbrella.

WILLY: Oh, Ben, how did you do it? What is the answer? Did you wind up the Alaska deal already?

BEN: Doesn't take much time if you know what you're doing. Just a short business trip. Boarding ship in an hour. Wanted to say good-by.

WILLY: Ben, I've got to talk to you.

BEN, *glancing at his watch:* Haven't the time, William.

WILLY, *crossing the apron to Ben:* Ben, nothing's working out. I don't know what to do.

BEN: Now, look here, William. I've bought timberland in Alaska and I need a man to look after things for me.

WILLY: God, timberland! Me and my boys in those grand outdoors!

BEN: You've a new continent at your doorstep, William. Get out of these cities, they're full of talk and time payments and courts of law. Screw on your fists and you can fight for a fortune up there.

WILLY: Yes, yes! Linda, Linda!

Linda enters as of old, with the wash.

LINDA: Oh, you're back?

BEN: I haven't much time.

WILLY: No, wait! Linda, he's got a proposition for me in Alaska.

LINDA: But you've got— *To Ben:* He's got a beautiful job here.

WILLY: But in Alaska, kid, I could—

LINDA: You're doing well enough, Willy!

BEN, *to Linda:* Enough for what, my dear?

LINDA, *frightened of Ben and angry at him:* Don't say those things to him! Enough to be happy right here, right now. *To Willy, while Ben laughs:* Why must everybody conquer the world? You're well liked, and the boys love you, and someday— *to Ben*—why, old man Wagner told him just the other day that if he keeps it up he'll be a member of the firm, didn't he, Willy?

WILLY: Sure, sure. I am building something with this firm, Ben, and if a man is building something he must be on the right track, mustn't he?

BEN: What are you building? Lay your hand on it. Where is it?

WILLY, *hesitantly:* That's true, Linda, there's nothing.

LINDA: Why? *To Ben:* There's a man eighty-four years old—

WILLY: That's right, Ben, that's right. When I look at that man I say, what is there to worry about?

BEN: Bah!

WILLY: It's true, Ben. All he has to do is go into any city, pick up the phone, and he's making his living and you know why?

BEN, *picking up his valise:* I've got to go.

WILLY, *holding Ben back:* Look at this boy!

Biff, in his high school sweater, enters carrying suitcase. Happy carries Biff's shoulder guards, gold helmet, and football pants.

WILLY: Without a penny to his name, three great universities are begging for him, and from there the sky's the limit, because it's not what you do, Ben. It's who you know and the smile on your face! It's contacts, Ben, contacts! The whole wealth of Alaska passes over the lunch table at the Commodore Hotel, and that's the wonder, the wonder of this country, that a man can end with diamonds here on the basis of being liked! *He turns to Biff.* And that's why when you get out on that field today it's important. Because thousands of people will be rooting for you and loving you. *To Ben, who has again begun to leave:* And Ben! when he walks into a business office his name will sound out like a bell and all the doors will open to him! I've seen it, Ben, I've seen it a thousand times! You can't feel it with your hand like timber, but it's there!

BEN: Good-by, William.

WILLY: Ben, am I right? Don't you think I'm right? I value your advice.

BEN: There's a new continent at your doorstep, William. You could walk out rich. Rich! *He is gone.*

WILLY: We'll do it here, Ben! You hear me? We're gonna do it here!

Young Bernard rushes in. The gay music of the Boys is heard.

BERNARD: Oh, gee, I was afraid you left already!

WILLY: Why? What time is it?

BERNARD: It's half-past one!

WILLY: Well, come on, everybody! Ebbets Field next stop! Where's the pennants? *He rushes through the wall-line of the kitchen and out into the living-room.*

LINDA, *to Biff:* Did you pack fresh underwear?

BIFF, *who has been limbering up:* I want to go!

BERNARD: Biff, I'm carrying your helmet, ain't I?

HAPPY: No, I'm carrying the helmet.

BERNARD: Oh, Biff, you promised me.

HAPPY: I'm carrying the helmet.

BERNARD: How am I going to get in the locker room?

LINDA: Let him carry the shoulder guards. *She puts her coat and hat on in the kitchen.*

BERNARD: Can I, Biff? 'Cause I told everybody I'm going to be in the locker room.

HAPPY: In Ebbets Field it's the clubhouse.

BERNARD: I meant the clubhouse. Biff!

HAPPY: Biff!

BIFF, *grandly, after a slight pause:* Let him carry the shoulder guards.

HAPPY, *as he gives Bernard the shoulder guards:* Stay close to us now.

Willy rushes in with the pennants.

WILLY, *handing them out:* Everybody wave when Biff comes out on the field. *Happy and Bernard run off.* You set now, boy?

The music has died away.

BIFF: Ready to go, Pop. Every muscle is ready.

WILLY, *at the edge of the apron:* You realize what this means?

BIFF: That's right, Pop.

WILLY, *feeling Biff's muscles:* You're comin' home this afternoon captain of the All-Scholastic Championship Team of the City of New York.

BIFF: I got it, Pop. And remember, pal, when I take off my helmet, that touchdown is for you.

WILLY: Let's go! *He is starting out, with his arm around Biff, when Charley enters, as of old, in knickers.* I got no room for you, Charley.

CHARLEY: Room? For what?

WILLY: In the car.

CHARLEY: You goin' for a ride? I wanted to shoot some casino.

WILLY, *furiously:* Casino! *Incredulously:* Don't you realize what today is?

LINDA: Oh, he knows, Willy. He's just kidding you.

WILLY: That's nothing to kid about!

CHARLEY: No, Linda, what's goin' on?

LINDA: He's playing in Ebbets Field.

CHARLEY: Baseball in this weather?

WILLY: Don't talk to him. Come on, come on! *He is pushing them out.*

CHARLEY: Wait a minute, didn't you hear the news?

WILLY: What?

CHARLEY: Don't you listen to the radio? Ebbets Field just blew up.

WILLY: You go to hell! *Charley laughs. Pushing them out:* Come on, come on! We're late.

CHARLEY, *as they go:* Knock a homer, Biff, knock a homer!

WILLY, *the last to leave, turning to Charley:* I don't think that was funny, Charley. This is the greatest day of his life.

CHARLEY: Willy, when are you going to grow up?

WILLY: Yeah, heh? When this game is over, Charley, you'll be laughing out of the other side of your face. They'll be calling him another Red Grange. Twenty-five thousand a year.

CHARLEY, *kidding:* Is that so?

WILLY: Yeah, that's so.

CHARLEY: Well, then, I'm sorry, Willy. But tell me something.

WILLY: What?

CHARLEY: Who is Red Grange?

WILLY: Put up your hands. Goddam you, put up your hands!

Charley, chuckling, shakes his head and walks away, around the left corner of the stage. Willy follows him. The music rises to a mocking frenzy.

WILLY: Who the hell do you think you are, better than everybody else? You don't know everything, you big, ignorant, stupid . . . Put up your hands!

Light rises, on the right side of the forestage, on a small table in the reception room of Charley's office. Traffic sounds are heard. Bernard, now mature, sits whistling to himself. A pair of tennis rackets and an overnight bag are on the floor beside him.

WILLY, *offstage:* What are you walking away for? Don't walk away! If you're going to say something say it to my face! I know you laugh at me behind my back. You'll laugh out of the other side of your goddam face after this game. Touchdown! Touchdown! Eighty thousand people! Touchdown! Right between the goal posts.

Bernard is a quiet, earnest, but self-assured young man. Willy's voice is coming from right upstage now. Bernard lowers his feet off the table and listens. Jenny, his father's secretary, enters.

JENNY, *distressed:* Say, Bernard, will you go out in the hall?

BERNARD: What is that noise? Who is it?

JENNY: Mr. Loman. He just got off the elevator.

BERNARD, *getting up:* Who's he arguing with?

JENNY: Nobody. There's nobody with him. I can't deal with him any more, and your father gets all upset everytime he comes. I've got a lot of typing to do, and your father's waiting to sign it. Will you see him?

WILLY, *entering:* Touchdown! Touch— *He sees Jenny.* Jenny, Jenny, good to see you. How're ya? Workin'? Or still honest?

JENNY: Fine. How've you been feeling?

WILLY: Not much any more, Jenny. Ha, ha! *He is surprised to see the rackets.*

BERNARD: Hello, Uncle Willy.

WILLY, *almost shocked:* Bernard! Well, look who's here! *He comes quickly, guiltily, to Bernard and warmly shakes his hand.*

BERNARD: How are you? Good to see you.

WILLY: What are you doing here?

BERNARD: Oh, just stopped by to see Pop. Get off my feet till my train leaves. I'm going to Washington in a few minutes.

WILLY: Is he in?

BERNARD: Yes, he's in his office with the accountant. Sit down.

WILLY, *sitting down:* What're you going to do in Washington?

BERNARD: Oh, just a case I've got there, Willy.

WILLY: That so? *Indicating the rackets:* You going to play tennis there?

BERNARD: I'm staying with a friend who's got a court.

WILLY: Don't say. His own tennis court. Must be fine people, I bet.

BERNARD: They are, very nice. Dad tells me Biff's in town.

WILLY, *with a big smile:* Yeah, Biff's in. Working on a very big deal, Bernard.

BERNARD: What's Biff doing?

WILLY: Well, he's been doing very big things in the West. But he decided to establish himself here. Very big. We're having dinner. Did I hear your wife had a boy?

BERNARD: That's right. Our second.

WILLY: Two boys! What do you know!

BERNARD: What kind of a deal has Biff got?

WILLY: Well, Bill Oliver—very big sporting-goods man—he wants Biff very badly. Called him in from the West. Long distance, carte blanche, special deliveries. Your friends have their own private tennis court?

BERNARD: You still with the old firm, Willy?

WILLY, *after a pause:* I'm—I'm overjoyed to see how you made the grade, Bernard, overjoyed. It's an encouraging thing to see a young man really—really— Looks very good for Biff—very— *He breaks off, then:* Bernard— *He is so full of emotion, he breaks off again.*

BERNARD: What is it, Willy?

WILLY, *small and alone:* What—what's the secret?

BERNARD: What secret?

WILLY: How—how did you? Why didn't he ever catch on?

BERNARD: I wouldn't know that, Willy.

WILLY, *confidentially, desperately:* You were his friend, his boyhood friend. There's something I don't understand about it. His life ended after that Ebbets Field game. From the age of seventeen nothing good ever happened to him.

BERNARD: He never trained himself for anything.

WILLY: But he did, he did. After high school he took so many correspondence courses. Radio mechanics; television; God knows what, and never made the slightest mark.

BERNARD, *taking off his glasses:* Willy, do you want to talk candidly?

WILLY, *rising, faces Bernard:* I regard you as a very brilliant man, Bernard. I value your advice.

BERNARD: Oh, the hell with the advice, Willy. I couldn't advise you. There's just one thing I've always wanted to ask you.

When he was supposed to graduate, and the math teacher flunked him—

WILLY: Oh, that son-of-a-bitch ruined his life.

BERNARD: Yeah, but, Willy, all he had to do was go to summer school and make up that subject.

WILLY: That's right, that's right.

BERNARD: Did you tell him not to go to summer school?

WILLY: Me? I begged him to go. I ordered him to go!

BERNARD: Then why wouldn't he go?

WILLY: Why? Why! Bernard, that question has been trailing me like a ghost for the last fifteen years. He flunked the subject, and laid down and died like a hammer hit him!

BERNARD: Take it easy, kid.

WILLY: Let me talk to you—I got nobody to talk to. Bernard, Bernard, was it my fault? Y'see? It keeps going around in my mind, maybe I did something to him. I got nothing to give him.

BERNARD: Don't take it so hard.

WILLY: Why did he lay down? What is the story there? You were his friend!

BERNARD: Willy, I remember, it was June, and our grades came out. And he'd flunked math.

WILLY: That son-of-a-bitch!

BERNARD: No, it wasn't right then. Biff just got very angry, I remember, and he was ready to enroll in summer school.

WILLY, surprised: He was?

BERNARD: He wasn't beaten by it at all. But then, Willy, he disappeared from the block for almost a month. And I got the idea that he'd gone up to New England to see you. Did he have a talk with you then?

Willy stares in silence.

BERNARD: Willy?

WILLY, *with a strong edge of resentment in his voice:* Yeah, he came to Boston. What about it?

BERNARD: Well, just that when he came back—I'll never forget this, it always mystifies me. Because I'd thought so well of Biff, even though he'd always taken advantage of me. I loved him, Willy, y'know? And he came back after that month and took his sneakers—remember those sneakers with "University of Virginia" printed on them? He was so proud of those, wore them every day. And he took them down in the cellar, and burned them up in the furnace. We had a fist fight. It lasted at least half an hour. Just the two of us, punching each other down the cellar, and crying right through it. I've often thought of how strange it was that I knew he'd given up his life. What happened in Boston, Willy?

Willy looks at him as at an intruder.

BERNARD: I just bring it up because you asked me.

WILLY, *angrily:* Nothing. What do you mean, "What happened?" What's that got to do with anything?

BERNARD: Well, don't get sore.

WILLY: What are you trying to do, blame it on me? If a boy lays down is that my fault?

BERNARD: Now, Willy, don't get—

WILLY: Well, don't—don't talk to me that way! What does that mean, "What happened?"

Charley enters. He is in his vest, and he carries a bottle of bourbon.

CHARLEY: Hey, you're going to miss that train. *He waves the bottle.*

BERNARD: Yeah, I'm going. *He takes the bottle.* Thanks, Pop. *He picks up his rackets and bag.* Good-by, Willy, and don't worry about it. You know, "If at first you don't succeed . . ."

WILLY: Yes, I believe in that.

BERNARD: But sometimes, Willy, it's better for a man just to walk away.

WILLY: Walk away?

BERNARD: That's right.

WILLY: But if you can't walk away?

BERNARD, *after a slight pause:* I guess that's when it's tough. *Extending his hand:* Good-by, Willy.

WILLY, *shaking Bernard's hand:* Good-by, boy.

CHARLEY, *an arm on Bernard's shoulder:* How do you like this kid? Gonna argue a case in front of the Supreme Court.

BERNARD, *protesting:* Pop!

WILLY, *genuinely shocked, pained, and happy:* No! The Supreme Court!

BERNARD: I gotta run. 'By, Dad!

CHARLEY: Knock 'em dead, Bernard!

Bernard goes off.

WILLY, *as Charley takes out his wallet:* The Supreme Court! And he didn't even mention it!

CHARLEY, *counting out money on the desk:* He don't have to— he's gonna do it.

WILLY: And you never told him what to do, did you? You never took any interest in him.

CHARLEY: My salvation is that I never took any interest in any-thing. There's some money—fifty dollars. I got an accountant inside.

WILLY: Charley, look . . . *With difficulty:* I got my insurance to pay. If you can manage it—I need a hundred and ten dollars.

Charley doesn't reply for a moment; merely stops moving.

WILLY: I'd draw it from my bank but Linda would know, and I . . .

CHARLEY: Sit down, Willy.

WILLY, *moving toward the chair:* I'm keeping an account of everything, remember. I'll pay every penny back. *He sits.*

CHARLEY: Now listen to me, Willy.

WILLY: I want you to know I appreciate . . .

CHARLEY, *sitting down on the table:* Willy, what're you doin'? What the hell is goin' on in your head?

WILLY: Why? I'm simply . . .

CHARLEY: I offered you a job. You can make fifty dollars a week. And I won't send you on the road.

WILLY: I've got a job.

CHARLEY: Without pay? What kind of a job is a job without pay? *He rises.* Now, look, kid, enough is enough. I'm no genius but I know when I'm being insulted.

WILLY: Insulted!

CHARLEY: Why don't you want to work for me?

WILLY: What's the matter with you? I've got a job.

CHARLEY: Then what're you walkin' in here every week for?

WILLY, *getting up:* Well, if you don't want me to walk in here—

CHARLEY: I am offering you a job.

WILLY: I don't want your goddam job!

CHARLEY: When the hell are you going to grow up?

WILLY, *furiously:* You big ignoramus, if you say that to me again I'll rap you one! I don't care how big you are! *He's ready to fight.*

Pause.

CHARLEY, *kindly, going to him:* How much do you need, Willy?

WILLY: Charley, I'm strapped. I'm strapped. I don't know what to do. I was just fired.

CHARLEY: Howard fired you?

WILLY: That snotnose. Imagine that? I named him. I named him Howard.

CHARLEY: Willy, when're you gonna realize that them things don't mean anything? You named him Howard, but you can't sell that. The only thing you got in this world is what you can sell. And the funny thing is that you're a salesman, and you don't know that.

WILLY: I've always tried to think otherwise, I guess. I always felt that if a man was impressive, and well liked, that nothing—

CHARLEY: Why must everybody like you? Who liked J. P. Morgan? Was he impressive? In a Turkish bath he'd look like a butcher. But with his pockets on he was very well liked. Now listen, Willy, I know you don't like me, and nobody can say I'm in love with you, but I'll give you a job because—just for the hell of it, put it that way. Now what do you say?

WILLY: I—I just can't work for you, Charley.

CHARLEY: What're you, jealous of me?

WILLY: I can't work for you, that's all, don't ask me why.

CHARLEY, *angered, takes out more bills:* You been jealous of me all your life, you damned fool! Here, pay your insurance. *He puts the money in Willy's hand.*

WILLY: I'm keeping strict accounts.

CHARLEY: I've got some work to do. Take care of yourself. And pay your insurance.

WILLY, *moving to the right:* Funny, y'know? After all the highways, and the trains, and the appointments, and the years, you end up worth more dead than alive.

CHARLEY: Willy, nobody's worth nothin' dead. *After a slight pause:* Did you hear what I said?

Willy stands still, dreaming.

CHARLEY: Willy!

WILLY: Apologize to Bernard for me when you see him. I didn't mean to argue with him. He's a fine boy. They're all fine boys, and they'll end up big—all of them. Someday they'll all play tennis together. Wish me luck, Charley. He saw Bill Oliver today.

CHARLEY: Good luck.

WILLY, *on the verge of tears:* Charley, you're the only friend I got. Isn't that a remarkable thing? *He goes out.*

CHARLEY: Jesus!

Charley stares after him a moment and follows. All light blacks out. Suddenly raucous music is heard, and a red glow rises behind the screen at right. Stanley, a young waiter, appears, carrying a table, followed by Happy, who is carrying two chairs.

STANLEY, *putting the table down:* That's all right, Mr. Loman, I can handle it myself. *He turns and takes the chairs from Happy and places them at the table.*

HAPPY, *glancing around:* Oh, this is better.

STANLEY: Sure, in the front there you're in the middle of all kinds a noise. Whenever you got a party, Mr. Loman, you just tell me and I'll put you back here. Y'know, there's a lotta people they don't like it private, because when they go out they like to see a lotta action around them because they're sick and tired to stay in the house by theirself. But I know you, you ain't from Hackensack. You know what I mean?

HAPPY, *sitting down:* So how's it coming, Stanley?

STANLEY: Ah, it's a dog's life. I only wish during the war they'd a took me in the Army. I coulda been dead by now.

HAPPY: My brother's back, Stanley.

STANLEY: Oh, he come back, heh? From the Far West.

HAPPY: Yeah, big cattle man, my brother, so treat him right. And my father's coming too.

STANLEY: Oh, your father too!

HAPPY: You got a couple of nice lobsters?

STANLEY: Hundred per cent, big.

HAPPY: I want them with the claws.

STANLEY: Don't worry, I don't give you no mice. *Happy laughs.* How about some wine? It'll put a head on the meal.

HAPPY: No. You remember, Stanley, that recipe I brought you from overseas? With the champagne in it?

STANLEY: Oh, yeah, sure. I still got it tacked up yet in the kitchen. But that'll have to cost a buck apiece anyways.

HAPPY: That's all right.

STANLEY: What'd you, hit a number or somethin'?

HAPPY: No, it's a little celebration. My brother is—I think he pulled off a big deal today. I think we're going into business together.

STANLEY: Great! That's the best for you. Because a family business, you know what I mean?—that's the best.

HAPPY: That's what I think.

STANLEY: 'Cause what's the difference? Somebody steals? It's in the family. Know what I mean? *Sotto voce:* Like this bartender here. The boss is goin' crazy what kinda leak he's got in the cash register. You put it in but it don't come out.

HAPPY, *raising his head:* Sh!

STANLEY: What?

HAPPY: You notice I wasn't lookin' right or left, was I?

STANLEY: No.

HAPPY: And my eyes are closed.

STANLEY: So what's the—?

HAPPY: Strudel's comin'.

STANLEY, *catching on, looks around:* Ah, no, there's no—

He breaks off as a furred, lavishly dressed girl enters and sits at the next table. Both follow her with their eyes.

STANLEY: Geez, how'd ya know?

HAPPY: I got radar or something. *Staring directly at her profile:* Oooooooo . . . Stanley.

STANLEY: I think that's for you, Mr. Loman.

HAPPY: Look at that mouth. Oh, God. And the binoculars.

STANLEY: Geez, you got a life, Mr. Loman.

HAPPY: Wait on her.

STANLEY, *going to the girl's table:* Would you like a menu, ma'am?

GIRL: I'm expecting someone, but I'd like a—

HAPPY: Why don't you bring her—excuse me, miss, do you mind? I sell champagne, and I'd like you to try my brand. Bring her a champagne, Stanley.

GIRL: That's awfully nice of you.

HAPPY: Don't mention it. It's all company money. *He laughs.*

GIRL: That's a charming product to be selling, isn't it?

HAPPY: Oh, gets to be like everything else. Selling is selling, y'know.

GIRL: I suppose.

HAPPY: You don't happen to sell, do you?

GIRL: No, I don't sell.

HAPPY: Would you object to a compliment from a stranger? You ought to be on a magazine cover.

GIRL, *looking at him a little archly:* I have been.

Stanley comes in with a glass of champagne.

HAPPY: What'd I say before, Stanley? You see? She's a cover girl.

STANLEY: Oh, I could see, I could see.

HAPPY, *to the Girl:* What magazine?

GIRL: Oh, a lot of them. *She takes the drink.* Thank you.

HAPPY: You know what they say in France, don't you? "Champagne is the drink of the complexion"—Hya, Biff!

Biff has entered and sits with Happy.

BIFF: Hello, kid. Sorry I'm late.

HAPPY: I just got here. Uh, Miss—?

GIRL: Forsythe.

HAPPY: Miss Forsythe, this is my brother.

BIFF: Is Dad here?

HAPPY: His name is Biff. You might've heard of him. Great football player.

GIRL: Really? What team?

HAPPY: Are you familiar with football?

GIRL: No, I'm afraid I'm not.

HAPPY: Biff is quarterback with the New York Giants.

GIRL: Well, that is nice, isn't it? *She drinks.*

HAPPY: Good health.

GIRL: I'm happy to meet you.

HAPPY: That's my name. Hap. It's really Harold, but at West Point they called me Happy.

GIRL, *now really impressed:* Oh, I see. How do you do? *She turns her profile.*

BIFF: Isn't Dad coming?

HAPPY: You want her?

BIFF: Oh, I could never make that.

HAPPY: I remember the time that idea would never come into your head. Where's the old confidence, Biff?

BIFF: I just saw Oliver—

HAPPY: Wait a minute. I've got to see that old confidence again. Do you want her? She's on call.

BIFF: Oh, no. *He turns to look at the Girl.*

HAPPY: I'm telling you. Watch this. *Turning to the Girl:* Honey? *She turns to him.* Are you busy?

GIRL: Well, I am . . . but I could make a phone call.

HAPPY: Do that, will you, honey? And see if you can get a friend. We'll be here for a while. Biff is one of the greatest football players in the country.

GIRL, *standing up:* Well, I'm certainly happy to meet you.

HAPPY: Come back soon.

GIRL: I'll try.

HAPPY: Don't try, honey, try hard.

The Girl exits. Stanley follows, shaking his head in bewildered admiration.

HAPPY: Isn't that a shame now? A beautiful girl like that? That's why I can't get married. There's not a good woman in a thousand. New York is loaded with them, kid!

BIFF: Hap, look—

HAPPY: I told you she was on call!

BIFF, *strangely unnerved:* Cut it out, will ya? I want to say something to you.

HAPPY: Did you see Oliver?

BIFF: I saw him all right. Now look, I want to tell Dad a couple of things and I want you to help me.

HAPPY: What? Is he going to back you?

BIFF: Are you crazy? You're out of your goddam head, you know that?

HAPPY: Why? What happened?

BIFF, *breathlessly:* I did a terrible thing today, Hap. It's been the strangest day I ever went through. I'm all numb, I swear.

HAPPY: You mean he wouldn't see you?

BIFF: Well, I waited six hours for him, see? All day. Kept sending my name in. Even tried to date his secretary so she'd get me to him, but no soap.

HAPPY: Because you're not showin' the old confidence, Biff. He remembered you, didn't he?

BIFF, *stopping Happy with a gesture:* Finally, about five o'clock, he comes out. Didn't remember who I was or anything. I felt like such an idiot, Hap.

HAPPY: Did you tell him my Florida idea?

BIFF: He walked away. I saw him for one minute. I got so mad I could've torn the walls down! How the hell did I ever get the idea I was a salesman there? I even believed myself that I'd been a salesman for him! And then he gave me one look and— I realized what a ridiculous lie my whole life has been! We've been talking in a dream for fifteen years. I was a shipping clerk.

HAPPY: What'd you do?

BIFF, *with great tension and wonder:* Well, he left, see. And the secretary went out. I was all alone in the waiting-room. I don't know what came over me, Hap. The next thing I know I'm in his office—paneled walls, everything. I can't explain it. I—Hap, I took his fountain pen.

HAPPY: Geez, did he catch you?

BIFF: I ran out. I ran down all eleven flights. I ran and ran and ran.

HAPPY: That was an awful dumb—what'd you do that for?

BIFF, *agonized:* I don't know, I just—wanted to take something, I don't know. You gotta help me, Hap, I'm gonna tell Pop.

HAPPY: You crazy? What for?

BIFF: Hap, he's got to understand that I'm not the man somebody lends that kind of money to. He thinks I've been spiting him all these years and it's eating him up.

HAPPY: That's just it. You tell him something nice.

BIFF: I can't.

HAPPY: Say you got a lunch date with Oliver tomorrow.

BIFF: So what do I do tomorrow?

HAPPY: You leave the house tomorrow and come back at night and say Oliver is thinking it over. And he thinks it over for a couple of weeks, and gradually it fades away and nobody's the worse.

BIFF: But it'll go on forever!

HAPPY: Dad is never so happy as when he's looking forward to something!

Willy enters.

HAPPY: Hello, scout!

WILLY: Gee, I haven't been here in years!

Stanley has followed Willy in and sets a chair for him. Stanley starts off but Happy stops him.

HAPPY: Stanley!

Stanley stands by, waiting for an order.

BIFF, *going to Willy with guilt, as to an invalid:* Sit down, Pop. You want a drink?

WILLY: Sure, I don't mind.

BIFF: Let's get a load on.

WILLY: You look worried.

BIFF: N-no. *To Stanley:* Scotch all around. Make it doubles.

STANLEY: Doubles, right. *He goes.*

WILLY: You had a couple already, didn't you?

BIFF: Just a couple, yeah.

WILLY: Well, what happened, boy? *Nodding affirmatively, with a smile:* Everything go all right?

BIFF, *takes a breath, then reaches out and grasps Willy's hand:* Pal . . . *He is smiling bravely, and Willy is smiling too.* I had an experience today.

HAPPY: Terrific, Pop.

WILLY: That so? What happened?

BIFF, *high, slightly alcoholic, above the earth:* I'm going to tell you everything from first to last. It's been a strange day. *Silence. He looks around, composes himself as best he can, but his breath keeps breaking the rhythm of his voice.* I had to wait quite a while for him, and—

WILLY: Oliver?

BIFF: Yeah, Oliver. All day, as a matter of cold fact. And a lot of—instances—facts, Pop, facts about my life came back to me. Who was it, Pop? Who ever said I was a salesman with Oliver?

WILLY: Well, you were.

BIFF: No, Dad, I was a shipping clerk.

WILLY: But you were practically—

BIFF, *with determination:* Dad, I don't know who said it first, but I was never a salesman for Bill Oliver.

WILLY: What're you talking about?

BIFF: Let's hold on to the facts tonight, Pop. We're not going to get anywhere bullin' around. I was a shipping clerk.

WILLY, *angrily:* All right, now listen to me—

BIFF: Why don't you let me finish?

WILLY: I'm not interested in stories about the past or any crap of that kind because the woods are burning, boys, you understand? There's a big blaze going on all around. I was fired today.

BIFF, *shocked:* How could you be?

WILLY: I was fired, and I'm looking for a little good news to tell your mother, because the woman has waited and the woman has suffered. The gist of it is that I haven't got a story left in my head, Biff. So don't give me a lecture about facts and aspects. I am not interested. Now what've you got to say to me?

Stanley enters with three drinks. They wait until he leaves.

WILLY: Did you see Oliver?

BIFF: Jesus, Dad!

WILLY: You mean you didn't go up there?

HAPPY: Sure he went up there.

BIFF: I did. I—saw him. How could they fire you?

WILLY, *on the edge of his chair:* What kind of a welcome did he give you?

BIFF: He won't even let you work on commission?

WILLY: I'm out! *Driving:* So tell me, he gave you a warm welcome?

HAPPY: Sure, Pop, sure!

BIFF, *driven:* Well, it was kind of—

WILLY: I was wondering if he'd remember you. *To Happy:* Imagine, man doesn't see him for ten, twelve years and gives him that kind of a welcome!

HAPPY: Damn right!

BIFF, *trying to return to the offensive:* Pop, look—

WILLY: You know why he remembered you, don't you? Because you impressed him in those days.

BIFF: Let's talk quietly and get this down to the facts, huh?

WILLY, *as though Biff had been interrupting:* Well, what happened? It's great news, Biff. Did he take you into his office or'd you talk in the waiting-room?

BIFF: Well, he came in, see, and—

WILLY, *with a big smile:* What'd he say? Betcha he threw his arm around you.

BIFF: Well, he kinda—

WILLY: He's a fine man. *To Happy:* Very hard man to see, y'know.

HAPPY, *agreeing:* Oh, I know.

WILLY, *to Biff:* Is that where you had the drinks?

BIFF: Yeah, he gave me a couple of—no, no!

HAPPY, *cutting in:* He told him my Florida idea.

WILLY: Don't interrupt. *To Biff:* How'd he react to the Florida idea?

BIFF: Dad, will you give me a minute to explain?

WILLY: I've been waiting for you to explain since I sat down here! What happened? He took you into his office and what?

BIFF: Well—I talked. And—and he listened, see.

WILLY: Famous for the way he listens, y'know. What was his answer?

BIFF: His answer was— *He breaks off, suddenly angry.* Dad, you're not letting me tell you what I want to tell you!

WILLY, *accusing, angered:* You didn't see him, did you?

BIFF: I did see him!

WILLY: What'd you insult him or something? You insulted him, didn't you?

BIFF: Listen, will you let me out of it, will you just let me out of it!

HAPPY: What the hell!

WILLY: Tell me what happened!

BIFF, *to Happy:* I can't talk to him!

A single trumpet note jars the ear. The light of green leaves stains the house, which holds the air of night and a dream. Young Bernard enters and knocks on the door of the house.

YOUNG BERNARD, *frantically:* Mrs. Loman, Mrs. Loman!

HAPPY: Tell him what happened!

BIFF, *to Happy:* Shut up and leave me alone!

WILLY: No, no! You had to go and flunk math!

BIFF: What math? What're you talking about?

YOUNG BERNARD: Mrs. Loman, Mrs. Loman!

Linda appears in the house, as of old.

WILLY, *wildly:* Math, math, math!

BIFF: Take it easy, Pop!

YOUNG BERNARD: Mrs. Loman!

WILLY, *furiously:* If you hadn't flunked you'd've been set by now!

BIFF: Now, look, I'm gonna tell you what happened, and you're going to listen to me.

YOUNG BERNARD: Mrs. Loman!

BIFF: I waited six hours—

HAPPY: What the hell are you saying?

BIFF: I kept sending in my name but he wouldn't see me. So finally he . . . *He continues unheard as light fades low on the restaurant.*

YOUNG BERNARD: Biff flunked math!

LINDA: No!

YOUNG BERNARD: Birnbaum flunked him! They won't graduate him!

LINDA: But they have to. He's gotta go to the university. Where is he? Biff! Biff!

YOUNG BERNARD: No, he left. He went to Grand Central.

LINDA: Grand— You mean he went to Boston!

YOUNG BERNARD: Is Uncle Willy in Boston?

LINDA: Oh, maybe Willy can talk to the teacher. Oh, the poor, poor boy!

Light on house area snaps out.

BIFF, *at the table, now audible, holding up a gold fountain pen:* . . . so I'm washed up with Oliver, you understand? Are you listening to me?

WILLY, *at a loss:* Yeah, sure. If you hadn't flunked—

BIFF: Flunked what? What're you talking about?

WILLY: Don't blame everything on me! I didn't flunk math— you did! What pen?

HAPPY: That was awful dumb, Biff, a pen like that is worth—

WILLY, *seeing the pen for the first time:* You took Oliver's pen?

BIFF, *weakening:* Dad, I just explained it to you.

WILLY: You stole Bill Oliver's fountain pen!

BIFF: I didn't exactly steal it! That's just what I've been explaining to you!

HAPPY: He had it in his hand and just then Oliver walked in, so he got nervous and stuck it in his pocket!

WILLY: My God, Biff!

BIFF: I never intended to do it, Dad!

OPERATOR'S VOICE: Standish Arms, good evening!

WILLY, *shouting:* I'm not in my room!

BIFF, *frightened:* Dad, what's the matter? *He and Happy stand up.*

OPERATOR: Ringing Mr. Loman for you!

WILLY: I'm not there, stop it!

BIFF, *horrified, gets down on one knee before Willy:* Dad, I'll make good, I'll make good. *Willy tries to get to his feet. Biff holds him down.* Sit down now.

WILLY: No, you're no good, you're no good for anything.

BIFF: I am, Dad, I'll find something else, you understand? Now don't worry about anything. *He holds up Willy's face:* Talk to me, Dad.

OPERATOR: Mr. Loman does not answer. Shall I page him?

WILLY, *attempting to stand, as though to rush and silence the Operator:* No, no, no!

HAPPY: He'll strike something, Pop

WILLY: No, no . . .

BIFF, *desperately, standing over Willy:* Pop, listen! Listen to

me! I'm telling you something good. Oliver talked to his partner about the Florida idea. You listening? He—he talked to
his partner, and he came to me . . . I'm going to be all right,
you hear? Dad, listen to me, he said it was just a question of
the amount!

WILLY: Then you . . . got it?

HAPPY: He's gonna be terrific, Pop!

WILLY, *trying to stand:* Then you got it, haven't you? You got
it! You got it!

BIFF, *agonized, holds Willy down:* No, no. Look, Pop. I'm
supposed to have lunch with them tomorrow. I'm just telling
you this so you'll know that I can still make an impression,
Pop. And I'll make good somewhere, but I can't go tomorrow,
see?

WILLY: Why not? You simply—

BIFF: But the pen, Pop!

WILLY: You give it to him and tell him it was an oversight!

HAPPY: Sure, have lunch tomorrow!

BIFF: I can't say that—

WILLY: You were doing a crossword puzzle and accidentally
used his pen!

BIFF: Listen, kid, I took those balls years ago, now I walk in
with his fountain pen? That clinches it, don't you see? I can't
face him like that! I'll try elsewhere.

PAGE'S VOICE: Paging Mr. Loman!

WILLY: Don't you want to be anything?

BIFF: Pop, how can I go back?

WILLY: You don't want to be anything, is that what's behind it?

BIFF, *now angry at Willy for not crediting his sympathy:* Don't take it that way! You think it was easy walking into that office after what I'd done to him? A team of horses couldn't have dragged me back to Bill Oliver!

WILLY: Then why'd you go?

BIFF: Why did I go? Why did I go! Look at you! Look at what's become of you!

Off left, The Woman laughs.

WILLY: Biff, you're going to go to that lunch tomorrow, or—

BIFF: I can't go. I've got no appointment!

HAPPY: Biff, for . . . !

WILLY: Are you spiting me?

BIFF: Don't take it that way! Goddammit!

WILLY, *strikes Biff and falters away from the table:* You rotten little louse! Are you spiting me?

THE WOMAN: Someone's at the door, Willy!

BIFF: I'm no good, can't you see what I am?

HAPPY, *separating them:* Hey, you're in a restaurant! Now cut it out, both of you! *The girls enter.* Hello, girls, sit down.

The Woman laughs, off left.

MISS FORSYTHE: I guess we might as well. This is Letta.

THE WOMAN: Willy, are you going to wake up?

BIFF, *ignoring Willy:* How're ya, miss, sit down. What do you drink?

MISS FORSYTHE: Letta might not be able to stay long.

LETTA: I gotta get up very early tomorrow. I got jury duty. I'm so excited! Were you fellows ever on a jury?

BIFF: No, but I been in front of them! *The girls laugh.* This is my father.

LETTA: Isn't he cute? Sit down with us, Pop.

HAPPY: Sit him down, Biff!

BIFF, *going to him:* Come on, slugger, drink us under the table. To hell with it! Come on, sit down, pal.

On Biff's last insistence, Willy is about to sit.

THE WOMAN, *now urgently:* Willy, are you going to answer the door!

The Woman's call pulls Willy back. He starts right, befuddled.

BIFF: Hey, where are you going?

WILLY: Open the door.

BIFF: The door?

WILLY: The washroom . . . the door . . . where's the door?

BIFF, *leading Willy to the left:* Just go straight down.

Willy moves left.

THE WOMAN: Willy, Willy, are you going to get up, get up, get up, get up?

Willy exits left.

LETTA: I think it's sweet you bring your daddy along.

MISS FORSYTHE: Oh, he isn't really your father!

BIFF, *at left, turning to her resentfully:* Miss Forsythe, you've just seen a prince walk by. A fine, troubled prince. A hardworking, unappreciated prince. A pal, you understand? A good companion. Always for his boys.

LETTA: That's so sweet.

HAPPY: Well, girls, what's the program? We're wasting time.

Come on, Biff. Gather round. Where would you like to go?

BIFF: Why don't you do something for him?

HAPPY: Me!

BIFF: Don't you give a damn for him, Hap?

HAPPY: What're you talking about? I'm the one who—

BIFF: I sense it, you don't give a good goddam about him. *He takes the rolled-up hose from his pocket and puts it on the table in front of Happy.* Look what I found in the cellar, for Christ's sake. How can you bear to let it go on?

HAPPY: Me? Who goes away? Who runs off and—

BIFF: Yeah, but he doesn't mean anything to you. You could help him—I can't! Don't you understand what I'm talking about? He's going to kill himself, don't you know that?

HAPPY: Don't I know it! Me!

BIFF: Hap, help him! Jesus . . . help him . . . Help me, help me, I can't bear to look at his face! *Ready to weep, he hurries out, up right.*

HAPPY, *starting after him:* Where are you going?

MISS FORSYTHE: What's he so mad about?

HAPPY: Come on, girls, we'll catch up with him.

MISS FORSYTHE, *as Happy pushes her out:* Say, I don't like that temper of his!

HAPPY: He's just a little overstrung, he'll be all right!

WILLY, *off left, as The Woman laughs:* Don't answer! Don't answer!

LETTA: Don't you want to tell your father—

HAPPY: No, that's not my father. He's just a guy. Come on,

we'll catch Biff, and, honey, we're going to paint this town! Stanley, where's the check! Hey, Stanley!

They exit. Stanley looks toward left.

STANLEY, *calling to Happy indignantly:* Mr. Loman! Mr. Loman!

Stanley picks up a chair and follows them off. Knocking is heard off left. The Woman enters, laughing. Willy follows her. She is in a black slip; he is buttoning his shirt. Raw, sensuous music accompanies their speech.

WILLY: Will you stop laughing? Will you stop?

THE WOMAN: Aren't you going to answer the door? He'll wake the whole hotel.

WILLY: I'm not expecting anybody.

THE WOMAN: Whyn't you have another drink, honey, and stop being so damn self-centered?

WILLY: I'm so lonely.

THE WOMAN: You know you ruined me, Willy? From now on, whenever you come to the office, I'll see that you go right through to the buyers. No waiting at my desk any more, Willy. You ruined me.

WILLY: That's nice of you to say that.

THE WOMAN: Gee, you are self-centered! Why so sad? You are the saddest, self-centeredest soul I ever did see-saw. *She laughs. He kisses her.* Come on inside, drummer boy. It's silly to be dressing in the middle of the night. *As knocking is heard:* Aren't you going to answer the door?

WILLY: They're knocking on the wrong door.

THE WOMAN: But I felt the knocking. And he heard us talking in here. Maybe the hotel's on fire!

WILLY, *his terror rising:* It's a mistake.

THE WOMAN: Then tell him to go away!

WILLY: There's nobody there.

THE WOMAN: It's getting on my nerves, Willy. There's somebody standing out there and it's getting on my nerves!

WILLY, *pushing her away from him:* All right, stay in the bathroom here, and don't come out. I think there's a law in Massachusetts about it, so don't come out. It may be that new room clerk. He looked very mean. So don't come out. It's a mistake, there's no fire.

The knocking is heard again. He takes a few steps away from her, and she vanishes into the wing. The light follows him, and now he is facing Young Biff, who carries a suitcase. Biff steps toward him. The music is gone.

BIFF: Why didn't you answer?

WILLY: Biff! What are you doing in Boston?

BIFF: Why didn't you answer? I've been knocking for five minutes, I called you on the phone—

WILLY: I just heard you. I was in the bathroom and had the door shut. Did anything happen home?

BIFF: Dad—I let you down.

WILLY: What do you mean?

BIFF: Dad . . .

WILLY: Biffo, what's this about? *Putting his arm around Biff:* Come on, let's go downstairs and get you a malted.

BIFF: Dad, I flunked math.

WILLY: Not for the term?

BIFF: The term. I haven't got enough credits to graduate.

WILLY: You mean to say Bernard wouldn't give you the answers?

BIFF: He did, he tried, but I only got a sixty-one.

WILLY: And they wouldn't give you four points?

BIFF: Birnbaum refused absolutely. I begged him, Pop, but he won't give me those points. You gotta talk to him before they close the school. Because if he saw the kind of man you are, and you just talked to him in your way, I'm sure he'd come through for me. The class came right before practice, see, and I didn't go enough. Would you talk to him? He'd like you, Pop. You know the way you could talk.

WILLY: You're on. We'll drive right back.

BIFF: Oh, Dad, good work! I'm sure he'll change it for you!

WILLY: Go downstairs and tell the clerk I'm checkin' out. Go right down.

BIFF: Yes, sir! See, the reason he hates me, Pop—one day he was late for class so I got up at the blackboard and imitated him. I crossed my eyes and talked with a lithp.

WILLY, laughing: You did? The kids like it?

BIFF: They nearly died laughing!

WILLY: Yeah? What'd you do?

BIFF: The thquare root of thixthy twee is . . . Willy bursts out laughing; Biff joins him. And in the middle of it he walked in!

Willy laughs and The Woman joins in offstage.

WILLY, without hesitation: Hurry downstairs and—

BIFF: Somebody in there?

WILLY: No, that was next door.

The Woman laughs offstage.

BIFF: Somebody got in your bathroom!

WILLY: No, it's the next room, there's a party—

THE WOMAN, *enters, laughing. She lisps this:* Can I come in? There's something in the bathtub, Willy, and it's moving!

Willy looks at Biff, who is staring open-mouthed and horrified at The Woman.

WILLY: Ah—you better go back to your room. They must be finished painting by now. They're painting her room so I let her take a shower here. Go back, go back . . . *He pushes her.*

THE WOMAN, *resisting:* But I've got to get dressed, Willy, I can't—

WILLY: Get out of here! Go back, go back . . . *Suddenly striving for the ordinary:* This is Miss Francis, Biff, she's a buyer. They're painting her room. Go back, Miss Francis, go back . . .

THE WOMAN: But my clothes, I can't go out naked in the hall!

WILLY, *pushing her offstage:* Get outa here! Go back, go back!

Biff slowly sits down on his suitcase as the argument continues offstage.

THE WOMAN: Where's my stockings? You promised me stockings, Willy!

WILLY: I have no stockings here!

THE WOMAN: You had two boxes of size nine sheers for me, and I want them!

WILLY: Here, for God's sake, will you get outa here!

THE WOMAN, *enters holding a box of stockings:* I just hope there's nobody in the hall. That's all I hope. *To Biff:* Are you football or baseball?

BIFF: Football.

THE WOMAN, *angry, humiliated:* That's me too. G'night. *She snatches her clothes from Willy, and walks out.*

WILLY, *after a pause:* Well, better get going. I want to get to the school first thing in the morning. Get my suits out of the closet. I'll get my valise. *Biff doesn't move.* What's the matter? *Biff remains motionless, tears falling.* She's a buyer. Buys for J. H. Simmons. She lives down the hall—they're painting. You don't imagine— *He breaks off. After a pause:* Now listen, pal, she's just a buyer. She sees merchandise in her room and they have to keep it looking just so . . . *Pause. Assuming command:* All right, get my suits. *Biff doesn't move.* Now stop crying and do as I say. I gave you an order. Biff, I gave you an order! Is that what you do when I give you an order? How dare you cry! *Putting his arm around Biff:* Now look, Biff, when you grow up you'll understand about these things. You mustn't— you mustn't overemphasize a thing like this. I'll see Birnbaum first thing in the morning.

BIFF: Never mind.

WILLY, *getting down beside Biff:* Never mind! He's going to give you those points. I'll see to it.

BIFF: He wouldn't listen to you.

WILLY: He certainly will listen to me. You need those points for the U. of Virginia.

BIFF: I'm not going there.

WILLY: Heh? If I can't get him to change that mark you'll make it up in summer school. You've got all summer to—

BIFF, *his weeping breaking from him:* Dad . . .

WILLY, *infected by it:* Oh, my boy . . .

BIFF: Dad . . .

WILLY: She's nothing to me, Biff. I was lonely, I was terribly lonely.

BIFF: You—you gave her Mama's stockings! *His tears break through and he rises to go.*

WILLY, *grabbing for Biff:* I gave you an order!

BIFF: Don't touch me, you—liar!

WILLY: Apologize for that!

BIFF: You fake! You phony little fake! You fake! *Overcome, he turns quickly and weeping fully goes out with his suitcase. Willy is left on the floor on his knees.*

WILLY: I gave you an order! Biff, come back here or I'll beat you! Come back here! I'll whip you!

Stanley comes quickly in from the right and stands in front of Willy.

WILLY, *shouts at Stanley:* I gave you an order . . .

STANLEY: Hey, let's pick it up, pick it up, Mr. Loman. *He helps Willy to his feet.* Your boys left with the chippies. They said they'll see you home.

A second waiter watches some distance away.

WILLY: But we were supposed to have dinner together.

Music is heard, Willy's theme.

STANLEY: Can you make it?

WILLY: I'll—sure, I can make it. *Suddenly concerned about his clothes:* Do I—I look all right?

STANLEY: Sure, you look all right. *He flicks a speck off Willy's lapel.*

WILLY: Here—here's a dollar.

STANLEY: Oh, your son paid me. It's all right.

WILLY, *putting it in Stanley's hand:* No, take it. You're a good boy.

STANLEY: Oh, no, you don't have to . . .

WILLY: Here—here's some more, I don't need it any more. *After a slight pause:* Tell me—is there a seed store in the neighborhood?

STANLEY: Seeds? You mean like to plant?

As Willy turns, Stanley slips the money back into his jacket pocket.

WILLY: Yes. Carrots, peas . . .

STANLEY: Well, there's hardware stores on Sixth Avenue, but it may be too late now.

WILLY, *anxiously:* Oh, I'd better hurry. I've got to get some seeds. *He starts off to the right.* I've got to get some seeds, right away. Nothing's planted. I don't have a thing in the ground.

Willy hurries out as the light goes down. Stanley moves over to the right after him, watches him off. The other waiter has been staring at Willy.

STANLEY, *to the waiter:* Well, whatta you looking at?

The waiter picks up the chairs and moves off right. Stanley takes the table and follows him. The light fades on this area. There is a long pause, the sound of the flute coming over. The light gradually rises on the kitchen, which is empty. Happy appears at the door of the house, followed by Biff. Happy is carrying a large bunch of long-stemmed roses. He enters the kitchen, looks around for Linda. Not seeing her, he turns to Biff, who is just outside the house door, and makes a gesture with his hands, indicating "Not here, I guess." He looks into the living-room and freezes. Inside, Linda, unseen, is seated, Willy's coat on her lap. She rises ominously and quietly and moves toward Happy, who backs up into the kitchen, afraid.

HAPPY: Hey, what're you doing up? *Linda says nothing but moves toward him implacably.* Where's Pop? *He keeps backing to the right, and now Linda is in full view in the doorway to the living-room. Is he sleeping?*

LINDA: Where were you?

HAPPY, *trying to laugh it off:* We met two girls, Mom, very fine types. Here, we brought you some flowers. *Offering them to her:* Put them in your room, Ma.

She knocks them to the floor at Biff's feet. He has now come inside and closed the door behind him. She stares at Biff, silent.

HAPPY: Now what'd you do that for? Mom, I want you to have some flowers—

LINDA, *cutting Happy off, violently to Biff:* Don't you care whether he lives or dies?

HAPPY, *going to the stairs:* Come upstairs, Biff.

BIFF, *with a flare of disgust, to Happy:* Go away from me! *To Linda:* What do you mean, lives or dies? Nobody's dying around here, pal.

LINDA: Get out of my sight! Get out of here!

BIFF: I wanna see the boss.

LINDA: You're not going near him!

BIFF: Where is he? *He moves into the living-room and Linda follows.*

LINDA, *shouting after Biff:* You invite him for dinner. He looks forward to it all day—*Biff appears in his parents' bedroom, looks around, and exits*—and then you desert him there. There's no stranger you'd do that to!

HAPPY: Why? He had a swell time with us. Listen, when I—*Linda comes back into the kitchen*—desert him I hope I don't outlive the day!

LINDA: Get out of here!

HAPPY: Now look, Mom . . .

LINDA: Did you have to go to women tonight? You and your lousy rotten whores!

Biff re-enters the kitchen.

HAPPY: Mom, all we did was follow Biff around trying to cheer him up! *To Biff:* Boy, what a night you gave me!

LINDA: Get out of here, both of you, and don't come back! I don't want you tormenting him any more. Go on now, get your things together! *To Biff:* You can sleep in his apartment. *She starts to pick up the flowers and stops herself.* Pick up this stuff, I'm not your maid any more. Pick it up, you bum, you!

Happy turns his back to her in refusal. Biff slowly moves over and gets down on his knees, picking up the flowers.

LINDA: You're a pair of animals! Not one, not another living soul would have had the cruelty to walk out on that man in a restaurant!

BIFF, *not looking at her:* Is that what he said?

LINDA: He didn't have to say anything. He was so humiliated he nearly limped when he came in.

HAPPY: But, Mom, he had a great time with us—

BIFF, *cutting him off violently:* Shut up!

Without another word, Happy goes upstairs.

LINDA: You! You didn't even go in to see if he was all right!

BIFF, *still on the floor in front of Linda, the flowers in his hand; with self-loathing:* No. Didn't. Didn't do a damned thing. How do you like that, heh? Left him babbling in a toilet.

LINDA: You louse. You . . .

BIFF: Now you hit it on the nose! *He gets up, throws the flowers in the wastebasket.* The scum of the earth, and you're looking at him!

LINDA: Get out of here!

BIFF: I gotta talk to the boss, Mom. Where is he?

LINDA: You're not going near him. Get out of this house!

BIFF, *with absolute assurance, determination:* No. We're gonna have an abrupt conversation, him and me.

LINDA: You're not talking to him!

Hammering is heard from outside the house, off right. Biff turns toward the noise.

LINDA, *suddenly pleading:* Will you please leave him alone?

BIFF: What's he doing out there?

LINDA: He's planting the garden!

BIFF, *quietly:* Now? Oh, my God!

Biff moves outside, Linda following. The light dies down on them and comes up on the center of the apron as Willy walks into it. He is carrying a flashlight, a hoe, and a handful of seed packets. He raps the top of the hoe sharply to fix it firmly, and then moves to the left, measuring off the distance with his foot. He holds the flashlight to look at the seed packets, reading off the instructions. He is in the blue of night.

WILLY: Carrots . . . quarter-inch apart. Rows . . . one-foot rows. *He measures it off.* One foot. *He puts down a package and measures off.* Beets. *He puts down another package and measures again.* Lettuce. *He reads the package, puts it down.* One foot— *He breaks off as Ben appears at the right and moves slowly down to him.* What a proposition, ts, ts. Terrific, terrific. 'Cause she's suffered, Ben, the woman has suffered. You understand me? A man can't go out the way he came in, Ben, a man has got to add up to something. You can't, you can't— *Ben moves toward him as though to interrupt.* You gotta consider, now. Don't answer so quick. Remember, it's a guaranteed twenty-thousand-dollar proposition. Now look, Ben, I want you to go through the ins and outs of this thing with me. I've got nobody to talk to, Ben, and the woman has suffered, you hear me?

BEN, *standing still, considering:* What's the proposition?

WILLY: It's twenty thousand dollars on the barrelhead. Guaranteed, gilt-edged, you understand?

BEN: You don't want to make a fool of yourself. They might not honor the policy.

WILLY: How can they dare refuse? Didn't I work like a coolie to meet every premium on the nose? And now they don't pay off? Impossible!

BEN: It's called a cowardly thing, William.

WILLY: Why? Does it take more guts to stand here the rest of my life ringing up a zero?

BEN, *yielding:* That's a point, William. *He moves, thinking, turns.* And twenty thousand—that *is* something one can feel with the hand, it is there.

WILLY, *now assured, with rising power:* Oh, Ben, that's the whole beauty of it! I see it like a diamond, shining in the dark, hard and rough, that I can pick up and touch in my hand. Not like—like an appointment! This would not be another damned-fool appointment, Ben, and it changes all the aspects. Because he thinks I'm nothing, see, and so he spites me. But the funeral— *Straightening up:* Ben, that funeral will be massive! They'll come from Maine, Massachusetts, Vermont, New Hampshire! All the old-timers with the strange license plates—that boy will be thunder-struck, Ben, because he never realized—I am known! Rhode Island, New York, New Jersey— I am known, Ben, and he'll see it with his eyes once and for all. He'll see what I am, Ben! He's in for a shock, that boy!

BEN, *coming down to the edge of the garden:* He'll call you a coward.

WILLY, *suddenly fearful:* No, that would be terrible.

BEN: Yes. And a damned fool.

WILLY: No, no, he mustn't, I won't have that! *He is broken and desperate.*

BEN: He'll hate you, William.

The gay music of the Boys is heard.

WILLY: Oh, Ben, how do we get back to all the great times? Used to be so full of light, and comradeship, the sleigh-riding in winter, and the ruddiness on his cheeks. And always some kind of good news coming up, always something nice coming up ahead. And never even let me carry the valises in the house, and simonizing, simonizing that little red car! Why, why can't I give him something and not have him hate me?

BEN: Let me think about it. *He glances at his watch.* I still have a little time. Remarkable proposition, but you've got to be sure you're not making a fool of yourself.

Ben drifts off upstage and goes out of sight. Biff comes down from the left.

WILLY, *suddenly conscious of Biff, turns and looks up at him, then begins picking up the packages of seeds in confusion:* Where the hell is that seed? *Indignantly:* You can't see nothing out here! They boxed in the whole goddam neighborhood!

BIFF: There are people all around here. Don't you realize that?

WILLY: I'm busy. Don't bother me.

BIFF, *taking the hoe from Willy:* I'm saying good-by to you, Pop. *Willy looks at him, silent, unable to move.* I'm not coming back any more.

WILLY: You're not going to see Oliver tomorrow?

BIFF: I've got no appointment, Dad.

WILLY: He put his arm around you, and you've got no appointment?

BIFF: Pop, get this now, will you? Everytime I've left it's been a fight that sent me out of here. Today I realized something about myself and I tried to explain it to you and I—I think I'm just not smart enough to make any sense out of it for you. To hell with whose fault it is or anything like that. *He takes Willy's arm.* Let's just wrap it up, heh? Come on in, we'll tell Mom. *He gently tries to pull Willy to left.*

WILLY, *frozen, immobile, with guilt in his voice:* No, I don't want to see her.

BIFF: Come on! *He pulls again, and Willy tries to pull away.*

WILLY, *highly nervous:* No, no, I don't want to see her.

BIFF, *tries to look into Willy's face, as if to find the answer there:* Why don't you want to see her?

WILLY, *more harshly now:* Don't bother me, will you?

BIFF: What do you mean, you don't want to see her? You don't want them calling you yellow, do you? This isn't your fault; it's me, I'm a bum. Now come inside! *Willy strains to get away.* Did you hear what I said to you?

Willy pulls away and quickly goes by himself into the house. Biff follows.

LINDA, *to Willy:* Did you plant, dear?

BIFF, *at the door, to Linda:* All right, we had it out. I'm going and I'm not writing any more.

LINDA, *going to Willy in the kitchen:* I think that's the best way, dear. 'Cause there's no use drawing it out, you'll just never get along.

Willy doesn't respond.

BIFF: People ask where I am and what I'm doing, you don't know, and you don't care. That way it'll be off your mind and you can start brightening up again. All right? That clears it, doesn't it? *Willy is silent, and Biff goes to him.* You gonna wish me luck, scout? *He extends his hand.* What do you say?

LINDA: Shake his hand, Willy.

WILLY, *turning to her, seething with hurt:* There's no necessity to mention the pen at all, y'know.

BIFF, *gently:* I've got no appointment, Dad.

WILLY, *erupting fiercely:* He put his arm around . . . ?

BIFF: Dad, you're never going to see what I am, so what's the use of arguing? If I strike oil I'll send you a check. Meantime forget I'm alive.

WILLY, *to Linda:* Spite, see?

BIFF: Shake hands, Dad.

WILLY: Not my hand.

BIFF: I was hoping not to go this way.

WILLY: Well, this is the way you're going. Good-by.

Biff looks at him a moment, then turns sharply and goes to the stairs.

WILLY, *stops him with:* May you rot in hell if you leave this house!

BIFF, *turning:* Exactly what is it that you want from me?

WILLY: I want you to know, on the train, in the mountains, in the valleys, wherever you go, that you cut down your life for spite!

BIFF: No, no.

WILLY: Spite, spite, is the word of your undoing! And when you're down and out, remember what did it. When you're rotting somewhere beside the railroad tracks, remember, and don't you dare blame it on me!

BIFF: I'm not blaming it on you!

WILLY: I won't take the rap for this, you hear?

Happy comes down the stairs and stands on the bottom step, watching.

BIFF: That's just what I'm telling you!

WILLY, *sinking into a chair at the table, with full accusation:* You're trying to put a knife in me—don't think I don't know what you're doing!

BIFF: All right, phony! Then let's lay it on the line. *He whips the rubber tube out of his pocket and puts it on the table.*

HAPPY: You crazy—

LINDA: Biff! *She moves to grab the hose, but Biff holds it down with his hand.*

BIFF: Leave it there! Don't move it!

WILLY, *not looking at it:* What is that?

BIFF: You know goddam well what that is.

WILLY, *caged, wanting to escape:* I never saw that.

BIFF: You saw it. The mice didn't bring it into the cellar! What is this supposed to do, make a hero out of you? This supposed to make me sorry for you?

WILLY: Never heard of it.

BIFF: There'll be no pity for you, you hear it? No pity!

WILLY, *to Linda:* You hear the spite!

BIFF: No, you're going to hear the truth—what you are and what I am!

LINDA: Stop it!

WILLY: Spite!

HAPPY, *coming down toward Biff:* You cut it now!

BIFF, *to Happy:* The man don't know who we are! The man is gonna know! *To Willy:* We never told the truth for ten minutes in this house!

HAPPY: We always told the truth!

BIFF, *turning on him:* You big blow, are you the assistant buyer? You're one of the two assistants to the assistant, aren't you?

HAPPY: Well, I'm practically—

BIFF: You're practically full of it! We all are! And I'm through with it. *To Willy:* Now hear this, Willy, this is me.

WILLY: I know you!

BIFF: You know why I had no address for three months? I stole a suit in Kansas City and I was in jail. *To Linda, who is sobbing:* Stop crying. I'm through with it.

Linda turns away from them, her hands covering her face.

WILLY: I suppose that's my fault!

BIFF: I stole myself out of every good job since high school!

WILLY: And whose fault is that?

BIFF: And I never got anywhere because you blew me so full of hot air I could never stand taking orders from anybody! That's whose fault it is!

WILLY: I hear that!

LINDA: Don't, Biff!

BIFF: It's goddam time you heard that! I had to be boss big shot in two weeks, and I'm through with it!

WILLY: Then hang yourself! For spite, hang yourself!

BIFF: No! Nobody's hanging himself, Willy! I ran down eleven flights with a pen in my hand today. And suddenly I stopped, you hear me? And in the middle of that office building, do you hear this? I stopped in the middle of that building and I saw— the sky. I saw the things that I love in this world. The work and the food and time to sit and smoke. And I looked at the pen and said to myself, what the hell am I grabbing this for? Why am I trying to become what I don't want to be? What am I doing in an office, making a contemptuous, begging fool of myself, when all I want is out there, waiting for me the minute I say I know who I am! Why can't I say that, Willy? *He tries to make Willy face him, but Willy pulls away and moves to the left.*

WILLY, *with hatred, threateningly:* The door of your life is wide open!

BIFF: Pop! I'm a dime a dozen, and so are you!

WILLY, *turning on him now in an uncontrolled outburst:* I am not a dime a dozen! I am Willy Loman, and you are Biff Loman!

Biff starts for Willy, but is blocked by Happy. In his fury, Biff seems on the verge of attacking his father.

BIFF: I am not a leader of men, Willy, and neither are you. You were never anything but a hard-working drummer who landed in the ash can like all the rest of them! I'm one dollar an hour, Willy! I tried seven states and couldn't raise it. A buck an hour! Do you gather my meaning? I'm not bringing home any prizes any more, and you're going to stop waiting for me to bring them home!

WILLY, *directly to Biff:* You vengeful, spiteful mut!

Biff breaks from Happy. Willy, in fright, starts up the stairs. Biff grabs him

BIFF, *at the peak of his fury:* Pop, I'm nothing! I'm nothing, Pop. Can't you understand that? There's no spite in it any more. I'm just what I am, that's all.

Biff's fury has spent itself, and he breaks down, sobbing, holding on to Willy, who dumbly fumbles for Biff's face.

WILLY, *astonished:* What're you doing? What're you doing? *To Linda:* Why is he crying?

BIFF, *crying, broken:* Will you let me go, for Christ's sake? Will you take that phony dream and burn it before something happens? *Struggling to contain himself, he pulls away and moves to the stairs.* I'll go in the morning. Put him—put him to bed. *Exhausted, Biff moves up the stairs to his room.*

WILLY, *after a long pause, astonished, elevated:* Isn't that— isn't that remarkable? Biff—he likes me!

LINDA: He loves you, Willy!

HAPPY, *deeply moved:* Always did, Pop.

WILLY: Oh, Biff! *Staring wildly:* He cried! Cried to me. *He is choking with his love, and now cries out his promise:* That boy—that boy is going to be magnificent!

Ben appears in the light just outside the kitchen.

BEN: Yes, outstanding, with twenty thousand behind him.

LINDA, *sensing the racing of his mind, fearfully, carefully:* Now come to bed, Willy. It's all settled now.

WILLY, *finding it difficult not to rush out of the house:* Yes, we'll sleep. Come on. Go to sleep, Hap.

BEN: And it does take a great kind of a man to crack the jungle.

In accents of dread, Ben's idyllic music starts up.

HAPPY, *his arm around Linda:* I'm getting married, Pop, don't forget it. I'm changing everything. I'm gonna run that department before the year is up. You'll see, Mom. *He kisses her.*

BEN: The jungle is dark but full of diamonds, Willy.

Willy turns, moves, listening to Ben.

LINDA: Be good. You're both good boys, just act that way, that's all.

HAPPY: 'Night, Pop. *He goes upstairs.*

LINDA, *to Willy:* Come, dear.

BEN, *with greater force:* One must go in to fetch a diamond out.

WILLY, *to Linda, as he moves slowly along the edge of the kitchen, toward the door:* I just want to get settled down, Linda. Let me sit alone for a little.

LINDA, *almost uttering her fear:* I want you upstairs.

WILLY, *taking her in his arms:* In a few minutes, Linda. I couldn't sleep right now. Go on, you look awful tired. *He kisses her.*

BEN: Not like an appointment at all. A diamond is rough and hard to the touch.

WILLY: Go on now. I'll be right up.

LINDA: I think this is the only way, Willy.

WILLY: Sure, it's the best thing.

BEN: Best thing!

WILLY: The only way. Everything is gonna be—go on, kid, get to bed. You look so tired.

LINDA: Come right up.

WILLY: Two minutes.

Linda goes into the living-room, then reappears in her bedroom. Willy moves just outside the kitchen door.

WILLY: Loves me. *Wonderingly:* Always loved me. Isn't that a remarkable thing? Ben, he'll worship me for it!

BEN, *with promise:* It's dark there, but full of diamonds.

WILLY: Can you imagine that magnificence with twenty thousand dollars in his pocket?

LINDA, *calling from her room:* Willy! Come up!

WILLY, *calling into the kitchen:* Yes! Yes. Coming! It's very smart, you realize that, don't you, sweetheart? Even Ben sees it. I gotta go, baby. 'By! 'By! *Going over to Ben, almost dancing:* Imagine? When the mail comes he'll be ahead of Bernard again!

BEN: A perfect proposition all around.

WILLY: Did you see how he cried to me? Oh, if I could kiss him, Ben!

BEN: Time, William, time!

WILLY: Oh, Ben, I always knew one way or another we were gonna make it, Biff and I!

BEN, *looking at his watch:* The boat. We'll be late. *He moves slowly off into the darkness.*

WILLY, *elegiacally, turning to the house:* Now when you kick off, boy, I want a seventy-yard boot, and get right down the field under the ball, and when you hit, hit low and hit hard, because it's important, boy. *He swings around and faces the audience.* There's all kinds of important people in the stands, and the first thing you know . . . *Suddenly realizing he is alone:* Ben! Ben, where do I . . . ? *He makes a sudden movement of search.* Ben, how do I . . . ?

LINDA, *calling:* Willy, you coming up?

WILLY, *uttering a gasp of fear, whirling about as if to quiet her*: Sh! *He turns around as if to find his way; sounds, faces, voices, seem to be swarming in upon him and he flicks at them, crying,* Sh! Sh! *Suddenly music, faint and high, stops him. It rises in intensity, almost to an unbearable scream. He goes up and down on his toes, and rushes off around the house.* Shhh!

LINDA: Willy?

There is no answer. Linda waits. Biff gets up off his bed. He is still in his clothes. Happy sits up. Biff stands listening.

LINDA, *with real fear*: Willy, answer me! Willy!

There is the sound of a car starting and moving away at full speed.

LINDA: No!

BIFF, *rushing down the stairs*: Pop!

As the car speeds off, the music crashes down in a frenzy of sound, which becomes the soft pulsation of a single cello string. Biff slowly returns to his bedroom. He and Happy gravely don their jackets. Linda slowly walks out of her room. The music has developed into a dead march. The leaves of day are appearing over everything. Charley and Bernard, somberly dressed, appear and knock on the kitchen door. Biff and Happy slowly descend the stairs to the kitchen as Charley and Bernard enter. All stop a moment when Linda, in clothes of mourning, bearing a little bunch of roses, comes through the draped doorway into the kitchen. She goes to Charley and takes his arm. Now all move toward the audience, through the wall-line of the kitchen. At the limit of the apron, Linda lays down the flowers, kneels, and sits back on her heels. All stare down at the grave.

Requiem

CHARLEY: It's getting dark, Linda.

Linda doesn't react. She stares at the grave.

BIFF: How about it, Mom? Better get some rest, heh? They'll be closing the gate soon.

Linda makes no move. Pause.

HAPPY, *deeply angered:* He had no right to do that. There was no necessity for it. We would've helped him.

CHARLEY, *grunting:* Hmmm.

BIFF: Come along, Mom.

LINDA: Why didn't anybody come?

CHARLEY: It was a very nice funeral.

LINDA: But where are all the people he knew? Maybe they blame him.

CHARLEY: Naa. It's a rough world, Linda. They wouldn't blame him.

LINDA: I can't understand it. At this time especially. First time in thirty-five years we were just about free and clear. He only needed a little salary. He was even finished with the dentist.

CHARLEY: No man only needs a little salary.

LINDA: I can't understand it.

BIFF: There were a lot of nice days. When he'd come home from a trip; or on Sundays, making the stoop; finishing the cellar; putting on the new porch; when he built the extra bathroom; and put up the garage. You know something, Charley, there's more of him in that front stoop than in all the sales he ever made.

CHARLEY: Yeah. He was a happy man with a batch of cement.

LINDA: He was so wonderful with his hands.

BIFF: He had the wrong dreams. All, all, wrong.

HAPPY, *almost ready to fight Biff:* Don't say that!

BIFF: He never knew who he was.

CHARLEY, *stopping Happy's movement and reply. To Biff:* Nobody dast blame this man. You don't understand: Willy was a salesman. And for a salesman, there is no rock bottom to the life. He don't put a bolt to a nut, he don't tell you the law or give you medicine. He's a man way out there in the blue, riding on a smile and a shoeshine. And when they start not smiling back—that's an earthquake. And then you get yourself a couple of spots on your hat, and you're finished. Nobody dast blame this man. A salesman is got to dream, boy. It comes with the territory.

BIFF: Charley, the man didn't know who he was.

HAPPY, *infuriated:* Don't say that!

BIFF: Why don't you come with me, Happy?

HAPPY: I'm not licked that easily. I'm staying right in this city, and I'm gonna beat this racket! *He looks at Biff, his chin set.* The Loman Brothers!

BIFF: I know who I am, kid.

HAPPY: All right, boy. I'm gonna show you and everybody

else that Willy Loman did not die in vain. He had a good dream. It's the only dream you can have—to come out number-one man. He fought it out here, and this is where I'm gonna win it for him.

BIFF, *with a hopeless glance at Happy, bends toward his mother:* Let's go, Mom.

LINDA: I'll be with you in a minute. Go on, Charley. *He hesitates.* I want to, just for a minute. I never had a chance to say good-by.

Charley moves away, followed by Happy. Biff remains a slight distance up and left of Linda. She sits there, summoning herself. The flute begins, not far away, playing behind her speech.

LINDA: Forgive me, dear. I can't cry. I don't know what it is, but I can't cry. I don't understand it. Why did you ever do that? Help me, Willy, I can't cry. It seems to me that you're just on another trip. I keep expecting you. Willy, dear, I can't cry. Why did you do it? I search and search and I search, and I can't understand it, Willy. I made the last payment on the house today. Today, dear. And there'll be nobody home. *A sob rises in her throat.* We're free and clear. *Sobbing more fully, released:* We're free. *Biff comes slowly toward her.* We're free . . . We're free . . .

Biff lifts her to her feet and moves out up right with her in his arms. Linda sobs quietly. Bernard and Charley come together and follow them, followed by Happy. Only the music of the flute is left on the darkening stage as over the house the hard towers of the apartment buildings rise into sharp focus, and

The Curtain Falls

The preceding is the standard 1958 Viking Compass text of *Death of a Salesman*, pagination unchanged. Other versions are the 1951 Bantam edition, out of print since 1955; and the Dramatists Play Service acting edition, containing technical details for staging.

CRITICISM AND ANALOGUES

EDITORIAL NOTE

In the critical section of this volume all footnotes are mine unless they carry the author's initials. Omissions, of course, are indicated by ellipses.

G. W.

Miller on *Death of a Salesman*

TRAGEDY AND THE COMMON MAN

In this age few tragedies are written. It has often been held that the lack is due to a paucity of heroes among us, or else that modern man has had the blood drawn out of his organs of belief by the skepticism of science, and the heroic attack on life cannot feed on an attitude of reserve and circumspection. For one reason or another, we are often held to be below tragedy—or tragedy above us. The inevitable conclusion is, of course, that the tragic mode is archaic, fit only for the very highly placed, the kings or the kingly, and where this admission is not made in so many words it is most often implied.

I believe that the common man is as apt a subject for tragedy in its highest sense as kings were. On the face of it this ought to be obvious in the light of modern psychiatry, which bases its analysis upon classic formulations, such as the Oedipus and Orestes complexes, for instances, which were enacted by royal beings, but which apply to everyone in similar emotional situations.

More simply, when the question of tragedy in art is not at issue, we never hesitate to attribute to the well-placed and the

From *The New York Times*, February 27, 1949, II, pp. 1, 3. Copyright 1949 by Arthur Miller. The description of tragedy in the modern world in the first paragraph is derived primarily from Joseph Wood Krutch's famous chapter "The Tragic Fallacy" from *The Modern Temper* (New York: Harcourt, Brace, 1929), pp. 115–143. Much of the terminology that Miller attempts to redefine comes from Aristotle's *Poetics*.

exalted the very same mental processes as the lowly. And finally, if the exaltation of tragic action were truly a property of the high-bred character alone, it is inconceivable that the mass of mankind should cherish tragedy above all other forms, let alone be capable of understanding it.

As a general rule, to which there may be exceptions unknown to me, I think the tragic feeling is evoked in us when we are in the presence of a character who is ready to lay down his life, if need be, to secure one thing—his sense of personal dignity. From Orestes to Hamlet, Medea to Macbeth, the underlying struggle is that of the individual attempting to gain his "rightful" position in his society.

Sometimes he is one who has been displaced from it, sometimes one who seeks to attain it for the first time, but the fateful wound from which the inevitable events spiral is the wound of indignity, and its dominant force is indignation. Tragedy, then, is the consequence of a man's total compulsion to evaluate himself justly.

In the sense of having been initiated by the hero himself, the tale always reveals what has been called his "tragic flaw," a failing that is not peculiar to grand or elevated characters. Nor is it necessarily a weakness. The flaw, or crack in the character, is really nothing—and need be nothing—but his inherent unwillingness to remain passive in the face of what he conceives to be a challenge to his dignity, his image of his rightful status. Only the passive, only those who accept their lot without active retaliation, are "flawless." Most of us are in that category.

But there are among us today, as there always have been, those who act against the scheme of things that degrades them, and in the process of action everything we have accepted out of fear or insensitivity or ignorance is shaken before us and examined, and from this total onslaught by an individual against the seemingly stable cosmos surrounding us—from this total examination of the "unchangeable" environment—comes the terror and the fear that is classically associated with tragedy.

More important, from this total questioning of what has previously been unquestioned, we learn. And such a process is not beyond the common man. In revolutions around the world, these past thirty years, he has demonstrated again and again this inner dynamic of all tragedy.

Insistence upon the rank of the tragic hero, or the so-called nobility of his character, is really but a clinging to the outward forms of tragedy. If rank or nobility of character was indispensable, then it would follow that the problems of those with rank were the particular problems of tragedy. But surely the right of one monarch to capture the domain from another no longer raises our passions, nor are our concepts of justice what they were to the mind of an Elizabethan king.

The quality in such plays that does shake us, however, derives from the underlying fear of being displaced, the disaster inherent in being torn away from our chosen image of what and who we are in this world. Among us today this fear is as strong, and perhaps stronger, than it ever was. In fact, it is the common man who knows this fear best.

Now, if it is true that tragedy is the consequence of a man's total compulsion to evaluate himself justly, his destruction in the attempt posits a wrong or an evil in his environment. And this is precisely the morality of tragedy and its lesson. The discovery of the moral law, which is what the enlightenment of tragedy consists of, is not the discovery of some abstract or metaphysical quantity.

The tragic right is a condition of life, a condition in which the human personality is able to flower and realize itself. The wrong is the condition which suppresses man, perverts the flowing out of his love and creative instinct. Tragedy enlightens—and it must, in that it points the heroic finger at the enemy of man's freedom. The thrust for freedom is the quality in tragedy which exalts. The revolutionary questioning of the stable environment is what terrifies. In no way is the common man debarred from such thoughts or such actions.

Seen in this light, our lack of tragedy may be partially accounted for by the turn which modern literature has taken toward the purely psychiatric view of life, or the purely sociological. If all our miseries, our indignities, are born and bred within our minds, then all action, let alone the heroic action, is obviously impossible.

And if society alone is responsible for the cramping of our lives, then the protagonist must needs be so pure and faultless as to force us to deny his validity as a character. From neither of these views can tragedy derive, simply because neither represents a balanced concept of life. Above all else, tragedy requires the finest appreciation by the writer of cause and effect.

No tragedy can therefore come about when its author fears to question absolutely everything, when he regards any institution, habit or custom as being either everlasting, immutable or inevitable. In the tragic view the need of man to wholly realize himself is the only fixed star, and whatever it is that hedges his nature and lowers it is ripe for attack and examination. Which is not to say that tragedy must preach revolution.

The Greeks could probe the very heavenly origin of their ways and return to confirm the rightness of laws. And Job could face God in anger, demanding his right and end in submission. But for a moment everything is in suspension, nothing is accepted, and in this stretching and tearing apart of the cosmos, in the very action of so doing, the character gains "size," the tragic stature which is spuriously attached to the royal or the highborn in our minds. The commonest of men may take on that stature to the extent of his willingness to throw all he has into the contest, the battle to secure his rightful place in his world.

There is a misconception of tragedy with which I have been struck in review after review, and in many conversations with writers and readers alike. It is the idea that tragedy is of necessity allied to pessimism. Even the dictionary says nothing more about the word than that it means a story with a sad or unhappy ending. This impression is so firmly fixed that I almost hesitate to claim that in truth tragedy implies more optimism in its author than does comedy, and that its final result ought to be the reinforcement of the onlooker's brightest opinions of the human animal.

For, if it is true to say that in essence the tragic hero is intent upon claiming his whole due as a personality, and if this struggle must be total and without reservation, then it automatically demonstrates the indestructible will of man to achieve his humanity.

The possibility of victory must be there in tragedy. Where pathos rules, where pathos is finally derived, a character has fought a battle he could not possibly have won. The pathetic is achieved when the protagonist is, by virtue of his witlessness, his insensitivity or the very air he gives off, incapable of grappling with a much superior force.

Pathos truly is the mode for the pessimist. But tragedy requires a nicer balance between what is possible and what is impossible. And it is curious, although edifying, that the plays we revere, century after century, are the tragedies. In them, and in them alone, lies the belief—optimistic, if you will, in the perfectibility of man.

It is time, I think, that we who are without kings, took up this bright thread of our history and followed it to the only place it can possibly lead in our time—the heart and spirit of the average man.

THE "SALESMAN" HAS A BIRTHDAY

Experience tells me that I will probably know better next year what I feel right now about the first anniversary of "Death of a Salesman"—it usually takes that long to understand anything. I suppose I ought to try to open some insights into the play. Frankly, however, it comes very fuzzily to mind at this date. I have not sat through it since dress rehearsal and haven't read it since the proofs went to the publisher. In fact, it may well be that from the moment I read it to my wife and two

From *The New York Times*, February 5, 1950, II, pp. 1, 3. Copyright 1950 by Arthur Miller.

friends one evening in the country a year ago last fall, the play cut itself off from me in a way that is incomprehensible.

I remember that night clearly, best of all. The feeling of disaster when, glancing up at the audience of three, I saw nothing but glazed looks in their eyes. And at the end, when they said nothing, the script suddenly seemed a record of a madness I had passed through, something I ought not admit to at all, let alone read aloud or have produced on the stage.

I don't remember what they said, exactly, excepting that it had taken them deeply. But I can see my wife's eyes as I read a —to me—hilarious scene, which I prefer not to identify. She was weeping. I confess that I laughed more during the writing of this play than I have ever done, when alone, in my life. I laughed because moment after moment came when I felt I had rapped it right on the head—the non sequitur, the aberrant but meaningful idea racing through Willy's head, the turn of story that kept surprising me every morning. And most of all the form, for which I have been searching since the beginning of my writing life.

Writing in that form was like moving through a corridor in a dream, knowing instinctively that one would find every wriggle of it and, best of all, where the exit lay. There is something like a dream's quality in my memory of the writing and the day or two that followed its completion.

I remember the rehearsal when we had our first audience. Six or seven friends. The play working itself out under the single bulb overhead. I think that was the first and only time I saw it as others see it. Then it seemed to me that we must be a terribly lonely people, cut off from each other by such massive pretense of self-sufficiency, machined down so fine we hardly touch any more. We are trying to save ourselves separately, and that is immoral, that is the corrosive among us.

On that afternoon, more than any time before or since, the marvel of the actor was all new to me. How utterly they believed what they were saying to each other!

To watch fine actors creating their roles is to see revealed the innocence, the naïve imagination of man liberated from the prisons of the past. They were like children wanting to show that they could turn themselves into anybody, thus opening their lives to limitless possibilities.

And Elia Kazan, with his marvelous wiles, tripping the latches of the secret little doors that lead into the always different personalities of each actor. That is his secret; not merely to know what must be done, but to know the way to implement the doing for actors trained in diametrically opposite schools, or not trained at all. He does not "direct," he creates a center point, and then goes to each actor and creates the desire to move toward it. And they all meet, but for different reasons, and seem to have arrived there by themselves.

Was there ever a production of so serious a play that was carried through with so much exhilarating laughter? I doubt it. We were always on the way, and I suppose we always knew it.

There are things learned—I think, by many people—from this production. Things which, if applied, can bring much vitality to our theatre.

There is no limit to the expansion of the audience imagination so long as the play's internal logic is kept inviolate. It is not true that conventionalism is demanded. They will move with you anywhere, they will believe right into the moon so long as you believe who tell them this tale. We are at the beginning of many explosions of form. They are waiting for wonders.

A serious theme is entertaining to the extent that it is not trifled with, not cleverly angled, but met in head-on collision. They will not consent to suffer while the creators stand by with tongue in cheek. They have a way of knowing. Nobody can blame them.

And there have been certain disappointments, one above all. I am sorry the self-realization of the older son, Biff, is not a weightier counterbalance to Willy's disaster in the audience mind.

And certain things more clearly known, or so it seems now. We want to give of ourselves, and yet all we train for is to take, as though nothing less will keep the world at a safe distance. Every day we contradict our will to create, which is to give. The end of man is not security, but without security we are without the elementary condition of humaneness.

A time will come when they will look back at us astonished that we saw something holy in the competition for the means of existence. But already we are beginning to ask of the great man, not what has he got, but what has he done for the world. We ought to be struggling for a world in which it will be possible to lay blame. Only then will the great tragedies be written, for where no order is believed in, no order can be breached, and thus all disasters of man will strive vainly for moral meaning.

And what have such thoughts to do with this sort of reminiscence? Only that to me the tragedy of Willy Loman is that he gave his life, or sold it, in order to justify the waste of it. It is the tragedy of a man who did believe that he alone was not meeting the qualifications laid down for mankind by those clean-shaven frontiersmen who inhabit the peaks of broadcasting and advertising offices. From those forests of canned goods high up near the sky, he heard the thundering command to succeed as it ricocheted down the newspaper-lined canyons of his city, heard not a human voice, but a wind of a voice to which no human can reply in kind, except to stare into the mirror at a failure.

So what is there to feel on this anniversary? Hope, for I know now that the people want to listen. A little fear that they want to listen so badly. And an old insistence—sometimes difficult to summon, but there none the less—that we will find a way beyond fear of each other, beyond bellicosity, a way into our humanity.

THE AMERICAN THEATER

. . . For instance, when we were searching for a woman to play Linda, the mother in *Death of a Salesman*, a lady came in whom we all knew but could never imagine in the part. We needed a woman who looked as though she had lived in a house dress all her life, even somewhat coarse and certainly less than brilliant. Mildred Dunnock insisted she was that woman, but she was frail, delicate, not long ago a teacher in a girl's college, and a cultivated citizen who probably would not be out of place in a cabinet post. We told her this, in effect, and she understood, and left.

And the next day the line of women formed again in the wings and suddenly there was Milly again. Now she padded herself from neck to hemline to look a bit bigger, and for a moment none of us recognized her, and she read again. As soon as she spoke we started to laugh at her ruse; but we saw, too, that she *was* a little more worn now, and seemed less well-maintained, and while she was not quite ordinary she reminded you of women who were. But we all agreed, when she was finished reading, that she was not right, and she left.

Next day she was there again in another getup and the next and the next, and each day she agreed with us that she was wrong; and to make a long story short when it came time to make the final selection it had to be Milly and she turned out to be magnificent. But in this case we had known her work; there was no doubt that she was an excellent actress. The number of talented applicants who are turned down because they are unknown is very large. Such is the crap-shooting chanciness

From *Holiday*, XVII (January 1955), 90–104. Copyright 1954 by Arthur Miller. The article, of which the last few paragraphs are printed here, is a view of American theater, at once practical and romantic, which begins with the assumption that there is a difference "between Show Business and the Theater. I belong to the Theater. . . ."

of the business, its chaos, and part of its charm. In a world where one's fate so often seems machined and standardized, and unlikely to suddenly change, these five blocks are like a stockade inside which are people who insist that the unexpected, the sudden chance, must survive. And to experience it they keep coming on all the trains.

But to understand its apparently deathless lure for so many it is necessary, finally, to have participated in the first production of a new play. When a director takes his place at the beaten-up wooden table placed at the edge of the stage, and the cast for the first time sit before him in a semicircle, and he gives the nod to the actor who has the opening lines, the world seems to be filling with a kind of hope, a kind of regeneration that, at the time, anyway, makes all the sacrifices worth while.

The production of a new play, I have often thought, is like another chance in life, a chance to emerge cleansed of one's imperfections. Here, as when one was very young, it seems possible again to attain even greatness, or happiness, or some otherwise unattainable joy. And when production never loses that air of hope through all its three-and-a-half-week rehearsal period, one feels alive as at no other imaginable occasion. At such a time, it seems to all concerned that the very heart of life's mystery is what must be penetrated. They watch the director and each other and they listen with the avid attention of deaf mutes who have suddenly learned to speak and hear. Above their heads there begins to form a tantalizing sort of cloud, a question, a challenge to penetrate the mystery of why men move and speak and act.

It is a kind of glamour that can never be reported in a newspaper column, and yet it is the center of all the lure theater has. It is a kind of soul-testing that ordinary people rarely experience except in the greatest emergencies. The actor who has always regarded himself as a strong spirit discovers now that his vaunted power somehow sounds querulous, and he must look within himself to find his strength. The actress who has made her way on her charm discovers that she appears not charming so much as shallow now, and must evaluate herself all over again, and create anew what she always took for granted. And the great performers are merely those who have been able to face themselves without remorse.

In the production of a good play with a good cast and a knowing director a kind of banding-together occurs; there is formed a fraternity whose members share a mutual sense of destiny. In these five blocks, where the rapping of the tapdancer's feet and the bawling of the phonographs in the recordshop doorways mix with the roar of the Broadway traffic; where the lonely, the perverted, and the lost wander like the souls in Dante's hell and the life of the spirit seems impossible, there are still little circles of actors in the dead silence of empty theaters, with a director in their center, and a new creation of life taking place.

There are always certain moments in such rehearsals, moments of such wonder that the memory of them serves to further entrap all who witness them into this most insecure of all professions. Remembering such moments the resolution to leave and get a "real" job vanishes and they are hooked again.

I think of Lee Cobb, the greatest dramatic actor I ever saw, when he was creating the role of Willy Loman in *Death of a Salesman*. When I hear people scoffing at actors as mere exhibitionists, when I hear them ask why there must be a theater if it cannot support itself as any business must, when I myself grow sick and weary of the endless waste and the many travesties of this most abused of all arts, I think then of Lee Cobb making that role and I know that the theater can yet be one of the chief glories of mankind.

He sat for days on the stage like a great lump, a sick seal, a mourning walrus. When it came his time to speak lines, he whispered meaninglessly. Kazan, the director, pretended certainty, but from where I sat he looked like an ant trying to prod an elephant off his haunches. Ten days went by. The other actors were by now much further advanced: Milly Dunnock, playing Linda, was already creating a role; Arthur Kennedy as Biff had long since begun to reach for his high notes; Cameron Mitchell had many scenes already perfected; but Cobb stared at them, heavy-eyed, morose, even persecuted, it seemed.

And then, one afternoon, there on the stage of the New Amsterdam way up on top of a movie theater on 42nd Street (this roof theater had once been Ziegfeld's private playhouse in the gilded times, and now was barely heated and misty with dust), Lee rose from his chair and looked at Milly Dunnock and there was a silence. And then he said, "I was driving along, you understand, and then all of a sudden I'm going off the road. . . ."

And the theater vanished. The stage vanished. The chill of an age-old recognition shuddered my spine; a voice was sounding in the dimly lit air up front, a created spirit, an incarnation, a Godlike creation was taking place; a new human being was being formed before all our eyes, born for the first time on this earth, made real by an act of will, by an artist's summoning up of all his memories and his intelligence; a birth was taking place above the meaningless traffic below; a man was here transcending the limits of his body and his own history. Through the complete concentration of his mind he had even altered the stance of his body, which now was strangely not the body of Lee Cobb (he was thirty-seven then) but of a sixty-year-old salesman; a mere glance of his eye created a window beside him, with the gentle touch of his hand on this empty stage a bed appeared, and when he glanced up at the emptiness above him a ceiling was there, and there was even a crack in it where his stare rested.

I knew then that something astounding was being made here. It would have been almost enough for me without even opening the play. The actors, like myself and Kazan and the producer, were happy, of course, that we might have a hit; but there was a good deal more. There was a new fact of life, there was an alteration of history for all of us that afternoon.

There is a certain immortality involved in theater, not created by monuments and books, but through the knowledge the actor keeps to his dying day that on a certain afternoon, in an empty and dusty theater, he cast a shadow of a being that was not himself but the distillation of all he had ever observed; all the unsingable heartsong the ordinary man may feel but never utter, he gave voice to. And by that he somehow joins the ages.

And that is the glamour that remains, but it will not be found in the gossip columns. And it is enough, once discovered, to make people stay with the theater, and others to come seeking it.

I think also that people keep coming into these five blocks because the theater is still so simple, so old-fashioned. And that is why, however often its obsequies are intoned, it somehow never really dies. Because underneath our shiny fronts of stone, our fascination with gadgets and our new toys that can blow the earth into a million stars, we are still outside the doorway through which the great answers wait. Not all the cameras in Christendom nor all the tricky lights will move us one step closer to a better understanding of ourselves, but only, as it always was, the truly written word, the profoundly felt gesture, the naked and direct contemplation of man which is the enduring glamour of the stage.

INTRODUCTION TO COLLECTED PLAYS

. . . The first image that occurred to me which was to result in *Death of a Salesman* was of an enormous face the height of the proscenium arch which would appear and then open up, and we would see the inside of a man's head. In fact, *The Inside of His Head* was the first title. It was conceived half in laughter, for the inside of his head was a mass of contradictions. The image was in direct opposition to the method of *All My Sons*—

From *Collected Plays* by Arthur Miller (New York: Viking, 1957), pp. 23–38. Copyright © 1957 by Arthur Miller. The complete Introduction (pp. 3–55) contains a general statement on playwriting and detailed comments on all the Miller plays from *All My Sons* through *A View from the Bridge*.

a method one might call linear or eventual in that one fact or incident creates the necessity for the next. The *Salesman* image was from the beginning absorbed with the concept that nothing in life comes "next" but that everything exists together and at the same time within us; that there is no past to be "brought forward" in a human being, but that he is his past at every moment and that the present is merely that which his past is capable of noticing and smelling and reacting to.

I wished to create a form which, in itself as a form, would literally be the process of Willy Loman's way of mind. But to say "wished" is not accurate. Any dramatic form is an artifice, a way of transforming a subjective feeling into something that can be comprehended through public symbols. Its efficiency as a form is to be judged—at least by the writer—by how much of the original vision and feeling is lost or distorted by this transformation. I wished to speak of the salesman most precisely as I felt about him, to give no part of that feeling away for the sake of any effect or any dramatic necessity. What was wanted now was not a mounting line of tension, nor a gradually narrowing cone of intensifying suspense, but a bloc, a single chord presented as such at the outset, within which all the strains and melodies would already be contained. The strategy, as with *All My Sons*, was to appear entirely unstrategic but with a difference. This time, if I could, I would have told the whole story and set forth all the characters in- one unbroken speech or even one sentence or a single flash of light. As I look at the play now its form seems the form of a confession, for that is how it is told, now speaking of what happened yesterday, then suddenly following some connection to a time twenty years ago, then leaping even further back and then returning to the present and even speculating about the future.

Where in *All My Sons* it had seemed necessary to prove the connections between the present and the past, between events and moral consequences, between the manifest and the hidden, in this play all was assumed as proven to begin with. All I was doing was bringing things to mind. The assumption, also, was that everyone knew Willy Loman. I can realize this only now, it is true, but it is equally apparent to me that I took it somehow for granted then. There was still the attitude of the unveiler, but no bringing together of hitherto unrelated things; only pre-existing images, events, confrontations, moods, and pieces of knowledge. So there was a kind of confidence underlying this play which the form itself expresses, even a naïveté, a self-disarming quality that was in part born of my belief in the audience as being essentially the same as myself. If I had wanted, then, to put the audience reaction into words, it would not have been "What happens next and why?" so much as "Oh, God, of course!"

In one sense a play is a species of jurisprudence, and some part of it must take the advocate's role, something else must act in defense, and the entirety must engage the Law. Against my will, *All My Sons* states, and even proclaims, that it is a form and that a writer wrote it and organized it. In *Death of a Salesman* the original impulse was to make that same procla-mation in an immeasurably more violent, abrupt, and openly conscious way. Willy Loman does not merely suggest or hint that he is at the end of his strength and of his justifications, he is hardly on the stage for five minutes when he says so; he does not gradually imply a deadly conflict with his son, an implica-tion dropped into the midst of serenity and surface calm, he is avowedly grappling with that conflict at the outset. The ulti-mate matter with which the play will close is announced at the outset and is the matter of its every moment from the first. There is enough revealed in the first scene of *Death of a Sales-man* to fill another kind of play which, in service to another dramatic form, would hold back and only gradually release it. I wanted to proclaim that an artist had made this play, but the nature of the proclamation was to be entirely "inartistic" and avowedly unstrategic; it was to hold back nothing, at any mo-ment, which life would have revealed, even at the cost of sus-pense and climax. It was to forego the usual preparations for scenes and to permit—and even seek—whatever in each character contradicted his position in the advocate-defense scheme of its jurisprudence. The play was begun with only one firm piece of knowledge and this was that Loman was to destroy himself. How it would wander before it got to that point I did not know and resolved not to care. I was convinced only that if I could make him remember enough he would kill himself, and the structure of the play was determined by what was needed to draw up his memories like a mass of tangled roots without end or beginning.

As I have said, the structure of events and the nature of its form are also the direct reflection of Willy Loman's way of thinking at this moment of his life. He was the kind of man you see muttering to himself on a subway, decently dressed, on his way home or to the office, perfectly integrated with his surroundings excepting that unlike other people he can no longer restrain the power of his experience from disrupting the superficial sociality of his behavior. Consequently he is working on two logics which often collide. For instance, if he meets his son Happy while in the midst of some memory in which Happy disappointed him, he is instantly furious at Happy, despite the fact that Happy at this particular moment deeply desires to be of use to him. He is literally at that terrible moment when the voice of the past is no longer distant but quite as loud as the voice of the present. In dramatic terms the form, therefore, *is* this process, instead of being a once-removed summation or indication of it.

The way of telling the tale, in this sense, is as mad as Willy and as abrupt and as suddenly lyrical. And it is difficult not to add that the subsequent imitations of the form had to collapse for this particular reason. It is not possible, in my opinion, to graft it onto a character whose psychology it does not reflect, and I have not used it since because it would be false to a more integrated—or less disintegrating—personality to pretend that the past and the present are so openly and vocally intertwined in his mind. The ability of people to down their past is normal, and without it we could have no comprehensible communication among men. In the hands of writers who see it as an easy way to elicit anterior information in a play it becomes merely a flashback. There are no flashbacks in this play but only a mobile concurrency of past and present, and this, again, because in his desperation to justify his life Willy Loman has destroyed the boundaries between now and then, just as anyone would do who, on picking up his telephone, discovered that this perfectly harmless act had somehow set off an explosion in his basement. The previously assumed and believed-in results of ordinary and accepted actions, and their abrupt and unforeseen—but apparently logical—effects, form the basic collision in this play, and, I suppose, its ultimate irony.

It may be in place to remark, in this connection, that while the play was sometimes called cinematographic in its structure, it failed as a motion picture. I believe that the basic reason— aside from the gross insensitivity permeating its film production—was that the dramatic tension of Willy's memories was destroyed by transferring him, literally, to the locales he had only imagined in the play. There is an inevitable horror in the spectacle of a man losing consciousness of his immediate surroundings to the point where he engages in conversations with unseen persons. The horror is lost—and drama becomes narrative—when the context actually becomes his imagined world. And the drama evaporates because psychological truth has been amended, a truth which depends not only on what images we recall but in what connections and contexts we recall them. The setting on the stage was never shifted, despite the many changes in locale, for the precise reason that, quite simply, the mere fact that a man forgets where he is does not mean that he has really moved. Indeed, his terror springs from his never-lost awareness of time and place. It did not need this play to teach me that the screen is time-bound and earth-bound compared to the stage, if only because its preponderant emphasis is on the visual image, which, however rapidly it may be changed before our eyes, still displaces its predecessor, while scene-changing with words is instantaneous; and because of the flexibility of language, especially of English, a preceding image can be kept alive through the image that succeeds it. The movie's tendency is always to wipe out what has gone before, and it is thus in constant danger of transforming the dramatic into narrative. There is no swifter method of telling a "story" but neither is there a more difficult medium in which to keep a pattern of relationships constantly in being. Even in those sequences which retained the real backgrounds for Willy's imaginary confrontations the tension between now and then was lost. I suspect this loss was due to the necessity of shooting the actors close-up—effectively eliminating awareness of their surroundings. The basic failure of the picture was a formal one. It did not solve, nor really attempt to find, a resolution for the problem of keeping the past constantly alive, and that friction, collision, and tension between past and present was the heart of the play's particular construction.

A great deal has been said and written about what *Death of a Salesman* is supposed to signify, both psychologically and from the socio-political viewpoints. For instance, in one periodical of the far Right it was called a "time bomb expertly placed under the edifice of Americanism," while the *Daily Worker* reviewer thought it entirely decadent. In Catholic Spain it ran longer than any modern play and it has been refused production in Russia but not, from time to time, in certain satellite countries, depending on the direction and velocity of the wind. The Spanish press, thoroughly controlled by Catholic orthodoxy, regarded the play as commendable proof of the spirit's death where there is no God. In America, even as it was being cannonaded as a piece of Communist propaganda, two of the largest manufacturing corporations in the country invited me to address their sales organizations in conventions assembled, while the road company was here and there picketed by the Catholic War Veterans and the American Legion. It made only a fair impression in London, but in the area of the Norwegian Arctic Circle fishermen whose only contact with civilization was the radio and the occasional visit of the government boat insisted on seeing it night after night—the same few people—believing it to be some kind of religious rite. One organization of salesmen raised me up nearly to patron-sainthood, and another, a national sales managers' group, complained that the difficulty of recruiting salesmen was directly traceable to the play. When the movie was made, the producing company got so frightened it produced a sort of trailer to be shown before the picture, a documentary short film which demonstrated how exceptional Willy Loman was; how necessary selling is to the economy; how secure the salesman's life really is; how idiotic, in short, was the feature film they had just spent more than a million dollars to produce. Fright does odd things to people.

On the psychological front the play spawned a small hill of doctoral theses explaining its Freudian symbolism, and there were innumerable letters asking if I was aware that the fountain pen which Biff steals is a phallic symbol.[1] Some, on the other hand, felt it was merely a fountain pen and dismissed the whole play. I received visits from men over sixty from as far away as California who had come across the country to have me write the stories of their lives, because the story of Willy Loman was exactly like theirs. The letters from women made it clear that the central character of the play was Linda; sons saw the entire action revolving around Biff or Happy, and fathers wanted advice, in effect, on how to avoid parricide. Probably the most succinct reaction to the play was voiced by a man who, on leaving the theater, said, "I always said that New England territory was no damned good." This, at least, was a fact.

That I have and had not the slightest interest in the selling profession is probably unbelievable to most people, and I very early gave up trying even to say so. And when asked what Willy was selling,[2] what was in his bags, I could only reply, "Himself." I was trying neither to condemn a profession nor particularly to improve it, and, I will admit, I was little better than ignorant of Freud's teachings when I wrote it. There was no attempt to bring down the American edifice nor to raise it higher, to show

---

[1] See Daniel E. Schneider's article, pp. 250–258. Most of the psychological assumptions about the play appeared first in it.

[2] Both Wolcott Gibbs and Kappo Phelan, reviewing the original production, assumed that Willy sold stockings, probably because he gave them to the Woman in Boston. For their reviews, see Bibliography.

up family relations or to cure the ills afflicting that inevitable institution. The truth, at least of my aim—which is all I can speak of authoritatively—is much simpler and more complex.

The play grew from simple images. From a little frame house on a street of little frame houses, which had once been loud with the noise of growing boys, and then was empty and silent and finally occupied by strangers. Strangers who could not know with what conquistadorial joy Willy and his boys had once re-shingled the roof. Now it was quiet in the house, and the wrong people in the beds.

It grew from images of futility—the cavernous Sunday afternoons polishing the car. Where is that car now? And the chamois cloths carefully washed and put up to dry, where are the chamois cloths?

And the endless, convoluted discussions, wonderments, arguments, belittlements, encouragements, fiery resolutions, abdications, returns, partings, voyages out and voyages back, tremendous opportunities and small, squeaking denouements—and all in the kitchen now occupied by strangers who cannot hear what the walls are saying.

The image of aging and so many of your friends already gone and strangers in the seats of the mighty who do not know you or your triumphs or your incredible value.

The image of the son's hard, public eye upon you, no longer swept by your myth, no longer rousable from his separateness, no longer knowing you have lived for him and have wept for him.

The image of ferocity when love has turned to something else and yet is there, is somewhere in the room if one could only find it.

The image of people turning into strangers who only evaluate one another.

Above all, perhaps, the image of a need greater than hunger or sex or thirst, a need to leave a thumbprint somewhere on the world. A need for immortality, and by admitting it, the knowing that one has carefully inscribed one's name on a cake of ice on a hot July day.

I sought the relatedness of all things by isolating their unrelatedness, a man superbly alone with his sense of not having touched, and finally knowing in his last extremity that the love which had always been in the room unlocated was now found.

The image of a suicide so mixed in motive as to be unfathomable and yet demanding statement. Revenge was in it and a power of love, a victory in that it would bequeath a fortune to the living and a flight from emptiness. With it an image of peace at the final curtain, the peace that is between wars, the peace leaving the issues above ground and viable yet.

And always, throughout, the image of private man in a world full of strangers, a world that is not home nor even an open battleground but only galaxies of high promise over a fear of falling.

And the image of a man making something with his hands being a rock to touch and return to. "He was always so wonderful with his hands," says his wife over his grave, and I laughed when the line came, laughed with the artist-devil's laugh, for it had all come together in this line, she having been made by him though he did not know it or believe in it or receive it into himself. Only rank, height of power, the sense of having won he believed was real—the galaxy thrust up into the sky by projectors on the rooftops of the city he believed were real stars.

It came from structural images. The play's eye was to revolve from within Willy's head, sweeping endlessly in all directions like a light on the sea, and nothing that formed in the distant mist was to be left uninvestigated. It was thought of as having the density of the novel form in its interchange of viewpoints, so that while all roads led to Willy the other characters were to feel it was their play, a story about them and not him.

There were two undulating lines in mind, one above the other, the past webbed to the present moving on together in him and sometimes openly joined and once, finally, colliding in the showdown which defined him in his eyes at least—and so to sleep.

Above all, in the structural sense, I aimed to make a play with the veritable countenance of life. To make one the many, as in life, so that "society" is a power and a mystery of custom and inside the man and surrounding him, as the fish is in the sea and the sea inside the fish, his birthplace and burial ground, promise and threat. To speak commonsensically of social facts which every businessman knows and talks about but which are too prosaic to mention or are usually fancied up on the stage as philosophical problems. When a man gets old you fire him, you have to, he can't do the work. To speak and even to celebrate the common sense of businessmen, who love the personality that wins the day but know that you've got to have the right goods at the right price, handsome and well-spoken as you are. (To some, these were scandalous and infamous arraignments of society when uttered in the context of art. But not to the businessmen themselves; they knew it was all true and I cherished their clear-eyed talk.)

The image of a play without transitional scenes was there in the beginning. There was too much to say to waste precious stage time with feints and preparations, in themselves agonizing "structural" bridges for a writer to work out since they are not why he is writing. There was a resolution, as in *All My Sons*, not to waste motion or moments, but in this case to shear through everything up to the meat of a scene; a resolution not to write an unmeant word for the sake of the form but to make the form give and stretch and contract for the sake of the thing to be said. To cling to the process of Willy's mind as the form the story would take.

The play was always heroic to me, and in later years the academy's charge that Willy lacked the "stature" for the tragic hero seemed incredible to me. I had not understood that these matters are measured by Greco-Elizabethan paragraphs which hold no mention of insurance payments, front porches, refrigerator fan belts, steering knuckles, Chevrolets, and visions seen not through the portals of Delphi but in the blue flame of the hot-water heater. How could "Tragedy" make people weep, of all things?

I set out not to "write a tragedy" in this play, but to show the truth as I saw it. However, some of the attacks upon it as a pseudo-tragedy contain ideas so misleading, and in some cases so laughable, that it might be in place here to deal with a few of them.

Aristotle having spoken of a fall from the heights, it goes without saying that someone of the common mold cannot be a fit tragic hero. It is now many centuries since Aristotle lived. There is no more reason for falling down in a faint before his *Poetics* than before Euclid's geometry, which has been amended numerous times by men with new insights; nor, for that matter, would I choose to have my illnesses diagnosed by Hippocrates rather than the most ordinary graduate of an American medical school, despite the Greek's genius. Things do change, and even a genius is limited by his time and the nature of his society.

I would deny, on grounds of simple logic, this one of Aristotle's contentions if only because he lived in a slave society. When a vast number of people are divested of alternatives, as slaves are, it is rather inevitable that one will not be able to imagine drama, let alone tragedy, as being possible for any but the higher ranks of society. There is a legitimate question of stature here, but none of rank, which is so often confused with it. So long as the hero may be said to have had alternatives of a magnitude to have materially changed the course of his life, it seems to me that in this respect at least, he cannot be debarred from the heroic role.

The question of rank is significant to me only as it reflects the question of the social application of the hero's career. There is no doubt that if a character is shown on the stage who goes through the most ordinary actions, and is suddenly revealed to be the President of the United States, his actions immediately assume a much greater magnitude, and pose the possibilities of much greater meaning, than if he is the corner grocer. But at the same time, his stature as a hero is not so utterly dependent upon his rank that the corner grocer cannot outdistance him as a tragic figure—providing, of course, that the grocer's career engages the issues of, for instance, the survival of the race, the relationships of man to God—the questions, in short, whose answers define humanity and the right way to live so that the world is a home, instead of a battleground or a fog in which disembodied spirits pass each other in an endless twilight.

In this respect *Death of a Salesman* is a slippery play to categorize because nobody in it stops to make a speech objectively stating the great issues which I believe it embodies. If it were a worse play, less closely articulating its meanings with its actions, I think it would have more quickly satisfied a certain kind of criticism. But it was meant to be less a play than a fact; it refused admission to its author's opinions and opened itself to a revelation of process and the operations of an ethic, of social laws of action no less powerful in their effects upon individuals than any tribal law administered by gods with names. I need not claim that this play is a genuine solid gold tragedy for my opinions on tragedy to be held valid. My purpose here is simply to point out a historical fact which must be taken into account in any consideration of tragedy, and it is the sharp alteration in the meaning of rank in society between the present time and the distant past. More important to me is the fact that this particular kind of argument obscures much more relevant considerations.

One of these is the question of intensity. It matters not at all whether a modern play concerns itself with a grocer or a president if the intensity of the hero's commitment to his course is less than the maximum possible. It matters not at all whether the hero falls from a great height or a small one, whether he is highly conscious or only dimly aware of what is happening, whether his pride brings the fall or an unseen pattern written behind clouds; if the intensity, the human passion to surpass his given bounds, the fanatic insistence upon his self-conceived role—if these are not present there can only be an outline of tragedy but no living thing. I believe, for myself, that the lasting appeal of tragedy is due to our need to face the fact of death in order to strengthen ourselves for life, and that over and above this function of the tragic viewpoint there are and will be a great number of formal variations which no single definition will ever embrace.

Another issue worth considering is the so-called tragic victory, a question closely related to the consciousness of the hero. One makes nonsense of this if a "victory" means that the hero makes us feel some certain joy when, for instance, he sacrifices himself for a "cause," and unhappy and morose because he dies without one. To begin at the bottom, a man's death is and ought to be an essentially terrifying thing and ought to make nobody happy. But in a great variety of ways even death, the ultimate negative, can be, and appear to be, an assertion of bravery, and can serve to separate the death of man from the death of animals; and I think it is this distinction which underlies any conception of a victory in death. For a society of faith, the nature of the death can prove the existence of the spirit, and posit its immortality. For a secular society it is perhaps more difficult for such a victory to document itself and to make itself felt, but, conversely, the need to offer greater proofs of the humanity of man can make that victory more real. It goes without saying that in a society where there is basic disagreement as to the right way to live, there can hardly be agreement as to the right way to die, and both life and death must be heavily weighted with meaningless futility.

It was not out of any deference to a tragic definition that Willy Loman is filled with a joy, however broken-hearted, as he approaches his end, but simply that my sense of his character dictated his joy, and even what I felt was an exultation. In terms of his character, he has achieved a very powerful piece of knowledge, which is that he is loved by his son and has been embraced by him and forgiven. In this he is given his existence, so to speak—his fatherhood, for which he has always striven and which until now he could not achieve. That he is unable to take this victory thoroughly to his heart, that it closes the circle for him and propels him to his death, is the wage of his sin, which was to have committed himself so completely to the counterfeits of dignity and the false coinage embodied in his idea of success that he can prove his existence only by bestowing "power" on his posterity, a power deriving from the sale of his last asset, himself, for the price of his insurance policy.

I must confess here to a miscalculation, however. I did not

realize while writing the play that so many people in the world do not see as clearly, or would not admit, as I thought they must, how futile most lives are; so there could be no hope of consoling the audience for the death of this man. I did not realize either how few would be impressed by the fact that this man is actually a very brave spirit who cannot settle for half but must pursue his dream of himself to the end. Finally, I thought it must be clear, even obvious, that this was no dumb brute heading mindlessly to his catastrophe.

I have no need to be Willy's advocate before the jury which decides who is and who is not a tragic hero. I am merely noting that the lingering ponderousness of so many ancient definitions has blinded students and critics to the facts before them, and not only in regard to this play. Had Willy been unaware of his separation from values that endure he would have died contentedly while polishing his car, probably on a Sunday afternoon with the ball game coming over the radio. But he was agonized by his awareness of being in a false position, so constantly haunted by the hollowness of all he had placed his faith in, so aware, in short, that he must somehow be filled in his spirit or fly apart, that he staked his very life on the ultimate assertion. That he had not the intellectual fluency to verbalize his situation is not the same thing as saying that he lacked awareness, even an overly intensified consciousness that the life he had made was without form and inner meaning.

To be sure, had he been able to know that he was as much the victim of his beliefs as their defeated exemplar, had he known how much of guilt he ought to bear and how much to shed from his soul, he would be more conscious. But it seems to me that there is of necessity a severe limitation of self-awareness in any character, even the most knowing, which serves to define him as a character, and more, that this very limit serves to complete the tragedy and, indeed, to make it at all possible. Complete consciousness is possible only in a play about forces, like *Prometheus*, but not in a play about people. I think that the point is whether there is a sufficient awareness in the hero's career to make the audience supply the rest. Had Oedipus, for instance, been more conscious and more aware of the forces at work upon him he must surely have said that he was not really to blame for having cohabited with his mother since neither he nor anyone else knew she was his mother. He must surely decide to divorce her, provide for their children, firmly resolve to investigate the family background of his next wife, and thus deprive us of a very fine play and the name for a famous neurosis. But he is conscious only up to a point, the point at which guilt begins. Now he is inconsolable and must tear out his eyes. What is tragic about this? Why is it not even ridiculous? How can we respect a man who goes to such extremities over something he could in no way help or prevent? The answer, I think, is not that we respect the man, but that we respect the Law he has so completely broken, wittingly or not, for it is that Law which, we believe, defines us as men. The confusion of some critics viewing *Death of a Salesman* in this regard is that they do not see that Willy Loman has broken a law without whose protection life is insupportable if not incomprehensible to him and to many others; it is the law which says that a failure in society and in business has no right to live. Unlike the law against incest, the law of success is not administered by statute or church, but it is very nearly as powerful in its grip upon men. The confusion increases because, while it is a law, it is by no means a wholly agreeable one even as it is slavishly obeyed, for to fail is no longer to belong to society, in his estimate. Therefore, the path is opened for those who wish to call Willy merely a foolish man even as they themselves are living in obedience to the same law that killed him. Equally, the fact that Willy's law—the belief, in other words, which administers guilt to him— is not a civilizing statute whose destruction menaces us all; it is rather, a deeply believed and deeply suspect "good" which, when questioned as to its value, as it is in this play, serves more to raise our anxieties than to reassure us of the existence of an unseen but humane metaphysical system in the world. My attempt in the play was to counter this anxiety with an opposing system which, so to speak, is in a race for Willy's faith, and it is the system of love which is the opposite of the law of success.

It is embodied in Biff Loman, but by the time Willy can perceive his love it can serve only as an ironic comment upon the life he sacrificed for power and for success and its tokens.

A play cannot be equated with a political philosophy, at least not in the way a smaller number, by simple multiplication, can be assimilated into a larger. I do not believe that any work of art can help but be diminished by its adherence at any cost to a political program, including its author's, and not for any other reason than that there is no political program—any more than there is a theory of tragedy—which can encompass the complexities of real life. Doubtless an author's politics must be one element, and even an important one, in the germination of his art, but if it is art he has created it must by definition bend itself to his observation rather than to his opinions or even his hopes. If I have shown a preference for plays which seek causation not only in psychology but in society, I may also believe in the autonomy of art, and I believe this because my experience with All My Sons and Death of a Salesman forces the belief upon me. If the earlier play was Marxist, it was a Marxism of a strange hue. Joe Keller is arraigned by his son for a willfully unethical use of his economic position; and this, as the Russians said when they removed the play from their stages, bespeaks an assumption that the norm of capitalist behavior is ethical or at least can be, an assumption no Marxist can hold. Nor does Chris propose to liquidate the business built in part on soldiers' blood; he will run it himself, but cleanly.

The most decent man in Death of a Salesman is a capitalist (Charley) whose aims are not different from Willy Loman's. The great difference between them is that Charley is not a fanatic. Equally, however, he has learned how to live without that frenzy, that ecstasy of spirit which Willy chases to his end. And even as Willy's sons are unhappy men, Charley's boy, Bernard, works hard, attends to his studies, and attains a worthwhile objective. These people are all of the same class, the same background, the same neighborhood. What theory lies behind this double view? None whatever. It is simply that I knew and know that I feel better when my work is reflecting a balance of the truth as it exists. A muffled debate arose with the success of *Death of a Salesman* in which attempts were made to justify or dismiss the play as a Left-Wing piece, or as a Right-Wing manifestation of decadence. The presumption underlying both views is that a work of art is the sum of its author's political outlook, real or alleged, and more, that its political implications are valid elements in its aesthetic evaluation. I do not believe this, either for my own or other writers' works.

The most radical play I ever saw was not *Waiting for Lefty* but *The Madwoman of Chaillot*. I know nothing of Giradoux's political alignment, and it is of no moment to me; I am able to read this play, which is the most open indictment of private exploitation of the earth I know about. By the evidence of his plays, Shaw, the socialist, was in love not with the working class, whose characters he could only caricature, but with the middle of the economic aristocracy, those men who, in his estimate, lived without social and economic illusions. There is a strain of mystic fatalism in Ibsen so powerful as to throw all his scientific tenets into doubt, and a good measure besides of contempt —in this radical—for the men who are usually called the public. The list is long and the contradictions are embarrassing until one concedes a perfectly simple proposition. It is merely that a writer of any worth creates out of his total perception, the vaster part of which is subjective and not within his intellectual control. For myself, it has never been possible to generate the energy to write and complete a play if I know in advance everything it signifies and all it will contain. The very impulse to write, I think, springs from an inner chaos crying for order, for meaning, and that meaning must be discovered in the process of writing or the work lies dead as it is finished. To speak, therefore, of a play as though it were the objective work of a propagandist is an almost biological kind of nonsense, provided, of course, that it is a play, which is to say a work of art. . . .

MORALITY AND MODERN DRAMA:
INTERVIEW WITH PHILLIP GELB

PHILLIP GELB: Mr. Miller, what about the apparent lack of positive moral values in modern drama?

ARTHUR MILLER: Not only modern drama, but literature in general, and this goes back a long, long distance in history, posits the idea of value, of right and wrong, good and bad, high and low, not so much by setting forth these values as such, but by showing, so to speak, the wages of sin. In other words, when, for instance, in *Death of a Salesman*, we are shown a man who dies for the want of some positive, viable human value, the play implies, and it could not have been written without the author's consciousness, that the audience did believe something different. In other words, by showing what happens when there are no values, I, at least, assume that the audience will be compelled and propelled toward a more intense quest for values that are missing. I am assuming always that we have a kind of civilized sharing of what we would like to see occur within us and in the world; and I think that the drama, at least mine, is not so much an attack but an exposition, so to speak, of the want of value, and you can only do this if the audience itself is constantly

From *Educational Theatre Journal*, X (October 1958), 190–202. Copyright © 1958 by *Educational Theatre Journal*. Reprinted by permission of *Educational Theatre Journal* and Phillip Gelb. A shorter version of this interview was one of thirteen half-hour taped programs entitled "Ideas and the Theatre," produced by KUOM of the University of Minnesota and distributed by the National Association of Educational Broadcasters. An editorial note accompanying the published interview says, "Mr. Miller, on reading the transcript, decided that, although he would wish to rephrase some of the things that he had said, on the whole it would be best to let it go as it was for 'the reader would undoubtedly know it was extemporaneous.'" The last few pages of the interview (199–202) are not reprinted here. They deal for the most part with politics and the theater and, although they contain interesting comments, personal and general, they are not immediately relevant to a discussion of "Salesman."

trying to supply what is missing. I don't say that's a new thing. The Greeks did the same thing. They may have had a chorus which overtly stated that this is what happens when Zeus' laws are abrogated or broken, but that isn't what made their plays great.

PHILLIP GELB: Reverend John Bachman at the Union Theological Seminary said something similar. He said that the *Death of a Salesman* is moral to the extent that it is a negative witness. Now at the same time he felt that your play could not do any kind of a job in terms of presenting positive answers; this, of course, in his view, was the job of religion. Do you feel that that dichotomy actually—

ARTHUR MILLER: It isn't always so. Ibsen used to present answers. Despite the fashion that claims he never presented answers, he of course did. In the *Doll's House* and even in *Hedda Gabler*, we will find—and in Chekhov, too—we will find speeches toward the ends of these plays which suggest, if they don't overtly state, what the alternative values are to those which misled the heroes or heroines of the action shown. The difference is that we are now a half century beyond that probably more hopeful time, and we've been through social revolution which these people hadn't witnessed yet. We have come to a kind of belated recognition that the great faith in social change as an amelioration or a transforming force of the human soul leaves something to be wanted. In other words, we originally, in the late nineteenth century, posed the idea that science would, so to speak, cure the soul of man by the eradication of poverty. We have eradicated poverty in large parts—well, in small parts of the world, but in significant parts of the world—and we're just as mean and ornery as we ever were. So that the social solution of the evil in man has failed—it seems so, anyway—and we are now left with a kind of bashful unwillingness to state that we still believe in life and that we still believe there is a conceivable standard of values. My feeling is, though, that we are in a transition stage between a mechanistic concept of man and an amalgam of both the rationalistic and what you could call the mystical or spiritualistic concept of him. I don't think either that man is without will or that society is impotent to change his deepest, most private self-conceptions. I think that the work of art, the great work of art, is going to be that work which finds space for the two forces to operate. So far, I will admit, the bulk of literature, not only on the stage but elsewhere, is an exposition of man's failure: his failure to assert his sense of civilized and moral life.

PHILLIP GELB: A situation came up just the other day—I teach speech at Hunter College—in which somebody made a speech proclaiming the values of deceit: manipulative techniques, sophistry, and the rest. Most everybody went along with it to the extent that they felt that the use of techniques was automatically deceitful. Techniques were equated with trickery and the negative. I pointed out that integrity and honor, responsibility, rationality, logic—a lot of these things can be used as techniques, too.

ARTHUR MILLER: That reminds me of a book by Thomas Mann about Moses, in which, with his tongue in his cheek probably, but certainly with high seriousness, he portrays Moses as being a man bedeviled by the barbaric backwardness of a stubborn people and trying to improve them and raise up their sights. He disappears into the wilderness, up on the mountain, and comes down after a considerable period of time with the Ten Commandments. Now the Ten Commandments, from the point of view that you've just been speaking about, is a technique. It is purely and simply a way of putting into capsule form what probably the most sensitive parts of the society were wishing could be stated so that people could memorize it and people could live by it. I am sure that there must have been a number of people that said it was a kind of deceit or dishonesty to try to pinpoint things that way, things that were otherwise amorphous and without form and which probably some old Jews felt were even irreligious to carve into stone—but it is a technique. The whole Bible is a technique; it has got a form. If you read the three Gospels of Matthew, Mark, and Luke you will see the tremendous effort being made to dramatize, to make vivid, an experience which probably none of them really saw—except possibly one. It was a job almost of spiritual propaganda. Why would they have to write this down? Why would they strive for the *mot juste*, for the perfect paragraph, for the most vivid image, which quite evidently they do? Technique is like anything else; it is deceitful only when it is used for deceitful purposes.

PHILLIP GELB: Mr. John Beaufort, the critic for the *Christian Science Monitor*, attacked Willy Loman as a sad character, a vicious character, who couldn't figure in dramatic tragedy because he never starts with any ideals to begin with.

ARTHUR MILLER: The trouble with Willy Loman is that he has tremendously powerful ideals. We are not accustomed to speaking of ideals in *his* terms, but if Willy Loman, for instance, had not had a very profound sense that his life as lived had left him hollow, he would have died contentedly polishing his car on some Sunday afternoon at a ripe old age.[1] The fact is that he has values. The fact that they cannot be realized is what is driving him mad, just as, unfortunately, it is driving a lot of other people mad. The truly valueless man, the man without ideals, is always perfectly at home anywhere because there cannot be conflict between nothing and something. Whatever negative qualities there are in the society or in the environment don't bother him because they are not in conflict with any positive sense that he may have. I think Willy Loman is seeking for a kind of ecstasy in life which the machine civilization deprives people of. He is looking for his selfhood, for his immortal soul, so to speak, and people who don't know the intensity of that quest think he is odd, but a lot of salesmen, in a line of work where ingenuity and individualism are acquired by the nature of the work, have a very intimate understanding of his problem; more so, I think, than literary critics who probably need strive less, after a certain point. A salesman is a kind of creative person. It is possibly idiotic to say so in a literary program, but they are; they have to get up in the morning and

---

[1] See page 168 for a similar image of Willy's dying while polishing the car. It is not surprising that, in an extemporaneous interview, Miller should echo written statements about his work.

conceive a plan of attack and use all kinds of ingenuity all day long just like a writer does.

PHILLIP GELB: I think this idea of "a plan of attack" comes back to what we were talking about before, about techniques that become deceitful. The whole concept of present advertising is involved. By techniques the public is sold things they don't really need. Your plan of attack therefore becomes vicious; only the technique makes them buy.

ARTHUR MILLER: Well, that's true. I see the point now. But compared to, let's say, the normal viciousness, if you want to use that term, of standard advertising techniques, Willy is a baby. I mean, Willy is naïve enough to believe in the goodness of his mission. There are highly paid advertising people who are utterly cynical about this business, and probably a lot of people call Willy vicious who would think of themselves as simply the pillars of society. Willy is a victim; he didn't originate this thing. He believes that selling is the greatest thing anybody can do.

PHILLIP GELB: This would seem to imply that Willy Loman, at least in terms of his problems and his anxieties, could be a lot of people. Now, Beaufort makes the statement, "If Willy Loman represented the whole mass of American civilization today, I think the country would be in a terrible state. I just can't accept Willy Loman as the average American citizen."

ARTHUR MILLER: It is obvious that Willy *can't* be an average American man, at least from one point of view; he kills himself. That's a rare thing in society, although it is more common than one could wish, and it's beside the point. As a matter of fact, that standard of "averageness" is not valid. It neither tells whether the character is a truthful character as a character, or a valid one. I can't help adding that that is the standard of socialist realism—which of course wasn't invented by socialists. It is the idea that a character in a play or in a book cannot be taken seriously unless he reflects some statistical average, plus his ability to announce the official aims of the society; and it is ridiculous. Hamlet isn't a typical Elizabethan, either. Horatio probably is. What is the difference? It has no point unless you are talking about, not literature, but patriotism. I didn't write *Death of a Salesman* to announce some new American man, or an old American man. Willy Loman is, I think, a person who embodies in himself some of the most terrible conflicts running through the streets of America today. A Gallup poll might indicate that they are not the majority conflicts; I think they are. But what's the difference?

PHILLIP GELB: Maybe I should have read this statement first. This was made by the critic for *Progressive* magazine, Martin Dworkin, and he considers that *Death of a Salesman* makes a strong message for an average American man because "Willy Loman is such a particular Willy Loman. He is not simply a slogan out of the 1930s; he is not a banner to be waved to liberate people; he is not a criticism of society." And then Dworkin points out that because Willy is so particular, therefore he does these other universal things. What about the theory of art and drama here that the best way to present a universal is in terms of a really specific story?

ARTHUR MILLER: It is the best. It is the hardest way, too, and it isn't given to many authors or to any single author many times to be able to do it. Namely, to create the universal from the particular. You have to know the particular in your bones to do that. As the few plays that are repeatedly done over generations and centuries show, they are generally, in our western culture anyway, those plays which are full of the most particular information about people. We don't do many Greek plays any more, in my opinion not because they lack wonderful stories—they have wonderful stories—but in our terms, in terms of particularization of characters, they are deficient. It doesn't mean the Greeks were bad playwrights. It means their aims were different. But we do do *Hamlet*, we do do *Macbeth*, we do a number of more mediocre plays as well; but the ones that last are the ones that we recognize most immediately in terms of the details of real human behavior in specific situations.

PHILLIP GELB: How do you apply that to T. S. Eliot and George Bernard Shaw? Do you feel that their people are very real or specific?

ARTHUR MILLER: I don't think T. S. Eliot would even claim that he is creating characters, in the realistic sense of the word. It is a different aim. It doesn't mean that he can't do it; I don't think he can, but I don't think he is trying to do it. I think he is trying to dramatize quite simply a moral, a religious dilemma. The same is true of Bernard Shaw excepting for occasional characters, usually women, in his plays. They are more psychologically real than anything, of course, T. S. Eliot has done to my knowledge, excepting perhaps for *Murder in the Cathedral*. But the aim in these plays is not the aim of "Salesman" or most American work. It is the setting forth of an irony, a dilemma, more or less in its own terms. I think all the characters in Shaw can be reduced to two or three, really, and nobody would mind particularly. You always know that it's Shaw speaking no matter what side of the argument is being set forth, and that is part of the charm. I think his great success is due to the fact that he made no pretense to do otherwise; he was observing the issues in the dilemma of life rather than the psychology of human beings.

PHILLIP GELB: I'd like to take issue with that and simply say that Shaw might be writing real people but they speak more eloquently, more intellectually than real people. Essentially, I am not sure that in *Pygmalion* the father isn't real. I don't think anybody would talk like that, but I think his motives are real. I think Higgins is a real person. I think Shaw simply is not happy with the inability of people to express themselves and so he says I will do it for them; but I never really felt that Shaw's people were not people.

ARTHUR MILLER: I would put it this way. Shaw is impatient with the insignificance of most human speech, most human thought, and most human preconceptions. It's not that his characters are not people; it is that they aren't insignificant people the way people usually are. When you strip from the human being everything that is not of significance, you may get a valid moment out of him, a valid set of speeches, a valid set of attitudes, but in the normal, naturalistic concept, they aren't real because the bulk of reality is, of course, its utter boredom, and its insignificance, and its irrelevancy, and Shaw is absolutely uninterested in that. Consequently, if you just take the significant part of the character, it will be true but if this is lifted out of the rest of the character's psychology, you can no longer speak in terms of normal psychological writing. I happen to like this sort of thing; I am not criticizing it. I think it is a great thing to be able to do. But it isn't the tapestry work, let us say, of a *Hamlet* where you are carried through moment to moment, from one thought to the next, including the boredom, including the irrelevancy, including the contradictions within him which are not thematic. That is to say, they have very little to do with his conflict with the king or his mother, but they have much to do with creating a background for the major preconceptions of the play. Shaw is always eliminating the insignificant background, and it's possibly because he had so much to say and there was so little time to say it. But you mentioned one of the minor characters in *Pygmalion*, like the father. I think, in general, aside from the women, it *is* the minor characters who are most realistically drawn. The major characters are too completely obsessed with the issues that are being set forth. One of the signs of an abrogation of regular psychology is that people stay on the theme. You know and I know, even in this little interview, that it is very difficult, if not impossible, to spontaneously stay on the subject. You read Shaw's plays and see how rarely people get off the subject; and that's what I mean when I say that it isn't psychology he is following, it is the theme.

PHILLIP GELB: Let's assume that Shaw is concerned with the intellectual or social significances and chooses his material accordingly. The statement has been made by anthropologist Solon Kimball that Tennessee Williams chooses materials by their psychological significances. Dr. Kimball says that while Williams' picture of a Southern community in part may be true, that this psychological orientation gives a distorted picture of the whole. Evidently even some truth to the community and to the psychology of characters is not enough. Do you feel that is true of Williams, or what do you think of the general idea?

ARTHUR MILLER: Williams is a realistic writer; realistic in the sense that I was just referring to—that is to say, realistic in the way that Shaw is not. I think Williams is primarily interested in passion, in ecstasy, in creating a synthesis of his conflicting feelings. It is perfectly all right, of course, for an anthropologist to make an observation that Williams' picture of the South is unrepresentative. It probably is, but at the same time, the intensity with which he feels whatever he does feel is so deep, is so great, that we do end up with a glimpse of another kind of reality; that is, the reality in the spirit rather than in the society. I think, as I said before, that the truly great work is that work which will show at one and the same time the power and force of the human will working with and against the force of society upon it. Probably Williams is less capable of delivering the second than he might be. Everybody has some blind spot. But, again, as with Willy Loman, I'm not ready to criticize a writer because he isn't delivering a typical picture. The most typical pictures of society I know are probably in the *Saturday Evening Post*, or on the soap operas. It is more likely to be typical of people to be humdrum and indifferent and without superb conflicts. When a writer sets out to create high climaxes, he automatically is going to depart from the typical, the ordinary, and the representative. The pity is, of course, that Williams works out of Southern material, I work out of big city material, so instantly our characters are compared in a journalistic sense to some statistical norm. Truly, I have no interest in the selling profession, and I am reasonably sure that Williams' interest in the sociology of the South is only from the point of view of a man who doesn't like to see brutality, unfairness, a kind of victory of the Philistine, etc. He is looking at it emotionally, and essentially I am, too. Inevitably, people are going to say that Willy Loman is not a typical salesman, or that Blanche Dubois is not a typical something else, but to tell you the truth, the writer himself couldn't be less interested.

PHILLIP GELB: You point out Shaw as dealing with the intellectual, the social, the moral; Eliot with the moral, the religious; Williams with the psychological. Eric Bentley made the statement that he thought, perhaps, Arthur Miller was the one writer today who had the most possibility of combining all of these things, and yet he also thought that this was impossible. Can it be done?

ARTHUR MILLER: Well, whether it can be done remains for me or somebody else to prove. But let me put it this way: we are living, or I'm living anyway, with a great consciousness of the incredible force of objective thought. As we speak, there is an object flying around in the sky, passing over this point, I think it is every hundred and some minutes, which was put up there by thinking men who *willed* it to go up there. The implications of this are as enormous as any statement by or on the part of Zeus, or Moses, or Shakespeare, or any feeling man. Now it may be a great bite to take, but I think the only thing worth doing—whether one can do it or not is an entirely different story, but aims are important—the only thing worth doing today in the theatre, from my point of view, is to synthesize the subjective drives of the human being with what is now demonstrably the case, namely, that by an act of will man can and has changed the world. Now it is said that nothing is new under the sun: this is. It is right under the sun and it is new. And it is only one of the things that are new. I have seen communities transformed by the act of a committee. I have seen the interior lives of people transformed by the decision of a company, or of a man, or of a school. In other words, it is old fashioned, so to speak, and it is not moot simply to go on asserting the helplessness of the individual. The great weight of evidence is upon the helplessness of man. This is true, I think, with variations: the great bulk of the weight of evidence is that we are not in command. And we're not, I'm not saying we are. But we surely have much more command than anybody, including Macbeth's Witches, could ever dream of, and somehow a form has to be devised which will account for this. Otherwise the drama is doomed to repeating and repeating *ad nauseum* the same pattern of striving, disillusion, and defeat. And I don't think it is a modern day phenomenon.

PHILLIP GELB: Gore Vidal made a statement similar to yours with almost an exact opposite conclusion. His point was that he felt the only influence he could be was in terms of man's ability to destroy and despair, and so he wrote a play in which he is going to destroy the world.[2] He said this facetiously, but since he didn't present any positive point of view, this led to the general topic of "the artist as the enemy"—perhaps the thing behind it is that many artists like to see the world destroyed. This isn't just a reporting; this is their own feeling.

ARTHUR MILLER: The enemy is the wrong word to me, although I would concede it. The artist is the outcast; he always will be. He is an outcast in the sense that he is to one side of the stream of life and absorbs it and is, in some part of himself, reserved from its implications; that is to say, a man like Vidal says we're out to destroy everything. I think that you can't see a thing when you are in the middle of it. To some extent, an artist has to step to one side of what is happening, divorce himself from his role as a citizen, and in that sense he becomes the enemy because he does not carry forth in himself and believe what is being believed around him. He is the enemy usually, I suppose, of the way things are, whatever way they are.

PHILLIP GELB: Does that mean, though, that he is always an inadequate reporter, too, because he is not a part? Is the artist perhaps in the least likely position to tell what might be true to most people?

ARTHUR MILLER: The trouble with literature is that writers have to be the ones who write it. It's always partial; it's always partisan, and it's always incomplete. When I say that writers have to be the ones to write it, I mean that in order to generate the energy to create a big novel, a big play, an involved poem, one has to be a species of fanatic. You have to think that that is really the only thing worth doing. Otherwise, you can't generate

---

[2] Vidal was presumably talking about *Visit to a Small Planet*, in which he backed away from the implications of his view of things and let his heroine save the world. For that reason, Miller's comment (p. 185) is all the more appropriate.

the intensity to do it well. And to that degree, by generating that intensity, you are blinding yourself to what does not fit into some preconceived pattern in your own mind. There's no doubt about that to me, and I think that probably lay behind Plato's prohibition of the artist in society. He was right in the sense that the artist doesn't know what he is doing, to some extent. That is, we pretend, or like to believe, that we are depicting the whole truth of some situation, when as a matter of fact, the whole truth is, by definition, made impossible by the fact that we are obsessed people. I don't know of a first class piece of work written by what I would call, or a psychologist would call, a balanced, adjusted fellow who could easily be, let us say, a good administrator for a complicated social mechanism of some sort. It doesn't work that way. We are not constituted that way; so consequently, to be sure, it will have to be partial. The impulse to do it is obsessive; it always is. One of the fairest, most just writers was Tolstoi, who was, to make it short, quite mad. I mean, you can't pretend that as a person he was judicious, balanced: he wasn't. Neither was Dostoevski. Neither, certainly, was Ibsen. Probably the most generously balanced man I know of was Chekhov. And I suspect that half of his psychological life we will never know. He was very reticent, and in those days there were no interviews of this sort, and if he didn't choose to write some essays describing his methods and personal life, you'd just know nothing about him.

PHILLIP GELB: I can get obsessive once or twice a year and maybe write a one-act play or something. The students have asked me this, "How do you take this obsessiveness and channel it into a discipline whereby you sit down and write regularly? Or is this always an individual problem?"

ARTHUR MILLER: I don't know how to write regularly. I wish I did. It's not possible to me. I suppose if one were totally dependent upon one's writing for a living and one's writing was of a kind that could be sold, like Dostoevski's was—he seems about the only big writer I know that wrote regularly, but he wrote regularly because he had to pay his gambling debts half the time and the sheriff was on his tail. I don't know what would have happened if he had been given a stipend of $10,000 a year. Well, he probably would have gambled it away and been in debt again, I guess. So he would have written regularly.

PHILLIP GELB: Now you're very well established. You don't have to look for a theatre, I imagine, just to see a play done. But do you feel that you might write more, or at least more regularly, if you were part of a group? I am thinking of the tradition of the writer as part of a theatre group—as it was with Shakespeare, the Greeks, Molière, even Shaw usually worked for some kind of company.

ARTHUR MILLER: I think that in the early life of a writer, in his beginning work,—and this would go for Shaw, O'Neill, and anybody you wanted to mention—a connection with a group of actors could be very valuable. But I think you will find that as he grows older a playwright dreads the prospect of his play being produced. I mean that seriously. There are so many stupid things that happen which destroy the most valuable, the most sensitive parts of a manuscript that, truthfully, if I seriously contemplated the production of a play as I was writing it, I don't know that I could write it. It is too dreadful a risk, and I don't care how well established you are; it is always the same risk. Your work can go down the drain because you have happened to hire an actor who simply does not have the sensitivity for that role and you didn't know it until the night before you opened. Think of that when you put in two, three, four years on a play, and you pick up a team of actors, so to speak, and put one guy in to pitch and another in to catch, and the catcher can't catch and the pitcher can't pitch, and there's your manuscript. And there's no critic alive who can tell the difference between a bad production and a bad script unless they are extremely bad in either direction. But where there is some reasonable excellence, nobody knows the difference. I have had plays that have failed in New York—*View from the Bridge* was one of them. I am sure that anybody who saw *View from the Bridge* in New York would not have recognized it in London. I had a great deal to do with the production there; it was a different mood, a different key, a different production, and I am sure anybody would have said it was a different play.[3]

PHILLIP GELB: In your case, your plays are going to be done for years and years, and you just can't be around, you don't know what kind of actors are going to do them. Any good playwright is at the mercy of a hundred and one different kinds of people, and personalities, and places. Why does one write for the theatre then?

ARTHUR MILLER: It is one of the minor curses of mankind, I suppose. I have a feeling that it is a way of seeing existence in terms of audible scenes. I was always a playwright. I was a playwright before I'd ever been in the theatre. I wrote my first play, which was produced in various places and was a play, after having seen only two.

PHILLIP GELB: From viewing current plays, one might conclude that maybe what makes most people write is antagonism, negative qualities: despair, getting even, spite.

ARTHUR MILLER: For myself, I can't write anything if I am sufficiently unhappy. A lot of writers write best when they are most miserable. I suppose my sense of form comes from a positive need to organize life and not from a desire to demonstrate the inevitability of defeat and death. If I feel miserable enough, I can't work. A lot of writers, I am aware, then are spurred on to express their disillusion. All I know about that really comes down to this—that we are doomed to live, and I suppose one had better make the best of it. I imagine that Vidal shares that fate with me and will continue to. He is probably taking some perverse pleasure in positing the destruction of the world, but I suspect he wouldn't enjoy it as much as he says he would.

PHILLIP GELB: You feel your need is to organize life and not to present the case for death and despair?

ARTHUR MILLER: It is a basic commitment for me, sitting here now in America. For another writer who is, let's say, a French writer, an Italian writer, and who has been through a

---

[3] It *was* a different play. The one-act "View," some of it written in verse of sorts, produced in New York, was revised into the two-act prose version done in London.

sufficiently profound social cataclysm, such as two world wars and a depression in-between in Europe, where he was faced with the ultimate disaster, it might seem foolish. My experience, though, is as valid as theirs. In other words, I can't pretend things are worse than they are, any more than they can pretend things are better. It is a commitment on my part that I don't see the point in proving again that we must be defeated. I didn't intend that—since you have mentioned "Salesman" so much in this interview—I didn't intend it in "Salesman." I was trying in "Salesman," in this respect, to set forth what happens when a man does not have a grip on the forces of life and has no sense of values which will lead him to that kind of a grip; but the implication was that there must be such a grasp of those forces, or else we're doomed. I was not, in other words, Willy Loman, I was the writer, and Willy Loman is there because I could see beyond him.

The Designer

JO MIELZINER

Jo Mielziner, scene designer and theater architecture consultant, was codesigner with Eero Saarinen of the Repertory Theater of New York's Lincoln Center and has designed the sets for more than two hundred and fifty productions for Broadway, London, and touring companies, including the original sets and lighting for *Death of a Salesman*.

DESIGNING A PLAY: *DEATH OF A SALESMAN*

September 24, 1948

My four months of living with *Death of a Salesman* began with a telephone call. . . .

Bloomgarden was sitting back from his desk, his feet up, deep in a manuscript. He removed a cigar from his mouth and said that he was rereading the script of an extraordinary play just completed by Arthur Miller. He called it a real "toughie." "At the end of his forty-odd scenes Miller says, 'The scenic solution to this production will have to be an imaginative and simple one. I don't know the answer, but the designer must work out something which makes the script flow easily.'"

Bloomgarden went on to say that they hoped to go into rehearsal in two weeks; Elia Kazan, who had read the script,

From *Designing for the Theatre* by Jo Mielziner (New York: Atheneum, 1965), Copyright © 1965 by Jo Mielziner, reprinted by permission of Atheneum Publishers. I have chosen only those selections from Mielziner's account in which the designer's problems and his solving them help to illuminate the play as a whole. They give an incomplete sense of what the book itself is like, an odd and amusing compound of hardheaded practicality and theater anecdotage.

had just called from Boston, where he was directing a new musical, *Love Life*, to say that he was anxious to take on the direction as soon as he was free. I took the script and went home to read.

I had previously had a fine time designing Tennessee Williams' *A Streetcar Named Desire* for Kazan, so I knew that if *Death of a Salesman* proved to be a tough job, I would have the support of a director with a strong visual imagination and a mind of his own. . . .

I started reading the Miller manuscript late that afternoon, and after supper I picked it up again. Script reading is always a slow process for me, but this time it was particularly laborious. It was not that the manuscript was overlong; I simply found it difficult to stick to the rule I had established many years before. This was to read a manuscript as if I were a member of an audience sitting out front, not as a scenic artist or as a director or even as a theatre man. I often go so far as to skip descriptions of scenes or business in these first readings. With *Death of a Salesman* I couldn't stick to my rule; the stage action was too complicated, and to follow the story line demanded an understanding of the sequence of scenes.

I began to understand what Bloomgarden had meant when he called it a "toughie." It was not only that there were so many different scenic locations but that the action demanded instantaneous time changes from the present to the past and back again. Actors playing a contemporaneous scene suddenly went back fifteen years in exactly the same setting—the Salesman's house. . . .

. . . a good scenic artist, without lacking respect for his author's contribution, should first make his own "breakdown" of the action, either in his mind or on paper. I always do mine on paper, as I did in rough form this night for *Death of a Salesman*. The designer should discover for himself what the author is saying in terms of the flow of action; he must examine the story as it unfolds and determine on his own where the most important scenes should be played. After these key scenes are fully identified, an intelligent design can begin to develop.

September 25, 1948

Early the next morning I glanced through the breakdown I had made. One thought came to me: in the scenes where the Salesman mentally goes back to the early years of his marriage, when his boys were young and the house was surrounded by trees and open country, I had to create something visually that would make these constant transitions in time immediately clear to the audience. My next thought was that, even if we ended up with a big stage, with plenty of stagehands, and I was able to design some mechanism for handling the large number of individual scenes, the most important visual symbol in the play—the real background of the story—was the Salesman's house. Therefore, why should that house not be the main set, with all the other scenes—the corner of a graveyard, a hotel room in Boston, the corner of a business office, a lawyer's consultation room,[1] and so on—played on a forestage? If I designed these little scenes in segments and fragments, with easily moved props and fluid lighting effects, I might be able, without ever lowering the curtain, to achieve the easy flow that the author clearly wanted.

By ten o'clock I had Bloomgarden on the telephone and we arranged to meet with Miller and Kazan later in the day. My calendar worried me. Kermit wanted *Death of a Salesman* to go into rehearsal in two weeks. This would leave me only six weeks in which to design and execute an extremely complex production. . . . But it wasn't other jobs that made me uneasy as much as it was my instinct that the new script would require a great deal of work by everyone if my basic idea for the setting proved to be acceptable. From long experience I knew that to delay an opening is usually too expensive for a producer even to consider; in addition, it sometimes means losing the services of important actors or of a top-notch director like Kazan.

---

[1] There is no scene in "Salesman" that takes place in a lawyer's consultation room. Perhaps Mielziner is thinking of the scene between Willy and Bernard that takes place in Charley's outer office. Since Mielziner began work with an early version of Miller's play, it is possible that he is referring to a scene that was later discarded. Similarly, his reference to a nonexistent character, Mr. Heiser (p. 196), may stem from an early script.

Just the same, after we had gathered in Bloomgarden's office, I described the way I envisioned the production design and the method of its operation. When I finished, there was a long—a much too long—pause. Then Kazan spoke up and said to Miller, "Art, this means a hell of a lot of work for me, and even more for you." And Kermit broke in with, "It means we can't possibly go into rehearsal in two weeks. I'll have to cancel my bookings out of town and in New York. It's up to you fellows to make the decisions. I'll go along if you feel you really need the time."

A long discussion followed. To Arthur Miller, a design scheme allowing him as author to blend scenes at will without even the shortest break for physical changes was a significant decision. To Kazan, with his strong sense of movement, stimulated by his already proven genius as a film director, the scheme would permit use of some of the best cinematic techniques. The decision to be made was not just a visual one; it would set the style in direction and performance, as well as in design.

Kazan had immediate commitments: he had to fly back to Boston that afternoon to a tryout of his musical. Miller had a great deal of rewriting to do, and felt that he didn't want to go ahead without constant conferences with his director. Bloomgarden had complex financial and booking adjustments to make. But they all finally agreed to postpone and, provided my ideas worked out, to rewrite. . . .

September 29, 1948

. . . In the five days that followed, I prepared about twenty sketches for *Death of a Salesman*. I decided to dispense with color at this time because it was more important to get the mood—the light and dark—and the feeling of isolation that lighting only a small segment of the setting would evoke. John Harvey[2] and his assistant went to work with my little ground plans, enlarging them to one half an inch to the foot. They were also going to build a model: the skeletonized version of the

---

[2] Mielziner's assistant.

Salesman's house—the focal point of the whole design—was
of the utmost importance and had to be developed three-
dimensionally in a model, even if no one but the director ever
looked at it. I was careful to start each sketch with the figures
of Willy Loman, the Salesman, or his sons, or his wife, not only
to intensify the dramatic mood of the sketch, but to control the
interrelation of all the elements of the stage picture including
the all-important human figure.

October 4, 1948

. . . The greatest conundrum was in the scene in which the
Salesman's two sons, as adults, go to bed in their attic bedroom
in full view of the audience and then must appear elsewhere on
the set a moment later as they were in their youth, entering
downstage dressed in football togs. How were we going to get
them out of bed and offstage without their being seen, when
both the beds and their own bodies under the covers were completely visible to the audience, and also provide for an instantaneous costume change?

I said, "Let me try this out: We can build an inner frame in
the beds that can act as an elevator. It can lower the boys quietly
from the attic bedroom down some seven feet to the stage in a
spot hidden from the audience by the set. From there they can
sneak backstage, make their changes, and appear in time."
"But," someone asked, "what's going to happen if the audience
sees their pillows and blankets suddenly flatten out?"

. . . I finally found the solution: the heads of the beds in the
attic room were to face the audience; the pillows, in full view
since there were to be no solid headboards, would be made of
papier mâché. A depression in each pillow would permit the
heads of the boys to be concealed from the audience, and they
would lie under the blankets that had been stiffened to stay in
place. We could then lower them and still retain the illusion of
their being in bed.

Whenever I use a special mechanism of this sort, I always
demonstrate it in full light at one of the early technical rehearsals. When I tried out this device, John Harvey was the

demonstrator; he is a good six feet one and probably weighed more than either Arthur Kennedy or Cameron Mitchell, who were to play the sons. He got into position in one of the beds, and we signaled the master property man, Joe Lynn, to lower the elevator. Engineers had recommended that the mechanism be electrically driven, but both Joe and John advised me that it would be safer to have a hand-driven winch that could be instantly stopped or reversed if anything went wrong. We had already determined that signals would be necessary: a red light, controlled by a button under the pillow on each bed, enabled each boy to indicate when he was in position, ready for the stagehand below to turn the crank of the winch that would lower the inner frame of the bed.

The mechanism worked perfectly in the first demonstration. Then Arthur Kennedy asked to try it. He climbed into the bed and, on cue, flashed his red light. As Joe Lynn worked the winch, we suddenly heard a frightening crunching and grinding noise. Kazan cried, "My God, I hope that isn't Kennedy's skull!" Fortunately for both the actor and the play, it turned out to be the papier-mâché pillow, which was half an inch too large and had jammed in the elevator. This was soon fixed, and on the next try we did it with stage lighting. The effect worked magnificently. Theatrical illusion had been achieved. . . .

October 15, 1948

. . . Anticipating the many lighting difficulties in *Death of a Salesman*, particularly in the scenes that used projections, I decided to have a preliminary check-up with my friend [Edward] Kook [of Century Lighting Company]. I outlined my problem: There must be a transformation of the Salesman's home from a house closely encircled by tenement buildings, which cut out all sunlight and view of the sky, to a vista of the same house years earlier, surrounded by open air and sunlit trees giving a feeling of leafy airiness. I showed him my design for the backdrop; instead of the customary rather opaque linen, I planned to use unbleached muslin, a much lighter material. On it I intended to have the surrounding buildings painted in translucent colors, particularly the windows, which would appear rather bright when lit from the rear. When the transformations to earlier times were to occur, I planned to use a number of projection units, like magic lanterns, both from the auditorium and from backstage, throwing leaf patterns on the backdrop and on parts of the house. As the lights behind the backdrop were faded out, the painted buildings on the front would, I hoped, virtually disappear as images of light, spring-like leaves and fresh greens were superimposed, liberating the house from the oppression of the surrounding structures and giving the stage a feeling of the free outdoors. This was an integral part of the Salesman's life story and had to be an easily recognized symbol of the spring-time of that life. . . .[3]

October 19, 1948

. . . I had reduced the Salesman's home to a series of three levels, with the frame outline of the house forming an open skeleton. Some of the doors were simply open framework; arches and windows were cut-outs of wood, but were drawn and painted with a good deal of quality in their line. Given this rather stark background, whatever props there were would have to be highly significant in character. One thing in particular loomed large: the icebox.

One of the best references in my library is not a work on theatre history or the fine arts; it is a torn and tattered collection of old Sears, Roebuck catalogues. One of the difficulties of re-search into period costumes or furnishings is that the illustrators of most of the books show what the upper crust was wearing or sitting on; when a designer wants to know about *hoi polloi*, it usually takes some concentrated digging. In 1929, which was the year I needed for the icebox, Sears, Roebuck was not attracting customers from Fifth Avenue or Newport, and so, in looking through the catalogues for that year, I found a picture of what

---

[3] For Mielziner's conception of the house, before and after the transfor-mation, see the color paintings in *Designing for the Theatre*, pp. 146–147. The volume also contains (pp. 28–29) reproductions of some of Mielziner's black-and-white sketches.

I had remembered as a refrigerator typical of the time—cast-iron Chippendale-type legs that were rather thin and ridiculous-looking, and condensation coils covered in white enamel and perched on top of the cabinet, looking for all the world like a mechanistic wedding cake.

Joe said he remembered the type very well, but added that they were hard to find, even in the best junkyards. However, he told me not to worry: "We'll allow ourselves enough time so that if we can't find one, we can make it. . . ."

November 1, 1948

. . . [Kazan's] chief concern after studying my model for "Salesman" was whether his actors would have enough room on the forestage to play the considerable number of scenes that we had placed there. We had agreed that the scenic effects for these episodes would have to be simple, but they would obviously involve a prop or two, and props have a way of taking up valuable playing space. Each scene would have to have enough of them to make it identifiable. The model showed only five feet of space between the footlight area and the beginning of the Salesman's house. This worried Kazan.

I had previously discussed, and was still seriously working on, the idea of extending the working stage beyond the footlights. This, of course, meant losing valuable seats in the first two rows, and both the producer and the general manager were concerned about the economics of the suggestion. . . .

December 8, 1948

I was still to face the possible battle over the lighting equipment, but, first, the time had come to pin down exactly what we were going to do about the forestage. Bloomgarden, Kazan, Miller, Max Allentuck, the general manager, and I met at the Morosco.

Del Hughes, the production stage manager, had been given my blueprint of the ground plan and had marked the stage floor with tape, indicating the location of the steps, platforms, exits, and entrances in relation to the footlight area. Kazan spent a silent half-hour moving thoughtfully around the stage, taking various positions, his head held down much of the time as he examined the marks on the floor; occasionally he would take a quick glance toward the forestage, mentally estimating where other actors would be when an actor was standing in the position that he, Kazan, was holding at the moment.

Suddenly he said, "Fine. But the real headache is out here," and he pointed to the space far downstage that I had asked for. He jumped over the footlights and landed in the aisle. He said, "Kerm, I'm afraid I'm going to kill at least a row and a half of seats." I could see Max Allentuck concernedly counting the doomed seats. We experimented back and forth, and then Kazan offered a compromise. He decided that we would have to eliminate only the center section of the first row, a total of eleven seats. This meant a loss of $323.40 per week in receipts, which can mount up over a year. But the request was urgent, and Bloomgarden readily agreed. I was to build a forestage in this area.

With some nervousness I next brought up the high costs of the lighting equipment. After an hour of talk we settled on two special follow-spots and, necessarily, two extra men to operate them. As Bloomgarden pointed out, it was like a director saying, "I need two more good actors for this scene." And his reply to my request was the same as it would have been to his hypothetical director: "If it's important, you shall have them."

December 10, 1948

. . . Bloomgarden asked me if I would meet with Alex North, the composer who had been engaged to do the music for *Death of a Salesman*. Everyone had agreed that the sound must be controlled with as much subtlety and care as the lights, increasing and diminishing almost imperceptibly. Since we had already planned to cover the orchestra pit with the forestage, where would the music be played, and what would the controlling mechanism be?

Using the blueprint of the ground plan, I reviewed the limitations with North and we concluded that we would use a dressing room as a control center and pipe the sound into the auditorium mechanically. Using headphones and a control speaker, the stage manager could then coordinate lighting cues with sound cues, for these two elements had to be in perfect harmony.

December 15, 1948

. . . During the previous weeks I had been receiving from Arthur Miller, scene by scene, the final version of the rehearsal script. Although he had done the basic rewriting, he had made no attempt to say how the transitions from one scene to another would be made. This was a problem for the director and the designer to work out together as we studied the model, the ground plan, and the cut-out cardboard symbols representing the props.

I pointed out to Kazan how difficult it would be in an office scene, for instance, to remove two desks, two chairs, and a hatrack (which the present script called for) and at the same time have an actor walk quickly across the stage and appear in "a hotel room in Boston where he meets a girl." I urged him to do even more cutting, not in the text but in the props called for in this latest version of the script. We finally got the office pared down to one desk and one chair. Then I suggested going so far as to use the same desk for both office scenes—first in Heiser's[4] office and then, with a change of other props, in Charley's office. As usual, Kazan's imagination rose to the suggestion. He replied, "Sure, let's cut this down to the bone—we can play on practically anything." This is effective abstraction, giving the spectator the opportunity to "fill in."

I had felt from the outset that the cemetery scene at the end of the play would be done on the forestage, and I had actually drawn up a design for a trick trapdoor out of which would rise the small gravestone that we thought necessary for this scene. I had shown Kazan the working drawing for the gravestone, ex-

---

[4] Heiser may simply be a slip of Mielziner's pen, but it may also be a name given at one stage of the writing to Howard Wagner, the only character other than Charley who has an office in the play.

plained how it would operate, and mentioned that because of union rules the man operating this mechanism would be doing this and nothing else, thereby adding a member to the crew for the sake of one effect. I had also mentioned that since the trap would be very close to the audience the sound of its opening might disturb the solemnity of the scene.

With some malice aforethought, I had also done a drawing showing the Salesman's widow sitting on the step leading to the forestage, with her two sons standing behind her, their heads bowed; on the floor at her feet was a small bouquet of flowers. The whole scene was bathed in a magic-lantern projection of autumn leaves. Here, again, leaves were symbolic. With this kind of lighting I thought I could completely obliterate the house in the background and evoke a sense of sadness and finality that might enable us to eliminate the gravestone itself.

My hints were not lost. "I get your point," Kazan said. "Let's do it without the gravestone. No matter how quietly you move it into place, everybody nearby is going to be so busy thinking, 'How is that done?' that they'll miss the mood of the scene."

. . . When we came to the scene in the Boston hotel room, Kazan said, "I don't need anything; just give me the feeling of a hotel room." I showed him a sketch of a panel of cheap wallpaper which I planned to project from the theatre balcony onto a background that was really a section of the trellis at one side of the Salesman's house. Projected images used in conjunction with scenery can be very valuable. In this case, the associations evoked by faded old wallpaper gave the audience a complete picture. Both the house and the exterior trellis faded away. The audience saw the Salesman in the cheap hotel room with that woman. I stress the phrase "in that room." Actors should never play against a scenic background but within the setting.

Kazan felt that the right actress cast in the role of the girl who visits Willy Loman in the hotel room, dressed in the right costume, plus the visual image of the wallpaper, would be enough to make this short scene come alive. There is no question that when a good actor is backed up by simple scenic treatment, his strong qualities are stressed. Of course, this can work in reverse, but Arthur Miller was lucky in the casting of "Salesman"; even the bit roles were played by vivid actors. . . .

December 24, 1948

. . . One example was the kitchen table for the Loman house. It would have been cheaper to buy one at a department store or a secondhand shop, but its color had to be right. I felt that in the Salesman's kitchen an old-fashioned oilcloth would have covered this table. But oilcloth is impossible to use on the stage because its shiny surface reflects too much light; and the moment the surface is sprayed down to kill the glare, the look of the oilcloth is lost. I knew from experience that glazed chintz with the right pattern plus a little over-painting by hand gives the impression of oilcloth. . . .

February 10, 1949

I was relaxed at the Broadway opening of *Death of a Salesman*. Here was a strong play. Audiences in Philadelphia had been tremendously enthusiastic. To me it was simply a question of how big a success the play would achieve. More than four months had passed since the initial phone call from Bloomgarden, and I felt I had done everything I was capable of doing to make the production visually effective and mechanically smooth-running. The performance *was* technically perfect. Artistically, the cast was superb, and they received a thunderous ovation. This type of reception is sometimes followed the next morning by cool reviews; but in this case the press was enthusiastic too. Contrary to custom, I even stayed up that night and went to a party. . . .

Reviews

ROBERT GARLAND

Robert Garland, newspaperman and columnist, was a drama critic for *The New York Journal-American* and International News Service until his death in 1955. He was also the author of many plays and scenarios.

AUDIENCE SPELLBOUND
BY PRIZE PLAY OF 1949

Here's my true report that, yesterday at the Morosco, the first-night congregation made no effort to leave the theatre at the final curtain-fall of Arthur Miller's *Death of a Salesman*. It's meant to make known to you the prevailing emotional impact of the new play by the author of *All My Sons*.

As a theatre reporter I'm telling you how that first-night congregation remained in its seats beyond the final curtain-fall. For a period somewhat shorter than it seemed, an expectant silence hung over the crowded auditorium. Then, believe me, tumultuous appreciation shattered the hushed expectancy.

It was, and will remain, one of the lasting rewards that I, as a professional theatregoer, have received in a long full life of professional theatregoing. In *Death of a Salesman*, Arthur Miller had given that first night congregation no ordinary new play to praise, to damn, or to ignore.

This, his most iconoclastic composition, is not easy on its congregation, first-night or later on. In writing what he wants to

From *The New York Journal-American*, February 11, 1949, p. 24. Reprinted by permission of The World Journal Tribune, Inc.

write, he has asked—demanded, rather—your sympathy as a fellow member of the bedeviled human race and your attention as an intelligent collaborator as well.

These, with everything else that's good, the author of "Death of a Salesman" received wholeheartedly last night. The play's playwright and playgoers were worthy of each other.

If Everyman will forgive me, in Arthur Miller's Salesman there's much of Everyman. Bothered, bewildered, but mostly bedeviled, as Willy Loman is, he's not a great deal different from the majority of his contemporaries. He, even as you and I, builds himself a shaky shelter of illusion.

You've the author's word that the motif of *Death of a Salesman* is the growth of illusion in even the most commonplace of mortals. In Willy Loman, the illusionist of the title, the individual is destroyed. And his progeny, Biff and Happy, are wrecked upon the rocks of reality.

Willy has created an image of himself which fails to correspond with Willy Loman as he is. According to the playwright, it's the size of the discrepancy that matters. In Salesman Loman, the discrepancy is so great that it finally slays him. Ironically, by his own unsteady hand.

In *Death of a Salesman*, the present and the past of Willy Loman exist concurrently—the "stream of consciousness" idea— until they collide in climax. Isn't it true that the Willy Lomans of this world are their own worst tragedy? At the Morosco, only Linda Loman can foresee the end.

And she, as wife and mother, is powerless to prevent it. This, to me, is the play's most tragic tragedy. She, too, is the play's most poignant figure. Not soon shall I forget her!

Forget Linda Loman, I mean, as Mildred Dunnock recreates her. For it is she, first as created by Mr. Miller, then as recreated by Miss Dunnock, whose all-too-human single-mindedness holds *Death of a Salesman* together. She, of all the Lomans, sees the Salesman as he is. And loves him!

Even so, the Salesman of Lee J. Cobb is a tour de force. In a part that's longer than Hamlet and almost as open to misinterpretation, Mr. Cobb is as right as he's resourceful. As Willy Loman, he manages to test your patience and break your heart. Frequently, both at the same time.

His boys—Biff and Happy—are sturdily three-dimensional as projected by Arthur Kennedy and Cameron Mitchell. And, as Charley, Howard Smith brings reality into the Lomans' illusory household. The others could scarcely be improved upon as neighbors, friends and ladies of the evening.

Although Arthur Miller's *Death of a Salesman* is programmed with Kermit Bloomgarden and Walter Fried as co-producers, it's also billed as Elia Kazan's production. You know what that means! And Jo Mielziner's high-flung imaginative setting is exactly what the playwright, the play and players call for . . .

Arthur Miller's *Death of a Salesman* at the Morosco is my personal prize-play of the 1948–1949 New York season. Here and now, I beat the Pulitzer people and the Critics' Circle to it.

WILLIAM HAWKINS

William Hawkins was a drama critic for *The New York World-Telegram & Sun* until his retirement in 1964. He is the author of two novels, *Big Red Pocketbook* and *Tell the Mischief*.

DEATH OF A SALESMAN
POWERFUL TRAGEDY

Death of a Salesman is a play written along the lines of the finest classical tragedy. It is the revelation of a man's downfall, in destruction whose roots are entirely in his own soul. The play builds to an immutable conflict where there is no resolution for this man in this life.

The play is a fervent query into the great American competitive dream of success, as it strips to the core a castaway from the race for recognition and money.

The failure of a great potential could never be so moving or so universally understandable as is the fate of Willy Loman, because his complete happiness could have been so easy to attain. He is an artisan who glories in manual effort and can be proud of the sturdy fine things he puts together out of wood and cement.

At eighteen he is introduced to the attention he might receive and the financial vistas he might travel by selling on the road. This original deception dooms him to a life of touring and a habit of prideful rationalization, until at sixty he is so far along his tangent that his efforts not to admit his resultant mediocrity are fatal.

Through most of this career runs the insistent legacy of "amounting to something" on his adopted terms, which he

From *The New York World-Telegram*, February 11, 1949, p. 16. Reprinted by permission of The World Journal Tribune, Inc.

forces on his favorite son. With indulgent adoration he unbalances the boy, demanding a mutual idolatry which he himself inevitably fails. If young Biff steals, it is courage. If he captains a football team, the world is watching.

In the end, after repeated failure, Biff sees the truth, too late to really penetrate his father's mind. The boy's tortured efforts to explain his own little true destiny can only crack open the years-long rift, and the salesman, with all his dream's lost shadows, has no alternative to death for his peace.

Often plays have been written that crossed beyond physical actuality into the realm of memory and imagination, but it is doubtful if any has so skillfully transcended the limits of real time and space. One cannot term the chronology here a flashback technique, because the transitions are so immediate and logical.

As Willy's mind wavers under the strain of his own failure and the antagonism of his boy, he recalls the early hopeful days. The course of the play runs so smoothly that it seems one moment the two sons have gone to bed upstairs in plain sight, weary and cynical, and an instant later they are tumbling in youthful exuberance to the tune of their father's delighted flattery.

Sometimes Willy recalls the chance he once had to join his rich adventurous brother, and as his desperation increases he begs Ben for some explanation of his deep confusion.

These illuminations of the man are so exquisitely molded into the form of the play that it sweeps along like a powerful tragic symphony. The actors are attuned to the text as if they were distinct instruments. Themes rise and fade, are varied and repeated. Again as in music, an idea may be introduced as a faint echo, and afterwards developed to its fullest part in the big scheme.

It is hard to imagine anyone more splendid than Lee J. Cobb is as Willy Loman, the salesman. To be big and broken is so contradictory. The actor subtly moves from the first realizations of defeat, into a state of stubborn jauntiness alternating with childlike fear in a magnificent portrait of obsolescence.

Only the rare young actor can sustain a role of hysterical intensity with any dignity, but Arthur Kennedy does it with the utmost taste and strength. It is a complicated role, now joyous, now bitter, sometimes surly then passionately outspoken. Kennedy rings these changes without faltering.

Willy's wife Linda is a truthfully blocked out character, gentle and delicate, yet fiercely loving and fiercely loyal.

Mildred Dunnock plays her with sincerity that comes only with surface simplicity and penetrating comprehension. The scenes where she defends and explains the father to her sons are done with heart-wringing reality.

JOHN MASON BROWN

John Mason Brown has been drama critic for *Theatre Arts Monthly,*
The New York Post, The New York World-Telegram, and *The*
Saturday Review, and has lectured in drama at the University of
Montana, Yale University, Middlebury College, and Harvard Uni-
versity. He is the author of seventeen books, among them *The*
Modern Theater in Revolt and *The Worlds of Robert E. Sherwood.*

[EVEN AS YOU AND I]

George Jean Nathan once described a certain actress's Camille
as being the first Camille he had ever seen who had died of
cartarrh. This reduction in scale of a major disease to an un-
pleasant annoyance is symptomatic of more than the acting
practice of the contemporary stage. Even our dramatists, at least
most of them, tend in their writing, so to speak, to turn t.b. into
a sniffle. They seem ashamed of the big things, embarrassed by
the raw emotions, afraid of the naked passions, and unaware of
life's brutalities and tolls.

Of understatement they make a fetish. They have all the reti-
cences and timidities of the overcivilized and undemonstrative.
They pride themselves upon writing around a scene rather than
from or to it; upon what they hold back instead of upon what
they release. They paint with pastels, not oils, and dodge the
primary anguishes as they would the primary colors.

Their characters belong to an anemic brood. Lacking blood,
they lack not only violence but humanity. They are the puppets
of contrivance, not the victims of circumstance or themselves.
They are apt to be shadows without substance, surfaces without
depths. They can be found in the *dramatis personae* but not in

From *Dramatis Personae* by John Mason Brown (New York: The Viking
Press, 1963), pp. 94–100, Copyright 1950 by John Mason Brown, all rights
reserved, reprinted by permission of The Viking Press, Inc. The title is the
one used when the review first appeared in *Saturday Review of Literature,*
XXXII (February 26, 1949), 30–32.

the telephone book. If they have hearts, their murmurings are seldom audible. They neither hear nor allow us to hear those inner whisperings of hope, fear, despair, or joy, which are the true accompaniment to spoken words. Life may hurt them, but they do not suffer from the wounds it gives them so that we, watching them, are wounded ourselves and suffer with them.

This willingness, this ability, to strike unflinchingly upon the anvil of human sorrow is one of the reasons for O'Neill's pre-eminence and for the respect in which we hold the best work of Clifford Odets and Tennessee Williams. It is also the source of Arthur Miller's unique strength and explains why his fine new play, *Death of a Salesman*, is an experience at once pulverizing and welcome.

Mr. Miller is, of course, remembered as the author of *Focus*, a vigorous and terrifying novel about anti-Semitism, and best known for *All My Sons*, which won the New York Critics Award two seasons back. Although that earlier play lacked the simplicity, hence the muscularity, of Mr. Miller's novel, it was notable for its force. Overelaborate as it may have been, it introduced a new and unmistakable talent. If as a young man's script it took advantage of its right to betray influences, these at least were of the best. They were Ibsen and Chekhov. The doctor who wandered in from next door might have been extradited from *The Three Sisters*. The symbolical use to which the apple tree was put was pure Ibsen. So, too, was the manner in which the action was maneuvered from the present back into the past in order to rush forward. Even so, Mr. Miller's own voice could be heard in *All My Sons*, rising strong and clear above those other voices. It was a voice that deserved the attention and admiration it won. It was not afraid of being raised. It spoke with heat, fervor, and compassion. Moreover, it had something to say.

In *Death of a Salesman* this same voice can be heard again. It has deepened in tone, developed wonderfully in modulation, and gained in carrying power. Its authority has become full-grown. Relying on no borrowed accents, it now speaks in terms of complete accomplishment rather than exciting promise. Indeed, it is released in a play which provides one of the modern theatre's most overpowering evenings.

How good the writing of this or that of Mr. Miller's individual scenes may be, I do not know. Nor do I really care. When hit in the face, you do not bother to count the knuckles which strike you. All that matters, all you remember, is the staggering impact of the blow. Mr. Miller's is a terrific wallop, as furious in its onslaught on the heart as on the head. His play is the most poignant statement of man as he must face himself to have come out of our theatre. It finds the stuffs of life so mixed with the stuffs of the stage that they become one and indivisible.

If the proper study of mankind is man, man's inescapable problem is himself—what he would like to be, what he is, what he is not, and yet what he must live and die with. These are the moving, everyday, all-inclusive subjects with which Mr. Miller deals in *Death of a Salesman*. He handles them unflinchingly, with enormous sympathy, with genuine imagination, and in a mood which neither the prose of his dialogue nor the reality of his probing can rob of its poetry. Moreover, he has the wisdom and the insight not to blame the "system," in Mr. Odets' fashion, for what are the inner frailties and shortcomings of the individual. His rightful concern is with the dilemmas which are timeless in the drama because they are timeless in life.

Mr. Miller's play is a tragedy modern and personal, not classic and heroic. Its central figure is a little man sentenced to discover his smallness rather than a big man undone by his greatness. Although he happens to be a salesman tested and found wanting by his own very special crises, all of us sitting out front are bound to be shaken, long before the evening is over, by finding something of ourselves in him.

Mr. Miller's Willy Loman is a family man, father of two sons. He is sixty-three and has grubbed hard all his life. He has never possessed either the daring or the gold-winning luck of his prospector brother, who wanders through the play as a somewhat shadowy symbol of success but a necessary contrast. Stupid, limited, and confused as Willy Loman may have been, however, no one could have questioned his industry or his loyalty to his family and his firm. He has loved his sons and, when they were growing up, been rewarded by the warmth of their returned love. He loves his wife, too, and has been unfaithful to her only because of his acute, aching loneliness when on the road.

He has lived on his smile and on his hopes; survived from sale to sale; been sustained by the illusion that he has countless friends in his territory, that everything will be all right, that he is a success, and that his boys will be successes also. His misfortune is that he has gone through life as an eternal adolescent, as someone who has not dared to take stock, as someone who never knew who he was. His personality has been his profession; his energy, his protection. His major ambition has been not only to be liked, but well liked. His ideal for himself and for his sons has stopped with an easy, back-slapping, sports-loving, locker-room popularity. More than ruining his sons so that one has become a woman chaser and the other a thief, his standards have turned both boys against their father.

When Mr. Miller's play begins, Willy Loman has reached the ebb-tide years. He is too old and worn out to continue traveling. His back aches when he stoops to lift the heavy sample cases that were once his pride. His tired, wandering mind makes it unsafe for him to drive the car which has carried him from one town and sale to the next. His sons see through him and despise him. His wife sees through him and defends him, knowing him to be better than most and, at any rate, well intentioned. What is far worse, when he is fired from his job he begins to see through himself. He realizes he is, and has been, a failure. Hence his deliberate smashup in his car in order to bring in some money for his family and make the final payment on his home when there is almost no one left who wants to live in it.

Although *Death of a Salesman* is set in the present, it finds time and space to include the past. It plays the agonies of the moment of collapse against the pleasures and sorrows of recollected episodes. Mr. Miller is interested in more than the life and fate of his central character. His scene seems to be Willy Loman's mind and heart no less than his home. What we see might just as well be what Willy Loman thinks, feels, fears, or remembers as what we see him doing. This gives the play a double and successful exposure in time. It makes possible the constant fusion of what has been and what is. It also enables it to achieve a greater reality by having been freed from the fetters of realism.

Once again Mr. Miller shows how fearless and perceptive an emotionalist he is. He writes boldly and brilliantly about the way in which we disappoint those we love by having disappointed ourselves. He knows the torment of family tensions, the compensations of friendship, and the heartbreak that goes with broken pride and lost confidence. He is aware of the loyalties, not blind but open-eyed, which are needed to support mortals in their loneliness. The anatomy of failure, the pathos of age, and the tragedy of those years when a life begins to slip down the hill it has labored to climb are subjects at which he excels.

The quality and intensity of his writing can perhaps best be suggested by letting Mr. Miller speak for himself, or rather by allowing his characters to speak for him, in a single scene, in fact, in the concluding one. It is then that Willy's wife, his two sons, and his old friend move away from Jo Mielziner's brilliantly simple and imaginative multiple setting, and advance to the footlights. It is then that Mr. Miller's words supply a scenery of their own. Willy Loman, the failure and suicide, has supposedly just been buried, and all of us are at his grave, including his wife who wants to cry but cannot and who keeps thinking that it is just as if he were off on another trip.

"You don't understand," says Willy's friend, defending Willy from one of his sons. "Willy was a salesman. And for a salesman, there is no rock bottom to the life. He don't put a bolt to a nut, he don't tell you the law or give you medicine. He's a man way out there in the blue, ridin' on a smile and a shoeshine. And when they start not smilin' back—that's an earthquake. And then you get yourself a couple spots on your hat, and you're finished. Nobody dast blame this man. A salesman is got to dream, boy. It comes with the territory."

The production of *Death of a Salesman* is as sensitive, human, and powerful as the writing. Elia Kazan has solved, and solved superbly, what must have been a difficult and challenging problem. He captures to the full the mood and heartbreak of the script. He does this without ever surrendering to sentimentality. He manages to mingle the present and the past, the moment and the memory, so that their intertwining raises no questions and causes no confusions. His direction, so glorious in its vigor, is no less considerate of those small details which can be both mountainous and momentous in daily living.

It would be hard to name a play more fortunate in its casting than *Death of a Salesman*. All its actors—especially Arthur Kennedy and Cameron Mitchell as the two sons, and Howard Smith as the friend—act with such skill and conviction that the line of demarcation between being and pretending seems abolished. The script's humanity has taken possession of their playing and is an integral part of their performances.

Special mention must be made of Lee J. Cobb and Mildred Dunnock as the salesman, Willy Loman, and his wife, Linda. Miss Dunnock is all heart, devotion, simplicity. She is unfooled but unfailing. She is the smiling, mothering, hard-worked, good wife, the victim of her husband's budget. She is the nourisher of his dreams, even when she knows they are only dreams; the feeder of his self-esteem. If she is beyond whining or nagging, she is above self-pity. She is the marriage vow—"for better for worse, for richer for poorer, in sickness and in health"—made flesh, slight of body but strong of faith.

Mr. Cobb's Willy Loman is irresistibly touching and wonderfully unsparing. He is a great shaggy bison of a man seen at that moment of defeat when he is deserted by the herd and can no longer run with it. Mr. Cobb makes clear the pathetic extent to which the herd has been Willy's life. He also communicates the fatigue of Willy's mind and body and that boyish hope and buoyancy which his heart still retains. Age, however, is his enemy. He is condemned by it. He can no more escape from it than he can from himself. The confusions, the weakness, the goodness, the stupidity, and the self-sustaining illusions which are Willy—all these are established by Mr. Cobb. Seldom has an average man at the moment of his breaking been characterized with such exceptional skill.

Did Willy Loman, so happy with a batch of cement when puttering around the house, or when acquaintances on the road smiled back at him, fail to find out who he was? Did this man, who worked so hard and meant so well, dream the wrong dream? At least he was willing to die by that dream, even when it had collapsed for him. He was a breadwinner almost to the end, and a breadwinner even in his death. Did the world walk out on him, and his sons see through him? At any rate he could boast one friend who believed in him and thought his had been a good dream, "the only dream you can have." Who knows? Who can say? One thing is certain. No one could have raised the question more movingly or compassionately than Arthur Miller.

HAROLD CLURMAN

Harold Clurman, regular drama critic of *The Nation*, is also well known as a director. He has lectured at the Carnegie Institute of Technology, was drama critic for *The New Republic* and *Tomorrow*, and was executive consultant of the Repertory Theater, Lincoln Center. He is the author of, among other books, *The Fervent Years* and *The Naked Image*, and the editor of *Famous American Plays of the 1930's* and *Seven Plays of the Modern Theater*.

[THE SUCCESS DREAM ON THE AMERICAN STAGE]

Arthur Miller's *Death of a Salesman* is one of the outstanding plays in the repertory of the American theatre. That its theme is not, strictly speaking, new to our stage—Arthur Richman's *Ambush* (1921), J. P. McEvoy's *The Potters* (1923), Elmer Rice's *The Adding Machine* (1923), George Kelly's *The Show-Off* (1924), Clifford Odets' *Awake and Sing* and *Paradise Lost* (1935) being in this respect its antecedents—does not in any way lessen its effect or significance. The value of *Death of a Salesman* lies in the fact that it states its theme with penetrating clarity in our era of troubled complacency.

Death of a Salesman is a challenge to the American dream. Lest this be misunderstood, I hasten to add that there are two versions of the American dream. The historical American dream is the promise of a land of freedom with opportunity and equality for all. This dream needs no challenge, only fulfillment. But

---

From *Lies Like Truth* by Harold Clurman (New York: Macmillan, 1958), pp. 68–72. Copyright 1949 by Harold Clurman. Reprinted by permission of the author and The Macmillan Co. The title used here comes from an article in *Tomorrow*, VIII (May 1949), 48–51, in which this review of "Salesman" first appeared (49–50) along with some general comments on the subject and a review of Clifford Odets' *The Big Knife* (reprinted, *Lies Like Truth*, pp. 49–52). For an earlier review of "Salesman" by Clurman, see "Attention!" *New Republic*, CXX (February 28, 1949), 26–28.

since the Civil War, and particularly since 1900, the American dream has become distorted to the dream of business success. A distinction must be made even in this. The original premise of our dream of success—popularly represented in the original boy parables of Horatio Alger—was that enterprise, courage and hard work were the keys to success. Since the end of the First World War this too has changed. Instead of the ideals of hard work and courage, we have salesmanship. Salesmanship implies a certain element of fraud: the ability to put over or sell a commodity regardless of its intrinsic usefulness. The goal of salesmanship is to make a deal, to earn a profit—the accumulation of profit being an unquestioned end in itself.

This creates a new psychology. To place all value in the mechanical act of selling and in self-enrichment impoverishes the human beings who are rendered secondary to the deal. To possess himself fully, a man must have an intimate connection with that with which he deals as well as with the person with whom he deals. When the connection is no more than an exchange of commodities, the man himself ceases to be a man, becomes a commodity himself, a spiritual cipher.

This is a humanly untenable situation. The salesman realizes this. Since his function precludes a normal human relationship, he substitutes an imitation of himself for the real man. He sells his "personality." This "personality," now become only a means to an end—namely, the consummated sale—is a mask worn so long that it soon comes to be mistaken, even by the man who wears it, as his real face. But it is only his commercial face with a commercial smile and a commercial aura of the well-liked, smoothly adjusted, oily cog in the machine of the sales apparatus.

This leads to a behavior pattern which is ultimately doomed; not necessarily because of the economic system of which it is the human concomitant, but quite simply because a man is not a machine. The death of Arthur Miller's salesman is symbolic of the breakdown of the whole concept of salesmanship inherent in our society.

Miller does not say these things explicitly. But it is the

strength of his play that it is based on this understanding, and that he is able to make his audience realize it no matter whether or not they are able consciously to formulate it. When the audience weeps at *Death of a Salesman*, it is not so much over the fate of Willy Loman—Miller's pathetic hero—but over the millions of such men who are our brothers, uncles, cousins, neighbors. The lovable lower-middle-class mole Willy Loman represents is related to a type of living and thinking in which nearly all of us—"professionals" as well as salesmen—share.

Willy Loman never acknowledges or learns the error of his way. To the very end he is a devout believer in the ideology that destroys him. He believes that life's problems are all solved by making oneself "well liked" (in the salesman's sense) and by a little cash. His wife knows only that he is a good man and that she must continue to love him. His sons, who are his victims, as he has been of the false dream by which he has lived, draw different conclusions from his failure. The younger boy, Hap, believes only that his father was an incompetent (as do many of the play's commentators), but he does not reject his father's ideal. (It is to be noted that in a very important sense Willy Loman is sympathetic precisely because of his failure to make himself a successful machine.) The older boy, Biff, comes to understand the falsity of his father's ideal and determines to set out on a new path guided by a recovery of his true self.

There are minor flaws in *Death of a Salesman*, such as the constant pointing to a secret in the older brother's past which is presumed to be the immediate cause of his moral breakdown —the secret turning out to be the boy's discovery of his father's marital infidelity. There is validity in this scene as part of the over-all picture of the father-son relationship. A shock such as the boy sustains here often serves to propel people into the unexplored territory of their subconscious, and may thus become the springboard for further and more basic questioning. Miller's error here is to make the boy's horror at his father's "deceit" appear crucial rather than contributory to the play's main line.

Some people have objected that the use of the stream-of-consciousness technique—the play dramatizes Willy's recollection of the past, and at times switches from a literal presentation of his memory to imaginary and semisymbolic representation of his thought—is confusing, and a sign of weakness in the author's grasp of his material.

These objections do not impress me. The limitations of *Death of a Salesman* are part of its virtues. The merit in Miller's treatment of his material lies in a certain clean, moralistic rationalism. It is not easy to make the rational a poetic attribute, but Miller's growth since *All My Sons* consists in his ability to make his moral and rationalistic characteristics produce a kind of poetry.

The truth of *Death of a Salesman* is conveyed with what might be compared to a Living Newspaper, documentary accuracy. With this there is a grave probity and a sensitivity that raise the whole beyond the level of what might otherwise have seemed to be only agitation and propaganda. Other playwrights may be more colorful, lyrical and rich with the fleshed nerves and substance of life; Miller holds us with a sense of his soundness. His play has an ascetic, slate-like hue, as if he were eschewing all exaggeration and extravagance; and with a sobriety that is not without humor, yet entirely free of frivolity, he issues the forthright commandment, "Thou shalt not be a damn' fool!"

Elia Kazan's production is first rate. It is true to Miller's qualities, and adds to them a swift directness, muscularity and vehemence of conviction. If any further criticism is in order I should say the production might have gained a supplementary dimension if it had more of the aroma of individual characterization, more intimacy, more of the quiet music of specific humanity—small, as the people in the play are small, and yet suggestive of those larger truths their lives signify.

Mildred Dunnock as the mother embodies the production's best features: its precision, clarity, purity of motive. Someone has said that the part might have been more moving if it had been played by an actress like Pauline Lord with all the magic overtones and "quarter tones" of her subtle sensibility. Concretely such a suggestion is, of course, irrelevant, but it points to a need I feel in the production as a whole more than to Miss Dunnock's particular performance.

Lee Cobb as the salesman is massively powerful and a commanding actor every step of the way. Yet I cannot help feeling that Cobb's interpretation is more akin to the prototype of a King Lear than to Willy Loman. What differentiates Willy from some similarly abused figure is his utter unconsciousness—even where the author gives him conscious lines—his battered pride, querulous innocence, wan bewilderment even within the context of protest and angry vociferation.

Cameron Mitchell as the younger son is eminently likable, but for the play's thesis he ought also to be something of a comic stinker. Arthur Kennedy, who plays the older son, is a truly fine actor, who loses some of his edge because the general high pitch of the production forces him to blunt his natural delicacy.

Jo Mielziner's scene design seems to me too complex in shape and too diverse in style to be wholly satisfactory for a functional set or for beautiful decoration. Neither this nor any of the other faults that may have been found in *Death of a Salesman* prevent it from remaining a cardinal event not only of this season but of many a long year in the American theatre.

ELEANOR CLARK

Eleanor Clark, novelist, short-story writer, and essayist, is the author of, among other books, *Rome and a Villa* and *The Oysters of Locmariaquer*.

OLD GLAMOUR, NEW GLOOM

It would seem that the success of Arthur Miller's, or Elia Kazan's, *Death of a Salesman* has been due largely to the feeling of depression with which one makes for the exit. The idea is that anything that can make you feel that glum must be good, true and above all important—and publicity aside, it must be admitted that this culturally lace-curtain notion has a few things to support it these days at the Morosco. These are, notably, a superb performance by Lee Cobb as the salesman, a beautifully flexible and elegant stylization of a small Brooklyn house by Jo Mielziner, and a production so slick and fast that you have hardly the time or the presumption to question it. Unfortunately, however, it becomes necessary to question just what it is that gives the play its brilliant down-in-the-mouth effect, since it would surely be hard for any but its most insensitive admirers to deny that although they came out from it stuffed full of gloom, they were strangely lacking in a sense either of pity or of illumination.

They have seen a good, or good enough, man driven to suicide, a family in despair, an illusion shattered, and a portrayal of American life that should, it seems, have given them the sharpest pang of all; they have been expressly invited to indulge the tragic sense and to carry away a conception of man's fate

---

From *Theatre Chronicle, Partisan Review*, Vol. XVI, No. 6 (June 1949), pp. 631–635. Copyright © 1949 by *Partisan Review*, reprinted by permission of *Partisan Review* and Eleanor Clark. Although the bulk of the glamour and gloom had to do with "Salesman," Miss Clark devoted a few pages (635–637) to a review of Sidney Kingsley's *Detective Story*.

as though from a production of *Oedipus Rex*, and what they have carried away instead is just that curious, rankling gloom. As the salesman's wife puts it after he has thrown himself under a train: "I can't cry. I want to cry, but I can't."[1] If an honest poll could be taken it might well turn out that a large majority of these admirers, including the critics, had been secretly telling themselves not only after the play but during it that they were not really bored, just a little tired that night. Or was it perhaps that the tragic sense with all it has undergone from the facts of recent times needs now some entirely different, some unimaginably new appeal, and this was too much to ask of a play?—better be grateful for this. But of course there is no reason to be grateful for something that pretends to be what it is not, and the fact of the matter is that these secret whisperings, if they occurred, were well justified. The play, with its peculiar hodgepodge of dated materials and facile new ones, is not tragedy at all but an ambitious piece of confusionism, such as in any other sphere would probably be called a hoax, and which has been put across by purely technical skills not unlike those of a magician or an acrobat.

Up to a point this might be considered no more than the usual operation of the second-rate mind as glamorized by Broadway. But there is a particular twist to the matter this time, which helps to explain how a subject that in its general lines was run ragged fifteen or twenty years ago should be able to turn up now as a vehicle for such large claims and such ponderous emotionalizing.

Certainly as representing the false dream aspect of American society Mr. Miller's salesman offers nothing very original. The old gag about the installment-plan frigidaire ("Once in my life

---

[1] Linda never says that she wants to cry and her reiteration of "I can't cry" is scattered through a long speech. The reviewer in the theater, with no text to refer to, has to make do with his memory or phrases scrawled on his program; so it is not surprising that Miss Clark can only approximate the line, as she does in most of the quotation in the review. It is less understandable that she thinks Willy threw himself under a train. Her inaccuracy is rather funny in the context of this paragraph in which she seems to know what is going on secretly inside the critics, although she is a little doubtful about what is going on openly on stage.

I'd like to own something outright before it's broke") are [sic] evidently still good for a laugh, and there is always a pocket of pathos reserved for the mortgage, but things have been sadder and funnier before. A slightly fresher breeze does blow at moments. Willy Loman calls for a genuine smile or two with his distinction between being "liked" and being "well-liked," and the perception behind this is accurate enough, even though in context it becomes one of the half-truths typical of the play. Willy's rock-bottom faith has been in the capacity to get along with people, to "make a good impression"; it is with this faith that he slides to old age and ruin while his brother Ben, who appears in some well-staged flashbacks, piles up a fortune in Alaska, and because of it at the end he is still pushing his favorite son Biff toward a failure worse than his own, the irony, as presented, lying not so much in the failure as in the denial of the man's true nature and talents along the way. Willy liked to work with his hands and had been happy when he was making a cement porch; and Biff, who had been happy as a ranch-hand in the West, has at the time of the play restlessly driven himself back home. In the end, after the suicide, it is the flashy son Hap, content with cheap success and easy women, who speaks of the salesman's dream as having been "good." Biff knows better—the dream was rotten though he speaks of his father nevertheless as a "prince"—and the wife knows better still; Willy was as good "as many other people." In short, he is the common man, and something or other has gone terribly wrong. The point is, what and why.

At first blush the answer seems fairly simple. Willy has a fatal flaw. He lives in a dream world; he can't face reality; he has always had excuses for his own failures ("the shop was closed for inventory") and has ruined Biff's life by indulging him all through his childhood in any whim including theft. It is a good theme. But it turns out not only that the author is saying a good deal more than this, but that he is also either very unclear as to his further meanings, or very anxious to present them and evade responsibility for them at the same time. It is, of course, the capitalist system that has done Willy in; the scene in which he is brutally fired after some forty years with the firm comes straight from the party line literature of the 'thirties; and the idea emerges lucidly enough through all the confused motivations of the play that it is our particular form of money economy that has bred the absurdly false ideals of both father and sons. It emerges, however, like a succession of shots from a duck-blind. Immediately after every crack the playwright withdraws behind an air of pseudo-universality, and hurries to present some cruelty or misfortune due either to Willy's own weakness, as when he refuses his friend's offer of a job after he has been fired, or gratuitously from some other source, as in the quite unbelievable scene of the two sons walking out on their father in the restaurant. In the end, after so much heaping of insult on injury, all one really knows about Willy Loman is that if the system doesn't kick him in the teeth he will do it himself—a well-known if wearisome tendency, that in itself might have dramatic possibilities, but that is neither particularly associated with salesmen nor adapted to the purposes of this play.

What it does lend itself to in this case is an intellectual muddle and a lack of candor that regardless of Mr. Miller's conscious intent are the main earmark of contemporary fellow-traveling. What used to be a roar has become a whine, and this particular piece of whining has been so expertly put over that it has been able to pass for something else, but behind all the fancy staging the old basic clumsiness and lack of humor are there. To be sure there are a few moments of ordinary Broadway sprightliness, as in the matter of the icebox, or Hap's little performance with the girls in the restaurant, but these are in passing.

The crucial scenes, like the general conception, are all heavily dead-pan, to an extent that floors the talents of every actor in the play but Mr. Cobb; Cameron Mitchell and Arthur Kennedy as the two sons do as well as possible with the script but both are driven by it at various points to over-act, and Mildred Dunnock in the part of the wife is obliged to keep up a tension of high-pitched nobility that would wear out one's tragic sense long before the end even if nothing else did. As for the clumsiness, it shows not only in the large aspects of the play but, rather surprisingly considering the general technical excellence of the job in a number of small ones too. That the much-stressed point of Willy's being deprived of working with his hands, and of his pride in that, is not a specific reflection on the money standards which are central to the play's action, but as remarked on by many writers over the last hundred years, has to do with modern mechanized society in whatever form, could perhaps be passed over. But nothing excuses the triteness and pseudo-psychoanalytic nature of the Boston scene, dragged in to explain Biff's failures, though he would have been far better perceived as a contemporary character without it. It is also annoying not to know what the salesman sells, and whether or not the insurance is going to be paid after his death, and to have the wife say in her final speech that they were just getting out of debt, with no previous explanation of how, and when in fact we have just seen Willy getting further into debt.[2]

These are details, but they indicate something of the speciousness of the play, which manages at every point to obscure both the real tragedy and the real comedy of the material. Willy is presumed to be losing his mind because he talks to himself, which permits the long series of flashbacks that give the play its illusion of liveliness, a form of madness that can at least, in the case, be called convenient; but all of us have seen and probably most of us have experienced delusions wilder and more illuminating than this. In the picture of Biff's unhappy restlessness Mr. Miller gives an impression of contemporaneity, but that is all; the true malaise of men of thirty now is a great deal more terrible than what happens to anyone in this play, and would not be a subject for a Broadway success. And so on. The play is made of such semi-perceptions, as can easily be appreci-

---

[2] For Miller on what Willy sells, see p. 161, and for other opinions the accompanying footnote. Ivor Brown (see p. 248) and Daniel E. Schneider (see p. 257) assume not only that the insurance paid off, but that Linda used the money for the last mortgage payment. This kind of circumstantial concern is amusing but not particularly relevant to the play, since the information, if given, would not alter our response to the scenes involving Willy as salesman and suicide and Linda as mourner.

ated by a glance at Eudora Welty's story, "Death of a Traveling Salesman," published some years ago.[3]

There are of course many possible approaches to the character of the salesman, and Miss Welty was humble in hers, but she succeeded nevertheless in some twenty pages in creating a figure of loneliness and haunting futility that conveys a truly tragic sense, and remains as a clear, echoing symbol in the mind. The story makes no claims, it says only what it has to say, at its own sure quiet pace, and its limitations are never violated, but it strikes deep and has been deeply felt and so they become irrelevant. If one chooses to take it that way, this is as strong a condemnation as one could wish of one of the abnormal, humanly stultifying aspects of our society, as represented by one of its most victimized as well as victimizing characters; and yet the effect, with all its continuing vibrations of meaning, has been achieved by nothing but a simple juxtaposition of a moment of the salesman's life with a pattern of simple, almost primitive love. There is no sound of whining here. It may be that this salesman too would have enjoyed working with his hands, but he is incapable of it; when his car rolls into a ditch another man has to haul it out for him, and he goes to his death in a dumb despair at the thought of that other man's life.

As against as strong and unpretentious a piece as this, Mr. Miller's use of his material seems even more unpleasantly pompous, and above all, flat. It can hardly have occurred to anyone to use such a word as, for instance, suggestiveness in connection with it. Everything is stated, two or three times over, all with a great air of something like poetry about it but actually with no remove, no moment of departure from the literal whatever; through scene after snappy scene the action ploughs along on a level of naturalism that has not even the virtue of being natural. A jumble of styles is maintained, with borrowings from the movies, the ballet and the Greeks, and at moments of particular significance the colloquial but unimagized language of the play becomes a trifle more genteel—"I search, and I search, and I search, and I can't understand," Willy's wife says after his sui-

ELEANOR CLARK 223

cide, though she has been foreseeing it and explaining it from
the beginning of the play. But such tricks, however skillfully
worked, are no substitute for real impact, and can only momen-
tarily hide the fact that this is a very dull business, which
departs in no way that is to its credit from the general
mediocrity of our commercial theater. . . .

T. C. WORSLEY

T. C. Worsley, British writer and critic, is the author of *The Fugitive Art*; *Dramatic Commentaries, 1947–1951*, co-author with W. H. Auden of *Education Today—and Tomorrow*, and co-author with John Dover Wilson of *Shakespeare's Histories at Stratford*.

POETRY WITHOUT WORDS

Death of a Salesman, the new play by the American Mr. Arthur Miller (whose *All My Sons* we saw last year) is at the moment, if we may trust reports, setting all New York weeping. At the Phoenix Theatre last week I did not observe any snuffling nor did I myself, though a ready enough snuffler, have to reach for my handkerchief once. I think it fairly describes the effect of the play to record that there was in the middle a good deal of that shifting of position and creaking of seats which indicate that attention is slipping: but that at the curtain fall the applause was long, loud and sincere. It was one of those comparatively rare plays, too, about which you are prepared to go on talking for two or three hours. But you may very likely find that you are not so much discussing the impact of the play itself as trying to account for the fact that the impact is so much smaller than it somehow ought to have been. Somehow much more expectation has been generated than ever gets satisfied. Immense care, elaboration, skill have been employed, and yet at the end we go away hungry. It is rather as if we had been invited to what promises to be a very grand dinner indeed. Jewels flash: starch gleams: the flowers on the table are exquisitely arranged: and heavens, we are dining off gold plate! And yet and yet . . . the soup when it comes doesn't it strike us as being a little thin? And how slow the service is! It takes a long time to reach the

---

From *New Statesman & Nation*, N.S. XXXVIII (August 6, 1949), pp. 146–147, reprinted by permission of *New Statesman*. The London production opened at the Phoenix Theatre, July 28, 1949.

sole. At least sole is what it is called on the menu. But doesn't it taste suspiciously like plaice? And only one minute fillet each! No doubt something more substantial will arrive presently. But no, what's this? The ladies are already rising and now the coffee essence is going round. Still, even if we are a little empty we cannot but admire immensely the ravishing little coffee cups in which it is served, all green and gold—Russian, don't you think they must be, in origin?

Mr. Miller in this play has joined the school of American playwrights (Saroyan, Thornton Wilder, Tennessee Williams) who are trying to break out of the constrictions of the naturalistic play form while at the same time retaining the realist contemporary subject. It is an attempt to make a poetic approach to every day life without using poetry—or even heightened speech. The characters are to remain as inarticulate as they are in real life; the "poetry" is to be supplied by symbols, by the handling, the time-switches, the lighting; the production, in short, is expected to do most of the work of evoking the heightened mood. Thus the Salesman of this play is living in a three-roomed Brooklyn house with his wife and two gone-to-the-bad sons. The stage design for this is skeletal; we see all three rooms at once, and we see, even more important, looming up behind, the great lowering claustrophobic cliff of concrete skyscraper in which their living space is embedded. A highly effective design this, by Jo Mielziner. He is also responsible for the lighting which focuses our attention on one room or another as the little scenes shift to and fro. Or he may bring us to the front of the stage for the "flashbacks" into the idealised past when the boys were young and loved their father and he could still hope for himself and for them; and this is "symbolised" by the leafy fringe projected in these scenes by a lantern on to the backcloth, shutting out the barren city landscapes to which their lives have now been reduced.

Willy Loman, a travelling salesman is at the end of his career. He is only sixty, but his life is sagging. He is worn out, worn out with travelling and with hoping and promising. The hopes have never materialised, the promises haven't been fulfilled, the travels are coming to an end—he is to lose his job this day. He still talks by habit as if he believed in a future, in turning some corner, in its all coming right. But the talk has already begun to fail to convince even himself. It is on his elder son, Biff, that his highest hopes have always centred—Biff, who adored him too, who was the star of the school football team, who was excused all his faults, adored and worshipped (all shown us in flashbacks). Why is Biff now at thirty a failure, and why does he now hate his Pop? Why did he suddenly stop loving him somewhere around seventeen? And why, the boys themselves wonder—Biff and Happy spotlighted in their bedroom on the first floor—has the old man started to go to pieces? He talks to himself all the time now, and all the time about the past and Biff. And why does he keep smashing up the car? This at least their mother can tell them—he is trying to kill himself and it's their fault; he's old and tired and disappointed in them. It takes the first half of the play to get us so far. But after the interval the pace does begin to quicken, through a final disappointment in Biff, to the climactic reconciliation between father and son. This releases Willy Loman ("He likes me . . . He likes me . . . Remarkable, most remarkable")[1] to walk out and kill himself.

There is no doubt that this play, episodic and rather rambling as it is, has a certain power. It creates a world and takes us into it. It gives off the feel of sincerity; it has evidently been deeply, even solemnly felt. On the other hand it is altogether slighter than the author or the producer seems to have any idea of. The whole atmosphere in the theatre is heavily scented with self-importance. There is a sad lack of contrast; there is hardly one moment's relief. The little theme is made to take itself much too seriously. In this sense it is sentimental: all the time it is being made to live far above its emotional and intellectual station.

The slightness derives partly from the fact that there are only one and a half characters to carry us along. The wife and the younger brother are on stage much of the time, it is true. But

[1] Worsley here gets the substance of Willy's line without getting its rhythm: "Isn't that—isn't that remarkable? Biff—he likes me!"

they aren't worked. They are really stooges, each given a character—she the perfect wife, he a girl-hungry bum—but they have
no real part in the emotional texture of the drama. The elder
son, Biff, comes alive only on the occasions when he comes in
conflict with his father. Mr. Kevin McCarthy makes a very vivid
character then of the young man fighting through the densities
of the family optimism to try to discover himself behind them.
But conflict only rises in the last quarter of the play and meanwhile the burden has fallen, too heavily, on Mr. Paul Muni as
the salesman. I don't quite see what more he could have done
for this character than he has, except perhaps to hasten the pace
and insist on cutting his part. He gets the shallow, weak charm
perfectly, the craving to be liked, the intoxication of optimism
and the shuffle and sag of failure. But he has to go on repeating
these without either words or actions to help him. In the end it
gets repetitious. We begin to shift in our seats, even while we
admire.

A contributory cause for this is the episodic time-switching
and place-switching. A friend of mine said to me recently of this
school of playwrights: They've discovered the secret of American audiences who, when they are in the theatre, would much
rather be in the cinema. These devices belong to the cinema
(and even at the cinema we have begun to groan when the
flashbacks start). The playwright's ace is concentration of interest and the Unities are the principle behind that concentration.
These switches keep dispersing the tension, which then needs to
be laboriously built up again time after time. I hope this play
will demonstrate to young playwrights here the barrenness of
such tricks.

But in the end it all boils down to one thing only—words.
Poetry is made with words; and in the poetic approach, nothing
but words will in the last analysis bring success. Mr. Kazan may
produce as brilliantly as he likes; he may bring out every device
of lighting, grouping, stylising, timing and designing to evoke
the play's moods. But none of them is an adequate substitute
for the words which just aren't there.

WILLIAM BEYER

William Beyer has taught at Drew University, Rutgers University, Columbia University, and Indiana University, and is Professor of English at Butler University. He is the author of *Keats and the Daemon King* and *The Enchanted Forest*.

THE STATE OF THE THEATRE:
THE SEASON OPENS

. . . According to all reports, the touring company of Miller's *Death of a Salesman*, starring Thomas Mitchell, is as distinguished and successful as the New York cast, starring Lee J. Cobb, and the London production with Paul Muni. An added distinction is the fact that The Viking Press published version of the play is rated a dual choice of the Book-of-the-Month Club. *Death of a Salesman* is a powerful and absorbing play, pithy and dynamic, and it is as engrossing reading as it is when seen played. We got the printed play before we saw the production and in some respects enjoyed the reading of it more than seeing it. *Death of a Salesman* is the revealing, touching narrative of a pathetic little man in the social scale, Willy Loman, an aging traveling salesman from Brooklyn, who loses his way in life, as so many men do, by mistaking false illusions for sound ideals, and who ruins himself in his diligent, blind pursuit of this immature gamble. The spurious values Willy freely elects to live by slowly undermine and eventually destroy him. The climax of his inglorious and fraudulent existence is precipitated by the sudden return of his elder son, Biff, broke as usual, from one of his periodic treks, "bumming," as his despairing mother puts it. Obviously a neurotic love between father and son is the basis of Biff's social maladjustment, for, since he worships and

From *School and Society*, LXX (December 3, 1949), pp. 363–364, reprinted by permission of *School and Society*. The "Salesman" review was only one item in a theatrical round-up, pp. 360–364.

seeks to emulate his father, he, too, never matures and so gambles on false illusions. Willy, boastful but unsuccessful "drummer" though he is at sixty-three, has never conceded his failure, nor has his devoted wife ever admitted it, and he still strives to "get by" on "a smile and a shoeshine." Willy has brought up his sons to follow the same superficial approach to life and has encouraged them in petty dishonesty and duplicity to gain their ends. He has, meanwhile, persisted stubbornly in brassily expounding his dubious code, cultivating spurious Rotarian camaraderie and striving only to maintain a "front." Characteristically enough, he has only a shrug and a wink for moral and spiritual values and substitutes cozy sentimentalities in their place. Compared to Biff, the tramp at thirty-four, Happy, also a bachelor in his thirties, has become a "Big Shot," a seventy-five-dollar-a-week merchandizing man, who ignores his aging father's plight and spends his money on women and liquor. Only when the repeated threat of Willy's suicide is uncovered do the two men, on their mother's frantic insistence, make a gesture to put the family on its feet. They concoct a hairbrained adolescent scheme, another one of the Loman pipe-dreams, but Biff, as usual, fumbles the ball, while Willy loses his position altogether. The situation explodes before the eyes of the gentle, helpless mother, and the family cracks up—Willy going to a suicide's grave, Biff to further aimless wandering, and Happy to his drink and dames. The last scene, at Willy's grave, is made eloquent by the devoted woman, capable of real nobility, who loves and loses her three men.

Miller has produced a challenging drama in *Death of a Salesman*, and it is a provocative, moving, and occasionally eloquent play which makes pertinent comment on the decadent values in our society. The play's structure drives its narrative home with emotional impact since Miller uses the familiar screen and radio technique. The play begins and ends in one basic setting, the Loman home, and flash-backs in the popular stream-of-consciousness style clarify the present dilemma in terms of past relevancies. Musical bridges between scenes dovetail them neatly together, for the music, being used thematically, is mood provoking and blends perfectly with the structure, which is organically valid and an artistic triumph. Sound craftsmanship is a commonplace in our theatre, but artistic creation is indeed a rarity, and Miller has achieved the latter here, which makes both the playwright and the play eventful. Psychologically, this neurotic father-son romance is for the greater part true, only once does it seem invalid to us, when Biff, as a youth, cracks up on finding his father intimate with a strange woman. As a basis to the neurosis Biff's reaction is inevitable, but when it turns instead on Biff's loyalty to his mother, for whom he has never indicated preference, only acceptance, it makes a stumbling block of what should be the cornerstone to the play's structure.

The play, it strikes us, is essentially the mother's tragedy, not Willy Loman's. Willy's plight is sad, true, but he is unimportant and too petty, commonplace, and immature to arouse more than pity, and the sons are of a piece with their father. Their aims, having been limited to their reach, stunt their stature as men and the subsequent impact of their failures on us. We can only sympathize since they reflect human frailties all too common among men. Within her circumscribed sphere of living, however, the mother makes of her love a star which her idealism places on high, and when it is destroyed her heavens are wiped out. What the mother stands for is important, and when she goes down the descent is tragic.

The superior quality of the play is fully matched in the expertness of Elia Kazan's sensitive and fluid direction, and there are brilliant performances given by Lee J. Cobb, as Willy Loman; Arthur Kennedy, as Biff; and Mildred Dunnock, as Mrs. Loman, with fine support by the rest of the company. Jo Mielziner's setting is striking and succeeds in enveloping the play with a romantic and nostalgic aura.

Essays on *Death of a Salesman*

JOHN GASSNER

John Gassner, theater historian and critic, taught at the University of Michigan, Columbia University, and Queens College, and for eleven years was Sterling Professor of Playwriting and Dramatic Literature at Yale University. He was the author of, among other books, *Masters of the Drama, Theatre at the Crossroads: Plays and Playwrights on the Mid-Century American Stage*, and *Directions in Modern Theatre and Drama*, and editor of many others, including *The Treasury of the Theatre* and the *Best American Plays* series.

DEATH OF A SALESMAN:
FIRST IMPRESSIONS, 1949

By far the most noteworthy contribution of the entire season was *Death of a Salesman,* winner of the Drama Critics Circle and Pulitzer awards, and a success of imposing proportions. The play inspired a triumphant production the equal of which it would be difficult to find in any other theatrical capital, so far as we can tell, except Paris. This drama also climaxed the young career of a playwright, Arthur Miller, whose emotional power and skill would have been received with respect anywhere since

From *The Theatre in Our Times* by John Gassner (New York: Crown Publishers, 1954), pp. 368–373, Copyright 1954 by John Gassner, reprinted by permission of Crown Publishers, Inc. and the author. The volume reprints two appraisals of the play, both written in 1949, of which this is the second. It first appeared, in slightly different form, as a contribution to one of Gassner's "Aspects of the Broadway Theatre" columns in *The Quarterly Journal of Speech*, XXXV (February 1949), 289–294.

the advent of prose realism. As projected in the theatre by Elia Kazan's roughly tender direction and Jo Mielziner's functional design, *Death of a Salesman* impressed most play reviewers as a superb work of art. Broadway superlatives are even more suspect than Broadway pejoratives, and both often conceal as much as they reveal. We must look closer at the play, therefore, if we are to understand its character and its place in our theatre.

The play is not quite the masterpiece of dramatic literature that the enthusiasts would have us believe. It is well written but is not sustained by incandescent or memorable language except in two or three short passages. Moreover, its hero, the desperate salesman Willy Loman, is too much the loud-mouthed dolt and emotional babe-in-the-woods to wear all the trappings of high tragedy with which he has been invested. For modern writers of the school of Molière and Shaw, Willy would have been an object of satirical penetration rather than mournful tenderness and lachrymose elegy. By contrast with contemporary dramatists of a poetic grain like O'Neill, Williams, and Anderson, Mr. Miller has written his story on the level of *drame bourgeois*. Although his intellect denies assent to the main character's fatuous outlook, some commonplaceness attends the sentiments of the writing, the overvaluation of Willy as a hero, and the selection of a bumptiously kind-hearted bourgeois, Charley, as the proper foil for the unsuccessful salesman. Charley is the model of right living because he was practical-minded and made a success of his business, and because his son Bernard married and became a lawyer who is now on his way to Washington to argue a case and takes his tennis rackets along, presumably to hobnob with successful people. No one in the play stands for values that would not gain the full approval of Bruce Barton and Dale Carnegie, in spite of the fact that their philosophy is shown to be invalid for Willy and Biff. The Promethean soul is mute in *Death of a Salesman*. The mind and the spirit that manifest themselves in it are rather earth-bound and not in themselves interesting.

Once these reservations are made, however, one cannot deny that the play has singular merits, that it is often moving and even gripping, that it is penetrative both in characterization and in social implication. It expresses a viewpoint of considerable importance when it exposes the delusions of "go-getting," "contacts"—inebriated philistinism by reducing it to the muddle of Willy's life, which is surely not an isolated case.

Miller has written a play remarkably apposite to an aspect of American life, and the audiences that are held by it and the many playgoers who are moved to tears pay him the tribute of recognition. Their interest and sympathy are engaged by the pathos of a man who gave all his life to a business only to be thrown on the scrap-heap, a householder whose pattern of life was interwoven with instalment plans with which he could hardly catch up, a doting father disappointed in his children, and an American *naïf* bemused by the worship of uncreative success and hollow assumptions that "personality" is the *summum bonum*.

A notable feature of the effectiveness of *Death of a Salesman* is that the author's judgments are not delivered down to the playgoer from some intellectual eminence but stem almost entirely from close identification with the outlook and thought-processes of the characters. This probably explains all that I find intrinsically commonplace in this otherwise powerful play. The playwright is not "outside looking in" but "inside looking out," and at least for the purposes of immediate effect it is less pertinent that he is not looking very far out than that he is so convincingly and sensitively inside his subject. Largely for this reason, too, Miller has also given the American theatre of social criticism its most unqualified success, for that theatre, ever since the nineteen-thirties when it became a distinct mode of playwriting, has tended to be argumentative and hortatory. (One can be argumentative, of course, if the brilliance of a Bernard Shaw infuses the argument with lambent intellection; and one can be hortatory, too, as in Shaw's speeches and Aristophanes' *parabases*, when fervor is not dulled by sociology. But one can hardly posit such qualities for most social drama in our time.) Instead of debating issues or denouncing Willy's and his society's errors, Miller simply demonstrates these in the life of his characters. He confines himself, moreover, to the particulars of normal behavior and environment, and nothing that Willy or his family does or says betrays the playwright as the inventor of special complications for the purpose of social agitation. The play does not even set up a conflict between two distinctly different sets of values, which, as I have indicated earlier, is in some respects a limitation of the work, as well as a merit. Even Charley's view of life which is contrasted to Willy's life is only a sensible conversion of it (it is merely a sensible materialism), and no challenging conversion by a character leads us out of the middle-class world. Willy's son Biff surmounts his father's attitude only in acquiring self-knowledge and resigning himself to being just an ordinary, dollar-an-hour citizen. Arthur Miller, in short, has accomplished the feat of writing a drama critical of wrong values and misguided conduct. It stabs itself into a playgoer's consciousness to a degree that may well lead him to review his own life and the lives of those who are closest to him. The conviction of the writing is, besides, strengthened by a quality of compassion rarely experienced in our theatre. One must be either extraordinarily snobbish or exceptionally obtuse to stand aloof from the play.

The virtues of *Death of a Salesman*, as well as the shortcomings, most of which are not likely to be apparent to most playgoers while the play is in progress, belong to the American theatre. They epitomize its norm of versimilitude, identification with the *dramatis personae*, and an objectivity midway between sentimentality and European ironic detachment.[1] These are democratic qualities, and the artistry of Miller's work is nothing if it is not democratic. Our most successful and substantial theatre, ever since the early experimental days of the Provincetown Playhouse, the Washington Players, and the Neigh-

---

[1] We can find that detachment virtually since *commedia dell' arte*, if not earlier, and there are excellent examples of it since Machiavelli's *Mandragola* and the comedies of Molière to Becque's *The Vultures* and Carl Sternheim's plays. In the American drama, ironic detachment crops up rarely; it does in Lillian Hellman's plays and has been viewed with some misgivings, as may be seen from the New York reviewers' critical reaction to *Another Part of the Forest*. [J.G.]

borhood Playhouse, has tended to be neither lowbrow nor highbrow; it has been almost inviolately "middlebrow."

There is, nevertheless, a world of difference between the average middle-class drama, so notably devoid of force and imagination, and *Death of a Salesman*. The latter impresses us as a triumph of poetic realism and it holds our attention as in a vise, and how this is possible in the case of a play so confined to the commonplaces of life is worth examining. It may throw light on what our dramatists can do, and often fail to do, with the realistic subject matter and dramaturgy to which they are devoted. It is a question of transmutation within the boundaries of realism, as may be gathered from the fact that there is hardly anything even in the reminiscent scenes, as the play alternates between actual scenes in the present and remembered ones, which is poetic or fantastic. The sole exception comes toward the end when Willy discusses his intended suicide with his elder brother Ben, who is now a figment of Willy's mind. When we call the play imaginative we must distinguish it, in the main, from such pieces as *Emperor Jones*, *The Hairy Ape*, *The Skin of Our Teeth*, and *The Madwoman of Chaillot*. Essentially, Miller affirms realism in the very process of transcending it. Most imaginative efforts to surmount humdrum realism in our theatre have either stylized or poeticized their matter. For all its ingenuity, *Death of a Salesman* does not seem noticeably "stylized" and is certainly not "literary."

Most decisive is the transmutation of the story itself, and with this a transformation of the character posited for Willy. An ordinary playwright would have regaled us with a lengthy recital of Willy's misfortunes as a superannuated white collar worker immolated on the Moloch of the business machine once his usefulness had ended. In Miller's treatment this is a subordinate part of the story, the main feature of which is the struggle between Willy and his son Biff, so that the pathos of failure is pitched higher than the sociological level. Miller had the wisdom to justify our concern with his blatant hero by making the wheel of the drama revolve around the one attribute that makes Willy extraordinary without being flagrantly atypical. My criticism that the play overvaluates a vacuous individual requires this important qualification: Willy, who is otherwise so unimpressive, is translated into a father for whom the love and success of his favorite son Biff is a paramount necessity and a consuming passion. He has been made into a dramatically charged father-hero, and as such becomes a heroic figure in active pursuit of the father-son ideal. He may be a fool, but he becomes a monolithic figure of some tragic dimension in this respect. This man who is a failure even as a bourgeois recalls somewhat the obsessed and self-consumed heroes of Elizabethan tragedy. Miller has created an intensification of humanity that lifts the drama above the level of the humdrum.

A second intensification is provided by Miller's over-all dramaturgic method. We are most familiar in our theatre with simple *horizontal* and simple *vertical* play building. The former is generally reserved for chronicles of famous lives and historical events, as in *Abe Lincoln in Illinois, Abraham Lincoln,* and *Victoria Regina.* It has not been employed successfully in American or English treatments of historically unimportant characters, so far as I can recall, except in *Milestones* and *Cavalcade,* and here at least the situations possessed historical importance. The vertical type of progression, however, has been standard in our drama. This type of play starts with some intention or plan on the part of a character, the character becomes embroiled in conflict as he tries to effectuate his desire, and ultimately, in the course of spiraling complications related to each other in accordance with the law of cause and effect, there are decisive consequences. Good examples of this procedure are provided by such comparatively recent plays as *The Little Foxes, Golden Boy, All My Sons, State of the Union,* and *Born Yesterday,* and quite as obviously by many other recent and older plays that have succeeded. Nevertheless, this technique has more often than not only exaggerated the defects of the average realistic play ever since the days of Dumas *fils.* The playgoer has been compelled to follow the unstimulating course of some commonplace individual capable of only humdrum desires and utterance forming an intention, then proceeding to encompass it and encountering opposition in ways that are either expected and therefore humdrum or unexpected and therefore likely to be contrived. It is noteworthy that Ibsen, who intensified the material of realism, also intensified its technique by adopting retrospective exposition and starting his realistic plays close to the crisis of the story. But most playwrights have lacked the highly dramatic feeling and imagination required by this procedure.

The point of attack in *Death of a Salesman* comes very near the turning point of the play. Miller's method is, moreover, not merely effectively vertical but at the same time circular—in the sense that the action starts with an already trapped individual and merely snaps the ring round him. The paramount question we are forced to ask of the play is not the usual "What is going to happen next?", "Will the hero win or lose?" or "How will his plan work out?"—questions to which a commonplace life in a commonplace situation can give only uninteresting answers. The important question, since the hero's fate is sealed from the beginning, is rather "What is really the matter and why?"— a question that points to basic realities. And if we are also bound to inquire "What more is going to happen?" the answer can be meaningful only in terms of answers to the prior question. Willy, a sixty-three-year-old salesman who no longer trusts himself to drive his car, comes back to his Brooklyn home instead of going on his prescribed trip. His sons decide to go into business and the older and more errant one, Biff, intends to ask a former employer, Oliver, for a loan, while Willy resolves to ask his employer for "an inside job." Willy is fired instead as a superannuated employee and Biff does not get a loan, disappearing instead with Oliver's fountain pen because petty thievery has been ingrained in him since boyhood. The disappointed Willy goes home in a distracted condition and kills himself. Out of these meager external materials, Miller has fashioned a comprehensive drama by pushing inward into motives and causes. He has done so mainly by employing a memory pattern by means of flashbacks into Willy's past life which are largely Willy's encounters with his younger and more confident self. The published play is aptly subtitled "Certain private conversations in two acts and a requiem."

Still, the resort to flashbacks is by itself too familiar to be remarkable. Sheer dramatic skill is a third factor in Miller's transmutation of the story of a man who devoted his life to selling instead of creating, of a salesman type described by his understanding friend Charley as "a man way out there in the blue, riding on a smile and a shoeshine" who is undone when people start not smiling back. I can only note here approvingly with respect to the flashbacks that each reminiscence springs from a *tension* in Willy. The reminiscence is not hurled at us as necessary information but presented as a compulsive act on Willy's part. In several instances, and especially in the crucial scene in which Willy recalls that his son's failure is largely the result of his having found him with a strange woman in a Boston hotel, the memory scene does not arise at once but crystallizes out of fluid and half-formed thoughts. In addition, it is noteworthy that no recollection is allowed to leave the play in a state of stasis. Not only does the over-all action move a step forward after such episodes, but these are both preceded and followed by bursts of conflict between Willy or the mother and the boys. Miller has, in addition, overcome stasis by a steady climb of discovery and revelation. If it is the nature of Willy to go to his death unenlightened, the son with whom he has identified his destiny wrings understanding out of his own and his father's predicaments, putting pretense aside.

These achievements, in sum, are vastly more important and harder to come by than the highly touted external means employed by the author—namely, the alternation of imagined and actual scenes well distributed and well lit on the stage space, and augmented by eerie off-stage flute music. The dramaturgic means are more effective, too, than attempts at symbolism in such details as Willy's small house being overshadowed by the apartment houses that grew up around it so that he can no longer grow anything in his backyard garden and more effective than the shadowy figure of Willy's elder brother Ben, the adventurer who employed jungle tactics in his pursuit of wealth and came out of the African jungle with a diamond mine in his possession. On closer examination, in fact, we may find Ben, who represents the spirit of social Darwinism or *laissez-faire*, an adventitious figure, theatrically effective but dramatically suspect as a motif. There is little doubt, then, that *Death of a Salesman*, praised though it be as a work of theatrical imagination, is essentially a victory for modern realism.

A. HOWARD FULLER

A. Howard Fuller was president of the Fuller Brush Company from 1943 to 1959.

A SALESMAN IS EVERYBODY

To be moved by a play and to comprehend it fully are two different things. It stands to reason that any real work of art admits of several interpretations and that the individual's subjective response will enter largely into his choice.

I was particularly moved by these lines spoken by Charley in the requiem:

Willy was a salesman; and for a salesman, there is no rock bottom to the life. He don't put a bolt to a nut, he don't tell you the law, or give you medicine. He's a man way out there in the blue, riding on a smile and a shoeshine; and when they start not smiling back— boy, that's an earthquake . . .

It has always seemed to me that in peacetime the professional salesman is the real hero of American society, the cutting edge of a free competitive economy who cheerfully exposes himself to the slings and arrows of outrageous fortune in order to present to the public new ideas embodied in the innumerable products constantly being produced by industry. This in many instances has been a thankless task. And yet out of just such enterprise

---

From *Fortune*, XXXIX (May 1949), pp. 79–80, Copyright 1949 by Time, Inc., reprinted by permission of *Fortune* and the Fuller Brush Company. This is an analysis of Miller's play by a successful contemporary salesman. It might be interesting at this point to take a look at an excerpt from a book on salesmanship published at about the time Willy, had he been a real rather than a fictional character, would have taken to the road. See pp. 367–370. Notice that Moody recommends *enthusiasm*, the quality which was largely responsible for Willy's difficulties, according to Fuller, who also praises it with restraint.

there has arisen in America the highest standard of living, the most powerful economy the world has ever known.

If the salesman can properly be called the hero of American society, it would be difficult to discover a more fitting hero for a modern tragedy. For in a very real sense Willy, with his slogans and enthusiasms, is symbolic of the true spirit of a large, an important, and, one might say, a decisive segment of American life.

I am reminded of a recent advertisement appearing in the magazines depicting a traveling merchant of the last century who brought the products of mill and factory to the rural areas of the still only partly settled West. The copy accompanying this picture paid fitting tribute to the great contributions made by such salesmen to the growth and development of this country. Surely just such traveling salesmen as Willy are in the great American tradition.

But if the salesman is a hero of modern industry, it is inevitable that he should sometimes fail. It is in this sense that Willy becomes a fitting subject for treatment in a tragedy such as Mr. Miller's new play. For selling is a tough business, exposing those who follow it as a trade to both physical and psychological stress. It is inevitable, therefore, that some salesmen should fall by the wayside. Willy was just such a failure.

It would appear that Willy does not concern himself with modern scientific merchandising techniques, but he does display great enthusiasm, with all the advantages and dangers which that entails. Nowadays enthusiasm is generally considered a good quality. But in the days of John Locke it was regarded with great suspicion and rightly so. Enthusiasm is the driving force behind any human enterprise. No achievement is possible without it. It is like the fuel that drives an automobile. But useful and necessary as gasoline may be, it can become a force for evil unless handled with intelligence. It can destroy and kill, as well as produce useful power.

Willy's enthusiasm, which is manifested in the slogans he sets such great store by, is not governed by intelligence. Willy is essentially a self-deluded man who has lost the power to distinguish between reality and the obsessions that come to dominate his life. He is also a dishonest man for whom one god, which might be called popularity, could justify a multitude of sins. His greatest offense is against his older son Biff—it is this that finally destroys him.

This offense against Biff will bear with some analysis. There is the classical Oedipus complex angle of course, but since it is patently self-evident in the play it need not be considered here. The significant problem between Willy and his older son is a struggle for power. Under the guise of paternal affection Willy would make Biff over into his own image and likeness by fair means or foul. It is for this that Willy blinds himself to the reality that Biff is essentially unsuited to play the role he has prescribed for him. It is for this that he gradually sacrifices his own career and even has automobile accidents on the road. Finally it is for this that Willy kills himself.

In order to escape this paternal tyranny, Biff takes refuge in kleptomania—he goes out West and he unconsciously uses the discovery of his father's faithlessness in the Boston hotel room as an excuse for his general waywardness. The tragedy in the situation derives from the fact that Willy, blinded by his enthusiasm and the obsessions arising therefrom, cannot make himself realize what should have been self-evident, that Biff cannot play the role that he desires for him, that his reluctance is more than mere willfulness. It goes without saying that just such conflicts between fathers and sons are all too common in real life. The tragedy is deepened in the play by the fact that Linda, the mother, invariably sides with Willy in the pursuit of his obsession toward Biff. The younger brother, Happy, though less affected than Biff, is nonetheless the victim of the neglect of the father, whose chief concern is always directed toward Biff. Happy suffers, accordingly, a general moral decline. From first to last, Willy is prepared to sacrifice all scruples in favor of his great god, popularity.

Concerning this play Mr. Miller has said, "The fact that

Willy Loman is by trade a salesman is important, but secondary. Central is that he has taken on a new—a social—personality which is calculated to ensure his material success. In so doing he has lost his essential—his real—nature, which is contradictory to his assumed one, until he is no longer able to know what *he* truly wants, what *he* truly stands for. In that sense he has sold himself. Obviously, then, his being a salesman has a double significance. For me he represents the salesman as a class, because he does sell merchandise and his life is bound up in the facts of actual salesmanship. However, in the deeper, psychological sense, he is Everyman who finds he must create another personality in order to make his way in the world, and therefore has sold himself."[1]

Truly Willy does represent any man whose illusions have made him incapable of dealing realistically with the problems of everyday life. He has sold himself by taking on an artificial personality that is wholly unrealistic. In pursuit of his delusions he ruins not only his private life but his career as well.

Mr. Miller's use of the expression Everyman would seem to offer a real clue to the widespread popularity that this modern tragedy has enjoyed since its first presentation. Nearly everyone who sees it can discover some quality displayed by Willy and his sons that exists in himself and in his friends and relatives. It is this close identity between the audience and the characters that lends such poignancy to the tragedy. It cannot be duplicated by a modern audience when viewing the classical tragedies of the Greeks and Elizabethans.

---

[1] This quotation is not from Miller's published remarks on the play. It presumably comes from private conversation or from the talk Miller gave to Fuller's sales department.

IVOR BROWN

Ivor Brown, British critic and author, has been drama critic for *The Manchester Guardian* and *The Saturday Review* and editor and honorary director of *The Observer*, and is Chairman of The British Drama League. Among his books are *J. B. Priestley, How Shakespeare Spent the Day*, and *Shaw in His Time*.

AS LONDON SEES WILLY LOMAN

Before the production of *Death of a Salesman* there was considerable publicity about this smashing New York success. One critic, writing after the opening—as critics usually do—remarked that he seemed to be the only person who had not reviewed the play in advance. Roughly, the story was that New Yorkers were so overwhelmed by Arthur Miller's tragedy of the defeated salesman that they sat sniffling and even sobbing and staggered into the street with tear-streaked faces.

I understand there was a certain amount of ballyhoo in all this. New York was certainly hard hit by the piece and accepted it as a tremendous and typical tragedy of a typical national figure; but that the flooded floors of the theatre had to be mopped up after tearful sessions is not true. It is a pity that so much was written in advance and such exaggeration used.

From the box-office point of view I doubt whether the insistently repeated information that a play has knocked the audience all of a heap in another metropolis is prudent. The recipients of the news are apt to say grimly, "Now let them

From *The New York Times Magazine* (August 28, 1949), pp. 11, 59, Copyright © 1949 by The New York Times Company, reprinted by permission of The New York Times Company and Ivor Brown. If Laurence Kitchin is correct, ten years after Brown found Willy Loman an uncongenial hero for English audiences, England had caught up with Miller's play; for Kitchin, Willy's preoccupation with things is particularly relevant to the England in which he writes. See Laurence Kitchin, *Mid-Century Drama* (London: Faber & Faber, 1960), p. 63.

show us," thus seeming to imply, "We're not simpletons or cry-babies. They won't get us fainting in the stalls."

When *Death of a Salesman* was given in London it was received with fair ovation and mainly respectful, appreciative notices. But I saw no signs of emotional collapse in the audience; nor have I heard of any since. What was praised was the imaginative staging and performance of a moving play about a poor, flashy, self-deceiving little man. Moving—but not overwhelming.

There were cheers for Paul Muni but no tears for Willy Loman, central figure of the play. I doubt whether one extra handkerchief has been sold by the haberdashers of the neighborhood.

Why the astonishing impact of this play upon Broadway? One point that has been made is that Americans can identify themselves with Willy because his outlook is so largely theirs, whatever his faults may have been. This matter of self-identification with the person or the story is, I think, very important in establishing success.

In Britain we notice it particularly in the case of radio characters. There are several family sagas which are given regular space on the air—"The McFlannels" in Scotland and Dr. Dale and his family of "Mrs. Dale's Diary" in England. Mrs. Dale comes on in the afternoons and there is dead silence for the "ordinary adventures of herself and her family" in myriads of parlors, kitchens and workshops.[1]

Let one of these chronicles be long enough established and public opinion will not allow it to be stopped. It just has to go on and on. Myriads of women are identifying themselves with Mrs. Dale. One proof of this close affection is that presents arrive at BBC marked for Mrs. Dale, not for the actress playing the part.

In Arthur Miller's character study, Willy Loman is carefully labeled a salesman. The word has more value in the United

---

[1] These are English soap operas. At this point, Brown is being nastier about Miller's play than his matter-of-fact, informational style suggests.

States than in Britain. Remember that Britain since 1939 has needed workers and buyers rather than drummers. Now, of course, it needs as never before salesmanship abroad. But at home the supply of goods was still so short until a year ago that little competitive salesmanship was needed. Rivalry is getting keen again but the commercial traveler, as we call the drummer, has never been the figure in English life that he has been in America. So this title, "Death of a Salesman," strikes home less strongly. There is not the same sense of a national type.

Then Willy has a pathetic faith in being liked. Here again Arthur Miller seems to have seized on an essential feature of American psychology. You cannot sell a book by the million in Britain by giving advice on how to make friends and so gain influence. Willy, in the play, reflects over and over again his belief that he is beloved of buyers and that to be beloved is to be a success. "The wonder of this country is that a man can end with diamonds on the basis of being liked."

Whether this is true of the United States, it is certainly untrue of England. We regard the very likeable fellow as one who will end in the way he began: Not starving, not a plutocrat, just making do. The diamond-set class are the unlikable—or at least so people think. We're suspicious of popularity hunters, the man with a fixed smile and a quip always ready. In the North especially a salesman would do much better if he were regarded as "Jannock" (i.e., genuine) than as "the life of the party."

Not that we austerely avoid or snub the good companion; we just don't think that he will get very far unless he's a good deal more than that.

This throws some light on the failure of Willy Loman to draw tears by the gallon from British eyes. The British are likely to despise Loman for an outlook on life (smiles into diamonds) which other nations regard as quite natural. And if you despise a man you naturally don't become frantically upset by his downfall.

Willy's fatal adulation of his supposedly wonderful sons is also outside British sympathy. Of course, there are doting par-

ents who spoil their children everywhere. But Loman's silly
encouragement of his boys to be "sports," which turns one of
them into a seedy seducer and the other into a drifting law-
breaker, is perhaps less intelligible in England than elsewhere,
despite our national taste for games.

At certain social levels, Britain may be called sport crazy. But
the majority keep their sense of values.

Again Loman's hunger for success through popularity makes
less appeal to British compassion since the way of life in Britain
is obviously less competitive. That Britain has gone too far in
its search for equality at the expense of liberty is my own opinion and that of millions of others, too. But whether right or
wrong, the fact is that while British parents like their boys and
girls to do well, they are chiefly eager to seek security for them
by finding jobs at the bottom of the ladder in big business or
in teaching or in civil service—a ladder up which it will be easy
to climb gradually if no silly mistakes are made.

This preoccupation with security is doubtless a natural weakness. But there it is, and those who value steady plodding
instead of success hunting by the good-at-games and smile-on-
your-buddy methods of Lomanism will hardly be struck with
horror when the little man is finally ruined by a tough employer.
This fellow applies the tests of success without mercy to
Loman's own inadequate performance as an aging salesman.

I take from my American friends the information that New
York has a very large and hard core of unhappiness at the heart
of it. This is attributed to the immense drive of a vast nation,
a great many of whose more ambitious members want to get to
Manhattan. Since everybody in New York cannot have the best
jobs or even good ones, and since pressure from the outside
continues unabated, many of the incomers must experience
frustration and disappointment.

Loman of Brooklyn is a typical New Yorker of the Failure
Fringe. He hasn't "made it" and he has bluffed and dodged to
pretend that he has. His wife sees through him, his brother-in-
law gives him doles, and still he bluffs. Still he masquerades as
a success. Pathetic? Yes, but its pathos is more easily recogniza-

ble in Brooklyn than in Balham.[2] Loman cannot fill the British playgoer with the compassion due a next door neighbor because he is not a Londoner's neighbor at all. He is just the subject of an efficient and well-acted play which one goes to see dispassionately, praises and before long forgets.

What has puzzled me about these Broadway tears for Willy Loman is the fact that the average shedder of those tears over a stage figure couldn't be bothered for one minute with Willy Loman if the poor little man came round in real life to beg a small loan. I don't say that he would grudge Loman the money, for Americans are uncommonly generous, but he would grudge him sympathy for Americans are quite ready to be tough. After all, there is almost nothing to be said for Loman, who lies to himself as to others, has no creed or philosophy of life beyond that of making money by making buddies, and cannot even be faithful to his helpful and long-suffering wife.

It occurred to me that New York's emotional response to the salesman whose leaving of life (modestly to enrich his family with insurance money) is his lonely piece of good conduct, may be due to a wide subconscious feeling that the fate of failure is too hard. The large, hard core of unhappiness is made to seem actual by the fictitious personage of Loman. So those who in their offices would brush him aside as just one more shabby and ineffective nuisance among a million may be sitting in their expensive seats to pay him the tribute of a sigh, even of a tear, since he is the symbol of all those failures on which alone success can be built.

Though some London critics declared themselves unmoved by *Death of a Salesman*, it is certainly a skillful piece of stagecraft, and the production deserves unreserved applause. It suits the mood of the time, both here and in America, because it makes the little man the hero. In that respect both publics are alike.

There are many points of psychological detail in which

---

[2] A district of London, largely residential. There may be some comparison between Balham and Brooklyn, but I suspect that Brown chose Balham (rather than, say, Fulham or Clapham) for the alliteration.

Loman is a stranger to British playgoers. But now the little man is everywhere the center of attraction and of sympathy. Thus news interest and a good production have been filling the Phoenix Theatre constantly.

Both nations accept the change of taste about suitable characters for tragedy. The classic hero, the Elizabethan hero, had to be a man of might, power and position. He fell because of some flaw in his character. The fall was greater because he was himself great. He was not a clown tumbling off his chair: he was a king crashing tremendously from his throne.

But now on both sides of the Atlantic we have stool tragedies, not throne tragedies. It is the clerk, not the king, who inspires the tragedian, Loman not Highman who throws Broadway into compassionate lamentation.

London too will like that. We recently had from the all-conquering Terence Rattigan a tragedy about the globe-trotting Alexander the Great.[3] It was not one of his box-office victories. Alexander the Great touches few hearts nowadays. But Loman the Little? There I think Britain and the United States are on common ground.

For that reason London support for the play has been abundant so far. The Age of the Common Man is the Age of the Shrimp, and Loman, because he pretends to be a prawn,[4] is really just a little shrimp. And nowadays we all are a dish of shrimps. The nations, not united on much, are at least united on that.

---

[3] *Adventure Story*, which opened at St. James's Theatre, March 17, 1949.

[4] In England, the prawn (our shrimp) is much larger than the crustacean the English call shrimp.

DANIEL E. SCHNEIDER, M.D.

Daniel Schneider, M.D., practicing psychoanalyst and author, has taught at the American Institute of Psychoanalysis and lectured at the University of Michigan and Columbia University. Among his books are *They Move with the Sun* and *The Psychoanalysis of Heart Attack*.

[PLAY OF DREAMS]

There are plays that remain with us a lifetime, like dreams that keep coming back again and again. Often one finds oneself saying: "I had a dream some time ago that I don't seem to be able to forget. And, what's more, I seem to be dreaming it over and over, each time a little different. But it's the same old familiar mysterious dream."

A powerful play has this same effect on us. It is perhaps the most compelling reason why we return many times to *Hamlet*. For a great work of art is as has already been indicated in this book, a dream turned inside out; a brilliant perception and portrayal of the impossible and impermissible ways in which we hurl ourselves against reality and, failing, dream out action and consequence as we sleep in our own inner universe of wishes.

From *The Psychoanalyst and the Artist* by Daniel Schneider (New York: Farrar, Straus and Co., 1950), pp. 246–255, Copyright 1950 by Daniel Schneider, reprinted by permission of International Universities Press. The analysis of "Salesman" forms part of Chapter Ten, "A Modern Playwright —Study of Two Plays by Arthur Miller," which devotes several pages (241–245) to *All My Sons*. Although Schneider's discussion of Miller is built on his examination of the two plays, the separate sections stand alone; the "Sons" references in the "Salesman" discussion are clear in context. The title used here is the one employed in *Theatre Arts*, XXXIII (October 1949), pp. 18–21, where the "Salesman" material appeared in a slightly modified form. When Miller was asked how he felt about Schneider's interpretation, he had the wit to say, "Impossible to 'agree' or 'disagree,' because I do not know my subconscious well enough." Quoted, W. David Sievers, *Freud on Broadway* (New York: Hermitage House, 1955), p. 395.

Sometimes it is a pleasant dream, like being magically able to fly. More often it has the quality of Arthur Miller's *Death of a Salesman*. More often it reveals the whole purpose of dreaming, night or day: to avoid pain, to repair the frustrations and humiliations of everyday life with which the common man is so familiar, and of which he is so frightened that he tries to glide over them, hoping that they won't add up into a seemingly ultimate, inevitable sum of exhaustion, despair and disillusionment.

It *is* like Willy Loman (low-man?) trying to keep up with the "maniac" of a refrigerator whose cost of operation eats up the very food it is designed to preserve, or like the twenty-five-year mortgage on the house which is empty of its sons by the time the father has paid for it literally with his life—and life insurance. The maniacal refrigerator, the life-sentencing mortgage, the ironic insurance: these things take on the aspect of sardonic gods of the mountain. They are symbols of one theme of the play—that describing a society in which man is a wandering peddler lured from reality by the pink clouds of magic sales talk; a world in which the burden of parenthood is enormous and where the common man has nothing to sell but himself, his pride, his youth.

The play begins with the classical requirement that its protagonist be at a turning-point in his life. And, as in the silver tree of Miller's earlier and excellent *All My Sons*, there is at the outset a cogent symbolization of the substance of the play: the Salesman comes home carrying wearily the two battered, black sample cases which are his cross. They are like the two sons he has carried through life; they are a burden we want him to set down with honor, but we sense almost at once that they are to be his coffin. It is obvious from his first words that he has lost command of them just as he has lost control of his sons, control of his car, control of his mind. The axe of final castration—insanity and suicide—has begun to fall. And, for a very definite reason, we learn at the beginning that his older brother Ben, the man who adventured and struck it rich, is dead. Ben becomes an increasingly obsessive vision to his disintegrating mind.

The form of his play is not that of "flashback" technique, though it has been described as such. It is rather the same technique as that of *Hamlet*: the technique of psychic projection, of hallucination, of the guilty expression of forbidden wishes dramatized.

Willy Loman, exhausted salesman, does not go back to the past. The past, as in hallucination, comes back to him; not chronologically as in flashback, but *dynamically with the inner logic of his erupting volcanic unconscious*. In psychiatry we call this "the return of the repressed," when a mind breaks under the invasion of primitive impulses no longer capable of compromise with reality.

To assess the extent to which the dramatization of the repressed makes the play, strip it of its hallucinatory exposition. Then the play is a dull picture of a broken-down, loud-mouthed, not too bright or presentable braggart of a salesman who comes home, irritable at his diminishing powers, disappointed in his sons, coddled by his wife who is full of solace but empty of excitement; a worn-out old man jealous of his relative's (next-door) success, and unable to obtain a more sedentary job better suited to his state of impending collapse. In the process of realization of his decay he quarrels with his badly brought-up sons, the older one (Biff) by now a petty thief and wanderer returned home, and the younger one (Hap) a rather dull, loud Babbitt who, very much like his father before him, has a deep sense of inferiority with respect to his older brother, and "knocks over the babes" and is "making good" as a salesman in a department store, but spends most of his money on the babes and his own apartment, a Lord-Salesman in embryo. Enough to make any father, even dimly aware of his faults, think of the futility of living and contemplate the gas-pipe.

But put back the hallucinatory experience and the play sings and shines. A lucidity is imparted to every gesture of the disintegrating Willy Loman. *It is visualized psychoanalytic interpretation woven into reality*. For example, near the end of the last act Willy comes out of the washroom of the restaurant, and is found on his knees by a waiter who cannot understand what is beautifully clear to the audience. For the audience has just shared Willy's hallucination of a scene of years ago, in which his son Biff caught him in a hotel room with a woman. Willy on his knees, shouting "I gave you an order, Biff!" creates an effect of great power placed next to the fact that his sons have just walked out on him to pursue a couple of chance women. Pounding his fist on the floor as he re-enacts the repressed scene of pleading with his son to forgive him for sexual philandering, Willy hammers at the present on the anvil of the past.

It is in this way that the magnificent transitions in *Death of a Salesman* are achieved. The first act moves from despair to false hope—false because we know right from the beginning that there is too much hatred (and similarity) between father and sons for the hope to be fulfilled. The older son Biff is too twisted ever to help the father set down his burden with honor. So too, the second act moves from a vestige of love to an orgy of hate, pity, and death.

The question arises as to what premise, in common with that of *All My Sons*, requires this particular dramatic form. When we examine its material we become aware that the same deep psychologic conflict dominates both plays. In both plays the sons become disillusioned with the father.

We must pursue the inner psychological theme. Willy Loman is not in the eyes of his sons just a man, but a god in decay. To his first son Biff, Willy was a god who would protect him from all misdemeanor, who could "fix" even a failure in mathematics; to his sons, Willy Loman was Salesman-Lord of New England. It is this illusion of sexless godhood that is shattered when Biff at seventeen comes to Boston on a surprise mission (to get his father to "fix" a math failure) and catches Willy with a lusty woman, then breaks down, weeps, and walks out on his father who is on his knees pleading for forgiveness, understanding, and lost godhood. This is the repressed scene of infidelity and smashed authority dramatized in the restaurant.

What theme is this? At what point does a son recognize finally and for all time that a father is not a sexless god but a

sexual man, prone to every human temptation? It is a variation
of the Oedipus theme, a variation which says: *he who pretends
to godhood over me must fulfill his godhood or be revealed as a
madman.*

Follow the second act from this point of view, and it is sheer
murder of a father by "all his sons"—an irrational Oedipal
blood-bath given seeming rationalization by the converging
social theme of the worn-out salesman. Willy Loman is really
brought low in this second act. Blow after blow descends upon
him until, symbolically castrated, shouting madly he is forced to
his knees, to pounding on the floor.

He is told he is no good as a salesman and never was—by his
dead boss's son to whom he was godfather, whom he named.
He is told by his nephew that at seventeen something happened
to Biff which destroyed the boy, a hint of Willy's infidelity. At
the restaurant where the feast of celebration (totem-feast) was
to have taken place, he is told by Biff that Biff has just compul-
sively stolen the fountain pen (genital) of a man who, Willy
imagined, might have started Biff on his hoped-for rehabilita-
tion. It is at this point that the father has to rush to the
bathroom—a piece of dramatic action which tells us, as explicitly
as we can be told, that the father is in castration-panic; and the
panic in the father is matched by the younger son's promotion
of a date with two "babes." The meaning of this episode can
hardly be missed. It is the ultimate act of father-murder; instead
of the totem-feast in which the sons recognize the father's authority and sexual rights, there is no dinner. There is only
abandonment. Emerging from the bathroom, re-living his own
sexual infidelity, Willy Loman—ex-god—has no recourse but to
shout in rage at the sexual assertion of the sons. And it is followed immediately by the mother's accusation against her sons
for their killing their father by their whoring. This is as close
to the original battle fought eons ago by man and his sons as
has ever been put upon the stage. It is this very thinly and yet
very adroitly disguised Oedipal murder which gives the play *its
peculiar symbolic prehistoric* power. It is not only modern man

exploited; it is also Neanderthal man raging against the restraint of civilization's dawn.

It is from this point on that the play in its last few minutes rises to critical intensity. The external contemporary social theme (announced by the mother near the end of the first act: "Attention—attention must finally be paid to such a man!") now converges and clashes with the eon-old psychological theme of the murdering, incestuous, whoring sons. Again, as in *All My Sons*, it is the mother fighting savagely for the father as she accuses the sons; it is the mother who sets off the older son's fury. It is she who has faced with the father the agonies of salesmanship, refrigerators, mortgages, life insurance, exhaustion and withering. Her rage at being old and dried-up is implicit as she fights like a she-tiger against the sons who have cast off the father for their own sexual philandering. It is thus she who is the protagonist of the external social theme: *a society that destroys fatherhood makes primitives (criminals) of its sons.*

In the last few minutes of the play, her confronting them ignites an explosive climax which is every dramatist's ambition. Biff, the protagonist of the Oedipal theme, goes into maniacal fury at the mother's defense of the father and exposes him as a philanderer and a fake, and is about to strike the tottering Willy. Then at the very last moment, because Biff, too, has lived by now and knows how tough civilization is against dreams and hopes, at the very last moment of conflict Biff is overtaken by pity and love and falls weeping into the stunned father's arms. This is an ultimate moment of climax rarely achieved in any theatre.

The tragedy now resolves itself powerfully upon its basic and hidden motivation: the guilt of a younger son for his hatred of his older brother, for Willy Loman is also a younger brother.

Willy reaffirms father-son love: "That boy is going to be magnificent!" he shouts, after saying incredulously, "He loves me!" But at the same time it is just this reconciliation between father and first son which must not be tolerated by the basic drive of the play. It is made to appear that Willy Loman can no longer endure this burden of fatherhood, this pity, this love of his first son, this evidence of authority which has failed, of fallen godhood. For again the repeated hallucination of *Willy's older brother Ben* appears, this time summoning Willy now to come away to new adventure (Death) in Ben's bragging, nagging refrain: "I was seventeen when I went into the jungle, and when I came out I was twenty-one and rich!" Here, in the play's final resolution, the entire necessity for the technique of hallucination becomes clear, though in fact it was announced at the very beginning of the play when Willy Loman commented that his older brother Ben, who struck it rich, is dead. Willy Loman, himself a younger brother (low-man on a totem pole), was determined in his time to "lick the system" by the magic of salesmanship and become "No. 1 Man"—a son with a deep guilty hatred for his older brother.

In this sense, the entire play has the aura of a dream, a wish of prehistoric proportion, its strength lying in its adroit social rationalization, in its superlative disguise of the role of the younger son Hap. It is as though Hap reported this dream:

"I had a strange dream last night. I dreamt that my father (who is a younger son and a salesman as I am) came home from one of his trips unable any longer to control his car. As he comes in, he is carrying two black, battered sample cases. They seem to have some ominous meaning as they weigh him down. In the dream he seems to be quite old and broken and starts shouting at my mother so loud that I and my brother Biff, who has come home from his wandering, hear him in our room upstairs where we lie sleeping. I explain to my brother that our father is losing his mind. As we listen, my father's older brother Ben, also a wanderer who struck it rich, is on my father's mind and he imagines that Ben is talking, calling to him.

"I persuade Biff to go into business with me and we plan to make good. But somehow Biff steals a fountain pen from the man who was to support our plan. (Biff used to steal, but my father let him get away with everything.) And my father plans to get a job from his boss's son, a position where he won't have to go on the road any more. My mother is very happy about all this because she is worried that my father is going to commit suicide. She is very happy about Biff's coming home and about his getting together with father, but pays little attention to me.

"But in the next scene of my dream, which seems to be the next day, everything goes wrong. My father is told by the boss's son, to whom my father was godfather, that he never was any good as a salesman. And the dinner we are to have with my father in a chop-house to celebrate doesn't come off, though we do meet there. It doesn't come off because nobody has succeeded—except me, because I still have my job. My father gets furious with Biff for stealing the fountain pen and Biff gets furious with my father for imagining that Biff ever could make good. Then I catch sight of a beautiful babe in the restaurant, and I tell her to get a girl friend, and Biff and I go off with the two of them to lay them all night. As we leave I seem to see my father rush into the bathroom and then come out and sink to his knees and shout and pound with his fist, something about giving Biff an order.

"In the last scene of the dream, when we get home, my mother goes into a rage and accuses us of whoring and of killing our father. Biff gets furious and begins to attack my father while I stand aside and watch, as though I were part of an audience at a play. Just as Biff is about to strike my father, he falls instead weeping into my father's arms. My father shouts: 'He loves me! . . . That boy is going to be magnificent!'

"Then Uncle Ben seems to call to my father—and this part is strange because I seem to see Ben as clearly as my father does, again as though it were a play of the inside of my father's mind. My father rushes out after Ben and gets killed by a car.[1]

"There is a tag-end to the dream. A sad little piece. It takes place at my father's grave. My mother moans that she doesn't understand it, especially since they had just made the last payment on the mortgage. Biff says that he is going away from the

---

[1] Since Dr. Schneider is filtering the play through his version of Happy, the suggestion in this line that an anonymous car killed Willy may not be a factual error, but his Happy's unwillingness to admit the suicide.

city. But not I. I vow that I'm going to lick the system and be No. 1 Man. It is very sad."

This is the dream of a younger, unpreferred son. No other analysis, it seems to me, can account for the increasing frequency of the vision of Ben, Willy's older and envied brother. In a sense, every first son "strikes it rich" in a younger son's eyes.

Death of a Salesman is an enduring play. It will be performed over and over for many years, because of its author's masterful exposition of the unconscious motivations in our lives. It is one of the most concentrated expressions of aggression and pity ever to be put on the stage. If Arthur Miller's *All My Sons* was aptly named, then this work is All Our Fathers.

GEORGE ROSS

George Ross, actor and writer, teaches English at the University of Tennessee, Martin branch.

DEATH OF A SALESMAN
IN THE ORIGINAL

A thoroughly satisfying translation is a rare thing in the theater, and even rare in the Yiddish theater. However, if *Toyt fun a Salesman* at the Parkway Theater in Brooklyn (through February 4 and perhaps longer) is nevertheless a unique experience, it is not for either of these reasons. Nor is it simply the fact that one finds it so apt, so almost inevitable, that this play of a Wandering Salesman should be presented to a Jewish audience. What one feels most strikingly is that this Yiddish play is really the original, and the Broadway production was merely—Arthur Miller's translation into English.

The vivid impression is that in translating from his mixed American-Jewish experience Miller tried to ignore or censor out the Jewish part, and as a result succeeded only in making the Loman family anonymous. What we saw on Broadway was a kind of American Everyman, an attempt at generalization which in fact ended in limitation. Not knowing who Willy Loman really was, what his real relation to American culture, we had to conclude that he was just what he was labeled—a salesman, and not a very bright one; and that his problems were those of a salesman. So, after all, the man who is supposed to have summed up the play by remarking, "That New England territory never *was* any good!" hadn't really missed the point. As for whatever was not included in the generalized "salesman," there we found ourselves saying, "Well, that's Willy Loman' character"—but here, too, we drew a blank. For, actually, what is character stripped of a particular milieu and culture? Americans, especially, manage better to be convincing when we are told what else they are besides "Americans," and to cut humanity down to the "common man" is to lose the human. Willy Loman's fate might have held a richer meaning—both particular and general— if we had known what he was besides a "salesman."

Clifford Odets—I mean the Odets of the 30's—comes to mind as a near relation of Miller's and points a lesson. Whatever else we may think of Odets as a playwright, the authenticity of his flavor and coloring, the realization of character and milieu, come from what he knew intimately with his physical and cultural senses; Arthur Miller, one feels, has almost deliberately deprived himself of some of the resources of his experience.

In the Yiddish production, what is inherently there may for the first time be seen full-bodied. The great success of Joseph Buloff's production is that it brings the play "home." The effect is remarkable. Buloff has caught Miller, as it were, in the act of changing his name, and has turned up the "original" for us. Where it fails of being the original, one tends to blame Miller's faulty English "translation" and Buloff's too exact fidelity to it. American tough talk and sex talk, for instance, become clumsy and embarrassing in Yiddish. "Strudel" in English might connote sensuality; in Yiddish it barely gets beyond being strudel. To speak of a whore as a *shtik flaish* is more savory but less brutal than the American "pig." American whores somehow become almost chaste in Yiddish, American sports less physical, less "rah-rah." Buloff was right to leave out the business of the bicycle-riding exercise and the school pennants, but in spite of such paring, such scenes don't succeed: Yiddish seems incapable of dealing with these areas of American life.

On the other side of the balance, and weighing much more

heavily, is the ease and grace with which the rather plain and often unidentifiable English becomes familiarly rich Yiddish. Except for the characters of the young men (Biff becomes Bill and Happy becomes Harry) and the loose women—there is the added difficulty that good young Jewish actors are harder to find than good young American actors—the language has a fluency and felicity which Miller might well envy. Particularly in the character of Willy Loman, whom Joseph Buloff acts as well as translates brilliantly: Willy speaks and behaves in Jewish idiom much more comfortably and eloquently than in American—and note that the translation is almost literal. Willy's repeated claim that his son has failed to find himself "for spite" becomes more connotative when "for spite" becomes "*af tsuloches*"; so many of a Jew's catastrophes seem to happen "*af tsuloches*." And Linda's (Willy's wife) impassioned "attention must be paid," while not at all unlikely in English, is not so embedded in the language and so frighteningly strong as "*gib achtung*." Here, and in many places, one felt in the English version as if Miller were thinking in Yiddish and unconsciously translating, as Odets often did more consciously; and sometimes when his English filters through the density of his background, it succeeds in picking up flavor on the way.

But beyond the apparent enhancement of language, of which I have given only a few characteristic instances, *Toyt fun a Salesman* is larger and more significant than *Death of a Salesman* by the discovery of Jewish character and Jewish situation in the play. How much more suggestive than Miller's bare hint of the salesman as poet-idealist living dangerously on a smile and a shoeshine, is the Yiddish Willy Loman, a Jewish salesman in America striving proudly and defensively to hold together his scattered family and himself, wandering off through all the cities with nothing really to sell but good will, trying desperately to be "known," "liked," accepted, and incidentally "not laughed at." Recall also Willy's exaggerated Americanism and his excessive attachment to his father through his older brother; his intense preoccupation with American sports and American gadgets, the "well-advertised refrigerator"; his unhappy dependence on the pinochle-playing Charley and on Charley's *yeshiva bocher*[1] son, Bernard.

And for the Jewish Willy, aren't there added interesting implications in his failure to become something he isn't, in his failure to know who he is, in his final division into two sons, one an unsuccessful sensualist, the other a bankrupt idealist? Even in the Yiddish, these elements are mere suggestions, and granted it is more the business of a play to suggest than to analyze—still one feels they might have been made with even sharper point if Mr. Buloff had felt freer than the English play allowed.

Something else, too, happens at the Parkway. The unalleviated grimness which never really attains to tragedy in the Broadway production slips here quite naturally into the moods of irony and pathos so familiar to Jews, and the whole tone is lightened in the way that Jews have always made their best jokes out of their cruelest experience. It is lightened, moreover, in favor of a deeper pathos rather than the more spurious "tragedy" of the English. And this pathos, I might add, is what the audience at the Parkway saw, indeed came prepared to see. It is for them, after all, a play about a Jewish *family*, not about an unsuccessful salesman, and they indicated freely their understanding of the problem of the threatened family when a son denounces his father, when a mother denounces her son, when a son and a father fall sobbing desperately into each other's arms.

It's unfortunate that Buloff, who is a fine actor, does not have the better company and more finished production that he deserves. His own acting is in the line of good Jewish realism. It

---

[1] A *yeshiva* is a Hebrew school. The phrase *yeshiva bocher* (schoolboy) connotes bookishness and, in this context, is affectionately pejorative, as "grind" is sometimes used on college campuses today.

is that larger, more lavish realism akin to the French, Italian, and Russian styles rather than the English and American which is so often both repressed and fussy. It is a physically generous style, but no less attentive to small natural detail and delicate psychological modulation. There was no need to explain Willy's schizophrenic conversations split between the real people and his dream people as a literary device or a stage convention; these speeches were right and necessary, as were also his frequent complete surrenders to dream. And they were righter than on Broadway, I believe, because of the appropriateness of this grander realism to the expressionist-realist style of the play itself.

Luba Kadison's Linda had quite as much force, feeling, and style as Buloff could have required. The same cannot be said for the rest of the support, except perhaps for Sam Gertler's Charley, who in fact added dimension to the role. Gertler's Charley was thoroughly smug and defiant in his ignorance of things American, especially sports, and he was smart enough to be sympathetic with rather than insulted by Willy; I seem to remember the Broadway Charley as less complete, quieter, almost apologetic, and not so fully in relation to Willy. Nathan Goldberg as Uncle Ben might have been more sinister and David Ellin as Bernard might better have suggested the earnest, the serious, the mental.

The set is a frugal copy of the original and the lighting gives little more than what is required in the script. The skeleton frame of the house is never quite part of the dream to which it belongs. The Yiddish theater in general finds it difficult to take properties and décor very seriously. The audience at the Parkway found the famous stage set which requires Willy to walk around through a skeleton doorway into his kitchen instead of by short cut through the imaginary wall quite funny. They found funny, too, Buloff's sensitively stylized fits of confusion; at one such moment a lady behind me remarked that he must be a *shiker*.[2] I suppose it's a matter of a *haimishe* audience refusing to see unhappiness as "neurosis," plain *tsores* as

---

[2] A drunk.

maladjustment."[3] What I myself found funny was that Yiddish should have no word for "salesman," unless it be "sale-es-man."

I don't think it would be altogether too facetious to propose as an interesting project to Arthur Miller that in the light of this production he make another try at a more imaginative translation of his material into English; the attempt might result in a more authentic and, by that same token, more moving play than we saw in the production on Broadway.

---

[3] A *haimishe* audience is made up of those people who might find themselves around a table, taking a glass of tea together. The phrase means more than "in-group." *Haimishe* comes from the word meaning "home," but it implies a wide range of things: practicality, matter-of-factness, awareness of one's surroundings and one's relatives and neighbors. Such a no-nonsense group, familiar with *tsores* (trouble), would refuse to give it a fancy psychological name.

JUDAH BIERMAN, JAMES HART, AND STANLEY JOHNSON

Judah Bierman and Stanley Johnson teach in the English Department at Portland State College. James Hart is Professor of American Literature at the University of California, Berkeley, and is the author of, among other books, *The Oxford Companion to American Literature*.

ARTHUR MILLER:
DEATH OF A SALESMAN

Unlike the dramas by Sophocles, Shakespeare, and Lorca, Arthur Miller's *Death of a Salesman* is a tragedy set in our own times, played out on our own scene, by characters who, however we regard the quality of their thought, speak in our own language and with our own peculiar accents. In one sense, therefore, we cannot claim that the play is foreign to us. For what we lose of *Oedipus* because we are not Athenians, and of *Othello* because we are not Elizabethans, and of *Blood Wedding* by not being Spaniards, that much, at least, is ours because we are Miller's American contemporaries. Even were we to reject his assumptions and deny his conclusions, we would still know the world Miller creates, because the apartment houses that cut off Willy's horizon cut off our own as well, and the three thousand miles from Brooklyn to San Francisco involve more a change of name and site than of setting.

Centering on the quality of the protagonist, most of the comment about this play has argued the question of whether Willy

---

From *The Dramatic Experience* by Judah Bierman, James Hart, and Stanley Johnson (Englewood Cliffs, N.J.: Prentice-Hall, 1958), pp. 490–493, Copyright © 1958 by Prentice-Hall, Inc., reprinted by permission of Prentice-Hall, Inc. This volume is a textbook, a collection of plays, in which, as this introductory essay indicates, "Salesman" is placed among the tragedies.

Loman has sufficient stature to be a tragic hero. There is an irony in this debate over the admission of Willy to the company of Oedipus and Othello: few commentators have recognized the significance of the play's structure, of its use of scenes that embody and, at the same time, illustrate the insubstantiality of the salesman's world of the smile and backslap; for the chosen structure indicates that Willy, though no less heroic—no less committed, that is, to his own dreams—is cast in a different mold than that used for the traditional hero. We begin, therefore, with what is most notable about the structure of the play itself, its treatment of time.

As in all tragedies, we first meet the hero a few moments before his end. But Miller's drama does not rely on the usual compressed expository report to acquaint us with the antecedent action necessary to an understanding of the hero's motives. Partly because the advance of modern psychology has made it easy for us to shift from the present to its root-experience in the past and back again, and partly because an illusion of such movement lies within the technical capacity of the modern stage, Miller has chosen actually to show us the scenes which made up the life that now dissolves before us. These he shows us as they exist in Willy's mind, that is, without any clear distinction as to the particular times at which they happened. Thus we come to witness, and not simply to know by report, the younger life of Willy Loman, who, some thirty-five years before, started his pilgrimage to the grave we now stand beside with his wife Linda, and his boys, Biff and Happy. This treatment of time, by putting emphasis on the earlier scenes, reduces the impact of the final suicide. On the other hand, it serves to raise that suicide to the level of sacrifice by linking it with Willy's early dreams.

Into his visualization of the last forty-eight hours of the hero's life, Miller introduces two other kinds of scenes: those involving guidance from Ben, and those involving the nurture of Biff. The first kind are objectifications of Willy's own insecurity, for Willy bows down to the image of Ben's success, finding in Ben's words —as in those of a Delphic oracle—both a guide for action and a reassurance that his own ideas are right. And the second kind of scene shows us Willy bending his son's knee before the idol of success, teaching him the liturgy of the smile, and making him to believe that over the door of heaven is inscribed: "Enter here only the well-liked." These scenes (and that other visualization of the past, the episode of the Woman in Boston), give dimension to the portrait of the protagonist. Without them, the play's theme-statements would be what they are sometimes unwittingly taken to be: sentimental idealizations of a failure. With them, it becomes clear that Willy's failure stems from the quality of his aspirations, and not of his spirit.

I don't say he's a great man. Willy Loman never made a lot of money. His name was never in the paper. He's not the finest character that ever lived. But he's a human being, and a terrible thing is happening to him. So attention must be paid. He's not to be allowed to fall into his grave like an old dog. Attention, attention must be finally paid to such a person.

The second is the epitaph that Charlie reads over his friend, Willy Loman—salesman, sixty-three, suspected suicide:

Nobody dast blame this man. You don't understand: Willy was a salesman. And for a salesman, there is no rock bottom to the life. He don't put a bolt to a nut, he don't tell you the law or give you medicine. He's a man way out there in the blue.

Now, in the first statement, Linda argues that Willy Loman, because he is a man, must have what all men must have: if his name is not to be written in the permanent records of Man, he must at least be able to hear the voices of his children. This minimal certificate of immortality he must have to keep him from oblivion. But Charlie, on the other hand, speaks of Willie as a salesman, not as a human being. There are men, he says, whose lives are built of necessity on nothing more substantial than the smile and the shine, whose satisfactions are no more enduring than dreams of bigger and still bigger orders. A man such as these cannot be blamed for his action if he chooses to die "dramatically" in a last attempt to gain for himself a more substantial place in the memory of men. Some commentators have in effect combined the two theme-statements, asserting that what Miller intended was an indictment of the American system for ruthlessly discarding its faithful servants. For them, Willy symbolizes the failure of the American capitalist ethos, its basic destruction of the humanity of man.

Each of these interpretations—the wife's, the friend's, and the critical view that combines them—points toward the meaning of the play, but each also raises questions that it leaves unanswered. Can we, for example, accept Linda's demand that "attention be paid," knowing as we do the shallowness of Willy's past? Does not this knowledge degrade him below the level of interest? Plain souls like this salesman are of interest to their families and to God; but we need greatness to inspire us. On the other hand, if Miller's concern lay with the tragedy of a salesman in a capitalist world, why did he not show us at least a successful salesman? Willy succeeds only with his batch of cement; he is a carpenter and a planter. But as a salesman he is a failure. Can he then be a valid symbol in an indictment of the capitalist world? Is he more than a symbol of failure?

These questions emphasize the danger, particularly acute in tragedy, of confusing the poetic statement with the whole meaning of the play; life as revealed in tragedy cannot be so easily summed up in a line or two of dialogue. The keys to meaning, on the contrary, are found in the plot, in the characters, and in the conflict that engages them. The conflict Miller chose to communicate his vision is that between Willy as a salesman and Willy as a man. Such a view of the conflict explains and justifies the author's uses of the past; each of the episodes can now be seen as making the same, insistent point: Willy suffers from his attempt to live by his business ethics. He is content to govern all his relationships, including those with his family, by the same standards that prevail when he is on the road. He cannot distinguish—as we do, and as the play insists we do— between the ethics of business (a little happy cheating now and then) and the sterner ethics of life.

Willy is blind to the fundamental contradiction between his

progress as a salesman and his self-realization as a man, and his blindness is almost allegorically reflected in his children. Like Willy, Happy lives the life of the business ethic. Like his father, he fails to understand that the smile is no safe-conduct pass through the jungle. Significantly, he is incapable of fruition; he is a philanderer, and wastes himself in a succession of casual, fruitless unions. He has the smell of women on him, in a play in which men cry out to assert their masculinity. Biff, on the other hand, reflects Willy's discontent. He does not understand what troubles him: who his father is. And the episode of the Woman in Boston sets him adrift because the episode is a combined revelation of Willy's key to successful selling and his recurrent attempts to blot out his feelings of inconsequentiality. Biff comes home and is symbolically set free only when he discovers himself as a nobody.

The whole question of Willy's hidden identity is curiously like that in *Oedipus*. The key words—he does not know who he is— point the parallel almost unmistakably. But before we rank the salesman with the king, we need to check one further structural element. From Aristotle to Maxwell Anderson the point of *recognition* has been fundamental in the structure of tragedy. Biff, as we have seen, finally recognizes his situation; he reports that in his flight with the pen, he has suddenly realized the falsity of his life. He discovers his own identity, even though he identifies himself as a nobody. But where is Willy's moment of recognition, and what does it amount to? How much does Willy really see, even after that climactic scene in which Biff, tendering his love, frees both himself and his father? The question we are really asking is whether Willy Loman recognizes anything equal in quality to that which drove Oedipus to his self-mutilation and Othello to his suicide. The answer is both yes and no.

The *impact* of his recognition is of equal quality: it drives him to decisive action. What is different and debased is the quality of the action taken, the solution envisioned. Unable to rise above the commercial values that have defined and limited his life, Willy comes to suicide only as a new answer to his old problem. He is giving Biff something in return for his tendered love; he will trade himself for the money which he still sees as the key to his son's success in life. What is debased is Willy's immature evaluation, and the equally immature response founded on it. It is the response of a man who chooses death, not because life has been made intolerable by a terrible burden of guilt, but because he believes that his death is the purchase price of a security he himself could never find.

But perhaps the best approach to Willy's place among tragic heroes is to ask of his death the same class of question that we ask of the others. Concerning the fall of Oedipus, ruler of Thebes, solver of the Sphinx's riddle, we ask, "Does this fall mean that man is driven by an insatiable desire to know (above all to know himself), but, at the same time, that this desire for self-knowledge leads ultimately to blindness and destruction?" As we witness the fall of Othello, prince of Moors, General of Venice, Governor of Cyprus, we ask, "Does this fall mean that we have in us all that seed of jealousy which, given a dark moment of despair, will germinate and flower into a passion that destroys all reason?" And of the bereavement of the Mother and the slayings of Leonardo and the Bridegroom,[1] are we not forced to ask, "Does this mean that the primitive hunger of the blood must always be satisfied, though it destroy the man, the family, and even the society through which it flows?" But, finally, what are we moved to ask of the death of Willy Loman? To what critical human issue does it point? Or is it merely another depressing episode, and, like his life, without significance? Who is Willy Loman that attention should be paid to him?

To answer that he is three million American salesmen—at least the equal of one Theban king or one Moorish general— is to evade the question. It is also an evasion to say that Willy is a common or Lo-man and hence ineligible to be the hero of a tragedy. The tragic vision is not focussed on the station or status of man, but on the motives of his soul. The stature of Othello and Oedipus and Leonardo comes not from their place but from the intensity of their living. They have had knowledge that

---

[1] In *Blood Wedding* by Federico García Lorca.

life is good; in them a human potential has been reached and, in the face of destruction, their manhood affirmed. It would solve our problem if we could insist that attention be paid to Willy Loman because in his living, whatever his station or work, he had lived, because in his human relations he had soared to what men are capable of. But even where he seems most successful, in the adoration given him by Biff and Happy, we know the shallowness of Willy's achievement; we know the falseness of his aspirations, and how their falsity keeps him from laying any real foundations for their future or his own.

Like Oedipus, Willy does not know who his father is or who his children are. But unlike Oedipus, who has the strength to discover the truth, as well as the strength to destroy himself, Willy has only the weakness of his ignorance. His self-destruction is not, like Othello's, an atonement and redress of balance by a figure who emerges from his torture with dearly bought wisdom; it is the despairing, ill-considered act of immaturity. If we reject Willy, it is because he is only potentially a hero. He never grows to full size, since, though he has something of the heroic spirit, he only vaguely comprehends that his life is without meaning or substance. We reject him because his life, the *unexamined* life, is not worth living. And yet, we cannot wholly reject him: the terror of Miller's vision, and the point at which it joins those of Sophocles and Shakespeare, is that it finally forces us to ask, "Have we created a society fundamentally so inimical to man that, in cutting him off from the sun and the earth, it threatens his very survival?"

GEORGE DE SCHWEINITZ

George de Schweinitz has taught at the University of Iowa and the University of Alabama, and is now Professor of English at West Texas State University.

DEATH OF A SALESMAN:
A NOTE ON EPIC AND TRAGEDY

For more than ten years Arthur Miller's *Death of a Salesman* has stirred up controversy. Is it really the tragedy its author so eloquently claims it to be?[1] One way of answering this question is to find some defining measures in the tragic tradition of Western culture and apply them to the play.

A glance back at Western literature shows immediately that tragedy and epic are often intermixed: witness *Paradise Lost* and *Moby-Dick*. In the epic, traditional value structures are probed and explored, perhaps re-created; in the tragedy, collisions between "units" in these structures precipitate catastrophe. The fundamental concern for such structures in both forms makes an intimate, and perhaps indissoluble, tie between tragedy and epic.

Besides being thus related, the epic and tragedy seem to have further characteristics in common: both seem to require a certain richness or maturity in homogeneous living in the society from which they come and both seem to reveal this characteristic by laying, or containing, a ground-plan for that culture. Though ostensibly portraits of the culture of one people or

---

From *Western Humanities Review*, XIV (Winter 1960), pp. 91–96, reprinted by permission of *Western Humanities Review* and George de Schweinitz.

[1] The author's original footnote cited "Tragedy and the Common Man" and the Introduction to *Collected Plays*, both of which are reprinted here, and "The Family in Modern Drama," *The Atlantic Monthly*, CXCVII (April 1956), pp. 35–41.

nation, they are, in fact, portraits of the projection of that people's or nation's culture, including, of course, its values, upon the whole universe. For as a man rises to epic or tragic heights, his view does not stop at the borders of his own native land.

One further characteristic common to epic and tragedy is that the protagonist in both must be accorded an unremitting respect as representative of the general type man. It is precisely here that the question concerning Willy Loman as such a protagonist has chiefly centered. Given the character he has, can he thus represent the general type man? I think he can and does, just as I think Ahab could and did, and in the remainder of the paper I shall consider why.

A generally three-part division of value characterized the Western epic and tragedy against which I am measuring *Death of a Salesman*. This division was objectified in a similarly three-part division of the universe in which it was contained. The gods (or God) ruled above; man occupied the earth, conceived of as a kind of "middle ground," and below was the Underworld or Hell. The realms of value corresponding to these divisions were, of course, first, the "divine" and the "human." On an equally simple basis, the realm of value of the Underworld or Hell corresponded to the corruption or negation of either or both of the other realms and thus to a condition of "no-value."

The focal questions about *Death of a Salesman* then are: is there here a structure of value in any way analogous to that of the older epic and tragic tradition (this does not mean: are the values the same?)? And, if so, does it receive objectification in anything like the way in which such structures did in the older tradition? In other words, in *Death of a Salesman* are there spatial or geographical equivalents for the basic divisions of value whose collisions produce the tragedy?

To answer these crucial questions, we must first recognize what in American history and tradition adhered to or deviated from this principally Old World structure. In *Moby-Dick* the tragedy was the outgrowth both of traumatic conditions in the protagonist and crises in his society. The combination of the two was both the story of a heroic rebel against the blind strokes of an impersonal and indifferent fate (the tragic part) and the story of "worlds" adrift in a universe whose age-old compartments of value were coming apart at the seams (the epic part). It was a case of individual trauma ruthlessly exploiting social and cultural crises and social and cultural crises mercilessly, yet unavoidably, aggravating individual trauma. One played into the other and there was no final separation of one from the other.

Let us say that by the middle of the twentieth century there was almost nothing left of this original value structure. By that time, in America, if a man found a stable and reliable value structure, it would almost certainly have to be something that he forged himself. Culturally, there were three main sources for his values: American history and tradition, which a man might or might not know enough to make use of; the frontier, which by the beginning of the twentieth century had largely become fantasized and associated with a folklore by which the citizen rationalized and covered over his naked drives for power and "success" (among the frontier's legacies was the political and social catchword "rugged individualism"); and the city, a complex reality which, while not exactly new in history, had achieved so dominant a place in the totality of twentieth century American experience that it constituted a third and final main source of value.

It will be seen at once that Arthur Miller takes for granted in this play that the individual's achieving a stable and reliable value structure in America is purely an empirical process. Such a structure is not something already formed—say, like Catholicism—into which the individual fits; rather, it is something he develops out of the crucible of his own highly heterogeneous experience. As Miller says himself, he is not writing in and of an age of faith, but in and of an age of secularism. The differences between these two types of culture to Miller is reflected in the fact that religious feeling, as normally understood, has absolutely no place in his play. In it God's name is mentioned only in vain.

This means that the "top" level of the traditional epic and

tragic division is empty. There is nobody or no group "up there." From "there," at least, there is no dispensing of perfect justice or eternal damnation. Willy, Biff, Linda, Howard, Charley and Happy pay it no heed; and neither does anybody, apparently, in their world. Whereas Ahab made a great commotion about turning the traditionally "top" level upside down, as it were, and becoming the "high" priest of the negation of the traditional "highest," for Willy and his world there is not even any question of protest because these things simply have no reality for him. If you had whispered in Willy's ear, in his mad and culturally dictated race for sales:

> As flies to wanton boys, are we to the gods
> They kill us for their sport.

you would have stopped him dead in his tracks—for a moment. What gods?

Willy's universe, then, is a drastically reduced one, compared even to Ahab's. But though for him a traditional "divine" has been so unequivocally removed, there must be something in its place—a "top" of some kind must still remain—or there would be no conflict, tragic or otherwise. We are now left with two realms of our original three: the "human," corresponding to earth in the old systemization, and the realm of "no-value," corresponding to the Underworld or Hell. Between these two we must find the "higher" and "lower" in value which form the poles between which a tragic protagonist is stretched. The "heaven" or "abode of the gods" of tradition is now to be found somewhere on earth, presumably somewhere within the territorial boundaries of the United States, maybe, in the form of an idea, hovering over, if never entering, the head of our hero Willy. The "hell" of tradition is, of course, as always, right beside it, ready to negate it or any lesser value, since "hell" is traditionally and unchangeably the negation of all value.

At this point it will be necessary to turn back to the three main sources of value that the play posits as possible for—to use Miller's word—the "average" American of this age, that is, for the American who, like Willy, has what Miller calls "the common materials of life" to work with. American history and tradition is the first of these, the frontier the second, and the city the third and last.

Each of these three main sources of value is clearly objectified or particularized in *Death of a Salesman*; that is, each is given a "vehicle" or correlative in the total action and each shares objectively—or realistically, to use Miller's term for this Ibsen-derived type of drama—in the total conflict leading to the catastrophe. To give their particular names, they are, first, New England, representing American history and tradition; second, Alaska and Africa, both frontiers in the sense of places ripe for economic development and exploitation; and third, New York, representing the city.

Let us take New England and examine its place in Willy's psychic as well as physical world. It is curious and significant that Willy, though late in life he is unable to make a living in New England, has nothing but good and kind thoughts about it. Earlier he had wanted to take the whole family there for a vacation. He never waxes rhapsodic about New York, but he does about New England. At times wistfulness and nostalgia come into his voice when he reminisces about New England. It has been the "field" that he has "ploughed"; it has yielded all the returns he has had for thirty years or more. It is "full of fine people" and "the cradle of the Revolution." To Willy, unlike New York, it is a place of historical significance in America; he even equates it with America. Instead of a geographical unit only, it is thus almost an essence to him, like the Pocahontas image, embodying an originally virginal and unspoiled America, in Hart Crane's *The Bridge*. Most important of all, it carries this high and imperishable image in Willy's mind; there old salesmen never die but only "fade away" to the hotel telephone where they carry on their extensive businesses amid increasing popularity and love.[2] Willy's heartfelt description of the sales-

---

[2] De Schweinitz, busy creating the image he wants, forgets that Willy says of Dave Singleman, "when he died—and by the way he died the death of a salesman, in his green velvet slippers in the smoker of the New York, New Haven and Hartford . . . ". Surely, that death would have fit the New England idealization de Schweinitz is after.

man over eighty who actually conducted business in this fashion suggests a worship of a state that appears as nothing less than the ideal. This is the salesman's Paradise. It may seem a tawdry one as Paradises go, but it may well be the best that a run-of-the-mill American salesman, with headquarters in New York in the mid-twentieth century, can imagine.

True, some of the deepest ironies of the play also develop from New England as the pole of "higher" value. For instance, as he gets older Willy can't make a living in it; New England is actually not one of the better sales territories. Willy presumably never makes enough in it to take his family on a vacation tour of its "beautiful towns." And as for its having "fine people" and being "the cradle of the Revolution," the positive side of both these values becomes in Willy's sales-soiled hands smirched and defaced; he commits adultery with one of these "fine people" and New England's vaunted "Revolution" thus becomes a merely personal, and sordid, infidelity.

Next, the frontier in the form of Alaska and Africa shapes up as a fairly constant "lower" pole of value, but still not the "lowest" (that is, the rock-bottom level of negation of value). If New England looms as the "higher" pole, the yearned-for ideal, or almost "religion," in the extensive revision of the traditional epic and tragic scheme that *Death of a Salesman* presents, then with the same logic the frontier comes forth as representative of a "middle" pole. The middle stage in the long and tortuous development of value toward a point of refinement deserving of the name of "religion" is generally called "magic." And it is certainly the magical properties of the names of these two places, neither of which is any part of the play's actual setting, that are made use of. Alaska and Africa represent "heavens" all right, but only in the crudest, most materialistic form; they are really lands of quick riches only. It is because of their deep embuement with an almost exclusive appeal to the senses that they get so instantaneous a reaction from a Willy who has never quite had the heart to be a sourdough, ready to fight both for his own and the other fellow's. But, as the recurring images and conversations with the exploiter Ben show, the magical names of Alaska and Africa tantalize Willy constantly and actually sound the theme song of his "middle" world of values which eventually takes him to his "nether-world"—the region, that is, where all values, and even life itself, are frozen for good.

Our epic and tragic "universe," twentieth-century American style, is now almost complete. What remains is only the "bottom" level, and that is the city, in this case New York. New York is the center of American business (America's chief day-to-day concern), and thus the natural "stand" of perhaps its most prevalent type, the salesman. New York is the infertile area, where seeds won't take root, though planted and replanted; where best friends go unrecognized; where infidelities are bred, though, in Willy's case, unconsummated (even an act of adultery, which is at least physically vital, is not possible for Willy in New York. "They don't need me in New York. I'm the New England man. I'm vital in New England."); where business loyalties and fair play do not last from one generation to another; where a gross premium is put on the showy, on success in a purely material or physical sense (witness Happy's financial and sexual success in this sense); and where, finally, sons like Happy, representing a basically infertile side of divided fathers like Willy, point up the play's traditionally tragic theme of a groping for self-knowledge by not even "knowing" their fathers when a luscious material or physical dividend catches and holds the eye. In brief, there is nothing about the city in this play that shows it to be anything but unfriendly to man, insidiously and increasingly so. Those who cope with it as Charley does do so by dint of a kind of philosophical legerdemain that leaves at least one side of their lives blank ("My salvation is that I never took any interest in anything."); the "whole" man does not grow in New York and New York is the last place to make a man "whole."

The scene in the restaurant, which may be considered the epitome of New York as here presented, comes closer to a picture of Hell than any other piece of modern literature—and certainly any other Realistic drama—I can think of. It is, in truth, the realm of "no-value," or of one value so pervasive that no other can survive beside it. Except for the still suffering and struggling Willy and Biff, everything in the restaurant is pure (though adept) negotiation with one and only one standard involved and that is exclusively of the sense world. The "pick-ups," Happy, and worst of all the bartender Stanley (because he is purely servile even in this lurid realm of "rugged individualists" of the senses)—these recall classic scenes of descents into the abyss more sharply than anything else in twentieth century American literature. And Happy's casually curt lie about his collapsing father ("He's just a guy.") is surely as close to the tragic terror as anything in American drama has yet come.

In summary, the "world" or "universe" of *Death of a Salesman*, while representing vast re-arrangements and shifts of poles of value, because of extraordinary changes in Western culture, especially as manifest in the United States, nevertheless still shows a basically traditional epic and tragic structure in that its poles of value are clearly located and distinguished one from another; in that they are also clearly objectified, as in the older tradition, but not allegorized, since Realistic drama stops short of tolerating allegory; and finally in that these poles of value, so located and objectified, precipitate the tragic situation and give a sense of a "universe" in the throes of unresolved conflict and agony.

JOSEPH A. HYNES

Joseph A. Hynes teaches English Literature at the University of Oregon and has written critical essays on Dickens and Henry James as well as Arthur Miller.

"ATTENTION MUST BE PAID . . ."

Because this essay presents an almost entirely unfavorable—not to say hostile—opinion of Arthur Miller's *Death of a Salesman*, I should like to say, non-Heepishly, that there would be no occasion for my remarks but for the undeniable power which has made of this play a theatrical triumph and a classroom perennial. Despite such vigor, however, structural difficulties of varying importance betray what seems the author's ultimate confusion. This pronouncement is no doubt brash, but will perhaps be found more nearly feasible if we consider the play in the light of some few requirements for the dramatic art and of one for the tragic art.

Certainly one of the first requirements for the dramatic gesture is probability. Given certain characters, locales, events, and situations, the audience ought to be able to accept the meshing of these elements without having to annihilate its disbelief. Because Willy Loman, for instance, is consistently schizophrenic, one has no difficulty making the transitions, with him, to and from past and present. But other phenomena are troublesome in varying degrees.

Although we grant that Willy, as a victim of what might be called "the American jock complex" and of Charley's laconically sane humor, might very probably shout that Ebbets Field holds "eighty thousand people," we have difficulty elsewhere. What, for instance, is the extent of the high school hero's popularity?

From *College English*, XXIII (April 1962), pp. 574–578, reprinted by permission of the National Council of Teachers of English and Joseph A. Hynes. The title, of course, comes from Linda's famous speech.

Considerable though such popularity does become, are we to believe that "the girls pay for" Biff? Or can we concede that the Loman basement is full of worshipful menials waiting to carry out the instructions of the quarterback hero? Such minor awkwardness accumulates. We wonder how Willy can clear seventy dollars' commission on a gross sale of two hundred dollars; yet when Linda says he will, we know we are to believe her. Again, Bernard's mere survival renders improbable his statement that he and Biff fought viciously for half an hour after Biff's return from Boston. And how are we to regard the more serious implications of Happy's effectively suggested sensuality, when we are asked to believe in the irresistibility of the yokel's approach which lures Miss Forsythe? And what of Happy's income? In a moment of passionate clearheadedness, Willy remarks that Happy earns seventy dollars a week; yet he manages an apartment and a plenitude of women, and has just paid for his father's vacation trip to Florida. We can perhaps close out this account of comparatively minor grievances by citing the basketballs and fountain pen which Biff steals from Bill Oliver. Supposing that these objects are symbols of the virility to which Biff thinks he can accede only by entering the man's world of Bill Oliver (everyone is always asking Willy or Biff when he is going to "grow up"), what about the inappropriateness of such devices? On the literal level, we envision a high school boy clandestinely staggering out of a stockroom under a *carton* of basketballs. On the symbolic level, we see no artistic need to provide symbols for Biff's repeatedly projected problem. But if symbols were wanted, why such improbable ones? (Contrast them, for instance, to the packet of seeds which Willy tries to plant in a sunless concrete yard.)

Such matters as these may be classified as slightly annoying violations of dramatic economy—lesser rents in Mr. Miller's theatrical fabric. Minor though they are, however, their inclusion seems additionally regrettable since—except possibly for Happy's encounter with Miss Forsythe—they serve no necessary function.

The details mentioned to this point do not account for, but

are symptoms of, a significant looseness in conception of character. A minor case in point is that of the woman in Boston, who is described as "quite proper-looking, Willy's age." One supposes that the woman's age and appearance are specified for a reason—possibly to render more likely Willy's pathetic assertion to Biff that "she's nothing to me" but a means of relieving loneliness; or possibly to show either that Willy is not the "fast" sort of traveling salesman attractive to the Miss Forsythes of this world, or that, in the unlikely event that he could have had a Forsythean, he is more interested in companionship than in sex. But what real purpose do Mr. Miller's specifications serve? Willy is lonely, of course, and we could understand this regardless of the variety of woman with whom we discovered him. But in fact it is clear that sex is what comforts Willy, and that his "road" character reveals him to be more vulgar than does his "home" character. No matter, then, how we sympathize with his isolation, we cannot see that the more superficial traits of his consoler matter much. What does matter is that Willy has found someone like himself in *character*, rather than merely in years or appearance. The woman is Willy's match in coarseness and unimaginative frivolousness, and perhaps in loneliness as well. Moreover, it makes no difference to *Biff* whether the woman is fifteen or sixty, plain or fancy. Mr. Miller's description appears, then, to qualify neither Biff's discovery nor ours.

A character whose portrayal is more crucially troublesome is Charley. For nearly the whole play he and Linda are the only ones who realize the seriousness of Willy's condition; and it is Charley who, in his gruffly humane way, tries to make a breadwinner of Willy and thereby help restore his dignity. It is Charley who has long since faced up to the "system," adapted himself to it by making the necessary compromises, and nevertheless salvaged a genuine humanity. His humanity and lack of illusion enable him to tell Willy pointedly that "the only thing you got in this world is what you can sell . . . you're a salesman, and you don't know that." True, it is Charley's regular tactic to be blunt with Willy. We may reasonably infer, however, that Charley believes what he says; that despite the obvious difference between himself and Howard Wagner, Charley also holds that "business is business." In short, Charley is both a warm person and a hard-nosed businessman. Yet in the "Requiem" we see him quite altered. Here he delivers the lines about some sort of Emersonian representative salesman—a typical or abstract salesman:

Nobody dast blame this man. . . . Willy was a salesman. And for a salesman, there is no rock bottom to the life. He don't put a bolt to a nut, he don't tell you the law or give you medicine. He's a man way out there in the blue, riding on a smile and a shoeshine. And when they start not smiling back—that's an earthquake. And then you get yourself a couple of spots on your hat, and you're finished. Nobody dast blame this man. A salesman is got to dream. . . . It comes with the territory.

What we have here, obviously, is sheer sentimentality—Nick Kenny[1] at the graveside. Why did Mr. Miller want a "Requiem," if not to sum up the life of Willy Loman? If not to establish what happened to Willy? If not somehow to impose the theme of the play? The "Requiem," however, does none of these things; and its plainest failure is Charley's speech. Like all sentimentality, this speech fails because it is untrue. It is untrue because it generalizes, against evidence incorporated into the play, about salesmen. It speaks of *the* salesman rather than of the particular salesman in question. Furthermore, it denies the character of Charley, who cannot possibly believe what he is saying, since his part is that of a clear-eyed realist—one who has no truck with well-groomed smiling stereotypes drifting on clouds from buyer to buyer. In fact, when we recall that Willy's initial misjudgment—a pitifully ironic one—was his unaccountable conclusion that old Dave Singleman (who went from train to hotel room and used the telephone, and not the handshake or the backslap) was successful because of his *personality*, we

---

[1] A syndicated poet, whose home paper was the *New York Daily Mirror*. According to the entry in *Celebrity Register*, Kenny once said of his urban-folksy outpourings, "My stuff has a sort of therapeutical value. It makes sick people feel better and it sometimes makes well people sick."

see that Mr. Miller has not only pulled Charley out of shape, but indeed ended the play by committing Charley to a mellow defense of Willy's wildest misconception. The result, when Charley's speech is coupled with Linda's tearfully ironic farewell, is that the audience is moved to tears—not because it sees Willy whole and clear, but because of this Hallmark-Card flourish at the curtain.

The tears and sense of depression common to viewers of the play are a fairly sound indication that we have here no tragedy. It is essential to make this point—certainly not a new one—in order to get at what appears to be the play's severest shortcoming: uncertainty of theme.

In his widely anthologized essay, "Tragedy and the Common Man," Mr. Miller argues two main points: 1) that nobility of rank and even of character is not essential to tragedy; and 2) that what is essential to tragedy is any man's willingness to give his all, against even impossible odds, for the purpose of establishing himself in dignity where he thinks he belongs. Though Mr. Miller never names his own play, it is clear that *Death of a Salesman* is the subject of his essay, and that he conceives of it as a tragedy.

The first of these two arguments one is at least theoretically inclined to concede, though nobility of rank and nobility of character are so interwoven in the plays whose tragic stature is universally acknowledged (*Hamlet* and *Oedipus Rex*, for instance), and though it is nearly impossible to find general agreement on the tragic stature of any play in which the central figure lacks at least nobility of character. (I assume here that a tragedy is primarily that of an individual protagonist, and only secondarily—if at all—that of a society.) But supposing that social position is ancillary, and supposing even that the so-called common man (that unfindable entity) can achieve tragedy if he lives and dies to realize his dignity, we are concerned with a play which contradicts its author's claims for it.

The minor annoyances listed at the outset of this essay, and the unaccountable description of Willy's lady friend, are inconsequential compared to the contradiction which permits Charley to change character and sentimentalize the ending. For Charley, of all people, is the one who should speak for Mr. Miller in response to Biff's reiteration that Willy "had all the wrong dreams" and "never knew who he was." But Charley changes the subject, in effect, and thereby leaves the play mired in imprecision.

In a sense it would be right for Charley to speak by remaining silent, granting thereby the truth of what Biff says—and of what Charley has said all along. One suspects, however, that Charley is made to say something "more final" than Biff's comment, because the play has to be made once again Willy's. Our attention has gradually focussed on Biff, until at the showdown Biff has taken over completely, by virtue of discovering himself to be "nothing" in Willy's ruling set of values, and by means of his violent and futile demonstration of love. He takes over because it is he who at last knows himself; because, ironically, it is he who, in Mr. Miller's own terms, manifests tragic potential by driving against all possibility into the brick wall of Willy's dementia, in order to restore Willy's dignity by making him see himself as Biff sees both of them.

And of course Charley's moonshine, setting as it does the tone of the "Requiem," only superficially returns our attention from Biff to Willy, and finally reminds us that Willy is not a tragic figure. For whatever else a tragic figure may be, he is one who has come to know himself. My assumption here is that traditional tragedy derives essentially from the protagonist's self-awareness. I mean not that Hamlet, say, knows *why* his will and his acts are at odds, but only that he knows this conflict to be the supreme fact of his life. Willy, on the other hand, and despite Biff's insistence that he is a "prince" (a lapse comparable to Charley's), evokes tears rather than exaltation precisely because he races joyfully to his death in the firm conviction that his conflict is resolved, when of course he has no idea what his conflict is. If self-awareness is basic to tragedy, then, it is impossible to say that Willy's tragedy is his *failure* to discover himself, or that we have here a different *kind* of tragedy. Finally, about this matter of classifying, I should perhaps mention what ought to be obvious: that attempts to assign a name arise not merely from some pointless academania for labels, but from a desire to *know* and name differences. Thus if one wishes to call Mr. Miller's play a tragedy, one must assign a new name to *Hamlet*.

The only one who gains self-awareness is Biff; but the play is Willy's. Because the play is indeed so clearly Willy's, the showdown lights up the play's flaw as tragedy. The main irony of the work is the effect upon Willy of Biff's appeal: Willy hears not a word, but is instead doomed to final nescience by Biff's love. This forceful irony, however, precludes tragedy, accounts for our quite nontragic feeling of depression, and introduces yet another confusion.

Mr. Miller distinguishes, in his essay, between tragedy and pathos:

> The possibility of victory must be there in tragedy. Where pathos rules, where pathos is finally derived, a character has fought a battle he could not possibly have won. The pathetic is achieved when the protagonist is, by virtue of his witlessness, his insensitivity, or the very air he gives off, incapable of grappling with a much superior force.
> Pathos truly is the mode for the pessimist. But tragedy requires a nicer balance between what is possible and what is impossible.

For Willy Loman, "victory" would have been realization not only of Biff's love for him, but of "who he was." But such a "victory" Willy "could not possibly have won," simply because he was created "incapable of grappling with a much superior force"—whether Biff's love or his own dream, the two forces which "his witlessness, his insensitivity," and his love for Biff prevent his seeing sanely. Mr. Miller is quite accurate in isolating the elements of pathos and pessimism, and in thus characterizing his own "Salesman." We sag because Willy hasn't a chance to know himself; to achieve tragic dimensions.

When we understand this much, however, we must ask, finally, what "wrong dreams" Willy had and who, in fact, "he was." These are the ultimate questions which the "Requiem" avoids. If the play is not a tragedy, we should nevertheless like to know what shape it does take. One way to approach this investigation is to ask precisely what causes Willy's collapse.

The proximate answer is that Willy's confusion, his identifying of two needs, overwhelms him. The two synonymous needs are 1) that Biff return his father's love, and 2) that Biff's love take the particular shape of his accepting Willy's "dream," and of thereby vindicating Willy's whole life. But we can be satisfied with this answer only while we allow Willy's "dream" to remain vague. When we solicit more precise information about the "dream" we find it composed, by Willy and Biff, of several elements: Ben's hard-fisted, independent acquisition of vast wealth; the geographical and economic freedom enjoyed by Willy's father, an improbable flute-hawking salesman of the plains, who "made more in a week than a man like [Willy] could make in a lifetime"; the fixed idea that Dave Singleman's ability to sell his product by telephone somehow revealed the pregnant power and value of being "well-liked"; the longing for sufficient peace of mind to enjoy his considerable manual skill and to raise chickens in the open air; the defensive insistence that he is popular and financially successful; and, to come full circle, the theory that Biff's high school popularity and athletic prowess will (must) inevitably make him as "successful" as Willy.

These elements are interwound so thoroughly that we cannot clearly distinguish cause from effect. And their interdependence is plainly deliberate: Mr. Miller wishes us to see that his "common man" would have been assuredly uncommon had he been able to untangle so many strands and find himself. But when we have seen how and why Willy is confused, we proceed to the confusion of his creator. Here we revert to the problem of theme.

Willy wants, in summary, three kinds of things: 1) love and respect; 2) freedom to work simply with his hands; and 3) "success" based on popularity in the "business world." Any attempt to distinguish between what he wants and what he thinks he wants is pointless, since the pathetic nature of the man is his blindness to this very distinction. But what does the playwright want? He is most vague about *why* the "dream" was "wrong." If Willy had taken advantage of his "one chance" to follow Ben to Alaska, it is probable that he would not have become a disciple of Dale Carnegie or have fought for Howard Wagner's brand of "success." Yet what could be more obvious than the criticism of the robber baron personified in Ben? Willy derives his values from Ben, and would have become another Ben in Alaska. On the other hand, if Willy had not been deluded and tactless in the "business world," he might have done well enough as a salesman. But if he had, would he have been different from Howard Wagner? Would he have been humanly adequate? (In this connection, incidentally, one may ask what real purpose is served by Biff's discovery in Boston. Biff would have been Willy-trained and miserable in business, whether or not he had made the trip to Boston; and, if we can judge by the author's sketch of Howard, Biff would have failed humanly even if he had sold merchandise triumphantly.)

Aside from locale, and from *abundance* of money or power, the point would seem to be that materialism must turn out poor specimens of humanity (e.g., Ben, Howard, and Happy). But if we are to see Willy as destroyed by materialistic values and by a "system" which shapes human lives so that, like mass-produced refrigerators, "when you've finally paid for them, they're used up," Charley and Bernard demonstrate plainly enough that one can manage one's affairs within such a "system" while remaining sane and decent. Conversely, if the "system" is *not* responsible for Willy's destruction, why are Happy, Ben, and Howard belabored as soullessly at home in it? It appears not that the author avoids a too-easy accusation in a complex situation, but that the complex possible causes largely cancel one another out.

The conclusion is not merely that Willy is nontragic, but that Mr. Miller, in supposing him tragic, implies his own uncertainty about Willy's trouble and about who Willy "was." He was not *the* Salesman of Charley's rhapsodic elocution-piece. He was not *only* the victim of an economic arrangement. And if the author speaks in Biff's assertion that Willy did not belong in the rat-race, we must suppose that "wrong" means "wrong for Willy" rather than "unfit for human participation"—in which case the social criticism of the play is severely maimed. No matter which way we turn to isolate "Willyness," we thus encounter evidence that if "attention must be paid" to Willy, the author's failure to pay it frustrates our attempt to do so. Willy is confused; but despite the force of this play, Mr. Miller's possible theme lies buried in his own confusion.

"Salesman" in Context: General Essays on Miller

WILLIAM WIEGAND

William Wiegand teaches English at San Francisco State College and is the author of, among other books, *The Treatment Man.*

ARTHUR MILLER
AND THE MAN WHO KNOWS

A little over a year ago, *Holiday Magazine* gave Arthur Miller, author of *Death of a Salesman* a chance to go home again.[1] They assigned him to write as part of their series on American colleges the story of the University of Michigan, as it was Then when Miller was a student there, and as it is Now. Miller stayed in Ann Arbor for about a week gathering material, then returned to New York and wrote the article, a highly sensitive and keenly nostalgic piece about how things had changed at Michigan, mostly about how impersonal they had become, and how, for some reason, the students were no longer making

From *The Western Review*, XXI (Winter 1957), 85–102. Reprinted by permission of William Wiegand and *The Western Review*.
[1] Arthur Miller, "University of Michigan," *Holiday*, XIV (December 1953), 68–70, 128–143.

themselves felt. It was the "hanging around the lamp post" that Miller missed; it was the failure of the student to experience that sense of being alive, that unique feeling of participation which Miller cherished in his own memories of college life.

The reaction of University officials to Miller's article was not cordial. Most of them were either hurt by it, or dismissed it as one Alumnus official did who remarked that "perhaps the University has not changed as much as Arthur Miller has." This may have been a consoling idea, but it was a diagnosis that was controverted by the evidence. The amazing thing was quite the opposite: Arthur Miller, far from having changed "so much," had not changed at all. He still believed in 1934-to-1938 with a passion that was undeniable. Nor was it so much a passion for the shadowy romance of anybody's college days, as it was a passion for the Values students held then (the capital "V" is Miller's). These Values were what made the difference, not specifically what was believed in those tarnished days, but the fact that anything was believed at all. The excitement of belief is what is gone, Miller says, and its absence portends, in his words, "a tragedy in the making."

As a man and a playwright who is deeply conscious of "tragedy" and whose voice has become of some importance on the stage today, the point of view implicitly suggested here raises some interesting questions about what Miller is. It offers a new suggestion perhaps that his work has been at least partly misunderstood, and this is important because *Death of a Salesman*, if not his other works too, has had an impact not only on critics but on popular audiences as well. Already, despite some controversial opinion about it, "Salesman" has been allowed the standing of a young classic. But where did it come from? "Classics" do not appear by means of magical processes; they come from somewhere and are obliged to be going some place. By definition, "classic" means "of or pertaining to a coherent system."

My feeling is that the foundations and ramifications of "Salesman" have not been properly understood on the level of anything like a system but have been worked out only in the obvious terms of a "tradition." Because of this, "Salesman" is left a mere *fait accompli*. It casts no shadow forward; it has only *been*, and this is sometimes fatal to classics. Provoked by the *Holiday* article, I would like to find this "system" by trying to factor "Salesman" out on the basis of something more alive than, say, Ibsenian realism or the disillusionment of the Thirties; more specifically, on the basis of the long and going career of Arthur Miller himself.

In writing "Salesman," Miller, first of all, accomplished something significant to the drama anthologists: he had tidied up a seventy-five year cycle in the theater. Titles like *From Ghosts to Death of a Salesman*, as John Gassner's latest collection is called, mean to suggest more, I think, than a simple bracketing of a group of recent plays. Gassner, in fact, has shown that Miller has taken the theater back to Ibsen while at the same time assimilating most of the major technical influences that have arisen since that time. Moreover, the ghosts of paternal sin that trouble Oswald Alving are very much the same as those that plague Biff Loman, but Miller makes the whole cycle glitter by showing off the enriched post-Ibsen heritage in projecting them. "Here [in 'Salesman']" Gassner writes, ". . . the expressionistic and realistic styles exist in a fused state."

In the process of describing the cycle, the epicycle—the literary history of Arthur Miller—has, however, been largely ignored. The reason for this is implied almost in passing, again by Gassner: "[Miller] had been working steadily toward excellence and had already distinguished himself with much thoughtful writing in his thirty-three years." In other words, if a *Death of a Salesman* was going to be written at that moment, what more natural, he seems to say, than that it should come from this seasoned professional, this winner of a Critics' Circle Award, this published novelist, this keen social conscience who was never associated with the "private sensibility" drama most of his fellow playwrights were producing? The same lack of real interest in Miller was shared by the play's less friendly critics who levied various reasonable, but impersonal complaints. Some dwelt, for example, on Willy Loman's failure as a tragic hero (a contention denied by some of the play's supporters). Others thought that the dialogue was "bad poetry." Eric Bentley said that the play was "vague" with a "blurring of outlines."[2]

So in general, "Salesman" was treated like a new baby whose arrival is not completely expected but is totally appropriate just the same because it is the product of an ideal marriage between a healthy, if nondescript, playwright and a dramatic tradition that has proved beautifully fertile after all. This fertility pre-occupied most of the offspring's strongest admirers. Those less impressed carped about the shape of Baby's fingernails perhaps, but showed no great interest as to what it was in Miller's genes that made them that way. Father was only Father, too much respected maybe, but also too much taken for granted. The reason for restoring Miller's parental rights, thus, is not that he has been resentful of the dandling wayfarers' attentions to his progeny, but that it has become almost impossible by now to determine how much of the play is Miller, how much is that of the "can-a-little-man-be-a-tragic-hero?" scholar, and how much belongs to that almost legendary businessman who weeps in the orchestra because Willy Loman reminds him so much either of his Uncle George or of his own secret self. With the perspective of five more years and the advantage of an additional play dur-ing that period, it should be possible to find specific character-istics of Miller—"Miller traditions," as it were—which may or may not be congruent with the social and dramatic traditions with which he is usually identified.

In order to do this, first of all it is perhaps necessary to dispose quickly of some of the prevalent popular opinions of what Miller is. The most common of these was recently reasserted when the State Department refused to allow Miller a passport to visit Europe last May, evidently on the grounds that his record sug-gested that he might be lured into making anti-American-way-of-life statements abroad. The fellow-traveler stigma is nothing new for him. *Life Magazine* helped wish it on him a few years back when they ran his name in an impromptu list of suspicious

---

[2] For Bentley's opinion of the play, see *In Search of Theater*, New York, Knopf, 1953, pp. 84–87.

intellectuals.[3] Whatever extra-literary factors may have operated in the diplomatic decision, Miller's work itself, it is clear, has not been Marxist for over ten years; I do not see that this is anything but obvious, unless, of course, one falls prey to the current confusion whereby peripheral criticism of The System is equated with "being a Red." Miller has, in fact, more often than not in his commentaries bent over backwards to be above politics, claiming to be interested strictly in the "moral dilemma" of our society.

But if he has himself shied away from doctrinaire interpretations of his plays, this has not stopped other people, some nominally Miller's friends, from attempting to define his ideology and from occasionally feeling insulted by the cloudiness of it. The Crucible, for example, was criticized by Robert Warshow in Commentary Magazine for waging a totally inadequate attack on McCarthyism,[4] a purpose the liberal wing necessarily presumed Miller did or should have had in writing the play. Warshow was at least an antidote to fuzzy-minded myopics like columnist Ed Sullivan, who inquired after The Crucible, why Miller hadn't rather written a play that praised our colonial heritage.

For the most part, then, it was only long after "Salesman" had become an institution that the vested-interest experts got concerned about the errors in Miller's ways. Generally, their disapproval was as whimsical as it was predisposed. However, without shaking off the spell of both the overzealous liberal "friends" on one hand and the Comintern mentalities in Washington on the other, it would be difficult to look at Miller's touchy early plays and see them as anything more than adolescent symptoms of his dislike of The System. The plays are part

---

[3] "Red Visitors Cause Rumpus," Life, XXVI (April 4, 1949), 39–43. The famous collection of Life-labeled "Dupes and Fellow Travelers," Miller among them, fills a two-page (42–43) spread.

[4] Robert Warshow, "The Liberal Conscience in The Crucible," Commentary, XV (March 1953), 265–271. Wiegand's one-sentence summary of Warshow's article does not (and does not intend to) give the flavor of the essay. It is useful now, not as Miller criticism, but as a document of the political tone of the times, a ritual attack on "liberal confusion."

of his artistic development, however, and seem fruitful, I think, because they contain the seeds of an important non-political premise in Miller's work—an idea which lay dormant after he left college only to reach full bloom later in the plays that have been written since the war. I will discuss this idea shortly.

II

Let us look first at the early work: two full-length plays which Miller wrote as an undergraduate at the University of Michigan. Both won awards in the University Avery Hopwood Contests, respectively, in 1936 and 1937. Both also were cast strictly in the Marxist mold of the Thirties.[5]

The earlier, *Honors at Dawn,* deals with an obtuse young proletarian named Max Zabriskie who is blacklisted by the capitalists after participating, rather unwittingly, in an abortive strike at the plant where he has worked. Once out of The System, he elects to go to college, the seat of integrity and idealism. His brother, a much better student than he, is already there, and unknown to Max is subsidized by the university to spy on campus radicals. When Max learns of his brother's perfidy and the even greater corruption of the university, his illusions about college are dispelled. Max leaves and works himself back into the union movement where with sound social conscience he participates in a real strike. The play climaxes with the hero beaten up, but with a sure sense that he has found "at dawn" the "honors" he was seeking at the university before he learned of their false foundation.

Miller's other Hopwood play, *No Villain,* was later revised and expanded into a drama called *They Too Arise* which won a national WPA award in 1938. This play revolves around the family of a middle-class garment manufacturer in New York and takes place during one of the labor crises in the industry. Abe

---

[5] These plays exist only in manuscript; copies are at the University of Michigan. A typescript of *They Too Arise* is in the New York Public Library.

Simon, the father, is determined to cross the picket lines to make deliveries which will save his small and shaky business. His older son Ben is his right bower, schooled in the family traditions but cynical about carrying them out. Arnie, the younger son, home from college for the summer, is called a Communist by his father and wears the title proudly. Arnie will not scab for his father against the strikers.

It becomes clear at last that only the big manufacturers will survive the strike. Ben, however, is offered a cheap out when given an opportunity to marry the daughter of one of the bigger enterprisers. Arnie's influence is too persuasive though. Ben rejects the marriage, the business folds, the old grandfather symbolically dies. With the two boys joined, it seems that Abe and his wife have little choice but to convert too. As the play ends, they are getting used to the idea, much as the Gordons did in Clifford Odets' *Paradise Lost*.

All this was before 1940. Out of school only a few years when the war broke out, Miller was immediately enlisted as a propaganda writer of sorts, much of his output being absorbed by radio and in sponsored one-act plays like *That They May Live*, a work dedicated to urging its audience to turn in OPA price ceiling violators. Margaret Mayorga, who includes this play in one of her annual collections, reports that in production the in-the-script interruption of the stage action by a man planted in the audience on several occasions almost started a riot. This indicated at least that Miller had a certain capacity to stir live audiences, although it must be presumed that this particular uprising occurred out of simple irritation with a loudmouth rather than any kind of *Waiting for Lefty* indignation against black market offenders.

In any case, Miller suddenly found himself on one hand writing social messages for money and on the other hand, on his own, for the stage he was writing a play with virtually no dialectic significance at all. This work, which reached Broadway in 1944, was called *The Man Who Had All the Luck*. It reads like part Willa Cather and part Sigmund Freud, involving in its plot a young gasoline-station operator who experiences such a series of good breaks that eventually he can't stand it any more. He finally succeeds in cooking up a situation that financially destroys him. His homespun wife, however, recognizes that his guilt feelings over his success must be alleviated somehow and cheerfully accepts the disaster, which unfortunately has little real impact since it is only financial.

The play ran less than a week on Broadway, the Cather elements turning out perhaps too bland, the Freud too thick (although Miller blames a bad production). He was at any rate a produced playwright on Broadway. Oddly enough, however, his major work (at this point) had not only no tinge of Marxism; it hardly had a point of view. For a young man like Miller, who was apparently interested in much more than mere craft, this was unusual. One might speculate whether or not he was still nursing a dialectic that had to remain dormant for the duration of the emergency.

By this time, however, the war was beginning to cast up specters more disturbing than price violators. Miller received an assignment from Hollywood to prepare himself for writing the screen play of *The Story of G. I. Joe*, the film version of Ernie Pyle's stories. A 4-F himself, Miller accepted the task enthusiastically. If the Marxists had long known what society was like, they had no ready answers for what war was like, and on his own he meant to find out.

The result of his tour of Army camps and war-casualty hospitals is reported in a book Miller wrote after he finished his film scenario. This work, *Situation Normal*, bridges the crucial gap, I think, between Miller of the early discipline and Miller of the later one. The book ends this way:

. . . you are over New York harbor now. In the plane the Navy flier buttons his jacket, fixes his tie, runs a comb through his hair, sets his battle ribbons straight. He stares, summing up his appointments for the day, the people to call, the important girl. He feels for his money, is assured. He counts the days ahead and mentally apportions a certain amount of cash to each, knowing, however, that he will soon forget how much he allowed himself to spend and will probably be broke in four days regardless of calculations. We land and he descends the steps to the ground and hurries into the airport building. He secludes himself in the phone booth and begins to pick up his life. Mother answers and is waiting for him. The girl picks up the phone at the very first ring and a party is being organized. Already odors of woman assail him and the sound of certain kinds of evening gowns. Hearing her voice he is filled with a dull longing for something from her, something he wishes he could sense between her words and among the various pitches in her voice. And he cannot find it there. One minute she is filled with pity for him, the next pride. He suffers for her and for his inability to know what it really is he wants her to feel. He recalls how easy it was to talk to the guys in the squadron, how simple to communicate without talking at all. She asks him how it was and he says it was pretty bad in the beginning but it got all right later on and suddenly he is very tired. Sad, strangely. He makes the date and hangs up. What the hell does he want her to do, know what it was like out there? How could she when she wasn't there? Maybe it's something she ought to want. Wanting him back, being glad he is back. . . it's like everything they had been doing out there added up to one thing—that he had gotten back at last and could go dancing and see his mother . . . His mother kisses him, walks him into the house where he smells the food. He washes in the old bathroom, finds a razor he has forgotten about, and starts to shave. For an instant, the curious notion strikes him that it will be good to get out of here again, it will be good to be going back. Exactly why, he doesn't know, but good it will be. Good to be going in one direction with the other guys. Good to have certain things mutually understood again. He goes downstairs and mother talks and he watches her. It is growing strange. He has found her with nothing more than joy at his returning. He wonders again what on earth he would have these people feel. God knows he doesn't want her calling him her hero. The heroes aren't coming home to mother any more. But they did change something by going out there, didn't they? Or did they? The newspaper on the chair looks up at him. "In the next war the probability is that the rocket bomb . . ." The next war. Well now, as easy as that. When are they going to start figuring out this war? His mother questions.

Between mouthfuls he answers his mother. "Well, in the beginning," he mutters, "it was pretty bad. But after a while . . . it was
all right." Oh, hell, let it go at that. It doesn't matter anyway.
   Does it?

This final "does it?" this apparently rhetorical question, is
what Miller has been trying to answer ever since. He has en-
deavored to show that the failure of people to communicate
with one another does matter, of course. It mattered to some
extent even in the very early plays. But after *Situation Normal*,
the idea became crucial: certain men know certain truths; people suffer and sometimes die because these truths fail to be
communicated. Consequently, his Navy flier quiet and puzzled,
always the square peg in the round hole, has since descended
from the clouds in the alter egos of Chris Keller in *All My
Sons*, Biff Loman in *Death of a Salesman*, and John Proctor in
The Crucible, all of whom found their supernal, ineffable awareness to be tragically incommunicable when they reached the
earth below.
   The repetition of the same situation and especially of the
same characters is, I think, the kind of thing Bentley was talking about when he speaks of "the blurring of outlines." Biff
Loman is an undelineated sensitive man, stamped from the
international archetype, likewise Chris and Proctor; all three of
these roles can be and incidentally were played on Broadway
by the same archetypically sensitive actor, Arthur Kennedy.
More specifically, in terms of the Navy flier, each of these characters may be described as a Man Who Knows (a term, by
the way, that Miller himself first used to designate one of the
dramatis personae in the one act play mentioned above). Inevitably in Miller's plays, the Man Who Knows is the character
with whom the major share of the audience's sympathy lies
(not to be confused with pity, the emotion necessarily felt
toward Willy Loman), and is the one who has the soundest
suspicion that something is wrong with the society around him.
Unfortunately, however, he can do nothing to forestall the
imminent tragedy.

Chris, Biff, and Proctor, of course, have still other similarities. All three express themselves in forceful colloquial dialogue, much as Odets' heroes do. Unlike Odets' men, however, the passion with which they speak does not conceal any personal fight with the devil inside. All of these Men seem to have been born right-thinking; even Proctor's dalliance with his young tormentress never seems particularly evil of him, but is merely a necessary thread of the plot. And Biff Loman's stealing is kleptomania, hence no breach of the Ten Commandments. What the Man Who Knows knows is what is true, what should be. Beyond his inborn wisdom, he is an innocent and helpless tool.

To complete the pattern in these three works are characters foiling the Man Who Knows, each of whom may be described as the Man Who Learns. These characters are wrong-thinking at the beginning, mostly because of pride, but they learn something by the end. Joe Keller, who manufactures defective airplane engines and kills twenty-one pilots, hears that his own son has committed suicide because of the disgrace, forcing him to accept the fact that they were, as he says, "all my sons." Because of his early misapprehension, Joe must kill himself too. Willy Loman never comes to a complete awareness of his mistake; that is the major impact and irony of *Death of a Salesman*. Still, even if there is no capacity to act on or talk about it, there is a Learning in "Salesman," a Learning that gets through to the audience and to Willy too: the dream is a sham and there can be no possibility of his surviving to test it further. Both Keller and Willy hence become victims, perhaps because they learn too late.

The pattern is varied slightly in *The Crucible*. The Man Who Learns here is the Reverend Hale, but unlike the earlier two plays, it is not he who suffers the death in the third act. But Hale takes the play over so completely from the victim, Proctor (who after all only Knows and is static) that the latter's martyrdom seems almost a sentimental afterthought. "I denounce these proceedings," Hale says at the curtain of the second last scene, but the tide of majority stupidity has already engulfed them. He is too late too, and this is his tragedy.

What is Miller's verdict on these people who learn so slowly and painfully? Well, as Uncle Charlie says at Willie Loman's funeral, "No one dast blame this man." No one dast blame any of them—Keller, Willy, Hale. But it is sad, Miller says, sad that the few who comprehend the truth from the first were powerless to communicate it so that it could be understood in time.

Miller's moral lesson ends in every case the same way. The false faith leads to martyrdom. In *All My Sons*, this faith is that "the world ends at the building line." In "Salesman," it is, of course, that material success is everything, and in *The Crucible*, the error is that witches exist and cast evil spells. In each case, a prevalent misapprehension sets the machine in motion. Whatever the nature of the false faith, someone must be martyred in the trial. This dramatic pattern is familiar, of course, in Greek tragedy.

Miller's three latest plays, in other words, aspire to more than what has been called "social drama." Note, for example, that the strong motif of retribution does not appear in his "optimistic" Marxist plays where false faiths in the university and in the business were respectively undermined without more than bloodying the hero a little. Similarly, there is, of course, no "Greek" expiation in the play Miller adapted for a New York production in 1951—Ibsen's *Enemy of the People*. The Man Who Knows in this work is entirely capable of communicating his truth even though people don't like it. Ibsen makes his point by showing Doctor Stockmann ostracized in his community. He does not need to award him martyrdom as a kind of consolation prize.

Of *Enemy of the People*, Miller writes in the preface to his adaptation the following:

. . . I believed this play could be alive for us because its central theme is, in my opinion, the central theme of our social life today. Simply, it is the question of whether the democratic guarantees protecting political minorities ought to be set aside in time of crises. More personally, it is the question of whether one's vision of the truth ought to be a source of guilt at a time when the mass of men condemn it as a dangerous and devilish lie. . .

Here again, in making a judgment on what is important, on what indeed is "*the* central theme of our social life today," he focuses on a problem specifically involving individual martyrdom. Also, in choosing quickly to treat the "question" of minority rights on an oblique personal level, he sees immediately what he wants to see in the play: a "source of guilt" or sin, even in Knowing, although there is no evidence that Stockmann feels anything of the kind. Miller reads a classic sin-and-retribution theme into the play.

According to Miller, what makes Ibsen a giant is not the boldness of his themes (which are of course no longer bold), but it is rather the eternal truth of his situations. Elsewhere in his preface, Miller says:

. . . I had a private wish to demonstrate that Ibsen is really pertinent today, that he is not "old-fashioned" and implicitly, that those who condemn him are themselves misleading our theater and our playwrights into a blind alley of senseless sensibility, triviality, and the inevitable waste of our dramatic talents; for it has become the fashion of plays to reduce the "thickness" of life to a fragile facsimile, to avoid portraying the complexities of life, the contradictions of character, the fascinating interplay of cause and effect that have long been part of the novel.

In working toward objectives like these in his own plays, Miller's point of view on the theater implicitly becomes directly opposite to those of playwrights like John Van Druten, for example. Van Druten has written: "The theater is ephemeral and plays are a perishable commodity . . . [Still] I see no reason for being ashamed of one's part in it, nor for avoiding the effort to do one's best at it."[6]

---

[6] See John Van Druten, *Playwright at Work* (New York: Harper, 1953), pp. 7–8.

Where Van Druten is "unashamed" but resigned, Miller is militant and determined that certain values are deathless. He glimpses them in Ibsen, and, as I have noted, pursues them even more hotly down old Hellenic corridors when he says, as Plato might have: "I don't see how you can write anything decent without using the question of right and wrong as the basis." And when he writes an *All My Sons*, which fits the dramatic specifications offered by Aristotle right down to recognition and peripety.

III

The consequences of Miller's adoption of classic moral values are complicated. Obviously, appropriating Sophocles' religion does not make one Sophocles, even if we ignore the large issue of respective lyric capacities. The question of how the values have been embraced and revealed remains. Miller's "expression," in other words, must stand up as drama. It must bear criticism. To this end, but in fear of interposing any rigidly abstract standards, either ancient or modern, I would like to make a few purely comparative judgments of Miller's plays, as drama, against those of two playwrights who have worked approximately in his milieu: again Ibsen and Odets. This comparison is only partially fair to Miller since we have, of course, a longer span of work by which to judge the other two dramatists.

The congruities between *An Enemy of the People* and *The Crucible* I have already partially noted. Both are stories of men who have, in Miller's words, a "vision of the truth [which is] condemned by the mass of men as a dangerous and devilish lie." If the likenesses are evident, there are also these important differences between the plays: Ibsen's hero, Stockmann, invites his own disaster by freely publishing the report on the pollution of the waters, which will destroy the economy of his village. He does this without compunction and with a cavalier kind of thoughtlessness. Miller's Proctor, on the other hand, is almost a casual victim of his village. His "sin" with the girl, which Miller tries to insist on, lies outside the immediate public concern and has no bearing on his fate. He appears, innocent, at the witch trials in order to defend his wife, herself unjustly branded. In time, Proctor finds himself accused too and eventually convicted. Offered an opportunity to confess and save his life, he refuses, preferring the martyr's death instead. Thus he dies gratuitously, bravely perhaps, but rather like the soldier on the battlefield who will not turn and run despite the fact he finds himself in a world he never made.

Stockmann has entered the battle in full tilt. His opponents have no choice but to defend themselves; the danger to them is apparent, and undoubtedly more real to us, in dramatic terms, than Salem's witches. The "villains" in *Enemy of the People* are not victims of a mere temporary, even if recurring, social delusion. They have power, but so does Stockmann. He is never reduced, as is Proctor, to go begging to his opponents for wisdom and justice. Unlike Proctor, he has a chance to win on his own terms. And, at the end, with rocks crashing through the window, he says: "We must live through this." He continues to make plans although he is well aware "there'll be a long night before it's day." The light of this "day" is what Miller never allows for, except as it may be seen in the gaudy fire that burns his martyr. He ends with the roll of drums and the suffering of a sad, but somewhat cheap, injustice. The curbstone "justice" that Stockmann gets, base as it is, seems in some proportion to his injury to the community. Esthetically, this ending has much better conscience than the ending of *The Crucible*.

Miller's sentimentality, at least in this area, may possibly be due to the fact that he is too glib an ideologist. It is so easy for him to fit the raw material into the "lesson" that there are no rough edges. Everything is schematized and smooth as glass. He writes, for instance, among much other prefatory and interpolative commentary in the published version of *The Crucible*, this:

In the countries of the Communist ideology, all resistance of any import is linked to the totally malign capitalist succubi and in America any man who is not reactionary in his view is open to the charge of alliance with the Red hell. Political opposition thereby is given an inhumane overlay which then justifies the abrogation of all normally applied customs of civilized intercourse. . .

While this sort of interlinear display is forgivable self-indulgence, it does invite suspicion that the cart is pulling the horse, or that everything in the play is too tightly yoked to its elaborately explicated intentions.

Even further in the direction of didacticism is Miller's decision in his adaptation of *Enemy of the People* to edit out certain speeches of Stockmann which, according to Miller, "have been taken to mean Ibsen was a Fascist." He devotes a short section of his preface to considering this matter, then finally says:

I have taken the justification for *removing those examples which no longer prove the theme* (italics mine)—examples I believe Ibsen would have removed were he alive today—the line in the original manuscript that reads: "There is no established truth[7] that can remain true for more than seventeen, eighteen, at most twenty years. . . ." The man who wrote A *Doll's House*, the clarion call for the equality of women, cannot be equated with a fascist. . . .

John Gassner, among others, has pointed out in detail how Ibsen is "one of the most deceptive of dramatists," how his inherent contradiction is a large part of his dramatic strength. To Miller, however, Ibsen was a man who occasionally wrote "tendentious speeches spoken into the blue" and had to be revised in order "to prove the theme."

This artistic nearsightedness in Miller is perhaps magnified when we compare him with Clifford Odets, a thesis dramatist who is roughly contemporary with Miller. The relationship between these two writers is a close one. Rather than saying, however, that Odets, who came first, was an influence on Miller, it is probably more accurate to say they were both influenced by similar backgrounds and similar economic experiences. Both began by writing Jewish family plays with strong Marxist

---

[7] Miller apparently distinguishes between "established" or pragmatic truth, and absolute truth. [W. W.]

themes. Later, the more strident leftism was sacrificed along with the ethnic settings. Both, though, continued to work with middle-class characters.

Miller repeats with astonishing frequency dramatic situations that Odets used first. In *Awake and Sing*, for example, an old man commits an "accident"-suicide in a futile effort to supply the scion of the family with much-needed insurance money. This is exactly the climax of *Death of a Salesman*. In *Paradise Lost*, Odets' favorite among his own plays, the personal history of Ben Gordon wholly anticipates that of Biff Loman. Ben's boyhood victory in a Madison Square Garden track meet parallels Biff's moment of glory in the Ebbets Field football game. Ben has medals and a statue of himself in the living room; his young bride says adoringly: "My Ben can be anything he wants," much as Biff Loman's mother says: "He could be a—anything in that suit!" Ben, like Biff, is unable to live up to his high school prestige, experiences a complete self-contempt, and winds up a petty gunman much as Biff does a thief.

The rougher similarities between the work of the two men are beyond count; *Golden Boy* and *Rocket to the Moon* both have echoes in "Salesman," for instance, and *Till The Day I Die* treats the same problem that *The Crucible* does. It is, however, the differences between their respective treatments rather than the similarities which suggest the particular nature of Miller's selectivity and emphasis. In the situations mentioned above, for example, Odets practically throws away Jacob Berger's suicide in *Awake and Sing*. To him this is matter for the second act and not the third. Dying is incidental to the living that is going on. No funeral eulogies are spoken for old Jacob but this does not mitigate the fact that it is a brave thing he has done rather than simply a terribly pathetic thing. Odets is thus able later to close the play with an unsentimental affirmation of the life-force, an entirely appropriate ending.

In *Paradise Lost*, for the second act curtain, Ben Gordon expires offstage in a rain of police bullets. But somehow Odets has saved this from simple pathos, too. Ben's fall never holds more than part of the stage and yet his flashy finish is no less a one than he has a right to. Because he is a man, he has traded confidences, cynically enough only with the person who is cuckolding him; he does not, like Biff Loman, weep self-reproach on the shoulders of his mother and father.

Both *Awake and Sing* and *Paradise Lost* are of Odets' Marxist period. These plays, however, survive despite the outdatedness of their particular message. The reason for this must be that Odets was either too slipshod a Communist, too artful a dramatist, or, more likely, both. Today the speeches fit the play like period furniture on the set—they would not really be missed if removed; at the same time they add something to the place and time and spirit of the occasion. But certainly it is unlikely that the plays could be produced in Moscow today since they never fulfill the political responsibility they invite. They are too Chekhovian.

Such evasion of "responsibility" Miller is incapable of. His primary dedication is to "prove the theme." The result is that Odets' plays, with their characters and individual scenes that transcend the gestalt, are often less than the sum of their parts; and, conversely, Miller's may seem more. But in Miller's case, we may ask: how large are the parts? His characters too often are flat and humorless. He shows no love for them and very little respect, except here and there the kind a schoolboy might hold for George Washington, and then not Washington the man but Washington the symbol. His people are passionate but bloodless. Where in Miller, for example, is there anybody with the heart of Moody in *Golden Boy*, Moe in *Awake and Sing*, or Prince in *Rocket to the Moon*, all superficially selfish characters?

To these same people, Miller seems able to offer only pity. "A man is a jellyfish," he has a character say in *The Man Who Had All the Luck*, "and a jellyfish can't swim no matter how he tries; it's the tide that pushes him every time. So just keep feeding and enjoy the water till you're thrown up on the beach." Although this particular character is a cynic, it is remarkable how often Miller reverts to comparisons of men with beasts of land or sea, particularly helpless ones. The best he will allow for human beings is a basically negative metaphor: "A man is not a piece of fruit," as Willy Loman says. Yet he is only animate enough to feel pain and to resist being peeled.

Miller sees no particular charm or other possibilities in the weaknesses of his characters. Their ineffectuality leaves them simply an object of pity or, vaguely, an inspiration for moral regeneration. They are examples, even sermons, because they sermonize. "Attention must be paid to such a man," Linda Loman says when she knows the tide is pushing Willy up on the beach. Joe Keller's wife shares Linda's undefined need for some sort of acknowledgment of the terrible situation. After Joe's crime has been confessed, Kate asks her son, "What more can we be [than 'sorry']?" Chris says, "You can be better." And even much earlier, Esther Simon in *They Too Arise*, speaks the weary final curtain line: "Yeh, we gotta learn; a lotta things we gotta learn." People are so hopelessly far away from grasping simple truths, Miller says, they have no right to bid for anything but pity at the moment.

The only major characters not defeated in their own terms and more or less from the outset are Proctor, and, in the novel *Focus*, Newman. Proctor is engulfed just the same. Newman, the timid personnel executive, arrives at a sort of bogus victory by ceasing at the end of the book to deny he is a Jew after being mistaken for one and abused because of it up until that point. This is doubly ironic because Newman has been somewhat anti-Semitic himself. Unfortunately, however, his acceptance of the Jewish identity that has been thrust upon him occurs while he is making a complaint in a police station; again society's brutality is too much for him to handle by himself. Like many of Miller's characters, he only wants to be let alone, but denied this, he wears the martyr's badge proudly, the Man Who Learns, in effect, how to adapt himself to what is perhaps the most ancient heritage of martyrdom in existence. Finding this role, he loses his fear. He learns late, like Willy Loman, Joe Keller, and the Reverend Hale, that he had been contaminated by the poison in the social sea. The realization may be relieving to the jellyfish, but will, of course, have no effect on the tidal waters.

Partly aware of this "relief," there have been recent efforts by some who, while attacking the drama of "senseless sensibility," have tried to build up a case for "tragedy of the common man." Longing for the tragical catharsis has become a shibboleth to modern critics, and those most friendly to the contemporary stage seem determined to fit certain modern plays into the classic formulae. Without much poking and prodding, Miller fits— if only, they seem to say, we can accept the protagonist as sufficiently symbolic of the society as classic royalty was. This is the nub of the problem.

A better question, it would seem to me, in the light of any close examination of Miller's characters, is not whether they are broad enough symbols but whether they are deep enough men. Is their power perhaps *merely* symbolic? Is Willy Loman a cross that Miller is shaking at us, its basic impact lying somewhere outside the play, in the house where Uncle George lives, for instance? Certainly Uncle George is no less real and no more mythic than Sacco and Vanzetti were, for instance, when liberal sentiment engendered by their conviction magnified Maxwell Anderson's *Winterset* into "tragedy" for a time, largely because it drew a recognizable parallel with a real situation fraught with social implication. Unwittingly or not, *The Crucible* does the same thing with the McCarthy bogey.

The danger of harvesting these extra-play dividends is obvious: in most cases, the symbol stifles any chance the individual character might have if left on his own. We are deluded by the symbol's mystic tribal sanction. We are lulled by a myth. In certain ways, it might even be contended that Miller's ritual pilgrimages in the coach of Human Truth lead only to a brave mirage quite as insubstantial as that sought by commercial writers who hitch up to the resplendent locomotive called The American Dream in order that all the passengers may feel familiar and easy in the club car.

It is ironic perhaps to associate a writer as "moral" and

Knowing as Miller with this kind of fallacy, and yet, like them, he is fundamentally reliant on response to ritual beliefs. His problem, consequently, is one which even the old minstrels had: how to make the singing of a legend seem fresh and pure and convincing. Right now, rather than being a tragedian, Arthur Miller is like the man who comes to a funeral and tells many traditional stories about the deceased, except you get the feeling he was anticipating the occasion of the epitaph even while he was witnessing the events.

In summary, Miller has been writing for the last ten years what might be called modern-dress versions of classical martyr-doms. While the beginning of his success as a dramatist was coincident with his discovery of a particular pattern for accomplishing this adaptation, the germ of it lay in his very early work as well. Although these works superficially called for political action, they indicated his instincts and interests were more deeply "tragic," if we accept the word with all its moral connotations. In *Situation Normal*, for instance, he expresses grievance with the producers of *The Story of G. I. Joe* when they revised his screenplay. "About three of them [soldiers] were going to die at first," Miller writes. "Then we cut it down to two, and finally I think only one died dead, the others ending up with wounds. It is very hard to kill a good character in Hollywood because the public seems to prefer pictures in which nobody dies . . ."

The discovery of the uncommunicated-truth pattern was a discipline for this kind of Lost Generation disillusionment. Miller afterwards no longer had to guess "about three" deaths were sufficient for his tragical purposes. He simply made a religion of absolute, but non-sectarian, truth, martyrs for which were to be drawn from the ranks of men who knew this truth but could not communicate it and men who did not know it at the start but came to learn it.

It is not unlikely that this "truth" represented some kind of substitute for the Marxist "truth" which had fortified Miller's early career and answered all the questions of life. After he abandoned it, he probably felt for a time something like his

Navy flier who realized in the limbo that the central principle of existence was lacking. The flier thinks: it would "be good to be going back. Exactly why, he doesn't know, but good it will be. Good to be going in one direction with the other guys. Good to have certain things mutually understood again." Vague things, to be sure, and a vague direction. But something.

It is no discredit to Miller that he needed a direction, nor no credit to Odets, for instance, that he did not. Ten years older than Miller, Odets had not grown up with the depression, with the sharp early sense of group identity that the whole "anti" movement offered. Miller, younger, perhaps more impressionable, was genuinely moved by the opportunities for martyrdom that are relished by hard-minded youth. Odets, on the other hand, was, as Harold Clurman's book on the Group Theater[8] indicates, more egocentric, more the *Naturkind* of the Twenties. He put on Marxism like a coat and took it off again as easily. But for Miller the loss of the old feeling is a tragedy. If there is at Michigan no communication among students and between students and faculty; if the ideals are lost in some old book or on some professor's muted tongue; if everything is really changed; then it is unbearably sad. He says, it may be, of course, that he does not know where to look any more. But truth and beauty were here somewhere. Their passing is a cause for genuine sorrow. This nostalgic sorrow is the emotional link with the Thirties Miller has never been able to cut.

Which brings us to the present and a look ahead to Miller's shortly-expected next play,[9] eagerly awaited in New York for reasons others have accurately expressed. Reasons like: Miller is always timely, he is not afraid of large emotions, he has a great gift for structure and dramatic development; if his techniques are largely traditional, he is aware of and has made impressive use of more experimental methods. He is "fresh" and poetic, with none of what has been called "the mystique of O'Neill

---

[8] *The Fervent Years* (New York: Knopf, 1945).

[9] The play was *A View from the Bridge*. Although Wiegand's article was not printed until 1957, it was apparently written before the New York opening of "View" in 1955.

and . . . the formality and generalized rhetoric of Anderson; [his work] never leaves the actual world! it does not cultivate naiveté; and it takes a responsible view of life in our society . . ." Clurman, Odets' old director, has also spoken of Miller's "humanistic jurisprudence."

All this, however, to be worthwhile, ought to be channeled past certain facts apparent about the writer: one, he does not give much to human goodness, intelligence, or charm; social vice inevitably defeats them. Two, a few men are in touch with truth and they suffer most because reality is so bad in comparison. Three, dying is the loudest proof of having lived.

Hence, this eclectic social consciousness of Arthur Miller is levered from hardly more than a single fulcrum of superstition: that the men who know are destined to be trampled upon, yet to arrive at this "knowing" is a man's only chance of saving his soul. Here I must argue with the Clurman opinion quoted above. Miller's superstition is not so "humanistic"; it belongs more to a mysticism which, unlike O'Neill's, minimizes the essential life-force of the little man, and which, in past eras, has often been a portent of monolithic and reactionary societies. This may be the shadow that *Death of a Salesman* is casting forward, and which makes the play unwittingly timely in a decade when they say that both God and the Kremlin are growing in strength every day. Standing against them and their temper in our time, the "fragile facsimiles" made by Miller's contemporaries, sadly enough, seem fragile indeed.

RAYMOND WILLIAMS

Raymond Williams is a lecturer at Cambridge University. Among his books are *Drama from Ibsen to Eliot, Culture and Society, The Long Revolution,* and *Modern Tragedy.*

THE REALISM OF ARTHUR MILLER

I

The most important single fact about the plays of Arthur Miller is that he has brought back into the theatre, in an important way, the drama of social questions. It has been fashionable, certainly in England, to reject such drama as necessarily superficial. In part, this rejection is in itself social, for it has shown itself in the context of a particular phase of consciousness: that widespread withdrawal from social thinking which came to its peak in the late nineteen-forties, at just the time when we were first getting to know Arthur Miller as a dramatist. Yet the rejection can be seen, also, as critically necessary, for there is little doubt that the dramatic forms in which social questions were ordinarily raised had become, in general, inadequate: a declined, low-pressure naturalism, or else the angularity of the self-conscious problem play, the knowingness of the post-expressionist social revue. To break out from this deadlock needed three things, in any order: a critical perception of why the forms were inadequate; effective particular experiment; a revival, at depth and with passion, of the social thinking itself. Arthur Miller is unquestionably the most important agent of this break-out, which as yet, however, is still scattered and uncertain. His five plays to date show a wide and fascinating range of experiment, and the introduction he has written to the collected edition of them shows an exceptionally involved and

From *Critical Quarterly*, I (Summer 1959), pp. 140–149, reprinted by permission of *Critical Quarterly* and Raymond Williams.

perceptive critical mind, both self-conscious and self-critical of the directions of his creative effort. Yet, while he could not have written his plays without these qualities, it is probably true that the decisive factor, in his whole achievement, is a particular kind and intensity of social thinking, which in his case seems both to underlie and to determine the critical scrutiny and the restless experimentation. In seeking to define the magnificent realism of the great tradition of nineteenth-century fiction, I wrote of that kind of work which "seeks to create and judge the quality of a whole way of life in terms of the qualities of persons":[1]

Neither element, neither the society nor the individual, is there as a priority. The society is not a background against which the personal relationships are studied, nor are the individuals merely illustrations of aspects of the way of life. Every aspect of personal life is radically affected by the quality of the general life, yet the general life is seen at its most important in completely personal terms.

I argued that this "social" tradition had broken down, in fiction, into the separate forms of the "personal" and the "sociological," and I would make the same analysis, with certain changes of detail, in the case of twentieth-century drama. The key to social realism, in these terms, lies in a particular conception of the relationship of the individual to society, in which neither is the individual seen as a unit nor the society as an aggregate, but both are seen as belonging to a continuous and in real terms inseparable process. My interest in the work of Arthur Miller is that he seems to have come nearer than any other post-war writer (with the possible exceptions of Albert Camus and Albrecht Goes) to this substantial conception. Looking at it from one point of view, he has restored active social criticism to the drama, and has written on such contemporary themes as the social accountability of business, the forms of the success-ethic, intolerance and thought-control, the nature of modern work-relations. Yet he has written "about" these in such a way

---

[1] See Raymond Williams, "Realism and the Contemporary Novel," *Partisan Review*, XXVI (Spring 1959), 200–213.

as to distinguish his work quite clearly from the ordinary socio-logical problem-play, for at his best he has seen these problems as living tissue, and his most successful characters are not merely "aspects of the way of life," but individuals who are ends and values in themselves:

He's a human being, and a terrible thing is happening to him. So attention must be paid . . . Attention, attention must be finally paid to such a person.

It is from this centre—a new or newly-recovered way of social thinking, which is also powerfully available as direct experi-ence—that any estimate of Arthur Miller as a dramatist must begin.

I I

Miller's first two published plays[2]—he had written seven or eight others before this success—are *All My Sons* (1947) and *Death of a Salesman* (1949). It is extremely interesting to com-pare these two, because while they are very different in method they are also quite obviously very deeply linked, in experience. *All My Sons* has been described as an Ibsenite play, and cer-tainly, if we restrict Ibsen to the kind of play he wrote between *The League of Youth* (1869) and *Rosmersholm* (1886), it is a relevant description. The similarities are indeed so striking that we could call *All My Sons* pastiche if the force of its conception were not so evident. It is perhaps that much rarer case, of a writer who temporarily discovers in an existing form an exact way of realising his own experience. At the center of the play is the kind of situation which was Ibsen's development of the device of the "fatal secret." Joe Keller, a small manufacturer, has (in a similar way to Consul Bernick in *Pillars of Society*) committed a social crime for which he has escaped responsi-bility. He acquiesced in the sending of defective parts to the American Air Force in wartime, and yet allowed another man to

---

[2] There were earlier published plays (see Bibliography), but none obvi-ously that Miller cared to put into *Collected Plays*.

take the consequences and imprisonment. The action begins after the war, and is basically on the lines of what has been called Ibsen's retrospective method (it was always much more than a device of exposition; it is a thematic forcing of past into present). The Ibsen method of showing first an ordinary domestic scene, into which, by gradual infiltration, the crime and the guilt enter and build up to the critical eruption, is exactly followed. The process of this destructive infiltration is carefully worked out in terms of the needs of the other characters— Keller's wife and surviving son, the girl the son is to marry, the neighbours, the son of the convict—so that the demonstration of social consequence, and therefore of Keller's guilt, is not in terms of any abstract principle, but in terms of personal needs and relationships, which compose a reality that directly enforces the truth. If Keller's son had not wanted to marry the convicted man's daughter (and they had been childhood friends; it was that neighbourhood which Keller's act disrupted); if his wife, partly in reaction to her knowledge of his guilt, had not maintained the superstition that their son killed in the war was still alive; if the action had been between strangers or business acquaintances, rather than between neighbours and neighbouring families, the truth would never have come out. Thus we see a true social reality, which includes both social relationships and absolute personal needs, enforcing a social fact—that of responsibility and consequence. This is still the method of Ibsen in the period named, and the device of climax—a concealed letter from Keller's dead son, who had known of his father's guilt—is again directly in Ibsen's terms.

The elements of theatrical contrivance in Ibsen's plays of this kind, and in *All My Sons*, are now sufficiently clear. Yet the total effect of such a play is undoubtedly powerful if its experience truly corresponds to its conventions. In historical terms, this is a bourgeois form, with that curious combination of a demonstrated public morality and an intervening fate, evident in the early 18th century domestic drama, and reaching its maturity in Ibsen. To a considerable extent, *All My Sons* is a successful late example of this form, but a point is reached, in

Miller's handling of the experience, where its limits are touched. For, as he rightly sees it, the social reality is more than a mechanism of honesty and right dealing, more than Ibsen's definition—

The spirits of Truth and Freedom, these are the pillars of society.[3]

Miller reaches out to a deeper conception of relationships, which he emphasises in his title. This is something more than honesty and uprightness: it is the quite different social conception of human brotherhood—

I think to him they were all my sons. And I guess they were, I guess they were.[4]

Moreover, Miller sees this in a social context, as he explains in the Introduction[5]:

Joe Keller's trouble . . . is not that he cannot tell right from wrong but that his cast of mind cannot admit that he, personally, has any viable connection with his world, his universe, or his society. He is not a partner in society, but an incorporated member, so to speak, and you cannot sue personally the officers of a corporation. I hasten to make clear that I am not merely speaking of a literal corporation but the concept of a man's becoming a function of production or distribution to the point where his personality becomes divorced from the actions it propels.

This concept, though Miller does not use the term, is the classical Marxist concept of alienation, and it is with alienation embodied both in a social action and in a personality that Miller is ultimately concerned. The true social reality—the needs and destinies of other persons—is meant to break down this alienated consciousness, and restore the fact of consequence,

---

[3] This is Lona Hessel's line in *Pillars of Society*, the last line in the play. It makes me uncomfortable when Williams assigns a character's lines to the author.

[4] This is the last line Joe Keller speaks before he goes off-stage to shoot himself.

[5] This quotation and those on the following pages are from Miller's Introduction to *Collected Plays*.

of significant and continuing relationships, in this man and in his society. But then it is at this point, as I see it, that the limits of the form are damaging. The words I have quoted, expressing Keller's realisation of a different kind of consciousness, have to stand on their own, because unlike the demonstration of ordinary social responsibility they have no action to support them, and moreover as words they are limited to the conversational resources so adequate elsewhere in the play, but wholly inadequate here to express so deep and substantial a personal discovery (and if it is not this it is little more than a maxim, a "sentiment"). It is at this point that we see the naturalist form—even a principled naturalism, as in Ibsen and Miller and so rarely in others; even this substantially and powerfully done—breaking down as it has so often broken down: partly for the reasons I argued in *Drama from Ibsen to Eliot*[6] (the inadequacy of conversational writing in any deep crisis); partly, I would now add, because the consciousness which the form was designed to express is in any serious terms obsolete, and was already, by Miller himself, being reached beyond.

There is an interesting account, in Miller's Introduction, of the genesis of *All My Sons*, relating it to a previous play and the discovery that

two of the characters, who had been friends in the previous drafts, were logically brothers and had the same father . . . The overt story was only tangential to the secret drama which its author was quite unconsciously trying to write . . . In writing of the father-son relationship and of the son's search for his relatedness there was a fullness of feeling I had never known before. The crux of *All My Sons* was formed; and the roots of *Death of a Salesman* were sprouted.

This is extremely important, not only as a clue to the plays named, but as indicating the way in which Miller, personally, came to the experience expressible as that of human brotherhood. In any sense that matters, this concept is always personally known and lived; as a slogan it is nothing. And the

---

[6] Raymond Williams, *Drama from Ibsen to Eliot* (London: Chatto & Windus, 1952).

complicated experience of inheritance from a father is perhaps one of the permanent approaches to this transforming consciousness. There is the creative complexity of the fact that a son, in many senses, replaces his father. There is dependence and the growth to independence, and both are necessary, in a high and moving tension. In both father and son there are the roots of guilt, and yet, ultimately they stand together as men— the father both a model and a rejected ideal; the son both an idea and a relative failure. But the model, the rejection, the idea and the failure are all terms of growth, and the balance that can be struck is a very deep understanding of relatedness and brotherhood. One way of looking at *All My Sons* is in these universal terms: the father, in effect, destroys one of his sons, and that son, in his turn, gives sentence of death on him, while at the same time, to the other son, the father offers a future, and the son, in rejecting it, destroys his father, in pain and love. Similarly, in *Death of a Salesman*, Willy Loman, like Joe Keller, has lived for his sons, will die for the son who was to extend his life, yet the sons, in their different ways, reject him, in one case for good reasons, and in effect destroy him. Yet the failure on both sides is rooted in love and dependence; the death and the love are deeply related aspects of the same relationship. This complex, undoubtedly, is the "secret drama" of which Miller writes, and if it is never wholly expressed it is clearly the real source of the extraordinary dramatic energy.

Death of a Salesman takes the moment of crisis in which Joe Keller could only feebly express himself, and makes of it the action of the whole play. Miller's first image was of

an enormous face . . . which would appear and then open up, and we would see the inside of a man's head. In fact, *The Inside of His Head* was the first title.

This, in dramatic terms, is expressionism, and correspondingly the guilt of Willy Loman is not in the same world as that of Joe Keller: it is not a single act, subject to public process, needing complicated grouping and plotting to make it emerge; it is, rather, the consciousness of a whole life. Thus the expressionist method, in the final form of the play, is not a casual experiment, but rooted in the experience. It is the drama of a single mind, and moreover.

it would be false to a more integrated—or less disintegrating—personality.

It is historically true that expressionism is attuned to the experience of disintegration. In general dramatic history, as in Miller's own development, it arises at that point where the limits of naturalism are touched and a hitherto stable form begins to break to pieces. Yet *Death of a Salesman* is actually a development of expressionism, of an interesting kind. As Miller puts it:

I had always been attracted and repelled by the brilliance of German expressionism after World War I, and one aim in "Salesman" was to employ its quite marvellous shorthand for humane "felt" characterisations rather than for purposes of demonstration for which the Germans had used it.

This is a fair comment on the "social expressionism" of, say, Toller, and the split of expressionism into "personal" and "social" kinds is related to the general dissociation which I earlier discussed. *Death of a Salesman* is an expressionist reconstruction of naturalist substance, and the result is not hybrid but a powerful particular form. The continuity from social expressionism remains clear, however, for I think in the end it is not Willy Loman as a man, but the image of the Salesman, that predominates. The social figure sums up the theme referred to as alienation, for this is a man who from selling things has passed to selling himself, and has become, in effect, a commodity which like other commodities will at a certain point be economically discarded. The persuasive atmosphere of the play (which the slang embodies so perfectly, for it is a social result of this way of living) is one of false consciousness—the conditioned attitudes in which Loman trains his sons—being broken into by real consciousness, in actual life and relationships. The expressionist method embodies this false consciousness much more powerfully than naturalism could do. In *All My Sons* it had to rest on a particular crime, which could then be seen as in a limiting way personal—Keller the black sheep in a white flock—although the fundamental criticism was of a common way of living and thinking. The "marvellous shorthand" is perfectly adapted to exposing this kind of illusion and failure. At the same time the structure of personal relationships, within this method, must be seen as in a sense arbitrary; it has nothing of the rooted detail which the naturalism of *All My Sons* in this respect achieved. The golden football hero, the giggling woman in the hotel, the rich brother, and similar figures seem to me to be clichés from the thinner world of a work like *Babbitt*, which at times the play uncomfortably resembles.[7] The final figure of a man killing himself for the insurance money caps the whole process of the life that has been demonstrated, but "demonstrated," in spite of Miller's comment on the Germans, is the word that occurs to one to describe it. The emotional power of the demonstration is considerable, and is markedly increased by the brilliant expressionist staging. Yet, by the high standards which Miller insists on, and in terms of the essential realism to which he seems to be reaching, the contrast of success and failure within both *All My Sons* and *Death of a Salesman* points finally to the radical and still unsolved difficulties of form.

III

The Crucible (1952) is a powerful and successful dramatisation of the notorious witch-trials of Salem, but it is technically less interesting than its predecessors just because it is based on a historical event which at the level of action and principled statement is explicit enough to solve, or not to raise, the difficult dramatic problems which Miller had previously set himself.

---

[7] For a detailed comparison of "Salesman" with *Babbitt* see Gordon W. Couchman, "Arthur Miller's Tragedy of Babbitt," *Educational Theatre Journal*, VII (October 1955), 206–211.

The importance of the witch-trials is that in them, in a clear and exciting way, the moral crisis of a society is explicit, is directly enacted and stated, in such a way that the quality of the whole way of life is organically present and evident in the qualities of persons. Through this action Miller brilliantly expresses a particular crisis—the modern witchhunt—in his own society, but it is not often, in our own world, that the issues and statements so clearly emerge in a naturally dramatic form. The methods explored in the earlier plays are not necessary here, but the problems they offered to solve return immediately, outside the context of this particular historical event. *The Crucible* is a fine play, but it is also a quite special case.

In *A Memory of Two Mondays* (1955), Miller returns to the direct dramatisation of modern living, and as if to underline the point made about *The Crucible* (of which, as the Introduction shows, he was completely aware) seeks to make a new form out of the very facts of inconsequence, discontinuity, and the deep frustrations of inarticulacy, which is at once a failure of speech and the wider inability of men to express themselves in certain kinds of work and working relationship. Instead of concentrating these themes in a particular history, pointed by plot or single crisis, he deploys them in the scattered form of a series of impressions, with the dramatic center in memory rather than in action or crisis. The work atmosphere is in some ways significantly caught, and there is always the mark of Miller's insight into the importance and passion of what many others dismiss as "ordinary" lives. There is an occasional flare of dramatic feeling, as in the last speech of Gus, but in general the tension is much lower than in the earlier plays, and the dramatic methods seem often mere devices. The Irish singer and reciter; the insets of flat sub-Auden verse; the lighting and scenic devices of the passing of time: these, at this tension, seem mechanical. And a central image of the play—when the workers clean the windows to let in a sight of sun and trees, and let in actually a view of a cat-house (brothel)—seems to me contrived. Miller's fertility of experiment is important, but experiment, as here, involves failure.

A *View from the Bridge* (1955; revised 1957)[8] brings back the intensity. The capacity to touch and stir deep human feeling was marked in the earlier plays, but Miller has said, interestingly (it is his essential difference from Tennessee Williams, with whom he is often linked):

The end of drama is the creation of a higher consciousness and not merely a subjective attack upon the audience's nerves and feelings.

The material of A *View from the Bridge* is to most people deeply disturbing, and Miller's first impulse was to keep it abstract and distant, to hold back

the empathic flood which a realistic portrayal of the same tale and characters might unloose.

But, in his own view, he went too far in this direction, and subsequently revised the play towards a more intense realism. The distancing element remains, however, in the use of a commentator, or *raisonneur*, and, though there are false notes in the writing of this part, it is an important reason for the play's success.

A *View from the Bridge* follows from the earlier works in that it shows a man being broken and destroyed by guilt. Its emphasis is personal, though the crisis is related to the intense primary relationships of an insecure and partly illegal group— a Brooklyn waterfront slum, with ties back to Italy, receiving unauthorised immigrants and hiding them within its own fierce loyalties. Eddie Carbone's breakdown is sexual, and the guilt, as earlier, is deeply related to love. And the personal breakdown leads to a sin against this community, when in the terror of his complicated jealousies Eddie betrays immigrants of his wife's kin to the external law.

At the centre of the drama again is the form of a relationship between parent and child, but here essentially displaced so that the vital relationship is between a man and the niece to whom he has been as a father. The girl's coming to adolescence pro-

---

[8] Although "View" was revised for its London production in October 1956, the revised edition was not published until 1957 in *Collected Plays*.

vokes a crisis which is no more soluble than if they had really been father and child, yet to a degree perhaps is more admissible into consciousness. Eddie is shown being destroyed by forces which he cannot control, and the complex of love and guilt has the effect of literal disintegration, in that the known sexual rhythms break down into their perverse variations: the rejection of his wife, as his vital energy transfers to the girl, and then the shattering crisis in which within the same rush of feeling he moves into the demonstration of both incestuous and homosexual desires. The crisis burns out his directions and meanings, and he provokes his death shouting "I want my name." This establishment of significance, after breakdown, through death, was the pattern of Joe Keller and Willy Loman; of John Proctor, in heroic stance, in *The Crucible*; of Gus, in a minor key, in *A Memory of Two Mondays*. We are at the heart, here, of Miller's dramatic pattern, and his work, in this precise sense, is tragedy—the loss of meaning in life turns to the struggle for meaning by death. The loss of meaning is always a personal history, though in Willy Loman it comes near to being generalized. Equally, it is always set in the context of a loss of social meaning, a loss of meaning in relationships. The point is made, and is ratifying, in the commentary in *A View from the Bridge*:

Now we are quite civilized, quite American. Now we settle for half . . .

and again, at the end:

. . . Something perversely pure calls to me from his memory—not purely good, but himself purely, for he allowed himself to be wholly known and for that I think I will love him more than all my sensible clients. And yet, it is better to settle for half, it must be! And so I mourn him—I admit it—with a certain alarm.

Tempted always to settle for half—for the loss of meaning and the loss of consequence endemic in the whole complex of personal and social relationships, the American way of living as Miller sees it—the heroes of these plays, because, however perversely, they are still attached to life, still moved by irresistible desires for a name, a significance, a vital meaning, break out and destroy themselves, leaving their own comment on the half-life they have experienced. Miller's drama, as he has claimed, is a drama of consciousness, and in reaching out for this new social consciousness—in which "every aspect of personal life is radically affected by the quality of the general life, yet the general life is seen at its most important in completely personal terms" —Miller, for all the marks of difficulty, uncertainty and weakness that stand within the intensity of his effort, seems clearly a central figure in the drama and consciousness of our time.

ALLAN SEAGER

Allan Seager is Professor of English at the University of Michigan and is the author of, among other books, *The Death of Anger* and A *Frieze of Girls: Memoirs as Fiction.*

THE CREATIVE AGONY OF
ARTHUR MILLER

Not long ago Arthur Miller was called by Kermit Bloomgarden, the producer, who asked him when he would have his next play ready. Show business is flourishing. Theatres are hard to find and Bloomgarden wanted to make sure he could rent one, not for the 1959 but for the 1960 season. Miller replied, "I don't know. I'm working on it, but I can't tell yet." Miller's answer indicates an area of knowledge that is usually blank or mysterious to the public, that is, just what Miller does when he "works" on a play. Theatregoers are impressed by the play they see. Critics quite properly can pronounce only on the finished work. They are concerned with the results of the playwright's art rather than with the art itself, one of whose chief elements is sheer stamina, and because they are so seldom described, few people are aware of the myriad of patient individual insights, the barren pauses, the earnest, even desperate stratagems, the lucky breaks, and the compromises that finally take shape as the play they see.

The play Miller is now working on ran, at one time, to two reams of paper typewritten. This comes to about a thousand pages; a finished play script is about a hundred and twenty. These pages were covered with dialogue, but it lacked the succinctness, the concentrated meaning, in fact, the poetry of dramatic speech. Miller was merely letting his characters talk,

From *Esquire*, LII (October 1959), pp. 123–126, Copyright © 1959 by *Esquire*, reprinted by permission of the author.

giving them their heads to say anything that might be remotely relevant to his purposes for them, not that these purposes were yet entirely clear. But after all this effort, the play did not come together and Miller got fed up. He dumped the two reams of paper into the wastebasket and they were taken out and burned. A waste? Hardly, for after a thousand pages of talk he knew his characters almost as well as he knows his friends. However, the work was at a standstill and Miller could not see how to give it the next push.

Familiar as they were by this time, the characters and principal actions were recalcitrant. Try as he would, Miller could not bring up the one intuition that would make the play a whole, make it, in effect, a play he could work on. Miller knows his craft and he realized it was time to stop trying. "Inspiration" is a word that has been blunted by high-school English teachers talking about the Romantic poets, but it was inspiration he was waiting for. This is not a gratuitous *éclaircissement*; it is the result of work, and, although you can toss a manuscript into the wastebasket, you can't toss it out of your head so easily. Miller turned his attention to other things, among them the script of *The Misfits*, a movie John Huston is making with Marilyn Monroe, but the gists and themes of the work he had already done gathered weight and meaning in some unworried, subliminal part of his mind until one day, abruptly, he had the crucial insight. It lay in the phrase, "to lay a hand on life." To explain why this phrase was essential or where its efficacy lay would probably require an impossibly minute history of the life and times of Arthur Miller, and the timing of the flash might elude even that. It was enough that the block was demolished and he could go to work again.

Miller says that work on a play is a "discovery of meaning," simultaneously the definition of a theme and its significance, but the theme of a play is not necessarily in its germ, its first beginning. Miller starts, not with any attempt to form a theme, but merely with something that interests him. This seems obvious enough, yet Flaubert wrote a great novel about the story of the Delamarre family which, he complained, did not interest him in the least. Literary psychologists have devoted a good deal of study to this phenomenon of interest, not much of it very fruitful. Excited laymen are always coming to writers with "a wonderful story you can use" and are disappointed when the writer remains listless, uninterested, in fact. What touches off Miller's interest may be a person, a human situation, a phrase, and he may not know why it does at the time. ("I want to make my plays out of evident truths," he says, but this kind of truth usually lies at the end of his labors, not the beginning.)

For instance, the origin of *All My Sons* seems clear and plausible because it adumbrates the major action of the play. It came out of an idle conversation with one of Miller's in-laws, who told of a woman in her neighborhood who turned in her own father for having shipped faulty materials to the government during the war. "The action astounded me," Miller said. "An absolute response to a moral command." Astonishment guarantees interest.

The beginnings of *Death of a Salesman* are more obscure, more difficult to explain. Miller was at work one night on another play. It was a warm evening in May and suddenly the character of the man who was to become Willy Loman drifted into his head, a memory of a man he had known. The accretion of ideas and emotions around this figure seemed to be instantaneous, and Miller wrote two-thirds of the first draft that night; the last third took him three months. After the play was running on Broadway, Miller was looking for something in his files and happened to find an old manuscript of a play he had begun at the University of Michigan about the same man. He had completely forgotten about it, but the man, a salesman in his life, had apparently gone on working in his head, unconsciously gathering the force that made the play come easily, and that the play released.

"What I am working for is the gasp," Miller says. "I used to stand at the back of the theatre when *Death of a Salesman* was playing and hear it." For a while after the play opened, he got phone calls and telegrams from salesmen saying things like this:

"I saw your play. I've just quit my job. What do I do now?" Two large corporations asked him to address their sales meetings. The total meaning of the play is not simple, but Miller felt he had been successful by his own standards when the salesmen themselves were struck so sharply by it. One salesman, as he was leaving the theatre, was overheard to say: "I always said that New England territory was no damned good."

The origins of *The Crucible* lay back in Miller's college years also. He had been fascinated then by the Salem witch trials, but they did not seem to be the stuff of a play until the McCarthy hysteria brought the story back to his mind and he noticed similarities. At this point, Miller had no play in mind, only the possibility of one. He went to the courthouse in Salem and said, "I'd like to see the record of some trials that took place here several years back." The clerk said, "Just when would that be?" "About 1695," Miller said. With unshakable aplomb, the clerk laid the big hand-written folios of the witch trials in front of him and he began to study them.

His decision to write a play out of them did not come, however, until he found that John Proctor was being mysteriously spared by Abigail Williams, who was clearly trying to hang his wife, and when it came out that Abigail had been the Proctors' servant girl. Miller says, "The pettiness of the inner reality compared to the perverse grandeur of the social paroxysm made a great impression. It was like my own situation then—trying to tell people that the great "issues" which the hysteria was allegedly about were covers for petty ambitions, hardheaded political drives, and the fantasies of very small and vengeful minds. Equally, I imposed the theme of Proctor's handing over his conscience to his wife and taking it back again with the resolve that he was good enough to hang. I felt that people in our time did not think themselves good enough to fight, were too privately guilty to withstand the accusations of guilt that were coming down daily from government and press." Once he had a beginning, Miller took many lines of the play directly from the court records.

These are the germs of three plays. The people and the situation or the people *in* the situation compelled his attention. Their actions excited him; that is, they interested him. It is doubtful whether he or any writer analyzes further at this stage. Objectively it is clear that the starting points of *All My Sons* and *The Crucible* were moral decisions of the highest seriousness, that one was topical and the other analogous to a contemporary situation, and that these starting points were discovered, not invented.

Unlike Terence Rattigan, who has said something like, "God forgive me if I ever write social drama," Miller maintains that a serious play can hardly be anything else. Acknowledged or not, the taints and blessings of society are there because the single man is immersed in it. "The fish is in the water; the water is in the fish," Miller says. Since the Depression exploded in his face when he was quite young, Miller has tended to use the social pressures of contemporary history in his plays. However, the presence of a new *Encyclopaedia Britannica* (a gift from his wife) at his elbow in his New York workroom indicates perhaps a shift of emphasis, perhaps a deepening of Miller's interest in history. He studied history in college, but the past had never concerned him anywhere near as much as the present. "I look things up in that all the time," he says of the *Encyclopaedia* "to remind myself of detail, to face the fact that there's so little I can really know; I use it to learn again what I once knew better. To know where you are you've got to know where you've been; there must be a couple of drops of blood in every one of us that are there because of the French Revolution, and another one or two because the Greeks fought at Marathon, and some because of Lincoln."

Miller has two places to work. One is a fourteen-by-fourteen split-shingle cabin behind his house at Roxbury, Connecticut. During the cold weather he customarily uses the cabin on week ends. (The first winter he tried to heat it with a stone fireplace, but the cabin was set wrong and the chimney wouldn't draw. Now he has a space heater and can write in comfort.) In the summer he's there for weeks at a time. The other place is an office in his apartment. It is a plainly furnished workroom with a desk, a sofa, a couple of chairs, a wall of books, and his files. The view from the single window is not of the Golfe-Juan or the ocean at Big Sur; it is merely uptown New York, and his desk faces away from it anyway. When Miller looks up he sees two beautiful photographs of his wife which, to many people, might be more distracting than the view from any window whatever.[1] But they are perhaps less so to Miller, who has only to stick his head out of the door and call to see the original.

What goes on in these rooms? What does Miller do when he works? Assuming that he has the germinal person or incident with him when he enters, he begins with notebooks. These are ordinary dime-store spiral notebooks. He does not sit down and fill the notebooks, writing smoothly like a clerk for five or six hours a day. He writes as things occur to him (with pauses for thought or reading in between), spasmodically, chaotically, with pen or pencil (he has no preference): aphorisms, scraps of dialogue invented or recalled, short or long poems left incomplete, drawings of sets for as-yet-unconceived plays, personal memoranda in which he talks to himself or asks himself the meaning of some dream or childhood incident, spurts of plotting which may suddenly reveal a whole act, or, with luck, the beginning, middle and end of a play. Here, at random, are some samples:

M. You ought to pay more attention to your wife.

D. That's all I do. I never knew you had to cultivate a wife until recently.

M. Well, you don't just plant them and let them grow by themselves.

D. Tells of his unhappiness.

Then. . . .

1. God! Who would ever have believed I would need sixty thousand dollars a year to live! And I'm not even living.

Then. . . .

Beware following the details to the loss of vision.

Then. . . .

---

[1] When this article was first published, Miller was married to Marilyn Monroe.

Beware following the vision to the loss of the details.

Then. . . .

It is first of all *ironic*. A man devoting his whole effort to avoiding a certain kind of disaster and discovering that it happened to him at the moment he changed his course to avoid it—the disaster was his challenge, the life that he never lived.

Then. . . .

S believes we are all living with an image of someone we are intent on deceiving—either by pretending to be like him or by trying to show hatred where there is only unrequited love. Deception is his *structure*.

Then. . . .

His question: Should he have adopted such a life?

My question: Did he really *adopt* anything?

Then. . . .

Remember the nature of his work. Remember pity. The erosion of the tentative commitment to a particular job for sixteen years.

Then. . . .

He calls her *perceptive*. It means she sees through him. He respects and fears her, therefore.

Then. . . .

I want to show that it is not some will-to-goodness that he lacks, but its definition; a firm image of the person he wishes to be. Therefore, the process is. . . . (Here follow some technical notes nobody would understand. A.M.)

Then. . . .

D. Sometimes I feel that a wild animal is trying to sit up inside of me. I don't know why that should be. I'm really not that dissatisfied.

He fears not only that something is going to happen to him but that nothing at all will. He is running away even from that toward which he is running. In a single hour, a day, he lives through all the extremes of his nature. Painfully timid, eagerly aggressive, easily aggressive, valiantly loyal, begrudgingly loyal, resentfully loyal; carnal, spiritual—and for moments he feels perfectly justified, adjusted to each. He is striving for peace by

rejecting each part of his nature by turns. The crisis comes
when she, in effect, can't locate him, challenges him to come
out. He cannot without bringing with him his sins.

Then. . . .

X. The great thing about Y is that he makes everybody feel
he's their best friend.

No!

. . . that they're *his* best friend.

Then. . . .

(A recalled speech by a man I know. A.M.)

"Blankman is a big Irishman. Did you see the revetment he
built in his back yard? His plan wasn't originally very desirable."
(This has no connection with any play, but is merely a handling
of a certain kind of diction that touches and amuses me. A.M.)

"And so on. A page of dialogue between a cop and a man he
is berating for attempting suicide *on his beat*; a page about the
difference between Matthew's version and Mark's, the former
fixing up the details of the story to make it more persuasive, the
latter writing like a witness; a paragraph to the effect that
hypocrisy is the friction in the creed, which, when it produces
more heat than power, must be brought down, redesigned.
And on."

During the early stages, "work" is the setting down of notes
like these, reminders of thinking. Some of them might be called
permanent observations on his craft applicable to any play, but
most of them have a connection, however tenuous, with the
theme, the over-all idea, he is trying to elucidate. And the little
decision as to whether a given note is worth putting down,
whether it is relevant or not, helps define what it is relevant *to*,
that is, the play he is trying to get to emerge as a whole.

All the time he is taking these notes by hand, Miller will be
writing scenes on the typewriter, "believing on certain mornings that the time is ripe to drive directly toward the stage," but,
again, "such false dawns can go on for months."

These successive acts of creation have little to do with logical
thought. For weeks at a time, Miller's attention may be fixed on
some character's face or on the feeling of revelation some experi-

ence has left behind. It is very hard to put one's feet on the desk (Miller is a long, gangling man and tends to do this) and merely think, day after day. The attention is slippery. These jottings, although most of them will be thrown away, fend off the devils of distraction and inertia that beset every writer. One other, a private devil of Miller's own, is a facility: "I could always write a good scene," he says, "but not always *the* scene," and he has to guard against false starts.

When the play begins to take shape in his mind at last, suddenly the aphorisms will disappear, the poems, the drawings, and there will be a whole notebook with nothing in it but dialogue and structural notes. Miller works at these until, again with luck and after no telling how long a time, the moment comes "when thinking is left behind. Everything is in the present tense and a play emerges which has resemblances but little else to the mass of notes left behind." It is, or it is similar to, an organic process, and comparisons with the bud and the flower or the chrysalis and the butterfly are obvious.

Miller sees his work as a constant effort to penetrate to a core of meaning in his material, a center of rich significance— a significance which has its own strict order: a dramatic order that he feels with all its nuances rather than an intellectual statement of meaning which could be summarized, say, in an essay. "There are two questions I ask myself over and over when I'm working, 'What do I mean? What am I trying to say?' " he says, but this meaning could not be contained in a flat linear statement or in an actor's lines, his pauses, or his gestures. The speeches and gestures are only implements. Ideally, the meaning lies in the minds of the man or woman in the audience, and the play in its entirety reveals it to them.

A finished script lying on a desk is still no more a play than the score of a symphony is the music. Both must be performed. Between Miller's desk and the rising of the curtain there are the producer, the director, the scene designer, and the actors. "From the time I finish the writing until the first performance, everything is a compromise," he says.

Death of a Salesman cost $65,000 to put on in 1949. Now, because of the rise in price of practically everything, Miller estimates that it would cost $140,000. The first task of a producer is to get up the money. There is little use in finding and renting a theatre, hiring a stage crew, and overseeing the dozens of chores like advertising and the printing of tickets unless the money is in sight. It is not hard to find investors for a Miller play, but, with costs mounting and wages increasing, the money is always something to think about.

Each director has his strengths and weaknesses and these must be balanced against the qualities of the script. There is one director who can handle scenes of physical action brilliantly, evoking almost a shimmer of meaning from the composition of the simplest movements. Another, by his reticence, can pull astonishing performances from actors, make them play over their heads. Another is personally so unpopular that, Miller says, "There are people in this town who, if this man came into their offices, would call the police," but he is fantastically conscientious and he has had a great many hits. The play must suit the director's peculiar talents for, ultimately, no matter how long and patiently he and Miller work together, it is the director's vision of the play that reaches the stage.

After the director, the scene designer must be selected. Each one naturally can do one kind of thing better than another. One's strong point may be the construction of a striking set; another can evoke the mood of the script through his lighting. "A set should be a metaphor of the whole play. For instance, the set of MacLeish's *J.B.* looks somewhat like a circus tent, but at the same time it suggests the whole world as the scene of Job's trials. It's very effective," Miller says. While he is writing, Miller has learned not to visualize the scene of the dramatic action too definitely. Any good scene designer must obviously be left room to develop his own conceptions and if Miller approached him with the sets rigidly erected in his own mind, the designer's freedom would be lost. "I had some notions about the set of *Death of a Salesman*, but when I saw Jo Mielziner's sketches for the set and his ideas about the lighting, I knew

they were better than anything I had imagined," Miller says.[2]
A concession like that is easy to make, but it demonstrates that
the stage performance is clearly not the flower of the playwright's efforts alone.

Miller has never yet written a part with a particular actor in
mind. He is present at all tryouts. An example of the kind of
compromise casting demands can be seen in the choosing of an
actor to play Willy Loman. Writing the play, Miller had taken
it for granted that Willy was a little guy, and at first several
small men, among them Ernest Truex, tried out for Miller and
Elia Kazan, the director. However, Lee J. Cobb, a large man,
was very anxious to get the part and he flew his own plane from
Hollywood to New York three times to read for Willy Loman.
The brilliance of his trial performances so impressed Miller and
Kazan that Cobb was hired and, in the memories of most playgoers today, he *is* Willy Loman. Once an actor has been selected
and rehearsed, he must be given some leeway in interpreting his
part, but this trust has its dangers. An actor in one of Miller's
plays had been doing a superb job during the first weeks of the
run. His performances showed great tact and a personal flair
that heightened the impact the play was making. Miller and the
director congratulated themselves for having picked him for the
role, but one day the actor casually asked Miller a question
which revealed that he understood neither his own part, its
relation to the play, nor the play as a whole. Miller was almost
afraid to answer, for fear he would let some light into the splendid darkness of the actor's conception. But Miller did answer
cautiously and the actor continued his fine work. It is enough
to freeze the blood.

Rehearsals last three-and-a-half to four weeks and it is then,
in the darkened theatre with his feet up on the seat in front of
him, that Miller puts in the twelve-hour day and, maybe, after
sending out for coffee, fourteen. Then the final touches are
given to the interpretation, the pace, the nuances of gesture, the

[2] For Mielziner's account of the first set of sketches, see p. 190.

timing of exits and entrances. There is always the line some actor cannot possibly say that must be rewritten. There is the piece of business that must somehow be made to come off now because the dates are fixed for the out-of-town tryout and the New York opening. And as the tension mounts, Miller's responsibility for his play lessens until on opening night it rests with the actors alone.

After the opening, what happens to the play depends on the critics and the public. If neither like it, it fails, obviously. If both do, it is a hit and there is a barrel of money in a hit. Investors have to wait until the play is off the nut before they make any profits, but the playwright's returns begin when the curtain goes up. The standard playwright's contract begins with five per cent of the gross receipts up to $4,000, seven and a half per cent from $4,000 to $8,000, and ten per cent over that. A few playwrights, among them Miller, can command a straight fifteen per cent, and a hit can mean an income of $5,000 a week during the run; this doubles if there is a road company.

Yet there is not an artist now living who has made fewer concessions to box-office standards than has Arthur Miller. It is not that he has a mission, a word that suggests nut-fooders and end-of-the-world guys with whiskers; rather he has an aim. "The playwright's function," he says, "is to tell the people what goes on." Leaving out such implications as the question, "Why don't they already know, considering all their sources of information?" and omitting such words as "commitment," and "engage," which have already been used about Miller and his work many times, it is possible to derive the meaning of this statement. What goes on is not good, as any of his plays will show. Miller's anxiety is spent in the gap between man as he is and man as he could be. (That it is *man*, and not people from Brooklyn or Americans, is clear from the success of his plays abroad.) Miller is perhaps less ready to believe than he once was that this gap can be narrowed by the passage of wise laws, the election of competent officials, or any organized gestures whatever. He is thinking more closely on man's lack of any profound concern with his own true nature and his consequent failure to recognize the true nature of his inevitable bonds with others. What goes on, in short, is a failure of love.

Miller said recently in conversation, "Writing a play is so damned tough that, when I finish one, I swear I'll never write anything again, not even a letter." He has recovered from this exhaustion every time, however, and it is practically certain that Kermit Bloomgarden can go ahead and rent a theater for the 1960 season.[8]

---

[8] If Bloomgarden rented a theater out of this practical certainty, he was disappointed. There was no new Miller play until 1964, when *After the Fall* was performed by the Lincoln Center Repertory Company at the ANTA–Washington Square Theater.

WILLIAM B. DILLINGHAM

William B. Dillingham teaches American Literature at Emory University and is author of *Frank Norris: The Fiction of Force* and co-editor with Hennig Cohen of *Humor of the Old Southwest*.

ARTHUR MILLER AND THE LOSS OF CONSCIENCE

Man's obligation to assume his rightful place in a world unified by love and a sense of responsibility is the central thesis of Arthur Miller's critical essays and the major theme of his plays. Tragedy occurs when a man fails to recognize his place in society or when he gives it up because of false values. Miller's goal as a serious playwright, he feels, is to point man toward "a world in which the human being can live as a naturally political, naturally private, naturally engaged person." Such a world was the Greek *polis*, where the people, Miller says, "were *engaged*, they could not imagine the good life excepting as it brought each person into close contact with civic matters. . . . The preoccupation of the Greek drama with ultimate law, with the Grand Design, so to speak, was therefore an expression of a basic assumption of the people, who could not yet conceive, luckily, that any man could longer prosper unless his polis prospered. The individual was at one with his society; his conflicts with it were, in our terms, like family conflicts the opposing sides of which nevertheless shared a mutuality of feeling and responsibility."[1]

Miller's tragedies are about men who are not "at one" with society because they have sinned against it or have refused to

From *Emory University Quarterly*, XVI (Spring 1960), pp. 40–50, reprinted by permission of William B. Dillingham.

[1] The quotations in this and the next paragraph are from "On Social Plays," Miller's introduction to *A View from the Bridge* (New York: Viking, 1955), 1–15.

assume their rightful place in it. Unfortunately, such men are representative products of the complex modern world, where man finds it difficult if not impossible to identify himself with society "except in the form of a truce with it." "The best we have been able to do," Miller writes, "is speak of a 'duty' to society, and this implies sacrifice or self-deprivation. To think of an individual fulfilling his subjective needs through social action . . . is difficult for us to imagine." Yet man can retain his integrity of "conscience" only if he is a part of the world of "feeling and responsibility" for others. For Miller, the loss of conscience is evidenced by a terrible unconsciousness, an un-awareness of fundamental values and of what constitutes human dignity. The pity and fear traditionally associated with the kathartic value of tragedy can best be experienced, Miller feels, by observing those who have lost conscience and have thereby been isolated from the "Grand Design." Central in the four tragedies, *All My Sons, Death of a Salesman, The Crucible,* and *A View from the Bridge,* is the loss of conscience (and the efforts to regain it).

Joe Keller of *All My Sons* has committed a grave antisocial act in allowing faulty and dangerous airplane engines to be sent from his wartime factory for use in combat. Keller represents, Miller has stated, "a threat to society," and his crime "is seen as having roots in a certain relationship of the individual to society, and to a certain indoctrination he embodies, which, if dominant, can mean a jungle existence for all of us no matter how high our buildings soar. And it is in this sense that loneliness is socially meaningful in these plays." Yet Joe Keller is not villainous. He does not exhibit in his personal life any of the brutality and cruelty generally associated with villains; indeed, he is a loving, dutiful husband and father. But it is precisely this virtuous love for his family that sows the seeds of tragedy. "Joe Keller's trouble," Miller writes, "is not that he cannot tell right from wrong but that his cast of mind cannot admit that he, personally, has any viable connection with his world, his universe, or his society. He is not a partner in society, but an incorporated member, so to speak, and you cannot sue personally the officers of a corporation."[2]

The implications of such family-centricity are apparent in the tragic design of the play. *All My Sons* is an excellent example of what Hegel considered the essence of tragedy: the conflict of two forces that are in themselves both good. Tragedy, writes Hegel, "consists in this, that within a collision of this kind both sides of the contradiction, if taken by themselves, are *justified*; yet, from a further point of view, they tend to carry into effect the true and positive content of their end and specific characterization merely as the negation and *violation* of the other equally legitimate power, and consequently in their ethical purport and relatively to this so far fall under *condemnation*." Reconciliation, according to Hegel, is the result of an act of "eternal justice," since this justice "is unable to tolerate the victorious issue and continuance in the truth of the objective world of such a conflict with any opposition to those ethical powers which are fundamentally and essentially concordant." Often these conflicting powers are "ethical life in its social universality and the family as the natural ground for moral relations."[3]

All My Sons illustrates well the Hegelian theory of tragedy, since its conflict is between these intrinsic goods, the family and society. Motivated by his desire to provide luxuries for his family and to leave something substantial for his son Chris to inherit, Joe Keller has worked his way from lowly beginnings to considerable wealth. "What the hell did I work for?" he asks Chris. "That's only for you, Chris, the whole shootin' match is for you!" Because of the pursuit of this "good" Joe Keller ordered his workers to ignore the imperfections in the airplane

---

[2] The Miller quotations on *All My Sons* here and those on the other plays that come later are from the Introduction to *Collected Plays*; for the section on "Salesman," see pp. 155–171.

[3] The Hegel quotations are from F. P. B. Osmaston's translation of *The Philosophy of Fine Art*, Vol. IV (London: Bell, 1920). It is most accessible in *Hegel on Tragedy*, ed. Anne and Henry Paolucci (Garden City, N.Y.: Doubleday Anchor, 1962).

engines and to ship them out. Twenty-one planes crashed in Australia, and twenty-one pilots died. Keller had not thought of these pilots who would fly with the imperfect engines; his only concern was to keep his factory operating so that he could hand it down to Chris. Not until the end of the play does Keller realize, in Miller's words, "the abomination of the anti-social action." Keller's extreme allegiance to a lesser good, the family, destroys his social consciousness; he becomes merely a shell, a man without conscience.

The brotherhood Keller had sinned against, Chris discovers while he is in the army. The men in his unit, Chris explains, "didn't die; they killed themselves for each other. I mean that exactly; a little more selfish and they'd 've been here today. And I got an idea—watching them go down. Everything was being destroyed, see, but it seemed to me that one new thing was made. A kind of—responsibility. Man for man." Keller, however, feels responsible to no one outside his family. "It don't excuse it that you did it for the family," his wife tells him. "There's something bigger than the family to him [Chris]." Not yet aware of the truth, Keller answers: "It's got to excuse it! . . . Nothin' is bigger! . . . Nothin's bigger than that. . . . If there's something bigger than that I'll put a bullet in my head!" Blindly devoted to the interests of the family, Joe Keller exemplifies the onesidedness which is, in Hegel's theory, always a part of tragic characters. "Despite the fact that the individual characters propose that which is itself essentially valid," Hegel states, "yet they are only able to carry it out under the tragic demand in a manner that implies contradiction, and with a onesidedness which is injurious."

Both Chris and his brother Larry feel the full impact of Joe Keller's antisocial action. Deeply shamed by his father's crime, Larry commits suicide in combat after writing his fiancee of his decision to take his own life. When Chris reads Larry's letter aloud, Keller finally sees that he has isolated himself from the world Chris and Larry had fought for. Before he shoots himself, he indicates powerfully but calmly his terrible recognition of this fact: "But I think to him [Larry] they were all my sons.

And I guess they were, I guess they were." Immediately preceding the sound of Keller's gun, Chris, here the spokesman for the playwright, sums up to his mother the necessity of being ruled by conscience, that is, of acting in accordance with a standard of values that embodies man's responsibility to his fellow beings: "You can be better! Once and for all you can know there's a universe of people outside and you're responsible to it, and unless you know that, you threw away your son because that's why he died."

Like Joe Keller, Willy Loman is characterized by his fanatic allegiance to a dream at the expense of conscience. In defending *Death of a Salesman* against the charge of being anticapitalistic, Miller has written: "The most decent man in *Death of a Salesman* is a capitalist whose aims are not different from Willy Loman's. The great difference between them is that Charley is not a fanatic." Willy insists upon trying to believe that he is a successful, "well-liked" salesman. Yet this is not a conception which he can really fulfill, as only Biff seems to admit. "They've laughed at Dad for years," Biff says, "and you know why? Because we don't belong in this nuthouse of a city! We should be mixing cement on some open plain, or—or carpenters. A carpenter is allowed to whistle!" Willy's false dream of his position in life is an expensive one. For he becomes, as Miller puts it, "a man superbly alone with his sense of not having touched . . . the image of private man in a world full of strangers, a world that is not home nor even an open battleground but only galaxies of high promise over a fear of falling." In short, *Death of a Salesman* is the portrait of a man who has given up conscience, that which is most fundamentally himself, for a place in society that can never be his. There was "more of him in that front stoop" he made with his hands, Biff says, "than in all the sales he ever made."

In losing his identity in an illusion of success and security, Willy Loman is strongly influenced by the same idea that dominated the Gatsbys and the Babbitts. Reared on the American success story, he watched his brother Ben go into the jungle poor and come out rich. Ben constantly exemplifies for Willy the glory of going from rags to riches. At times Willy actually questions the values he is stressing to his sons and admits that he feels "temporary" about himself. In this state of mind he seeks advice of Ben: "Ben, how should I teach them?" Ben's answer is the "American dream" in summary: "William, when I walked into the jungle, I was seventeen. When I walked out I was twenty-one. And, by God, I was rich!" Reassured, Willy feels that Ben has reached the end of the rainbow, and he is ready to follow him: "That's just the spirit I want to imbue them with! To walk into a jungle! I was right! I was right! I was right!"

Willy encounters another aspect of the American dream in his wife Linda, for whom security is the most important goal in life. Paradoxically, Linda genuinely loves and respects her husband, but she is a contributing cause in his tragedy. From the first she believes in Willy as the "well-liked" supersalesman. When he complains of his small number of sales, her confidence in him is unshaken: "Well, next week you'll do better," she tells him. At times Willy seems on the verge of recognizing his mediocrity as a salesman, but Linda resupplies him with the stuff his dreams are made on. "I don't know the reason for it," Willy tells Linda, "but they just pass me by. I'm not noticed." In answer Linda offers more encouragement than understanding: "But you're doing wonderful, dear." And when Willy has a chance to give up selling to go to Alaska, she convinces him that he should not go, that security is everything.

Probably Willy Loman would have failed in Alaska as he did at home, but the important point is that Linda believed in the illusion of her husband as the successful salesman perhaps more than Willy himself did. And instead of encouraging him to be himself—to be a carpenter or a plumber or a bricklayer—and to identify himself with real and fundamental values, she urges him to remain as he is, "alone, without the sense of having touched," in the name of security. Linda's emphasis on material security and her failure in understanding are reflected in her final speech at Willy's graveside: "Forgive me, dear. I can't cry. I don't know what it is, but I can't cry. I don't understand it. Why did you ever do that? . . . Why did you do it? I search and search and I search, and I can't understand it, Willy. I made the last payment on the house today. Today, dear. And there'll be nobody home. We're free and clear."

Death of a Salesman, then, is quite obviously concerned with what Miller terms the loss of conscience, and is not unlike *All My Sons* in its tragic pattern. Both Joe Keller and Willy Loman fit Hegel's description of the tragic hero, the character who seeks a "good" too far or in the wrong way so that he loses his identity, his necessary values, and is carried to destruction. Willy Loman is in search of success, in itself a good. His tragedy is partly the fault of his environment, especially Ben and Linda, who give him a false conception of success, and partly his own fault since he is so fanatically devoted to this goal. Miller has stated that the whole play "had all come together" in Linda's line over Willy's grave: "He was always so wonderful with his hands." The work with his hands was the "rock," the real values, with which Willy could have identified himself. But to him, Miller writes, "only rank, height of power, the sense of having won . . . was real—the galaxy thrust up into the sky by projectors on the rooftops of the city he believed were real stars." For Joe Keller the highest good is the family; for Willy Loman it is success. In both cases, the catastrophe occurs when the totality of good asserts itself, that is, when the tragic hero realizes—but too late—that he has magnified his ideal out of proportion.

But *Death of a Salesman*, as Miller has pointed out, is not meant to be a pessimistic play. If it focuses on Willy Loman's loss of conscience, it is also the story of Biff Loman and his struggle to regain his identity. Biff's values were distorted by his father, who felt it unimportant that his son was a thief as long as the boy was well-liked. Biff suddenly changes, however, when he discovers the woman in Willy's hotel room. He then sees Willy Loman as he has never seen him before, false to others and to himself. And through his determination not to follow Willy's example, not to go through life pretending, Biff is able to find himself. At his father's grave he tells Happy, "I know who I am." He has gained what Willy never found, his rightful position in society.

As in *All My Sons*, so again in *The Crucible*, Arthur Miller has emphasized the necessity for man's fidelity to others as well as to himself by stressing the horror of the antisocial act. In *The Crucible* Miller has dramatized the Salem witch hunt, one of the most terrible examples of how man may sin against his fellow beings. In his remarks on the play Miller has made it quite clear that he meant to compare the witch hunt with the McCarthy investigations. During this time of "McCarthyism," Miller has written, "conscience was no longer a private matter but one of state administration." He continues: "I saw men handing conscience to other men and thanking other men for the opportunity of doing so. I wished for a way to write a play that would be sharp, that would lift out of the morass of subjectivism the squirming, singled, defined process which would show that the sin of public terror is that it divests man of conscience, of himself. It was a theme not unrelated to those that invested the previous plays."

Although the theme is the same, the tragic hero of *The Crucible* is different from the heroes of the other plays. John Proctor, unlike Joe Keller, refuses to commit the antisocial action. That is, he loses his life because he will not admit that he is a witch, a confession that would save his own life but make the others who would not confess seem guilty and thereby justify the trials. He refuses to sign the confession because it would mean handing his conscience to the judges, as he puts it, a loss of his "name." When Danforth asks why he will not sign, Proctor replies: "Because it is my name! Because I cannot have another in my life! Because I lie and sign myself to lies! Because I am not worth the dust on the feet of them that hang! How may I live without my name?" John Proctor is not an especially good or brave person. Indeed, he has previously committed adultery with the chief accuser of the witches, Abigail Williams, and this relationship is one of the main causes of the witch hunt. Abigail desires Proctor's wife to hang so that she may have him. Proctor has felt his guilt strongly, and, as Miller tells us, "has come to regard himself as a kind of fraud." His adultery and guilt have prevented him from feeling at one with his community. From his wife, too, he has been spiritually and mentally separated since his sin. But Proctor, like Biff Loman, finds himself during the course of the play. He openly admits to the community that he is a "lecher" in order to save his wife, and after again feeling himself a part of the same brotherhood with the noble Rebecca Nurse and Giles Cory, the two "witches" who refuse to sign a false confession, he will not lose what he has gained. The central crucible, or trial, of *The Crucible* is John Proctor's personal test. He has a choice between life without conscience or death. He chooses to save his identity, his "name," even though it means his death.

In *The Crucible* as in *All My Sons* and *Death of a Salesman* there is discovery as well as loss of conscience. Chris Keller finds on the field of battle a world of love and responsibility to others while his father isolates himself from this same world by sending out the faulty engines. Biff Loman begins to find himself at the moment when Willy Loman's isolation is objectified in his act of adultery. And while John Proctor gains what his wife calls "his goodness," others, especially the leaders of the witch hunt, surrender their values and human dignity. Of this group, John Hale is the most important. Indeed he narrowly misses being the tragic hero of the play. William Wiegand sees *The Crucible* as John Hale's tragedy. "Hale takes the play over so completely from the victim, Proctor," writes Wiegand, "that the latter's martyrdom seems almost a sentimental afterthought."[4] Like Joe Keller and Willy Loman, Hale is intent upon following a "good," in his case ridding the world of evil. But he does not foresee the consequences of the Salem witch hunt and is partly responsible for a heinous atrocity against humanity. Recognizing the harm he has done in the name of good, Hale says to Elizabeth Proctor: "I came into this village like a bridegroom to his beloved, bearing gifts of high religion; the very crowns of

4 See p. 300.

holy law I brought, and what I touched with my bright confidence, it died; and where I turned the eye of my great faith, blood flowed up." When he desires to stop the trials, the terror has already spread too far and he is helpless. Since he has lost his perspective in his zeal to seek out the devil, he has compromised his conscience and cut himself off from man.

The effects of Hale's isolation are clearly reflected in his changing physical appearance. When Hale makes his second entrance, Miller describes him as "different now—drawn a little, and there is a quality of deference, even guilt, about his manner now." Hale's third and last appearance reveals him as still further decayed under the weight of guilt and isolation. He is now a man "steeped in sorrow, exhausted, and more direct than he ever was." John Hale, then, is to be placed in the same company with Joe Keller and Willy Loman. He discovers too late that the good he pursues has made him onesided and therefore brought him into conflict with the rest of life.

In *A View from the Bridge* the plot again focuses on an anti-social action, Eddie Carbone's betrayal of the immigrants. The longshoreman, Eddie Carbone, has taken his wife's niece into his home and supplied her needs as if she were his own child. As Catherine approaches young womanhood, however, his love for her becomes more than that of father for daughter. The coming of the immigrants Rodolpho and Marco stimulates his passion for Catherine. And when Rodolpho and Catherine indicate their desire to be married, Eddie must make a choice: he may simply acquiesce in the marriage of Catherine and thus fight against the intense passion he has for her, or he may keep Catherine in his household but only by betraying Rodolpho and Marco, who are guilty of illegal entry, to the authorities. After going to Mr. Alfieri, the lawyer, to inquire if the law will aid him in stopping Catherine's marriage to Rodolpho, Eddie succumbs to his passion and causes not only Rodolpho and Marco to be arrested but also two other immigrants whom he does not even know.

In betraying Rodolpho and Marco, Eddie violates a code of behavior with which he has previously identified himself. Early in the play Eddie indicates his accordance with the idea of helping immigrants in order that they may get a start. "It's an honor, B." he tells his wife. "I mean it. I was just thinkin' before, comin' home, suppose my father didn't come to this country, and I was starvin' like them over there . . . and I had people in America could help me a couple of months? The man would be honored to lend me a place to sleep." Commenting on Eddie's loss of conscience, Miller has written: "The maturing of Eddie's need to destroy Rodolpho was consequently seen in the context which could make it of real moment, for the betrayal achieves its true proportions as it flies in the face of the mores administered by Eddie's conscience—which is also the conscience of his friends, co-workers, and neighbors and not just his own autonomous creation." Eddie's action thus not only prevents the immigrants from feeding their starving families in Italy but also isolates him from his society, which recognizes the need of man to help his brothers. Eddie's need to reidentify himself with his society is suggested by his asking Marco to give him back his "name." "I want my name, Marco," Eddie says. "Now gimme my name." To Eddie Carbone as well as to John Proctor, name symbolizes a connection, a communion, with one's fellow beings without which we become hollow.

The settings and the social order in Arthur Miller's tragedies are modern. Even in *The Crucible*, where Miller goes to history for his plot and setting, there is an intended parallel to a modern situation. His primary interest, however, is traditional, for he is chiefly concerned with the individual and with the problem of moral decision. If his characters live in the modern world depicted by determinists like Dreiser and Galsworthy, they, like the heroes of Shakespeare and Hawthorne, must make their own choices. Tragedy occurs when they lose conscience, when they choose to ignore their responsible place in society. For this age Miller represents an unusual synthesis: the artist who is profoundly concerned with both the *polis* and the integrity and responsibility of the individual.

GERALD WEALES

ARTHUR MILLER:
MAN AND HIS IMAGE

He's got his stance, he's got his pace, he's got his control down to a pinpoint. He's almost original sometimes. When it comes to throwin' a ball, he's all there.
—AUGIE BELFAST in *The Man Who Had All the Luck*

Arthur Miller is one of those playwrights, like Thornton Wilder, whose reputation rests on a handful of plays. The quality of that reputation changes from year to year, from critic to critic, but now, five years after the production of his most recent play (the revision of *A View from the Bridge*), it is generally conceded, even by those who persist in not admiring his work, that Miller is one of the two playwrights of the postwar American theater who deserve any consideration as major dramatists. Tennessee Williams is the other.

There are many ways of approaching Miller's work. In the late forties, after *All My Sons* and *Death of a Salesman*, popular reviewers tended to embrace him enthusiastically, while consciously intellectual critics, displaying the carefulness of their kind, hoped that in explaining him they might explain him away. For a time, his plays were lost in discussions of the author's politics, past and present, or were buried beneath the pointless academic quibble about whether or not they are true tragedies. Miller's own defensiveness on these two points helped feed the controversy. In the last few years, however, with no new Miller play to stir up opinion, his work has begun to be considered outside the immediate context that produced it.

From *American Drama Since World War II* by Gerald Weales (New York: Harcourt, Brace & World, 1962), pp. 3-17, Copyright © 1962 by Gerald Weales, reprinted by permission of Harcourt, Brace & World, Inc.

Even so, there is no single handle by which to grasp his works. Because each of his four chief plays is built on a family situation—"Sons" and "Salesman" on the father-son conflict, *The Crucible* and "View" on the triangle—the plays can be treated as domestic dramas. Because they obviously criticize or comment upon the structure of society, they may be considered conventional social plays; still, as Eric Bentley has pointed out,[1] noting the chief motivating force in most of the plots, they are as much sexual as social dramas. There are probably enough biographical reflections in the plays to send the psychological critic in search of personal analogies; Maurice Zolotow, for instance, interrupts the psycho-anecdotage of *Marilyn Monroe* long enough to point out that both "Crucible" and "View" deal with marital problems caused by the attraction of an older man to a younger woman and to suggest that they stem from the fact that the author could not get Miss Monroe out of his mind between his first meeting with her in 1950 and his marriage to her in 1956.

Any of these approaches, even Zolotow's, may manage to say something valid about Miller's plays. To me, however, the most profitable way of looking at his work is through his heroes and through the concern of each, however inarticulate, with his identity—his *name*, as both John Proctor and Eddie Carbone call it. Perhaps the simplest way to get at what Miller is doing in these plays is to force a path through the confounding prose of his general comments on contemporary drama and on the kind of play he hopes he has written. Although his opinions on the nature of drama are scattered through interviews, introductions, and occasional articles for *The New York Times*, the bulk of his theoretical writing is contained in four essays: "On Social Plays," printed as an introduction to *A View from the Bridge* (1955); "The Family in Modern Drama," originally a lecture given at Harvard (*Atlantic Monthly*, April 1956); Introduction to the *Collected Plays* (1957); "The Shadows of the Gods" (*Harper's*, August 1958). Although each of these essays has a

---

[1] Eric Bentley, "Theatre," *New Republic*, CXXXIII (December 19, 1955), 22. This (pp. 21-22) is his review of *A View from the Bridge*.

particular job to do, a recurring idea about the possibilities of modern drama seeps through the ponderousness of all of them, climbs over the barriers of Miller's Germanic fondness for definition and redefinition. For Miller, the serious playwright writes social drama, but that genre, for him, is not simply "an arraignment of society's evils." Just as he refuses to accept the standard definition of the social play, a product of the thirties, so too he rejects the drama which he sees as most representative of contemporary American theater, the play in which the characters retreat into self-preoccupation and give little hint that there is a society outside themselves. The true social drama, the "Whole Drama," as he calls it, must recognize that man has both a subjective and an objective existence, that he belongs not only to himself and his family, but to the world beyond.

Since Miller's plays were written before these essays were, it is probably safe to assume that the theorizing is *ex post facto* in more ways than one, and that his general conclusions about the drama are based, in part, on what he thinks he has done as a playwright; his ready use of "Salesman" as an example strengthens such an assumption. I have no trouble accepting his belief that the best of drama has always dealt with man in both a personal and a social context, but his generalizations are most useful as approaches to his own work. His plays are family-centered, obviously, because our drama the last few years has been uncomfortable in any context larger than the family; his heroes, however, are more than failed husbands and fathers because he has recognized that the most impressive family plays, from *Oedipus* through *Hamlet* to *Ghosts*, have modified the concept of the family and of the individual under the pressure of society.

Each of his heroes is involved, in one way or another, in a struggle that results from his acceptance or rejection of an image that is the product of his society's values and prejudices, whether that society is as small as Eddie Carbone's neighborhood or as wide as the contemporary America that helped form Willy Loman. Miller's work has followed such a pattern from the beginning. Even Ben, the hero of *They Too Arise*, a now happily forgotten prize winner from the mid-thirties, has to decide whether he is to be the man that his middle-class, small-businessman father expects or the comrade that his radical brother demands; the play ends, of course, in leftist affirmation, but the conflict has been in terms of opposed images, both of which are assumed to have validity for Ben. The hero of *The Man Who Had All the Luck* (1944), Miller's first produced play, accepts the town's view of him as a man who has succeeded through luck not ability; he assumes that all luck must turn and, in his obsession, almost brings disaster on his head until his wife convinces him that he should reject the town's rationalizing bromide and accept the principle that man makes his own luck. In his novel *Focus* (1945), a fantasy-tract, his anti-Semitic hero finally accepts the label that his neighbors force on him; he admits that he is a Jew. Most of Miller's short stories reflect the same kind of preoccupation with the self that someone else expects the hero to be; in one of his most recent stories, "I Don't Need You Any More" (*Esquire*, December 1959), the five-year-old hero's idea of himself is formed on half-understood perceptions picked up from his parents and the adult world they live in, the only society that he recognizes outside himself. The lament and the longing implicit in Martin's thought—"If only he *looked* like his father and his brother!"—is a small echo of the bewilderment that haunts all the Miller heroes who do the right things and come to the wrong ends.

In *All My Sons* (1947), Miller's first successful play, Joe Keller, who is admittedly a good husband and a good father, fails to be the good man, the good citizen that his son Chris demands. "I'm his father and he's my son, and if there's something bigger than that I'll put a bullet in my head!" Chris makes clear that, for him, there is something bigger than the family, and Joe commits suicide. Much more interesting than the unmasking and punishment of Joe's crime (he shipped out cracked cylinder heads during the war and let his partner take the blame and go to jail) is Joe as a peculiarly American product. He is a self-made man, a successful businessman "with the imprint of the machine-shop worker and boss still upon him." There is nothing ruthless about Joe, no hint of the robber baron in his make-up; his ambitions are small—a comfortable home for his family, a successful business to pass on to his sons —but he is not completely fastidious in achieving his goals. Not only has he accepted the American myth of the primacy of the family, his final excuse for all his actions, but he has adopted as a working instrument the familiar attitude that there is a difference between morality and business ethics. Not that he could ever phrase it that way. "I'm in business, a man is in business. . . ." he begins his explanation, his plea for understanding, and moves on to that dimly lit area where the other man's culpability is his forgiveness.

When Miller at last moves in on Joe, brings Chris and discovery to destroy him, there is no longer any possibility of choice. His fault, according to Miller and Chris, is that he does not recognize any allegiance to society at large; his world, as he mistakenly says of that of his dead son Larry, "had a forty-foot front, it ended at the building line." Joe's shortness of vision, however, is a product of his society. Even Chris shares his goals: "If I have to grub for money all day long at least at evening I want it beautiful. I want a family, I want some kids, I want to build something I can give myself to." The neighbors, in the figure of Sue, respect Joe's methods: "They give him credit for being smart." At the end of the play, finally confronted with another alternative ("But I think to him they were all my sons"), Joe Keller, in killing himself, destroys the image that he has accepted.

There is a disturbing patness about *All My Sons*, an exemplary working out of the conflict that is as didactic as Chris's more extended speeches. With *Death of a Salesman* (1949), Miller escapes into richness. The ambiguity that occasionally touches the characters in the earlier play, that makes the supposedly admirable idealist son sound at times like a hanging judge, suffuses the playwright's second success, his finest play. It might be possible to reduce the play to some kind of formula, to suggest that Biff's end-of-the-play declaration, "I know who

I am, kid," is a positive statement, a finger pointing in some veri-
fiable direction, a refutation of all the beliefs to which Willy
clings and for which he dies. Miller suggests, in his Introduction
to the *Collected Plays*, that Biff does embody an "opposing
system" to the "law of success" which presumably kills Willy,
but there are almost as many contradictions in Miller's Introduction as there are in his play. Since the last scene, the
Requiem, is full of irony—Charley's romantic eulogy of the
Salesman, Linda's failure to understand ("I made the last payment on the house today. . . . We're free and clear"), Happy's
determination to follow in his father's failed footsteps—there is
no reason to assume that some of the irony does not rub off
on Biff. We have been with the lying Lomans so long, have
seen them hedge their bets and hide their losses in scene after
self-deluding scene, that it is at least forgivable if we respect
Willy's integrity as a character (if not as a man) and suspect
that Biff is still his son. The play after all, ends with the funeral;
there is no sequel.

When we meet Willy Loman, he, like Joe Keller, is past the
point of choice, but his play tells us that there are at least three
will-of-the-wisp ideals—father figures, all—that Willy might
have chosen to follow. The first is his own father, the inventor,
the flute maker, the worker-with-his-hands, who walked away
one day and left the family to shift for itself. His is the flute
melody that opens the play, "small and fine, telling of grass and
trees and the horizon." From what we hear of him, he was a
man who did not make his fortune because he did not know
that a fortune was a thing worth making and, if his desertion
of his family means anything, he needed the world's good
opinion as little as he needed its idea of conventional success.
The chances of Willy's going the way of his father are as dead
as the frontier, of course; so when the flute appears in the play
it is no more than a suggestion of a very vague might-have-been.
Nor is the second possible choice, that embodied in the figure
of Ben, a likely one for Willy; it is difficult to imagine him
among the business buccaneers. For that reason, perhaps, Miller
has chosen to make a comic caricature of Ben: "Why, boys,

when I was seventeen I walked into the jungle, and when I was twenty-one I walked out. And by God I was rich." Ben, with his assurance, his ruthlessness ("Never fight fair with a stranger, boy"), his connections in Africa and Alaska, looms a little larger than life in Willy's mind, half cartoon, half romance. There is romance enough—liberally laced with sentiment—in the ideal that Willy does choose, Dave Singleman, the old salesman who, at eighty-four, could, through the strength of his personality, sit in a hotel room and command buyers. Willy admires Singleman for dying "the death of a salesman, in his green velvet slippers in the smoker of the New York, New Haven and Hartford," without ever recognizing that there is more than one way to kill a salesman.

Willy can no more be Dave Singleman than he can be his father or his brother Ben. From the conflicting success images that wander through his troubled brain comes Willy's double ambition—to be rich and to be loved. As he tells Ben, "the wonder of this country [is] that a man can end with diamonds here on the basis of being liked!" From Andrew Carnegie, then, to Dale Carnegie. Willy's faith in the magic of "personal attractiveness" as a way to success carries him beyond cause and effect to necessity; he assumes that success falls inevitably to the man with the right smile, the best line, the most charm, the man who is not only liked, but well liked. He has completely embraced the American myth, born of the advertisers, that promises us love and a fortune as soon as we clear up our pimples, stop underarm perspiration, learn to play the piano; for this reason, the brand names that turn up in Willy's speeches are more than narrow realism. He regularly confuses labels with reality. In his last scene with Biff, Willy cries out, "I am not a dime a dozen! I am Willy Loman, and you are Biff Loman!" The strength and the pathos of that cry lie in the fact that Willy still thinks that the names should mean something; it is effective within the play because we have heard him imply that a punching bag is good because "It's got Gene Tunney's signature on it," and that a city can be summed up in a slogan—"Big clock city, the famous Waterbury clock."

The distance between the actual Willy and Willy as image is so great when the play opens that he can no longer lie to himself with conviction; what the play gives us is the final disintegration of a man who has never even approached his idea of what by rights he ought to have been. His ideal may have been the old salesman in his green velvet slippers, but his model is that mythic figure, the traveling salesman of the dirty joke. Willy tries to be a kidder, a caution, a laugh-a-minute; he shares his culture's conviction that personality is a matter of mannerism and in the sharing develops a style that is compounded of falseness, the mock assurance of what Happy calls "the old humor, the old confidence." His act, however, is as much for himself as it is for his customers. The play shows quite clearly that from the beginning of his career Willy has lied about the size of his sales, the warmth of his reception, the number of his friends. It is true that he occasionally doubts himself, assumes that he is too noisy and undignified, that he is not handsome enough ("I'm fat. I'm very—foolish to look at"), but usually he rationalizes his failure. His continuing self-delusion and his occasional self-awareness serve the same purpose; they keep him from questioning the assumptions that lie beneath his failure and his pretense of success. By the time we get to him, his struggle to hold on to his dream (if not for himself, then for his sons) has become so intense that all control is gone; past and present are one to him, and so are fact and fiction. A suggestion becomes a project completed; a possibility becomes a dream fulfilled. When Biff tries to give him peace by making him realize, and accept the realization, that he is a failure and a mediocrity and see that it makes no difference, Willy hears only what he wants to hear. He takes Biff's tears not only as an evidence of love, which they are, but as a kind of testimonial, an assurance that Willy's way has been the right one all along. Once again secure in his dream ("that boy is going to be magnificent"), he goes to his suicide's death, convinced that, with the insurance money, Biff will be—to use Willy's favorite nouns—a hero, a prince.

Joe Keller and Willy Loman find ready-made societal images

to attach themselves to and both become victims of the attachment. Society is not nearly so passive in Miller's next play, *The Crucible* (1953). Salem tries to force John Proctor to accept a particular image of himself, but he chooses to die. Although there are occasional voices in the earlier plays (the neighbors in *All My Sons*, the bartender in *Death of a Salesman*) who speak for society, Miller operates for the most part on the assumption that his audience knows and shares the ideas that work on the Kellers and the Lomans. He cannot be that certain in *The Crucible*. Whether we are to accept his Salem as historical or as an analogy for the United States in the early fifties, Miller needs to create a mood of mass hysteria in which guilt and confession become public virtues. For this reason, Proctor is not so intensively on stage as the protagonists of the earlier plays are; the playwright has to work up a setting for him, has to give his attention to the accusers, the court, the town.

Now that Joe McCarthy is dead and Roy Cohn is running Lionel trains, it has become customary to consider *The Crucible* outside the context in which it was written. Since the play is not simply a tract, there is good sense in that attitude; whatever value the play comes to have will be intrinsic. Still, there is something to be learned about John Proctor from Arthur Miller's opinions at the time the play was written. About six months after the play was produced, the *Nation* (July 3, 1954) published Miller's "A Modest Proposal for Pacification of the Public Temper," a not very successful attempt at Swiftian satire. What the piece does do is make quite clear that Miller believed that the America of that moment, like the Salem of his play, was going in for a kind of group therapy that demanded each man's *mea culpa*. It would be simple enough to dissect Miller's use of Salem and to show, as so many critics have, that the Massachusetts witch hunts are not analogous to the postwar Communist hunts, but such an exercise is finally beside the point. The important thing is that Miller found Salem both relevant and dramatically useful. A resurrection of the political situation at this time is valuable only because it is quite obvious that Miller's involvement with that situation dictated his treatment of the material. I am not thinking of the villainous Danforth, the ambitious Parris, the greedy Putnam, the envious Abigail, each of whom uses the cryings-out to his own advantage, although Miller was plainly intent on questioning the sincerity of accusers and investigators in general. It is John Proctor who shows most clearly Miller's attitude. His hero might have been another Willy Loman, another Joe Keller, an accepter not a defier of society, and his play would have had just as much—perhaps more—propaganda value. There is such a character in the play—the Reverend John Hale, the witch expert, who breaks under the strain of the trials—and one can make a good case for Hale as the protagonist of *The Crucible*. Although Hale is a much more interesting character than Proctor, it is Proctor's play and here Miller has produced, as he has not in his earlier plays, a romantic hero. It seems likely that Miller's opposition to the investigations and particularly to the form they took, the ritual naming of names, made him want a conventional hero, not, as usual, a victim-hero. When he appeared before the House Committe on Un-American Activities in June 1956, there was dignity in his refusal to give names, in his willingness to describe his past without apologizing for it, in his simple, "I accept my life." Ironically, not even Elizabeth's "He have his goodness now" can make Proctor's dignity convincing. The simplicity of the real situation is impossible on stage. Miller's need to push Proctor to his heroic end causes him to bring to *The Crucible* too many of the trappings of the standard romantic play; the plot turns on that moment in court when Elizabeth, who has never lied before, lies out of love of her husband and condemns him by that act. This is a sentimental mechanism almost as outrageous as the hidden-letter trick in the last act of *All My Sons*. There is excitement enough in the scene to hold an audience, but the attention that such a device demands is quite different from that required by John Proctor's struggle of conscience.

Although Proctor is never completely successful as a character, Miller makes a real effort to convince us that he is more than the blunt, not so bright good man he appears to be; and once again Miller works in terms of societal concepts. The Proctor who appears in the novelistic notes that Miller has sprinkled through the text of the published play is not quite the Proctor of the play itself; but there are similarities. We are to assume that Proctor is a solid man, but an independent one, not a man to fit lightly into anyone else's mold. When we meet him, however, he is suffering under a burden of guilt—intensified by his belief that Elizabeth is continually judging him. Miller makes it clear that in sleeping with Abigail Williams, Proctor has become "a sinner not only against the moral fashion of the time, but against his own vision of decent conduct." In Act III, when he admits in open court that he is a lecher, he says, "A man will not cast away his good name." When he is finally faced with the choice of death or confession (that he consorted with the devil), his guilt as an adulterer becomes confused with his innocence as a witch; one sin against society comes to look like another, or so he rationalizes. In the last act, however, Elizabeth in effect absolves him of the sin of adultery, gives him back the name he lost in court, and clears the way for him to reject the false confession and to give his life: "How may I live without my name?"

Eddie Carbone in *A View from the Bridge* (1955; revised 1956) also dies crying out for his name, but when he asks Marco to "gimme my name" he is asking for a lie that will let him live and, failing that, for death. Eddie is unusual among the Miller heroes in that he accepts the rules and prejudices of his society, an Italian neighborhood in Brooklyn, and dies because he violates them. Early in the play, Eddie warns Catherine to be closemouthed about the illegal immigrants (the "submarines") who are coming to live with them; he tells her with approbation about the brutal punishment meted out to an informer. By the end of the play, the "passion that had moved into his body, like a stranger," as Alfieri calls it, so possesses Eddie that to rid himself of the presence of Rodolpho he is willing to commit an act that he abhors as much as his society does. Miller's own comments on the play and the lines that he gives to Alfieri, a cross between the Greek chorus and Mary

Worth, indicate that he sees Eddie in the grip of a force that is almost impersonal in its inevitability, its terribleness, "the awesomeness of a passion which . . . despite even its destruction of the moral beliefs of the individual, proceeds to magnify its power over him until it destroys him." The action in "View" seems to me somewhat more complicated than the clean line Miller suggests; its hero is more than a leaf blown along on winds out of ancient Calabria. Eddie chooses to become an informer; his choice is so hedged with rationalization—his convincing himself that Rodolpho is homosexual, that he is marrying Catherine for citizenship papers—that he is never conscious of his motivation. He comes closer and closer to putting a label on his incestuous love for Catherine (although technically she is his niece, functionally she is his daughter) and his homosexual attraction to Rodolpho (how pathetically he goes round and round to keep from saying *queer*). By comparison, informing is a simpler breach of code, one that has justification in the world outside the neighborhood. It is almost as though he takes on the name *informer* to keep from wearing some name that is still more terrible to him, only to discover that he cannot live under the lesser label either.

"It is not enough any more to know that one is at the mercy of social pressures," Miller writes in "On Social Plays"; "it is necessary to understand that such a sealed fate cannot be accepted." Each of his four heroes is caught in a trap compounded of social and psychological forces and each one is destroyed. Miller is concerned that their deaths not be dismissed as insignificant, the crushing of little men by big forces. His description of Eddie Carbone expresses his opinion of all his heroes: "he possesses or exemplifies the wondrous and humane fact that he too can be driven to what in the last analysis is a sacrifice of himself for his conception, however misguided, of right, dignity, and justice."

Playwrights, however, have always been better at telling men how to die than how to live. A dramatist in opposition is always more comfortable than one in affirmation. When Miller chooses to be a social critic, in the old-fashioned sense, it is apparent what he is against. Although he disavows any blanket attack on capitalism, both "Salesman" and "Sons" contain explicit criticism of a business-oriented society in which corruption, selfishness, indifference, are the norms. The political and governmental targets are obvious enough in "Crucible"; in "View" there is an implicit condemnation of a social system that turns men into submarines. Back in the childhood of his career as a playwright, the days of *They Too Arise*, Miller might have been able to conceive of some kind of political action as a cure for such societal wrongs, but it has become increasingly clear that his concern is with personal morality, the individual's relation to a society in which the virtuous goals (Joe Keller's sense of family, Willy Loman's idea of success) are almost as suspect as the vicious methods. When there is a concrete situation, a problem like that of Joe Keller's cylinder heads, Miller has no difficulty; who in the audience is going to suggest that Keller was right in sending them out? It is with those other alternatives—the ones embedded in generalizations—that the trouble arises.

Biff can say, at the end of *Death of a Salesman*, "He had the wrong dreams," but we have seen enough of Willy to know that for this man there is probably no right dream. Still, Biff suggests that there is: "there's more of him in that front stoop than in all the sales he ever made." And Charley seems to agree: "He was a happy man with a batch of cement." The play is filled with references to Willy's pride in working with his hands, his desire for a garden. This theme that so pervades "Salesman" is hit glancingly in some of the other plays, in John Proctor's obvious love for his farm and in Eddie Carbone's pleasure in working a shipload of coffee. Smell, touch, taste, the physical contact between a man and his work, a man and the thing created—this is at least part of the alternative. It is a sentimental possibility, a compounding of two quasi-literary myths—the thirties' insistence on the dignity of labor coupled with the older back-to-nature idea. Reduced to its simplest, it is the respectable commonplace that a man is happiest doing work that he likes.

The rest of the "right dream" is not so concrete. It has to do with the relation of one man to another (a man to society, Miller might say), but it can only be defined in terms of the great words, the words that we use on state occasions. The fascination of Miller's plays is that he knows so well the way a society edits the meaning of the grand abstractions and forces (or entices) men to embrace them. Implicit in his work, however, is the possibility of a society that might not lead the Willys of this world astray. In *Situation Normal*, a volume of reportage that grew out of his army-camp research for the movie *The Story of G.I. Joe*, Miller insists that the main purpose of the book is to find the Belief (he uses the capital letter) that is sending men into war. When he finds it ("And that Belief says, simply, that we believe all men are equal"), it is traditional and it is honorable, but it is as amorphous as Chris Keller's *brotherhood*. Chris embodies the idea that a good society will follow when men choose not to live only for themselves. Vague as this idea is, it does represent a kind of commitment; Miller's characters, however, can effectively express or represent that commitment only in terms of opposition.

In Miller's most recent work, *The Misfits* (1961), both in the movie and the cinema novel (as his publisher calls it), there has been a change of attitude. It can be seen most clearly in two ideas that have preoccupied Miller the last few years: one is his assumption that in our society the hero is reduced to the misfit; the other is the chief dramatic cliché of the fifties, faith in the curative powers of love. To understand this change clearly, one must go back to *Death of a Salesman*, begin with Biff, who is, after all, the prototype of the Miller misfit. Uncomfortable in Willy's competitive world, Biff goes west, becomes an outdoors bum—like Gay, Guido, and Perce in *The Misfits*. Although "Salesman" is too ambiguous, too good a play to allow Biff to wear a single label, it implies at least that there is something positive in Biff's choice. Certainly, as late as 1955, in the novelistic notes he added to the Bantam edition of the play, Miller was to describe Happy as "less heroically cast" than Biff, a phrase that suggests that Biff is somehow heroic. The same year, however, in "On Social Plays," Miller shook his head sadly over the state of the hero, said that "our common sense reduces him to the size of a complainer, a misfit." "Salesman" suggests reasons for this reduction in size in Biff's case; he is "lost," to use a cliché that Miller shares with Linda Loman, the queen of the bromides, but the implication is that he is incapacitated by his sense of guilt at having rejected his father and his father's dream. Although there are suggestions of psychological dislocation in the story version of "The Misfits" (*Esquire*, October 1957), it is primarily the story of three men who have no place in the world of job, home, and family. "Well, it's better than wages," says Gay of their pathetic roundup of wild horses, and Perce answers, "Hell, yes. Anything's better than wages." Using the roundup as plot, the story insists that, even though the West might once have been big enough for a man or horse to be proud and free, the mustang has become dogfood and the mustanging hero, a dogfood-hunting bum. In this form, "The Misfits" is a kind of twilight of the gods, and it has the dignity and sadness that such a theme demands.

In the later versions, the movie and the novel, the regret turns to therapy. Although Miller has often criticized the sentimentality of contemporary drama, his commitment to the generalized good seems finally to have forced him to embrace the last decade's faith in love as an anodyne. In the Introduction to *Collected Plays*, published the year that "The Misfits" first appeared, Miller says that in "Salesman" he wanted to set up "an opposing system which, so to speak, is in a race for Willy's faith, and it is the system of love which is the opposite of the law of success." There is no such thing in the play. Biff obviously loves Willy as much as he hates him, but this fact hardly constitutes a system; nor is it presented as a possible opposite to Willy's desire for success. Miller is simply trying to read back into the earlier play a concept of love that comes too late to save Willy, but just in time to destroy the hero-misfit. The movie and the novel pick up the psychological hints of the story, develop them at great length and indicate that these men are not misfits in the grand tradition of Daniel Boone and Kit

Carson; they are would-be conformists looking for a home. At the end of the movie, Perce is going back to wages, to the mother and ranch he lost when she remarried after the death of his father. Guido is still crying out in anger, but there is more frustration than principle in his cries. It is with Gay that the sentimentality is most obvious. As he and Roslyn drive off at the end of *The Misfits,* after he has released the wild horse and with it any claim he has to independence, she says, "How do you find your way back in the dark?" He answers, "Just head for that big star straight on. The highway's under it; take us right home." It has been suggested that this end is as ironic as the Requiem of "Salesman," but there is too much evidence against such an interpretation: Miller's remarks about love and Biff, the sudsiness that pervades the prose and the characters in the novel, the clichés (John Huston's as well as Miller's) that fill the movie.

It is too early to tell whether *The Misfits* is an anomaly or an indication, whether—when and if he returns to the theater—Miller will again concern himself with society and its effects on men or, like so many of his contemporaries, crawl into the personal solution to public problems. Whatever happens, it is necessary to say that Miller's early work for the theater has earned him an important place in American drama. The faults of his plays are obvious enough. *All My Sons,* for all its neatness, tends to go to pieces in the last act when the recognition of Joe's guilt no longer comes from the interaction of characters, but from the gratuitous introduction of Larry's letter. In *Death of a Salesman,* peripheral characters such as Howard and Bernard are completely unbelievable and Miller has not saved them, as he has Ben, by turning them into obvious caricatures. There are distressing structural faults in *The Crucible,* violations of the realistic surface of the play, such as the unlikely scene in Act I in which Proctor and Abigail are left alone in the sick girl's bedroom. Nor was it such a good idea for Miller to attempt, in that play, to suggest the language of the period; the lines are as awkward and as stagily false as those in John Drinkwater's *Oliver Cromwell.* The pretentiousness of Alfieri's speeches in *A View from the Bridge*, the conscious attempt to make an analogy between Red Hook and Calabria, reduces the impact of Eddie Carbone's story; any connection between Eddie and the passion-ridden heroes of old should have been made implicitly.

Miller's virtues, however, outweigh these faults. The theme that recurs in all his plays—the relationship between a man's identity and the image that society demands of him—is a major one; in one way or another it has been the concern of most serious playwrights. A big theme is not enough, of course; Miller has the ability to invest it with emotion. He is sometimes sentimental, sometimes romantic about both his characters and their situations; but sentiment and romance, if they can command an audience without drowning it, are not necessarily vices. Even in *A Memory of Two Mondays*, in which he peoples his stage with stereotypes, he manages, in the end, to make Bert's departure touching. The test of the good commercial playwright is the immediate reaction of an audience; the test of the good playwright is how well his plays hold up under continuing observation. Each time I go back to *All My Sons*, to *The Crucible*, to *A View from the Bridge*, the faults become more ominous, but in each of these plays there are still scenes that work as effectively as they did when I first saw the play. *Death of a Salesman* is something else again. It does not merely hold its own, it grows with each rereading. Those people who go in for good-better-best labels—I am not one of them—would be wise, when they draw up their list of American plays, to put *Death of a Salesman* very near the top.

Analogues

WALTER D. MOODY

Walter D. Moody wrote *Men Who Sell Things* at about the same time Willy Loman would have been learning the trade.

THE KNOW-IT-ALL SALESMAN

The only shots that count are the shots that hit. —ROOSEVELT

Many a man who takes himself very seriously is regarded as a huge joke by others.

Many a fool is vain and self-deceptive; many a man of great power is modest to the last degree.

It does not follow that because air is life it has any application to salesmanship; but perhaps that is the reason why some salesmen blow so hard.

A noted and witty preacher once said: "The general pulpit style of America is about like this: Here I am, the Rev. Jeremiah Jones, D-o-c-t-o-r of D-i-v-i-n-i-t-y, saved by the grace of God, with a message to deliver. If you will repent and believe what I believe, you will be saved; and if you don't, you will be damned; and I don't care much if you are."

Self-assertiveness is an invaluable quality in salesmanship when properly harnessed, but it can be overworked.

The Know-it-all Salesman claims a large share of the limelight wherever possible. He seeks to impress every one with

From *Men Who Sell Things* by Walter D. Moody (Chicago: A. C. McClurg, 1909), pp. 111–116.

whom he comes in contact with an idea of his astonishing zeal, and by a melodramatic display of activity.

If a man is going to be efficient and successful, he must think more about his work than about himself. The salesman who wants to get to the top by intelligent devotion to work has no time for self-worship.

Salesmanship is like a great river coursing its way onward through the innumerable channels and branches of the world's activities, the shores of which are strewn with wrecks and failures, who held their own personalities as paramount to their work. If the quality of a salesman's work will pass muster with the head of his house, his personality will shine through it unushered by any effort on his part.

Salesmen that talk as though they were well pleased with themselves do not find many in their neighborhood who are well pleased with them. Whenever a salesman gets more self-consciousness than he has sense, he's going to talk foolishness most of the time. Selling-talk and foolishness do not mix well, the one must suffer at the expense of the other.

You associate with salesmanship thought, wisdom, and a reasonable amount of self-restraint, don't you? Now, some salesmen say that they don't have to study, and they don't need the advice of their sales manager. They can paddle their own canoes.

The president of a great house travelling many men appropriated a large sum to be invested in the education of his corps of salesmen through the organization and equipment of a class in scientific salesmanship.

A few weeks after the study had been installed, he went to one of his salesmen and inquired how he was getting along with the work. The reply was: "The author of that course don't know anything about our line. He can't learn me nothing."

And sure enough he could not.

When selling goods, that salesman just opened his mouth and let come out of it what would, and it was generally filled with air. That is all such a mouth can be filled with. There is many an old air-gun salesman shooting around over his territory. You can't bring down big game with an air-gun.

Three things are necessary to enable a salesman to put up a good selling-talk—knowledge, judgment, and enthusiasm. Buyers associate those qualities with every good selling-talk they hear.

No one will ever do anything for you that you can do for yourself. The sales manager in your house has too much to do to go running around posting lazy salesmen that have no disposition to learn anything new.

You show me a salesman that feels he is all-sufficient in his own knowledge, one who doesn't have to keep posted on the latest and best of everything that will aid him in holding and gaining prestige with his trade and his house, and I will show you an Air-gun. I write with safety, for of course there are no Air-guns around your house. I refer to those in the house of your neighbor down in the next block.

The next thing to an Air-gun is an old Powder-gun—one with nothing in it but powder. No trade is ever secured with that. The Powder-gun Salesman shoots at his trade without any shot. His customers enjoy it as much as he does—none of them ever get bagged. But whenever a salesman puts a shell filled with shot into the magazine of his selling-talk and lays the barrel on solid judgment, and takes careful aim, training the sight on the sale he is bent on securing, and fires, he is sure to hit the bull's-eye.

After his shot tells, he can stop and apologize: "I didn't mean to hit you there. I aimed here." That is a salesman who aims where he hits, and hits where he aims.

The greatest power any house ever had is a game salesman— never afraid of competition. And the greatest drawback is the Shotless Salesman, who aims at nothing in particular, and misses everything. He is in the same category with his fussy friend who is afraid of hurting somebody's feelings if he takes careful aim.

Don't let any one say of you that you talk too much of yourself and your affairs.

A reasonable degree of self-assurance is a good thing; the best of salesmen practise and live self-confidence and self-assertiveness to a certain measure; but the overworking of these qualities is the cause of the failure of many a bright salesman. You are obliged to have something more.

Salesmanship does not consist of what you profess, but it consists of what you are, what you do, and how well you do it. When the doing follows the being, the result swells your sales, increases your chances for ultimate success.

There is no objection to a man professing salesmanship. There is no quarrel with a salesman as long as he lives on a level with what he professes; but when he gets down below that, the sales manager should go for him. When the salesman mixes too much of himself with what he is trying to sell, he is not living on a level with his profession. Self-sufficiency does not secure efficiency.

The real worker must forget self; business is the main thing.

It is hard for the Know-it-all Salesman to realize that nobody is always right.

The man who either will not or cannot efface himself enough in performing his duties will find it exceedingly difficult to get along. He cannot hope to win the approval of those above him in authority, or to make lasting friends of his customers. He is like a man toiling up an icy glacier without the aid of an alpenstock. The most arduous effort too often means a sudden plunge into the yawning abyss.

EUDORA WELTY

Eudora Welty, novelist and short-story writer, is the author of *The Wide Net and Other Stories*, *The Golden Apples*, *The Ponder Heart*, *The Bride of the Innisfallen*, and *The Shoe Bird*.

DEATH OF A TRAVELING SALESMAN

R. J. Bowman, who for fourteen years had traveled for a shoe company through Mississippi, drove his Ford along a rutted dirt path. It was a long day! The time did not seem to clear the noon hurdle and settle into soft afternoon. The sun, keeping its strength here even in winter, stayed at the top of the sky, and every time Bowman stuck his head out of the dusty car to stare up the road, it seemed to reach a long arm down and push against the top of his head, right through his hat—like the practical joke of an old drummer, long on the road. It made him feel all the more angry and helpless. He was feverish, and he was not quite sure of the way.

This was his first day back on the road after a long siege of influenza. He had had very high fever, and dreams, and had become weakened and pale, enough to tell the difference in the mirror, and he could not think clearly. . . . All afternoon, in the midst of his anger, and for no reason, he had thought of his dead grandmother. She had been a comfortable soul. Once more Bowman wished he could fall into the big feather bed that had been in her room. . . . Then he forgot her again.

This desolate hill country! And he seemed to be going the wrong way—it was as if he were going back, far back. There was not a house in sight. . . . There was no use wishing he were back in bed, though. By paying the hotel doctor his bill he

From *A Curtain of Green and Other Stories* by Eudora Welty (New York: Harcourt, Brace & World, 1941), pp. 231–253, Copyright 1941 by Eudora Welty, reprinted by permission of Harcourt, Brace & World, Inc. and Russell and Volkening, Inc.

had proved his recovery. He had not even been sorry when the pretty trained nurse said good-bye. He did not like illness, he distrusted it, as he distrusted the road without signposts. It angered him. He had given the nurse a really expensive bracelet, just because she was packing up her bag and leaving.

But now—what if in fourteen years on the road he had never been ill before and never had an accident? His record was broken, and he had even begun almost to question it. . . . He had gradually put up at better hotels, in the bigger towns, but weren't they all, eternally, stuffy in summer and drafty in winter? Women? He could only remember little rooms within little rooms, like a nest of Chinese paper boxes, and if he thought of one woman he saw the worn loneliness that the furniture of that room seemed built of. And he himself—he was a man who always wore rather wide-brimmed black hats, and in the wavy hotel mirrors had looked something like a bullfighter, as he paused for that inevitable instant on the landing, walking downstairs to supper. . . . He leaned out of the car again, and once more the sun pushed at his head.

Bowman had wanted to reach Beulah by dark, to go to bed and sleep off his fatigue. As he remembered, Beulah was fifty miles away from the last town, on a graveled road. This was only a cow trail. How had he ever come to such a place? One hand wiped the sweat from his face, and he drove on.

He had made the Beulah trip before. But he had never seen this hill or this petering-out path before—or that cloud, he thought shyly, looking up and then down quickly—any more than he had seen this day before. Why did he not admit he was simply lost and had been for miles? . . . He was not in the habit of asking the way of strangers, and these people never knew where the very roads they lived on went to; but then he had not even been close enough to anyone to call out. People standing in the fields now and then, or on top of the haystacks, had been too far away, looking like leaning sticks or weeds, turning a little at the solitary rattle of his car across their countryside, watching the pale sobered winter dust where it chunked out behind like big squashes down the road. The stares of these distant people had followed him solidly like a wall, impenetrable, behind which they turned back after he had passed.

The cloud floated there to one side like the bolster on his grandmother's bed. It went over a cabin on the edge of a hill, where two bare chinaberry trees clutched at the sky. He drove through a heap of dead oak leaves, his wheels stirring their weightless sides to make a silvery melancholy whistle as the car passed through their bed. No car had been along this way ahead of him. Then he saw that he was on the edge of a ravine that fell away, a red erosion, and that this was indeed the road's end.

He pulled the brake. But it did not hold, though he put all his strength into it. The car, tipped toward the edge, rolled a little. Without doubt, it was going over the bank.

He got out quietly, as though some mischief had been done him and he had his dignity to remember. He lifted his bag and sample case out, set them down, and stood back and watched the car roll over the edge. He heard something—not the crash he was listening for, but a slow, unuproarious crackle. Rather distastefully he went to look over, and he saw that his car had fallen into a tangle of immense grapevines as thick as his arm, which caught it and held it, rocked it like a grotesque child in a dark cradle, and then, as he watched, concerned somehow that he was not still inside it, released it gently to the ground.

He sighed.

Where am I? he wondered with a shock. Why didn't I do something? All his anger seemed to have drifted away from him. There was the house, back on the hill. He took a bag in each hand and with almost childlike willingness went toward it. But his breathing came with difficulty, and he had to stop to rest.

It was a shotgun house, two rooms and an open passage between, perched on the hill. The whole cabin slanted a little under the heavy heaped-up vine that covered the roof, light and green, as though forgotten from summer. A woman stood in the passage.

He stopped still. Then all of a sudden his heart began to behave strangely. Like a rocket set off, it began to leap and expand into uneven patterns of beats which showered into his brain, and he could not think. But in scattering and falling it made no noise. It shot up with great power, almost elation, and fell gently, like acrobats into nets. It began to pound profoundly, then waited irresponsibly, hitting in some sort of inward mockery first at his ribs, then against his eyes, then under his shoulder blades, and against the roof of his mouth when he tried to say, "Good afternoon, madam." But he could not hear his heart—it was as quiet as ashes falling. This was rather comforting; still, it was shocking to Bowman to feel his heart beating at all.

Stock-still in his confusion, he dropped his bags, which seemed to drift in slow bulks gracefully through the air and to cushion themselves on the gray prostrate grass near the doorstep.

As for the woman standing there, he saw at once that she was old. Since she could not possibly hear his heart, he ignored the pounding and now looked at her carefully, and yet in his distraction dreamily, with his mouth open.

She had been cleaning the lamp, and held it, half blackened, half clear, in front of her. He saw her with the dark passage behind her. She was a big woman with a weather-beaten but unwrinkled face; her lips were held tightly together, and her eyes looked with a curious dulled brightness into his. He looked at her shoes, which were like bundles. If it were summer she would be barefoot. . . . Bowman, who automatically judged a woman's age on sight, set her age at fifty. She wore a formless garment of some gray coarse material, rough-dried from a washing, from which her arms appeared pink and unexpectedly round. When she never said a word, and sustained her quiet pose of holding the lamp, he was convinced of the strength in her body.

"Good afternoon, madam," he said.

She stared on, whether at him or at the air around him he

could not tell, but after a moment she lowered her eyes to show that she would listen to whatever he had to say.

"I wonder if you would be interested—" He tried once more. "An accident—my car . . ."

Her voice emerged low and remote, like a sound across a lake. "Sonny he ain't here."

"Sonny?"

"Sonny ain't here now."

Her son—a fellow able to bring my car up, he decided in blurred relief. He pointed down the hill. "My car's in the bottom of the ditch. I'll need help."

"Sonny ain't here, but he'll be here."

She was becoming clearer to him and her voice stronger, and Bowman saw that she was stupid.

He was hardly surprised at the deepening postponement and tedium of his journey. He took a breath, and heard his voice speaking over the silent blows of his heart. "I was sick. I am not strong yet. . . . May I come in?"

He stooped and laid his big black hat over the handle on his bag. It was a humble motion, almost a bow, that instantly struck him as absurd and betraying of all his weakness. He looked up at the woman, the wind blowing his hair. He might have continued for a long time in this unfamiliar attitude; he had never been a patient man, but when he was sick he had learned to sink submissively into the pillows, to wait for his medicine. He waited on the woman.

Then she, looking at him with blue eyes, turned and held open the door, and after a moment Bowman, as if convinced in his action, stood erect and followed her in.

Inside, the darkness of the house touched him like a professional hand, the doctor's. The woman set the half-cleaned lamp on a table in the center of the room and pointed, also like a professional person, a guide, to a chair with a yellow cowhide seat. She herself crouched on the hearth, drawing her knees up under the shapeless dress.

At first he felt hopefully secure. His heart was quieter. The room was enclosed in the gloom of yellow pine boards. He could see the other room, with the foot of an iron bed showing, across the passage. The bed had been made up with a red-and-yellow pieced quilt that looked like a map or a picture, a little like his grandmother's girlhood painting of Rome burning.

He had ached for coolness, but in this room it was cold. He stared at the hearth with dead coals lying on it and iron pots in the corners. The hearth and smoked chimney were of the stone he had seen ribbing the hills, mostly slate. Why is there no fire? he wondered.

And it was so still. The silence of the fields seemed to enter and move familiarly through the house. The wind used the open hall. He felt that he was in a mysterious, quiet, cool danger. It was necessary to do what? . . . To talk.

"I have a nice line of women's low-priced shoes . . ." he said.

But the woman answered, "Sonny 'll be here. He's strong. Sonny 'll move your car."

"Where is he now?"

"Farms for Mr. Redmond."

Mr. Redmond. Mr. Redmond. That was someone he would never have to encounter, and he was glad. Somehow the name did not appeal to him. . . . In a flare of touchiness and anxiety, Bowman wished to avoid even mention of unknown men and their unknown farms.

"Do you two live here alone?" He was surprised to hear his old voice, chatty, confidential, inflected for selling shoes, asking a question like that—a thing he did not even want to know.

"Yes. We are alone."

He was surprised at the way she answered. She had taken a long time to say that. She had nodded her head in a deep way too. Had she wished to affect him with some sort of premonition? he wondered unhappily. Or was it only that she would not help him, after all, by talking with him? For he was not strong enough to receive the impact of unfamiliar things without a little talk to break their fall. He had lived a month in which nothing had happened except in his head and his body—

an almost inaudible life of heartbeats and dreams that came back, a life of fever and privacy, a delicate life which had left him weak to the point of—what? Of begging. The pulse in his palm leapt like a trout in a brook.

He wondered over and over why the woman did not go ahead with cleaning the lamp. What prompted her to stay there across the room, silently bestowing her presence upon him? He saw that with her it was not a time for doing little tasks. Her face was grave; she was feeling how right she was. Perhaps it was only politeness. In docility he held his eyes stiffly wide; they fixed themselves on the woman's clasped hands as though she held the cord they were strung on.

Then, "Sonny's coming," she said.

He himself had not heard anything, but there came a man passing the window and then plunging in at the door, with two hounds beside him. Sonny was a big enough man, with his belt slung low about his hips. He looked at least thirty. He had a hot, red face that was yet full of silence. He wore muddy blue pants and an old military coat stained and patched. World War? Bowman wondered. Great God, it was a Confederate coat. On the back of his light hair he had a wide filthy black hat which seemed to insult Bowman's own. He pushed down the dogs from his chest. He was strong, with dignity and heaviness in his way of moving. . . . There was the resemblance to his mother.

They stood side by side. . . . He must account again for his presence here.

"Sonny, this man, he had his car to run off over the prec'pice an' wants to know if you will git it out for him," the woman said after a few minutes.

Bowman could not even state his case.

Sonny's eyes lay upon him.

He knew he should offer explanations and show money—at least appear either penitent or authoritative. But all he could do was to shrug slightly.

Sonny brushed by him going to the window, followed by the eager dogs, and looked out. There was effort even in the way he was looking, as if he could throw his sight out like a rope. Without turning Bowman felt that his own eyes could have seen nothing: it was too far.

"Got me a mule out there an' got me a block an' tackle," said Sonny meaningfully. "I *could* catch me my mule an' git me my ropes, an' before long I'd git your car out the ravine."

He looked completely around the room, as if in meditation, his eyes roving in their own distance. Then he pressed his lips firmly and yet shyly together, and with the dogs ahead of him this time, he lowered his head and strode out. The hard earth sounded, cupping to his powerful way of walking—almost a stagger.

Mischievously, at the suggestion of those sounds, Bowman's heart leapt again. It seemed to walk about inside him.

"Sonny's goin' to do it," the woman said. She said it again, singing it almost, like a song. She was sitting in her place by the hearth.

Without looking out, he heard some shouts and the dogs barking and the pounding of hoofs in short runs on the hill. In a few minutes Sonny passed under the window with a rope, and there was a brown mule with quivering, shining, purple-looking ears. The mule actually looked in the window. Under its eyelashes it turned target-like eyes into his. Bowman averted his head and saw the woman looking serenely back at the mule, with only satisfaction in her face.

She sang a little more, under her breath. It occurred to him, and it seemed quite marvelous, that she was not really talking to him, but rather following the thing that came about with words that were unconscious and part of her looking.

So he said nothing, and this time when he did not reply he felt a curious and strong emotion, not fear, rise up in him.

This time, when his heart leapt, something—his soul—seemed to leap too, like a little colt invited out of a pen. He stared at the woman while the frantic nimbleness of his feeling made his head sway. He could not move; there was nothing he could do, unless perhaps he might embrace this woman who sat there growing old and shapeless before him.

But he wanted to leap up, to say to her, I have been sick and I found out then, only then, how lonely I am. Is it too late? My heart puts up a struggle inside me, and you may have heard it, protesting against emptiness. . . . It should be full, he would rush on to tell her, thinking of his heart now as a deep lake, it should be holding love like other hearts. It should be flooded with love. There would be a warm spring day . . . Come and stand in my heart, whoever you are, and a whole river would cover your feet and rise higher and take your knees in whirlpools, and draw you down to itself, your whole body, your heart too.

But he moved a trembling hand across his eyes, and looked at the placid crouching woman across the room. She was still as a statue. He felt ashamed and exhausted by the thought that he might, in one more moment, have tried by simple words and embraces to communicate some strange thing—something which seemed always to have just escaped him . . .

Sunlight touched the furthest pot on the hearth. It was late afternoon. This time tomorrow he would be somewhere on a good graveled road, driving his car past things that happened to people, quicker than their happening. Seeing ahead to the next day, he was glad, and knew that this was no time to embrace an old woman. He could feel in his pounding temples the readying of his blood for motion and for hurrying away.

"Sonny's hitched up your car by now," said the woman. "He'll git it out the ravine right shortly."

"Fine!" he cried with his customary enthusiasm.

Yet it seemed a long time that they waited. It began to get dark. Bowman was cramped in his chair. Any man should know enough to get up and walk around while he waited. There was something like guilt in such stillness and silence.

But instead of getting up, he listened. . . . His breathing restrained, his eyes powerless in the growing dark, he listened uneasily for a warning sound, forgetting in wariness what it would be. Before long he heard something—soft, continuous, insinuating.

"What's that noise?" he asked, his voice jumping into the dark. Then wildly he was afraid it would be his heart beating so plainly in the quiet room, and she would tell him so.

"You might hear the stream," she said grudgingly.

Her voice was closer. She was standing by the table. He wondered why she did not light the lamp. She stood there in the dark and did not light it.

Bowman would never speak to her now, for the time was past. I'll sleep in the dark, he thought, in his bewilderment pitying himself.

Heavily she moved on to the window. Her arm, vaguely white, rose straight from her full side and she pointed out into the darkness.

"That white speck's Sonny," she said, talking to herself.

He turned unwillingly and peered over her shoulder; he hesitated to rise and stand beside her. His eyes searched the dusky air. The white speck floated smoothly toward her finger, like a leaf on a river, growing whiter in the dark. It was as if she had shown him something secret, part of her life, but had offered no explanation. He looked away. He was moved almost to tears, feeling for no reason that she had made a silent declaration equivalent to his own. His hand waited upon his chest.

Then a step shook the house, and Sonny was in the room. Bowman felt how the woman left him there and went to the other man's side.

"I done got your car out, mister," said Sonny's voice in the dark. "She's settin' a-waitin' in the road, turned to go back where she come from."

"Fine!" said Bowman, projecting his own voice to loudness. "I'm surely much obliged—I could never have done it myself— I was sick. . . ."

"I could do it easy," said Sonny.

Bowman could feel them both waiting in the dark, and he could hear the dogs panting out in the yard, waiting to bark when he should go. He felt strangely helpless and resentful. Now that he could go, he longed to stay. From what was he being deprived? His chest was rudely shaken by the violence of his heart. These people cherished something here that he could not see, they withheld some ancient promise of food and warmth and light. Between them they had a conspiracy. He thought of the way she had moved away from him and gone to Sonny, she had flowed toward him. He was shaking with cold, he was tired, and it was not fair. Humbly and yet angrily he stuck his hand into his pocket.

"Of course I'm going to pay you for everything—"

"We don't take money for such," said Sonny's voice belligerently.

"I want to pay. But do something more . . . Let me stay—tonight. . . ." He took another step toward them. If only they could see him, they would know his sincerity, his real need! His voice went on, "I'm not very strong yet, I'm not able to walk far, even back to my car, maybe, I don't know—I don't know exactly where I am—"

He stopped. He felt as if he might burst into tears. What would they think of him!

Sonny came over and put his hands on him. Bowman felt them pass (they were professional too) across his chest, over his hips. He could feel Sonny's eyes upon him in the dark.

"You ain't no revenuer come sneakin' here, mister, ain't got no gun?"

To this end of nowhere! And yet *he* had come. He made a grave answer. "No."

"You can stay."

"Sonny," said the woman, "you'll have to borry some fire."

"I'll go git it from Redmond's," said Sonny.

"What?" Bowman strained to hear their words to each other.

"Our fire, it's out, and Sonny's got to borry some, because its dark an' cold," she said.

"But matches—I have matches—"

"We don't have no need for 'em," she said proudly. "Sonny's goin' after his own fire."

"I'm goin' to Redmond's," said Sonny with an air of importance, and he went out.

After they had waited a while, Bowman looked out the window and saw a light moving over the hill. It spread itself out like a little fan. It zig-zagged along the field, darting and swift, not like Sonny at all. . . . Soon enough, Sonny staggered in, holding a burning stick behind him in tongs, fire flowing in his wake, blazing light into the corners of the room.

"We'll make a fire now," the woman said, taking the brand. When that was done she lit the lamp. It showed its dark and light. The whole room turned golden-yellow like some sort of flower, and the walls smelled of it and seemed to tremble with the quiet rushing of the fire and the waving of the burning lampwick in its funnel of light.

The woman moved among the iron pots. With the tongs she dropped hot coals on top of the iron lids. They made a set of soft vibrations, like the sound of a bell far away.

She looked up and over at Bowman, but he could not answer. He was trembling. . . .

"Have a drink, mister?" Sonny asked. He had brought in a chair from the other room and sat astride it with his folded arms across the back. Now we are all visible to one another, Bowman thought, and cried, "Yes sir, you bet, thanks!"

"Come after me and do just what I do," said Sonny.

It was another excursion into the dark. They went through the hall, out to the back of the house, past a shed and a hooded well. They came to a wilderness of thicket.

"Down on your knees," said Sonny.

"What?" Sweat broke out on his forehead.

He understood when Sonny began to crawl through a sort of tunnel that the bushes made over the ground. He followed, startled in spite of himself when a twig or a thorn touched him gently without making a sound, clinging to him and finally letting him go.

Sonny stopped crawling and, crouched on his knees, began to dig with both his hands into the dirt. Bowman shyly struck matches and made a light. In a few minutes Sonny pulled up a jug. He poured out some of the whisky into a bottle from his coat pocket, and buried the jug again. "You never know who's liable to knock at your door," he said, and laughed. "Start back," he said, almost formally. "Ain't no need for us to drink outdoors, like hogs."

At the table by the fire, sitting opposite each other in their chairs, Sonny and Bowman took drinks out of the bottle, passing it across. The dogs slept; one of them was having a dream.

"This is good," said Bowman. "This is what I needed." It was just as though he were drinking the fire off the hearth.

"He makes it," said the woman with quiet pride.

She was pushing the coals off the pots, and the smells of corn bread and coffee circled the room. She set everything on the table before the men, with a bone-handled knife stuck into one of the potatoes, splitting out its golden fiber. Then she stood for a minute looking at them, tall and full above them where they sat. She leaned a little toward them.

"You all can eat now," she said, and suddenly smiled.

Bowman had just happened to be looking at her. He set his cup back on the table in unbelieving protest. A pain pressed at his eyes. He saw that she was not an old woman. She was young, still young. He could think of no number of years for her. She was the same age as Sonny, and she belonged to him. She stood with the deep dark corner of the room behind her, the shifting yellow light scattering over her head and her gray formless dress, trembling over her tall body when it bent over them in its sudden communication. She was young. Her teeth were shining and her eyes glowed. She turned and walked slowly and heavily out of the room, and he heard her sit down on the cot and then lie down. The pattern on the quilt moved.

"She's goin' to have a baby," said Sonny, popping a bite into his mouth.

Bowman could not speak. He was shocked with knowing what was really in this house. A marriage, a fruitful marriage. That simple thing. Anyone could have had that.

Somehow he felt unable to be indignant or protest, although some sort of joke had certainly been played upon him. There was nothing remote or mysterious here—only something private.

The only secret was the ancient communication between two people. But the memory of the woman's waiting silently by the cold hearth, of the man's stubborn journey a mile away to get fire, and how they finally brought out their food and drink and filled the room proudly with all they had to show, was suddenly too clear and too enormous within him for response. . . .

"You ain't as hungry as you look," said Sonny.

The woman came out of the bedroom as soon as the men had finished, and ate her supper while her husband stared peacefully into the fire.

Then they put the dogs out, with the food that was left.

"I think I'd better sleep here by the fire, on the floor," said Bowman.

He felt that he had been cheated, and that he could afford now to be generous. Ill though he was, he was not going to ask them for their bed. He was through with asking favors in this house, now that he understood what was there.

"Sure, mister."

But he had not known yet how slowly he understood. They had not meant to give him their bed. After a little interval they both rose and looking at him gravely went into the other room.

He lay stretched by the fire until it grew low and dying. He watched every tongue of blaze lick out and vanish. "There will be special reduced prices on all footwear during the month of January," he found himself repeating quietly, and then he lay with his lips tight shut.

How many noises the night had! He heard the stream running, the fire dying, and he was sure now that he heard his heart beating too, the sound it made under his ribs. He heard breathing, round and deep, of the man and his wife in the room across the passage. And that was all. But emotion swelled patiently within him, and he wished that the child were his.

He must get back to where he had been before. He stood weakly before the red coals and put on his overcoat. It felt too heavy on his shoulders. As he started out he looked and saw that the woman had never got through with cleaning the lamp.

On some impulse he put all the money from his billfold under its fluted glass base, almost ostentatiously.

Ashamed, shrugging a little, and then shivering, he took his bags and went out. The cold of the air seemed to lift him bodily. The moon was in the sky.

On the slope he began to run, he could not help it. Just as he reached the road, where his car seemed to sit in the moonlight like a boat, his heart began to give off tremendous explosions like a rifle, bang bang bang.

He sank in fright onto the road, his bags falling about him. He felt as if all this had happened before. He covered his heart with both hands to keep anyone from hearing the noise it made.

But nobody heard it.

TENNESSEE WILLIAMS

Tennessee Williams' plays include *The Glass Menagerie, A Streetcar Named Desire, The Rose Tattoo, Camino Real, Cat on a Hot Tin Roof, Suddenly Last Summer,* and *The Night of the Iguana.* He is the author of, among other books, *The Roman Spring of Mrs. Stone,* a novel, and *The Knightly Quest,* a collection of short stories.

THE LAST OF
MY SOLID GOLD WATCHES

This play is inscribed to Mr. Sidney Greenstreet,
for whom the principal character was hopefully conceived.

Ce ne peut être que la fin du monde, en avançant.

—RIMBAUD

Characters
MR. CHARLIE COLTON
A NEGRO, *a porter in the hotel*
HARPER, *a traveling salesman*

SCENE: *A hotel room in a Mississippi Delta town. The room has looked the same, with some deterioration, for thirty or forty years. The walls are mustard-colored. There are two windows with dull green blinds, torn slightly, a ceiling-fan, a white iron bed with a pink counterpane, a washstand with rose-buds painted on the pitcher and bowl, and on the wall a colored lithograph of blind-folded Hope with her broken lyre.*

The door opens and Mr. Charlie Colton comes in. He is a legendary character, seventy-eight years old but still "going strong." He is lavish of flesh, superbly massive and with a kingly

From *27 Wagons Full of Cotton and Other One-Act Plays* by Tennessee Williams (Norfolk, Conn.: New Directions, 1953), pp. 73–85, Copyright 1945, 1953 by Tennessee Williams, all rights reserved, reprinted by permission of New Directions Publishing Corp. and Martin Secker Warburg Ltd.

dignity of bearing. Once he moved with a tidal ease and power. Now he puffs and rumbles; when no one is looking he clasps his hand to his chest and cocks his head to the warning heart inside him. His huge expanse of chest and belly is crisscrossed by multiple gold chains with various little fobs and trinkets suspended from them. On the back of his head is a derby and in his mouth a cigar. This is "Mistuh Charlie"—who sadly but proudly refers to himself as "the last of the Delta drummers." He is followed into the room by a Negro porter, as old as he is— thin and toothless and grizzled. He totes the long orange leather sample cases containing the shoes which Mr. Charlie is selling. He sets them down at the foot of the bed as Mr. Charlie fishes in his pocket for a quarter.

MR. CHARLIE, *handing the coin to the Negro*: Hyunh!

NEGRO, *breathlessly*: Thankyseh!

MR. CHARLIE: Huh! You're too old a darkey to tote them big heavy cases.

NEGRO, *grinning sadly*: Don't say that, Mistuh Charlie.

MR. CHARLIE: I reckon you'll keep right at it until yuh drop some day.

NEGRO: That's right, Mistuh Charlie.

Mr. Charlie fishes in his pocket for another quarter and tosses it to the Negro, who crouches and cackles as he receives it.

MR. CHARLIE: Hyunh!

NEGRO: Thankyseh, thankyseh!

MR. CHARLIE: Now set that fan in motion an' bring me in some ice-water by an' by!

NEGRO: De fan don' work, Mistuh Charlie.

MR. CHARLIE: Huh! Deterioration! Everything's going downhill around here lately!

NEGRO: Yes, suh, dat's de troof, Mistuh Charlie, ev'ything's goin' down-hill.

MR. CHARLIE: Who all's registered here of my acquaintance? Any ole-timers in town?

NEGRO: Naw, suh, Mistuh Charlie.

MR. CHARLIE: "Naw-suh-Mistuh-Charlie" 's all I get any more! You mean to say I won't be able to scare up a poker-game?

NEGRO, *chuckling sadly*: Mistuh Charlie, you's de bes' judge about dat!

MR. CHARLIE: Well, it's mighty slim pickin's these days. Ev'ry time I come in a town there's less of the old and more of the new and by God, nigguh, this new stand of cotton I see around the Delta's not worth pickin' off th' ground! Go down there an' tell that young fellow, Mr. Bob Harper, to drop up here for a drink!

NEGRO, *withdrawing*: Yes, suh.

MR. CHARLIE: It looks like otherwise I'd be playin' solitaire!

The Negro closes the door. Mr. Charlie crosses to the window and raises the blind. The evening is turning faintly blue. He sighs and opens his valise to remove a quart of whisky and some decks of cards which he slaps down on the table. He pauses and clasps his hand over his chest.

MR. CHARLIE—*ominously to himself*: Boom-boom-boom-boom-boom! Here comes th' parade!

After some moments there comes a rap at the door.

Come awn in!

Harper, a salesman of thirty-five, enters. He has never known the "great days of the road" and there is no vestige of grandeur in his manner. He is lean and sallow and has a book of colored comics stuffed in his coat pocket.

HARPER: How is the ole war-horse?

MR. CHARLIE, *heartily*: Mighty fine an' dandy! How's the young squirrel?

HARPER: Okay.

MR. CHARLIE: That's the right answer! Step on in an' pour you'self a drink! Cigar?

HARPER, *accepting both*: Thanks, Charlie.

MR. CHARLIE, *staring at his back with distaste*: Why do you carry them comic sheets around with yuh?

HARPER: Gives me a couple of laughs ev'ry once and a while.

MR. CHARLIE: Poverty of imagination!

Harper laughs a little resentfully.

You can't tell me there's any real amusement in them things.

He pulls it out of Harper's coat pocket.

"Superman," "The Adventures of Tom Tyler!" Huh! None of it's half as fantastic as life itself! When you arrive at my age—which is seventy-eight—you have a perspective of time on earth that astounds you! Literally astounds you! Naw, you say it's not true, all of that couldn't have happened! And for what *reason*? Naw! You begin to wonder. . . . Well . . . You're with Schultz and Werner?

HARPER: That's right, Charlie.

MR. CHARLIE: That concern's comparatively a new one.

HARPER: I don't know about that. They been in th' bus'ness fo' goin' on twenty-five years now, Charlie.

MR. CHARLIE: Infancy! Infancy! You heard this one, Bob? A child in its infancy don't have half as much fun as adults—in their adultery!

He roars with laughter. Harper grins. Mr. Charlie falls silent abruptly. He would have appreciated a more profound response. He remembers the time when a joke of his would precipitate a tornado. He fills up Harper's glass with whisky.

HARPER: Ain't you drinkin'?

MR. CHARLIE: Naw, suh. Quit!

HARPER: How come?

MR. CHARLIE: Stomach! Perforated!

HARPER: Ulcers?

Mr. Charlie grunts. He bends with difficulty and heaves a sample case onto the bed.

I had ulcers once.

MR. CHARLIE: *Ev'ry* drinkin' man has ulcers once. Some *twice.*

HARPER: You've fallen off some, ain't you?

MR. CHARLIE, *opening the sample case:* Twenty-seven pounds I lost since August.

Harper whistles. Mr. Charlie is fishing among his samples.

Yay-*ep!* Twenty-seven pounds I lost since August.

He pulls out an oxford which he regards disdainfully.

Hmmm . . . A waste of cow-hide!

He throws it back in and continues fishing.

A man of my age an' constitution, Bob—he oughtn't to carry so much of that—adipose tissue! It's—

He straightens up, red in the face and puffing.

—a terrible strain—on the *heart!* Hand me that other sample—over yonder. I wan' t' show you a little eyeful of queenly footwear in our new spring line! Some people say that the Cosmopolitan's not abreast of the times! That is an allegation which

I deny and which I intend to disprove by the simple display of one little calf-skin slipper!

Opening up the second case: Here we are, Son!

Fishing among the samples: You knew ole "Marblehead" Langner in Friar's Point, Mississippi.

HARPER: Ole "Marblehead" Langner? Sure.

MR. CHARLIE: They found him dead in his bath-tub a week ago Satiddy night. *Here's* what I'm lookin' faw!

HARPER: "Marblehead"? Dead?

MR. CHARLIE: *Buried!* Had a Masonic funeral. I helped carry th' casket. Bob, I want you t' look at this Cuban-heel, shawl-tongue, perforated toe, calf-skin Misses' sport-oxford!

He elevates it worshipfully.

I want you to look at this shoe—and tell me what you think of it in plain language!

Harper whistles and bugs his eyes.

Ain't that a piece of *real* merchandise, you squirrel? Well, suh, I want you t' know—!

HARPER: Charlie, that certainly is a piece of merchandise there!

MR. CHARLIE: Bob, that piece of merchandise is only a small indication—of what our spring line consists of! You don't have to pick up a piece of merchandise like that—with I.S.C. branded on it!—and examine it with the microscope t' find out if it's quality stuff as well as quality *looks!* This ain't a shoe that Mrs. Jones of Hattiesburg, Mississippi, is going to throw back in your face a couple or three weeks later because it come to pieces like *card*-board in th' first *rain!* No, suh—I want you to know! We got some pretty fast-movers in our spring line—I'm layin' my samples out down there in th' lobby first thing in th' mornin'—I'll pack 'em up an' be gone out of town by *noon*— But by the Almighty Jehovah I bet you I'll have to *wire* the office to mail me a bunch of *brand*-new order-books at my next stopping-off place, Bob! *Hot* cakes! *That's* what I'm sellin'!

He returns exhaustedly to the sample case and tosses the shoe back in, somewhat disheartened by Harper's vaguely benevolent contemplation of the brass light-fixture. He remembers a time when people's attention could be more securely riveted by talk. He slams the case shut and glances irritably at Harper who is staring very sadly at the brown carpet.

Well, suh—

He pours a shot of whisky.

It was a mighty shocking piece of news I received this afternoon.

HARPER, *blowing a smoke ring*: What piece of news was that?

MR. CHARLIE: The news about ole Gus Hamma—one of the old war-horses from *way* back, Bob. He and me an' this boy's daddy, C. C., used t' play poker ev'ry time we hit town together in this here self-same room! Well, suh, I want you t' know—

HARPER, *screwing up his forehead*: I think I heard about that. Didn't he have a stroke or something a few months ago?

MR. CHARLIE: He *did*. An' partly *recovered*.

HARPER: Yeah? Last I heard he had t' be fed with a spoon.

MR. CHARLIE, *quickly*: He did an' he partly recovered! He's been goin' round, y'know, in one of them chairs with a 'lectric motor on it. Goes chug-chug-chuggin' along th' road with th' butt of a cigar in his mouth. Well, suh, yestuddy in Blue Mountain, as I go out the Elks' Club door I pass him comin' in, bein' helped by th' nigguh—"Hello! Hiyuh, Gus!" That was at six-fifteen. Just half an hour later Carter Bowman stepped inside the hotel lobby where I was packin' up my sample cases an' give me the information that ole Gus Hamma had just now burnt himself to death in the Elks' Club lounge!

HARPER, *involuntarily grinning*: What uh yuh talkin' about?

MR. CHARLIE: Yes, suh, the ole war-horse had fallen asleep with that nickel cigar in his mouth—set his clothes on fire—and burnt himself right up like a piece of paper!

HARPER: I don't believe yuh!

MR. CHARLIE: Now, why on earth would I be lyin' to yuh about a thing like that? He burnt himself right up like a piece of paper!

HARPER: Well, ain't that a bitch of a way for a man to go?

MR. CHARLIE: *One* way—*another* way—!

Gravely: Maybe you don't *know* it—but all of us ole-timers, Bob, are disappearin' *fast!* We all gotta quit th' road one time or another. Me, I reckon I'm pretty nearly the last of th' Delta drummers!

HARPER, *restively squirming and glancing at his watch*: The last—of th' Delta drummers! How long you been on th' road?

MR. CHARLIE: Fawty-six yeahs in Mahch!

HARPER: I don't believe yuh.

MR. CHARLIE: Why would I tell you a lie about something like that? No, suh, I want you t' know—I want you t' know—Hmmm. . . . I lost a mighty good customer this week.

HARPER, *with total disinterest, adjusting the crotch of his trousers*: How's that, Charlie?

MR. CHARLIE, *grimly*: Ole Ben Summers—Friar's Point, Mississippi . . . Fell over dead like a bolt of lightning had struck him just as he went to pour himself a drink at the Cotton Planters' Cotillion!

HARPER: Ain't that terrible, though! What was the trouble?

MR. CHARLIE: Mortality, that was the trouble! Some people think that millions now living are never going to *die*. I don't think that—I think it's a misapprehension not borne out by the facts! We go like flies when we come to the end of the summer . . . And who is going to prevent it?

He becomes depressed.

Who—is going—to prevent it!

He nods gravely.

The road is changed. The shoe industry is changed. These times are—revolution!

He rises and moves to the window.

I don't like the way that it looks. You can take it from me—the world that I used to know—the world that this boy's father used t' know—the world we belonged to, us old time war-horses!—is slipping and sliding away from under our shoes. Who is going to prevent it? The ALL LEATHER slogan don't sell shoes any more. The stuff that a shoe's made of is not what's going to sell it any more! No! STYLE! SMARTNESS! APPEARANCE! That's what counts with the modern shoe-purchaser, Bob! But try an' tell your style department that. Why, I remember the time when all I had to do was lay out my samples down there in the lobby. Open up my order-book an' write out orders until my fingers *ached!* A *sales*-talk was not *necessary*. A store was a place where people sold merchandise and to sell merchandise the retail-dealer had to obtain it from the wholesale manufacturer, Bob! Where they get merchandise now I do not pretend to know. But it don't look like they buy it from wholesale dealers! Out of the air—I guess it materializes! Or maybe stores don't *sell* stuff any more! Maybe I'm living in a world of illusion! I recognize that possibility, too!

HARPER, *casually, removing the comic paper from his pocket*: Yep—yep. You must have witnessed some changes.

MR. CHARLIE: Changes? A mild expression. Young man—I have witnessed—a REVOLUTION!

Harper has opened his comic paper but Mr. Charlie doesn't notice, for now his peroration is really addressed to himself.

Yes, a *revolution!* The atmosphere that I *breathe* is not the same! Ah, well—I'm an old war-horse.

He opens his coat and lifts the multiple golden chains from his vest. An amazing number of watches rise into view. Softly, proudly he speaks.

Looky here, young fellow! You ever seen a man with this many watches? How did I *acquire* this many time-pieces?

Harper has seen them before. He glances above the comic sheet with affected amazement.

At every one of the annual sales conventions of the Cosmopolitan Shoe Company in St. Louis a seventeen-jewel, solid-gold, Swiss-movement Hamilton watch is presented to the ranking salesman of the year! Fifteen of those watches have been awarded to me! I think that represents something! I think that's *something* in the way of achievement! . . . Don't *you?*

HARPER: Yes, *siree!* You bet I *do*, Mistuh Charlie!

He chuckles at a remark in the comic sheet. Mr. Charlie sticks out his lips with a grunt of disgust and snatches the comic sheet from the young man's hands.

MR. CHARLIE: Young man—I'm talkin' to *you*, I'm talkin' for your *benefit*. And I expect the courtesy of your attention until I am through! I may be an old war-horse. I may have received— the last of my solid gold watches . . . But just the same—good manners are still a part of the road's tradition. And part of the *South's* tradition. Only a young peckerwood would look at the comics when old Charlie Colton is talking.

HARPER, *taking another drink*: Excuse me, Charlie. I got a lot on my mind. I got some business to attend to directly.

MR. CHARLIE: And directly you shall attend to it! I just want you to know what I think of this new world of yours! I'm not one of those that go howling about a Communist being stuck in the White House now! I don't say that Washington's been took over by Reds! I don't say all of the wealth of the country is in the hands of the Jews! I like the Jews and I'm a friend to the niggers! I *do* say *this*—however. . . . The world I knew is gone—gone—gone with the wind! My pockets are full of watches which tell me that my time's just about over!

A look of great trouble and bewilderment appears on his massive face. The rather noble tone of his speech slackens into a senile complaint.

All of them—pigs that was slaughtered—carcasses dumped in the river! Farmers receivin' payment *not* t' grow wheat an' corn an' *not* t' plant cotton! All of these alphabet letters that's sprung up all about me! Meaning—unknown—to men of my generation! The rudeness—the lack of respect—the newspapers full of strange items! The terrible—fast—dark—rush of events in the world! Toward what and where and why! . . . I don't pretend to have any knowledge of now! I only say—and I say this very humbly—I don't understand—what's happened. . . . I'm one of them monsters you see reproduced in museums—out of the dark old ages—the giant *rep*-tiles, and the dino-whatever-you-call-ems. But—I *do* know *this*! And I state it without any shame! Initiative—self-reliance—independence of character! The old sterling qualities that distinguished one man from another—the clay from the potters—the potters from the clay—are—

Kneading the air with his hands: How is it the old song goes? . . . Gone with the roses of *yesterday*! Yes—with the *wind*!

HARPER, *whose boredom has increased by leaps and bounds*: You old-timers make one mistake. You only read one side of the vital statistics.

MR. CHARLIE, *stung*: What do you mean by that?

HARPER: In the papers they print people *dead* in one corner and people *born* in the next and usually *one* just about levels *off* with the *other*.

MR. CHARLIE: Thank you for that information. I happen to be the godfather of several new infants in various points on the road. However, I think you have missed the whole point of what I was saying.

HARPER: I don't think so, Mr. Charlie.

MR. CHARLIE: Oh, yes, you have, young fellow. My point is this: the ALL LEATHER slogan is not what sells any more—not in shoes and not in humanity, neither! The emphasis isn't on quality. Production, production, yes! But out of inferior goods! *Ersatz*— that's what they're making 'em out of!

HARPER, *getting up*: That's your opinion because you belong to the past.

MR. CHARLIE, *furiously*: A piece of impertinence, young man! I expect to be accorded a certain amount of respect by whipper-snappers like you!

HARPER: Hold on, Charlie.

MR. CHARLIE: I belong to—tradition. I am a *legend*. Known from one end of the Delta to the other. From the Peabody hotel in Memphis to Cat-Fish Row in Vicksburg. Mistuh Charlie— *Mistuh Charlie!* Who knows *you?* What do *you* represent? A line of goods of doubtful value, some kike concern in the East! Get out of my room! I'd rather play solitaire, than poker with men who're no more solid characters than the jacks in the deck!

He opens the door for the young salesman who shrugs and steps out with alacrity. Then he slams the door shut and breathes heavily. The Negro enters with a pitcher of ice water.

NEGRO, *grinning*: What you shoutin' about, Mistuh Charlie?

MR. CHARLIE: I lose my patience sometimes. Nigger—

NEGRO: Yes, suh?

MR. CHARLIE: You remember the way it used to be.

NEGRO, *gently*: Yes, suh.

MR. CHARLIE: I used to come in town like a conquering hero!

Why, my God, nigger—they all but laid red carpets at my feet! Isn't that so?

NEGRO: That's so, Mistuh Charlie.

MR. CHARLIE: This room was like a *throne*-room. My samples laid out over there on green velvet cloth! The ceiling-fan *going*— now *broken!* And over here—the wash-bowl an' pitcher removed and the table-top *loaded* with *liquor!* In and out from the time I arrived till the time I left, the men of the road who knew me, to whom I stood for things commanding respect! Poker—continuous! Shouting, laughing—hilarity! Where have they all gone to?

NEGRO, *solemnly nodding*: The graveyard is crowded with folks we knew, Mistuh Charlie. It's mighty late in the day!

MR. CHARLIE: Huh!

He crosses to the window.

Nigguh, it ain't even late in the day any more—

He throws up the blind.

It's NIGHT!

The space of the window is black.

NEGRO, *softly, with a wise old smile*: Yes, suh . . . *Night*, Mistuh Charlie!

Curtain

IRWIN SHAW

Irwin Shaw's novels include *The Young Lions*, *The Troubled Air*, and *Two Weeks in Another Town*; he has written a number of plays, of which *Bury the Dead* is the best known, and is the author of two short-story collections, *Act of Faith and Other Stories* and *Mixed Company*.

THE EIGHTY-YARD RUN

The pass was high and wide and he jumped for it, feeling it slap flatly against his hands, as he shook his hips to throw off the halfback who was diving at him. The center floated by, his hands desperately brushing Darling's knee as Darling picked his feet up high and delicately ran over a blocker and an opposing linesman in a jumble on the ground near the scrimmage line. He had ten yards in the clear and picked up speed, breathing easily, feeling his thigh pads rising and falling against his legs, listening to the sound of cleats behind him, pulling away from them, watching the other backs heading him off toward the sideline, the whole picture, the men closing in on him, the blockers fighting for position, the ground he had to cross, all suddenly clear in his head, for the first time in his life not a meaningless confusion of men, sounds, speed. He smiled a little to himself as he ran, holding the ball lightly in front of him with his two hands, his knees pumping high, his hips twisting in the almost girlish run of a back in a broken field. The first halfback came at him and he fed him his leg, then swung at the last moment, took the shock of the man's shoulder without breaking stride, ran right through him, his cleats biting securely into the turf. There was only the safety man now, coming warily at him, his arms crooked, hands spread. Darling tucked the ball in,

From *Mixed Company* by Irwin Shaw (New York: Random House, 1941), pp. 13–28, Copyright 1941 by Irwin Shaw, reprinted by permission of Random House, Inc., and Jonathan Cape Ltd.

spurted at him, driving hard, hurling himself along, his legs pounding, knees high, all two hundred pounds bunched into controlled attack. He was sure he was going to get past the safety man. Without thought, his arms and legs working beautifully together, he headed right for the safety man, stiff-armed him, feeling blood spurt instantaneously from the man's nose onto his hand, seeing his face go awry, head turned, mouth pulled to one side. He pivoted away, keeping the arm locked, dropping the safety man as he ran easily toward the goal line, with the drumming of cleats diminishing behind him.

How long ago? It was autumn then, and the ground was getting hard because the nights were cold and leaves from the maples around the stadium blew across the practice field in gusts of wind, and the girls were beginnnig to put polo coats over their sweaters when they came to watch practice in the afternoons. . . . Fifteen years. Darling walked slowly over the same ground in the spring twilight, in his neat shoes, a man of thirty-five dressed in a double-breasted suit, ten pounds heavier in the fifteen years, but not fat, with the years between 1925 and 1940 showing in his face.

The coach was smiling quietly to himself and the assistant coaches were looking at each other with pleasure the way they always did when one of the second stringers suddenly did something fine, bringing credit to them, making their $2000 a year a tiny bit more secure.

Darling trotted back, smiling, breathing deeply but easily, feeling wonderful, not tired, though this was the tail end of practice and he'd run eighty yards. The sweat poured off his face and soaked his jersey and he liked the feeling, the warm moistness lubricating his skin like oil. Off in a corner of the field some players were punting and the smack of leather against the ball came pleasantly through the afternoon air. The freshmen were running signals on the next field and the quarterback's sharp voice, the pound of the eleven pairs of cleats, the "Dig, now *dig!*" of the coaches, the laughter of the players all somehow made him feel happy as he trotted back to midfield, listening to the applause and shouts of the students along the

sidelines, knowing that after that run the coach would have to
start him Saturday against Illinois.

Fifteen years, Darling thought, remembering the shower after
the workout, the hot water steaming off his skin and the deep
soapsuds and all the young voices singing with the water stream-
ing down and towels going and managers running in and out
and the sharp sweet smell of oil of wintergreen and everybody
clapping him on the back as he dressed and Packard, the captain, who took being captain very seriously, coming over to him
and shaking his hand and saying, "Darling, you're going to go
places in the next two years."

The assistant manager fussed over him, wiping a cut on his
leg with alcohol and iodine, the little sting making him realize
suddenly how fresh and whole and solid his body felt. The manager slapped a piece of adhesive tape over the cut, and Darling
noticed the sharp clean white of the tape against the ruddiness
of the skin, fresh from the shower.

He dressed slowly, the softness of his shirt and the soft
warmth of his wool socks and his flannel trousers a reward
against his skin after the harsh pressure of the shoulder harness
and thigh and hip pads. He drank three glasses of cold water,
the liquid reaching down coldly inside of him, soothing the
harsh dry places in his throat and belly left by the sweat and
running and shouting of practice.

Fifteen years.

The sun had gone down and the sky was green behind the
stadium and he laughed quietly to himself as he looked at
the stadium, rearing above the trees, and knew that on Saturday
when the 70,000 voices roared as the team came running out
onto the field, part of that enormous salute would be for him.
He walked slowly, listening to the gravel crunch satisfactorily
under his shoes in the still twilight, feeling his clothes swing
lightly against his skin, breathing the thin evening air, feeling
the wind move softly in his damp hair, wonderfully cool behind
his ears and at the nape of his neck.

Louise was waiting for him at the road, in her car. The top
was down and he noticed all over again, as he always did when

he saw her, how pretty she was, the rough blonde hair and the large, inquiring eyes and the bright mouth, smiling now.

She threw the door open. "Were you good today?" she asked.

"Pretty good," he said. He climbed in, sank luxuriously into the soft leather, stretched his legs far out. He smiled, thinking of the eighty yards. "Pretty damn good."

She looked at him seriously for a moment, then scrambled around, like a little girl, kneeling on the seat next to him, grabbed him, her hands along his ears, and kissed him as he sprawled, head back, on the seat cushion. She let go of him, but kept her head close to his, over his. Darling reached up slowly and rubbed the back of his hand against her cheek, lit softly by a street lamp a hundred feet away. They looked at each other, smiling.

Louise drove down to the lake and they sat there silently, watching the moon rise behind the hills on the other side. Finally he reached over, pulled her gently to him, kissed her. Her lips grew soft, her body sank into his, tears formed slowly in her eyes. He knew, for the first time, that he could do whatever he wanted with her.

"Tonight," he said. "I'll call for you at seven-thirty. Can you get out?"

She looked at him. She was smiling, but the tears were still full in her eyes. "All right," she said. "I'll get out. How about you? Won't the coach raise hell?"

Darling grinned. "I got the coach in the palm of my hand," he said. "Can you wait till seven-thirty?"

She grinned back at him. "No," she said.

They kissed and she started the car and they went back to town for dinner. He sang on the way home.

Christian Darling, thirty-five years old, sat on the frail spring grass, greener now than it ever would be again on the practice field, looked thoughtfully up at the stadium, a deserted ruin in the twilight. He had started on the first team that Saturday and every Saturday after that for the next two years, but it had never been as satisfactory as it should have been. He never had broken away, the longest run he'd ever made was thirty-five yards, and that in a game that was already won, and then that kid had come up from the third team, Diederich, a blank-faced German kid from Wisconsin, who ran like a bull, ripping lines to pieces Saturday after Saturday, plowing through, never getting hurt, never changing his expression, scoring more points, gaining more ground than all the rest of the team put together, making everybody's all-American, carrying the ball three times out of four, keeping everybody else out of the headlines. Darling was a good blocker and he spent his Saturday afternoons working on the big Swedes and Polacks who played tackle and end for Michigan, Illinois, Purdue, hurling into huge pile-ups, bobbing his head wildly to elude the great raw hands swinging like meat-cleavers at him as he went charging in to open up holes for Diederich coming through like a locomotive behind him. Still, it wasn't so bad. Everybody liked him and he did his job and he was pointed out on the campus and boys always felt important when they introduced their girls to him at their proms, and Louise loved him and watched him faithfully in the games, even in the mud, when your own mother wouldn't know you, and drove him around in her car keeping the top down because she was proud of him and wanted to show everybody that she was Christian Darling's girl. She bought him crazy presents because her father was rich, watches, pipes, humidors, an icebox for beer for his room, curtains, wallets, a fifty-dollar dictionary.

"You'll spend every cent your old man owns," Darling protested once when she showed up at his rooms with seven different packages in her arms and tossed them onto the couch.

"Kiss me," Louise said, "and shut up."

"Do you want to break your poor old man?"

"I don't mind. I want to buy you presents."

"Why?"

"It makes me feel good. Kiss me. I don't know why. Did you know that you're an important figure?"

"Yes," Darling said gravely.

"When I was waiting for you at the library yesterday two girls saw you coming and one of them said to the other, 'That's Christian Darling. He's an important figure.' "

"You're a liar."

"I'm in love with an important figure."

"Still, why the hell did you have to give me a forty-pound dictionary?"

"I wanted to make sure," Louise said, "that you had a token of my esteem. I want to smother you in tokens of my esteem."

Fifteen years ago.

They'd married when they got out of college. There'd been other women for him, but all casual and secret, more for curiosity's sake, and vanity, women who'd thrown themselves at him and flattered him, a pretty mother at a summer camp for boys, an old girl from his home town who'd suddenly blossomed into a coquette, a friend of Louise's who had dogged him grimly for six months and had taken advantage of the two weeks that Louise went home when her mother died. Perhaps Louise had known, but she'd kept quiet, loving him completely, filling his rooms with presents, religiously watching him battling with the big Swedes and Polacks on the line of scrimmage on Saturday afternoons, making plans for marrying him and living with him in New York and going with him there to the night clubs, the theaters, the good restaurants, being proud of him in advance, tall, white-teethed, smiling, large, yet moving lightly, with an athlete's grace, dressed in evening clothes, approvingly eyed by magnificently dressed and famous women in theater lobbies, with Louise adoringly at his side.

Her father, who manufactured inks, set up a New York office for Darling to manage and presented him with three hundred accounts, and they lived on Beekman Place with a view of the river with fifteen thousand dollars a year between them, because everybody was buying everything in those days, including ink. They saw all the shows and went to all the speakeasies and spent their fifteen thousand dollars a year and in the afternoons Louise went to the art galleries and the matinees of the more serious plays that Darling didn't like to sit through and Darling slept with a girl who danced in the chorus of *Rosalie* and with the wife of a man who owned three copper mines. Darling played squash three times a week and remained as solid as a stone barn and Louise never took here eyes off him when they were in the same room together, watching him with a secret, miser's smile, with a trick of coming over to him in the middle of a crowded room and saying gravely, in a low voice, "You're the handsomest man I've ever seen in my whole life. Want a drink?"

Nineteen twenty-nine came to Darling and to his wife and father-in-law, the maker of inks, just as it came to everyone else. The father-in-law waited until 1933 and then blew his brains out and when Darling went to Chicago to see what the books of the firm looked like he found out all that was left were debts and three or four gallons of unbought ink.

"Please, Christian," Louise said, sitting in their neat Beekman Place apartment, with a view of the river and prints of paintings by Dufy and Braque and Picasso on the wall, "please, why do you want to start drinking at two o'clock in the afternoon?"

"I have nothing else to do," Darling said, putting down his glass, emptied of its fourth drink. "Please pass the whisky."

Louise filled his glass. "Come take a walk with me," she said. "We'll walk along the river."

"I don't want to walk along the river," Darling said, squinting intensely at the prints of paintings by Dufy, Braque and Picasso.

"We'll walk along Fifth Avenue."

"I don't want to walk along Fifth Avenue."

"Maybe," Louise said gently, "you'd like to come with me to some art galleries. There's an exhibition by a man named Klee. . . ."

"I don't want to go to any art galleries. I want to sit here and drink Scotch whisky," Darling said. "Who the hell hung those goddam pictures up on the wall?"

"I did," Louise said.

"I hate them."

"I'll take them down," Louise said.

"Leave them there. It gives me something to do in the afternoon. I can hate them." Darling took a long swallow. "Is that the way people paint these days?"

"Yes, Christian. Please don't drink any more."

"Do you like painting like that?"

"Yes, dear."

"Really?"

"Really."

Darling looked carefully at the prints once more. "Little Louise Tucker. The middle-western beauty. I like pictures with horses in them. Why should you like pictures like that?"

"I just happen to have gone to a lot of galleries in the last few years . . ."

"Is that what you do in the afternoon?"

"That's what I do in the afternoon," Louise said.

"I drink in the afternoon."

Louise kissed him lightly on the top of his head as he sat there squinting at the pictures on the wall, the glass of whisky held firmly in his hand. She put on her coat and went out without saying another word. When she came back in the early evening, she had a job on a woman's fashion magazine.

They moved downtown and Louise went out to work every morning and Darling sat home and drank and Louise paid the bills as they came up. She made believe she was going to quit work as soon as Darling found a job, even though she was taking over more responsibility day by day at the magazine, interviewing authors, picking painters for the illustrations and covers, getting actresses to pose for pictures, going out for drinks with the right people, making a thousand new friends whom she loyally introduced to Darling.

"I don't like your hat," Darling said, once, when she came in in the evening and kissed him, her breath rich with martinis.

"What's the matter with my hat, Baby?" she asked, running her fingers through his hair. "Everybody says it's very smart."

"It's too damned smart," he said. "It's not for you. It's for a rich, sophisticated woman of thirty-five with admirers."

Louise laughed. "I'm practicing to be a rich, sophisticated

woman of thirty-five with admirers," she said. He stared soberly at her. "Now, don't look so grim, Baby. It's still the same simple little wife under the hat." She took the hat off, threw it into a corner, sat on his lap. "See? Homebody Number One."

"Your breath could run a train," Darling said, not wanting to be mean, but talking out of boredom, and sudden shock at seeing his wife curiously a stranger in a new hat, with a new expression in her eyes under the little brim, secret, confident, knowing.

Louise tucked her head under his chin so he couldn't smell her breath. "I had to take an author out for cocktails," she said. "He's a boy from the Ozark Mountains and he drinks like a fish. He's a Communist."

"What the hell is a Communist from the Ozarks doing writing for a woman's fashion magazine?"

Louise chuckled. "The magazine business is getting all mixed up these days. The publishers want to have a foot in every camp. And anyway, you can't find an author under seventy these days who isn't a Communist."

"I don't think I like you to associate with all those people, Louise," Darling said. "Drinking with them."

"He's a very nice, gentle boy," Louise said. "He reads Ernest Dowson."

"Who's Ernest Dowson?"

Louise patted his arm, stood up, fixed her hair. "He's an English poet."

Darling felt that somehow he had disappointed her. "Am I supposed to know who Ernest Dowson is?"

"No, dear. I'd better go in and take a bath."

After she had gone, Darling went over to the corner where the hat was lying and picked it up. It was nothing, a scrap of straw, a red flower, a veil, meaningless on his big hand, but on his wife's head a signal of something . . . big city, smart and knowing women drinking and dining with men other than their husbands, conversation about things a normal man wouldn't know much about, Frenchmen who painted as though they used their elbows instead of brushes, composers who wrote whole symphonies without a single melody in them, writers who knew all about politics and women who knew all about writers, the movement of the proletariat, Marx, somehow mixed up with five-dollar dinners and the best-looking women in America and fairies who made them laugh and half-sentences immediately understood and secretly hilarious and wives who called their husbands "Baby." He put the hat down, a scrap of straw and a red flower, and a little veil. He drank some whisky straight and went into the bathroom where his wife was lying deep in her bath, singing to herself and smiling from time to time like a little girl, paddling the water gently with her hands, sending up a slight spicy fragrance from the bath salts she used.

He stood over her, looking down at her. She smiled up at him, her eyes half closed, her body pink and shimmering in the warm, scented water. All over again, with all the old suddenness, he was hit deep inside him with the knowledge of how beautiful she was, how much he needed her.

"I came in here," he said, "to tell you I wish you wouldn't call me 'Baby.' "

She looked up at him from the bath, her eyes quickly full of sorrow, half-understanding what he meant. He knelt and put his arms around her, his sleeves plunged heedlessly in the water, his shirt and jacket soaking wet as he clutched her wordlessly, holding her crazily tight, crushing her breath from her, kissing her desperately, searchingly, regretfully.

He got jobs after that, selling real estate and automobiles, but somehow, although he had a desk with his name on a wooden wedge on it, and he went to the office religiously at nine each morning, he never managed to sell anything and he never made any money.

Louise was made assistant editor, and the house was always full of strange men and women who talked fast and got angry on abstract subjects like mural painting, novelists, labor unions. Negro short-story writers drank Louise's liquor, and a lot of Jews, and big solemn men with scarred faces and knotted hands who talked slowly but clearly about picket lines and battles with guns and leadpipe at mine-shaft-heads and in front of factory gates. And Louise moved among them all, confidently, knowing what they were talking about, with opinions that they listened to and argued about just as though she were a man. She knew everybody, condescended to no one, devoured books that Darling had never heard of, walked along the streets of the city, excited, at home, soaking in all the million tides of New York without fear, with constant wonder.

Her friends liked Darling and sometimes he found a man who wanted to get off in the corner and talk about the new boy who played fullback for Princeton, and the decline of the double wing-back, or even the state of the stock market, but for the most part he sat on the edge of things, solid and quiet in the high storm of words. "The dialectics of the situation . . . The theater has been given over to expert jugglers . . . Picasso? What man has a right to paint old bones and collect ten thousand dollars for them? . . . I stand firmly behind Trotsky . . . Poe was the last American critic. When he died they put lilies on the grave of American criticism. I don't say this because they panned my last book, but . . ."

Once in a while he caught Louise looking soberly and consideringly at him through the cigarette smoke and the noise and he avoided her eyes and found an excuse to get up and go into the kitchen for more ice or to open another bottle.

"Come on," Cathal Flaherty was saying, standing at the door with a girl, "you've got to come down and see this. It's down on Fourteenth Street, in the old Civic Repertory, and you can only see it on Sunday nights and I guarantee you'll come out of the theater singing." Flaherty was a big young Irishman with a broken nose who was the lawyer for a longshoreman's union, and he had been hanging around the house for six months on and off, roaring and shutting everybody else up when he got in an argument. "It's a new play, *Waiting for Lefty*; it's about taxi-drivers."

"Odets," the girl with Flaherty said. "It's by a guy named Odets."

"I never heard of him," Darling said.

"He's a new one," the girl said.

"It's like watching a bombardment," Flaherty said. "I saw it last Sunday night. You've got to see it."

"Come on, Baby," Louise said to Darling, excitement in her eyes already. "We've been sitting in the Sunday *Times* all day, this'll be a great change."

"I see enough taxi-drivers every day," Darling said, not because he meant that, but because he didn't like to be around Flaherty, who said things that made Louise laugh a lot and whose judgment she accepted on almost every subject. "Let's go to the movies."

"You've never seen anything like this before," Flaherty said. "He wrote this play with a baseball bat."

"Come on," Louise coaxed, "I bet it's wonderful."

"He has long hair," the girl with Flaherty said. "Odets. I met him at a party. He's an actor. He didn't say a goddam thing all night."

"I don't feel like going down to Fourteenth Street," Darling said, wishing Flaherty and his girl would get out. "It's gloomy."

"Oh, hell!" Louise said loudly. She looked coolly at Darling, as though she'd just been introduced to him and was making up her mind about him, and not very favorably. He saw her looking at him, knowing there was something new and dangerous in her face and he wanted to say something, but Flaherty was there and his damned girl, and anyway, he didn't know what to say.

"I'm going," Louise said, getting her coat. "I don't think Fourteenth Street is gloomy."

"I'm telling you," Flaherty was saying, helping her on with her coat, "it's the battle of Gettysburg, in Brooklynese."

"Nobody could get a word out of him," Flaherty's girl was saying as they went through the door. "He just sat there all night."

The door closed. Louise hadn't said good night to him. Darling walked around the room four times, then sprawled out on the sofa, on top of the Sunday *Times*. He lay there for five minutes looking at the ceiling, thinking of Flaherty walking down the street talking in that booming voice, between the girls, holding their arms.

Louise had looked wonderful. She'd washed her hair in the afternoon and it had been very soft and light and clung close to her head as she stood there angrily putting her coat on. Louise was getting prettier every year, partly because she knew by now how pretty she was, and made the most of it.

"Nuts," Darling said, standing up. "Oh, nuts."

He put on his coat and went down to the nearest bar and had five drinks off by himself in a corner before his money ran out.

The years since then had been foggy and downhill. Louise had been nice to him, and in a way, loving and kind, and they'd fought only once, when he said he was going to vote for Landon. ("Oh, Christ," she'd said, "doesn't *anything* happen inside your head? Don't you read the papers? The penniless Republican!") She'd been sorry later and apologized for hurting him, but apologized as she might to a child. He'd tried hard, had gone grimly to the art galleries, the concert halls, the bookshops, trying to gain on the trail of his wife, but it was no use. He was bored, and none of what he saw or heard or dutifully read made much sense to him and finally he gave it up. He had thought, many nights as he ate dinner alone, knowing that Louise would come home late and drop silently into bed without explanation, of getting a divorce, but he knew the loneliness, the hopelessness, of not seeing her again would be too much to take. So he was good, completely devoted, ready at all times to go anyplace with her, do anything she wanted. He even got a small job, in a broker's office, and paid his own way, bought his own liquor.

Then he'd been offered the job of going from college to college as a tailor's representative. "We want a man," Mr. Rosenberg had said, "who as soon as you look at him, you say, 'There's a university man.'" Rosenberg had looked approvingly at Darling's broad shoulders and well-kept waist, at his carefully brushed hair and his honest, wrinkle-less face. "Frankly, Mr.

Darling, I am willing to make you a proposition. I have inquired about you, you are favorably known on your old campus, I understand you were in the backfield with Alfred Diederich."

Darling nodded. "Whatever happened to him?"

"He is walking around in a cast for seven years now. An iron brace. He played professional football and they broke his neck for him."

Darling smiled. That, at least, had turned out well.

"Our suits are an easy product to sell, Mr. Darling," Rosenberg said. "We have a handsome, custom-made garment. What has Brooks Brothers got that we haven't got? A name. No more."

"I can make fifty, sixty dollars a week," Darling said to Louise that night. "And expenses. I can save some money and then come back to New York and really get started here."

"Yes, Baby," Louise said.

"As it is," Darling said carefully, "I can make it back here once a month, and holidays and the summer. We can see each other often."

"Yes, Baby." He looked at her face, lovelier now at thirty-five than it had ever been before, but fogged over now as it had been for five years with a kind of patient, kindly, remote boredom.

"What do you say?" he asked. "Should I take it?" Deep within him he hoped fiercely, longingly, for her to say, "No, Baby, you stay right here," but she said, as he knew she'd say, "I think you'd better take it."

He nodded. He had to get up and stand with his back to her, looking out the window, because there were things plain on his face that she had never seen in the fifteen years she'd known him. "Fifty dollars is a lot of money," he said. "I never thought I'd ever see fifty dollars again." He laughed. Louise laughed, too.

Christian Darling sat on the frail green grass of the practice field. The shadow of the stadium had reached out and covered him. In the distance the lights of the university shone a little mistily in the light haze of evening. Fifteen years. Flaherty even now was calling for his wife, buying her a drink, filling whatever bar they were in with that voice of his and that easy laugh. Darling half-closed his eyes, almost saw the boy fifteen years ago reach for the pass, slip the halfback, go skittering lightly down the field, his knees high and fast and graceful, smiling to himself because he knew he was going to get past the safety man. That was the high point, Darling thought, fifteen years ago, on an autumn afternoon, twenty years old and far from death, with the air coming easily into his lungs, and a deep feeling inside him that he could do anything, knock over anybody, outrun whatever had to be outrun. And the shower after and the three glasses of water and the cool night air on his damp head and Louise sitting hatless in the open car with a smile and the first kiss she ever really meant. The high point, an eighty-yard run in the practice, and a girl's kiss and everything after that a decline. Darling laughed. He had practiced the wrong thing, perhaps. He hadn't practiced for 1929 and New York City and a girl who would turn into a woman. Somewhere, he thought, there must have been a point where she moved up to me, was even with me for a moment, when I could have held her hand, if I'd known, held tight, gone with her. Well, he'd never known. Here he was on a playing field that was fifteen years away and his wife was in another city having dinner with another and better man, speaking with him a different, new language, a language nobody had ever taught him.

Darling stood up, smiled a little, because if he didn't smile he knew the tears would come. He looked around him. This was the spot. O'Connor's pass had come sliding out just to here . . . the high point. Darling put up his hands, felt all over again the flat slap of the ball. He shook his hips to throw off the halfback, cut back inside the center, picked his knees high as he ran gracefully over two men jumbled on the ground at the line of scrimmage, ran easily, gaining speed, for ten yards, holding the ball lightly in his two hands, swung away from the halfback diving at him, ran, swinging his hips in the almost girlish manner of a back in a broken field, tore into the safety man, his shoes drumming heavily on the turf, stiff-armed, elbow locked, pivoted, raced lightly and exultantly for the goal line.

It was only after he had sped over the goal line and slowed to a trot that he saw the boy and girl sitting together on the turf, looking at him wonderingly.

He stopped short, dropping his arms. "I . . ." he said, gasping a little, though his condition was fine and the run hadn't winded him. "I—once played here."

The boy and the girl said nothing. Darling laughed embarrassedly, looked hard at them sitting there, close to each other, shrugged, turned and went toward his hotel, the sweat breaking out on his face and running down into his collar.

Topics for Discussion
and Papers

(*C. P. Noyes and Malcolm Cowley*)

This book presents a wide diversity of opinions about *Death of a Salesman*. That so many things have been said about it is another testimony to its lasting vitality. No other American play of this century has provoked such long-continued arguments about its real nature. The principal questions it has raised are mentioned in Part II of the introduction. For instance, there is the great question of the genre to which it belongs. By any accepted definition of the word, is *Death of a Salesman* a tragedy? Is it better described as social criticism (and of what sort)? Or is it a play of still another species? How should the story of Willy Loman be interpreted? For the convenience of the student, these questions and others are here presented as topics suitable for research papers or class discussion.

It is well to repeat Gerald Weales's remark in the Introduction that he assembled this volume "in the hope that the reader will be forced to defend or to modify his own view of the play from the attacks or the seductions of critics who cannot see it that way at all." Before discussing or writing a paper on any of these topics, the student must form his own opinion, which should be based on a close reading of the play.

1. *Tragedy*. Aristotle defined tragedy as "the imitation of an action that is serious [or noble, or important] and also, as having magnitude, complete in itself; in language with pleasurable accessories . . . in a dramatic, not in a narrative form; with incidents arousing pity and fear, wherewith to accomplish

the catharsis of such emotions" (Ingram Bywater's translation of the *Poetics*). At a later point in the same treatise, Aristotle speaks of peripety (or reversal) and recognition or discovery (for which his term was "anagnorisis") as desirable elements in the plot of a tragedy. Critics for more than two thousand years have been explaining or expanding or altering his definition, as well as applying it to specific plays.

The discussion continues among the critics represented in the present volume, a number of whom base their judgment of *Death of a Salesman* on whether it complies, or fails to comply, with what they regard as the permanent laws of tragedy. Four of the essays to be consulted in this connection are "Arthur Miller: *Death of a Salesman*," by Bierman, Hart, and Johnson (perhaps the student's best way into the subject); "*Death of a Salesman*: A Note on Epic and Tragedy," by George de Schweinitz; "Arthur Miller and the Loss of Conscience," by William B. Dillingham; and, for a negative report on the play, "Attention Must Be Paid . . . " by Joseph A. Hynes. Arthur Miller himself enters the debate with his article "Tragedy and the Common Man," in which he rejects at least one of the Aristotelian requirements, and in which he also replies to a famous essay by Joseph Wood Krutch, "The Tragic Fallacy" (1929). Krutch had accepted Aristotle's definition, but had maintained that tragedies cannot be written in the modern era because we have ceased to believe that any human action is serious or "noble" in the Aristotelian sense.

Krutch's essay, not included in this volume, can be found in his book *The Modern Temper* (pp. 115–143 of the original edition). It is recommended to students who undertake library research. Four later books on tragedy are *Tragic Themes in Western Literature* by Cleanth Brooks (1955), *Spirit of Tragedy* by Herbert J. Muller (1956), the widely praised *Vision of Tragedy* by Richard B. Sewall (1959), and *Tragedy: Vision and Form*, edited by Robert W. Corrigan (1965).

Most of the arguments about *Death of a Salesman* as a tragedy come under four headings, each of which refers to one of the phrases in Aristotle's definition, and each of which gives rise to a number of questions. Any one of the headings might be discussed in a paper.

The first heading is the seriousness (or "nobility") and magnitude of *Death of a Salesman*. Is its action large or impressive enough to be an appropriate subject for a tragedy? Has Willy Loman the stature required of a tragic hero, so that we admire as well as pity him in his misfortune? Or, instead of being a hero, is he merely a victim and a deluded fool?

The second heading is discovery or recognition, which Aristotle seems to have regarded as the recognition of one character by another—e.g., that of Ulysses by his old nurse— but which modern critics prefer to interpret as the hero's recognition of his own nature. Does Willy achieve that tragic self-awareness at the end of the play, or does he die still clinging to an illusion? (See Bierman, Hart, and Johnson; also Harold Clurman's "The Success Dream on the American Stage"; also Arthur Miller's "Introduction to *Collected Plays*," where he argues that if Willy had not been aware of his separation from enduring values, "he would have died contentedly while polishing his car.") Is Miller's argument persuasive? If we refuse to accept it, might we say that Biff is the character who undergoes a tragic self-recognition ("I know who I am, kid")? Or do we question that recognition (See Gerald Weales's Introduction) on the ground that it may be only another of the Loman illusions?

The third heading is language, which Aristotle took for granted should be poetry, and which he said should be provided "with pleasing accessories." Is the language of *Death of a Salesman* effective in presenting the story? Is it too colloquial and prosaic for a tragedy? Does it rise to tragic heights, and if so, in which passages?

The fourth heading is the emotions evoked from the audience. Aristotle says that a tragedy should arouse pity and fear, but in such a way as to accomplish a catharsis or purging of such emotions. In regard to *Death of a Salesman*, some critics object that there is no purging of emotions and that the Requiem is designed to draw tears from the audience instead of raising it to a tragic exaltation. Is the objection justified, or is it pedantic? Does the Requiem leave us with "an image of peace," as it would seem that Miller intended it to do? Miller believes, contrary to Aristotle, that "the tragic feeling is invoked in us when we are in the presence of a character who is ready to lay down his life, if need be, to secure one thing—his sense of personal dignity" ("Tragedy and the Common Man"). Would this statement apply to all tragedies? What is the actual feeling, tragic or otherwise, aroused in a student by the play?

2. *Social Criticism.* Obviously *Death of a Salesman* implies some vigorous criticisms of American society, but critics do not agree as to what the criticisms are or exactly what they mean. Is the play a general attack on capitalism? That is how Eleanor Clark interprets it (see "Old Glamour, New Gloom"). She says, "It is, of course, the capitalist system that has done Willy in; the scene in which he is brutally fired after some forty years with the firm comes straight from the party line literature of the 'thirties." Are there other scenes and characters that conflict with Miss Clark's interpretation?

Harold Clurman ("The Success Dream on the American Stage") says, "The death of Arthur Miller's salesman is symbolic of the breakdown of the whole concept of salesmanship inherent in our society." Is this a true statement? Or is there as much truth in the opposite view expressed by A. Howard Fuller of the Fuller Brush Company ("A Salesman Is Everybody")— namely, that Willy's failure is caused by a personal delusion that not only ruined his private life but made him a bad salesman?

It is clear that Willy is the victim of false values imposed on him by the dream of success. By contrast, what does the play suggest as true values?

3. *Other Readings.* Of these there is a considerable variety. Raymond Williams ("The Realism of Arthur Miller") says that Miller has rediscovered an important type of social drama in which "every aspect of personal life is radically affected by the quality of the general life, yet the general life is seen at its most important in completely personal terms." Daniel E. Schneider ("Play of Dreams") interprets *Death of a Salesman* as an Oedipal drama, a conflict between father and sons (combined with another conflict between older and younger brothers). William Wiegand ("Arthur Miller *and the Man Who Knows*") says that *Death of a Salesman* and Miller's other plays as well are concerned with a failure of communication: someone (Biff in this case) painfully acquires knowledge, but is unable to impart it to others in time to prevent a catastrophe. Gerald Weales ("Arthur Miller: Man and His Image") views the work through "his heroes and through the concern of each, however inarticulate, with his identity—his name." Which of these interpretations seems most persuasive to the student? If satisfied with none of them, can he offer his own statement of what *Death of a Salesman* is about?

4. *Technique.* Several critics suggest that the technique of *Death of a Salesman* is a combination of naturalism and expressionism, the latter being defined (*Columbia Encyclopedia*) as a "term used to describe works of art in which the representation of nature is distorted to communicate an inner vision." Thus, Raymond Williams says that the play "is an expressionist reconstruction of naturalist substance, and the result is not hybrid but a powerful particular form." Aided by Miller's "Introduction to *Collected Plays*," the student should try to see for himself how the play is put together. How does Miller solve the dramatist's age-old problem of imparting information about the past lives of his characters? How does he manage the transition from naturalistic scenes in the Loman house to expressionistic re-enactments of Willy's past life? How did Jo Mielziner ("Designing a Play") embody the expressionist ele-

ments of the play in his stage design? How effectively is music employed as a background for the action?

5. *The Characters*. In the Greek sense of the word, Willy Loman is clearly the protagonist of the drama—that is, the principal actor—but many critics question whether he is the character with whom the audience tends to identify. As principal keys to the drama, Biff, Linda, and even the younger son, Happy, are each mentioned in one or more of the essays in this volume. George Ross ("*Death of a Salesman* in the Original") reviews a Yiddish production of the play and reports that the audience regarded it as, "after all, a play about a Jewish *family*" (his italics). For that special audience, the family as a whole— not any of its members, even the father—became the protagonist of the drama. Because of these conflicting views, a paper might answer the question, "Which of the characters most engages your sympathy, and why?"

Two of the more important questions regarding Willy Loman (his tragic stature and his recognition of, or failure to recognize, his own nature) were suggested in the paragraphs dealing with *Death of a Salesman* as a tragedy. But other questions remain, and one of them is whether Willy is a universal figure. Ivor Brown ("As London Sees Willy Loman") regards him as peculiarly American and says that Englishmen find it hard to sympathize with his fate. On the other hand, Miller himself (see his statement quoted in the Fuller essay) says that "in the deeper, psychological sense, [Willy] is Everyman who finds he must create another personality in order to make his way in the world. . . . "

Are we to agree with Miller (and with Gerald Weales's essay "Arthur Miller: Man and His Image") that the central conflict in the play is between Willy's identity as a person and the false image of himself demanded by society? And what of Willy's identity as a father? "He has achieved a very powerful piece of knowledge," Miller says in the "Introduction to *Collected Plays*," "which is that he is loved by his son and has been embraced by him and forgiven. In this sense he is given his existence, so to speak—his fatherhood, for which he has always striven and which until now he could not achieve." How important to an understanding of the play is the father-son conflict, particularly as analyzed by Dr. Schneider?

As for the many questions suggested by Biff, Linda, Happy, and the minor characters, there is no purpose in repeating them here. Gerald Weales states them in the last pages of his introduction.

6. *Symbols.* A symbol in a work of art is a word or object, given unusual stress, that suggests a range of meanings beyond the surface meaning. Jo Mielziner, the stage designer of the original production, was very conscious of symbols at work in the play. He says in "Designing a Play" that a pattern of leaves projected on the backdrop "was an integral part of the Salesman's life story, and had to be an easily recognized symbol of the springtime of that life." The two heavy sample cases that bowed the Salesman's shoulders when he carried them were so effective as symbols of age and discouragement that they were used on posters advertising the play. What other objects shown on the stage or mentioned in the dialogue seem to have a symbolic value? What range of meanings does each of them symbolize?

7. *Analogues.* The selections at the end of the book offer subjects for papers. For example, compare Willy Loman with R. J. Bowman in Eudora Welty's "Death of a Traveling Salesman." Or compare him with Mr. Charlie Colton in Tennessee Williams' "The Last of My Solid Gold Watches." Or compare Biff with the hero of Irwin Shaw's "The Eighty-Yard Run."

8. *Critical Appraisal.* For a more ambitious paper, the student might attempt an original critical appraisal of *Death of a Salesman,* using the essays in this book to support his points, but making sure that his principal argument depends on his own reading of the play and, for a longer paper, of others by the same author.

Bibliography

WORKS BY ARTHUR MILLER

The entries here are listed chronologically under genre. There is no attempt to be all-inclusive, particularly in the listing of articles and interviews. Material which deals too narrowly with plays other than *Death of a Salesman* has been passed over.

PLAYS (The date in parentheses is of the first production)

The Pussycat and the Expert Plumber Who Was a Man, in *One Hundred Non-Royalty Radio Plays,* William Kozlenko, ed. New York: Greenberg, 1941, pp. 20–30.

William Ireland's Confession, in *One Hundred Non-Royalty Radio Plays,* pp. 512–521.

That They May Win (1943), in *The Best One-Act Plays of 1944,* Margaret Mayorga, ed. New York: Dodd, Mead, 1945, pp. 45–59.

The Man Who Had All the Luck (1944), in *Cross-Section,* Edwin Seaver, ed. New York: L. B. Fischer, 1944, pp. 486–552. (This is a pre-production version of the play.)

Grandpa and the Statue, in *Radio Drama in Action,* Erik Barnouw, ed. New York: Farrar and Rinehart, 1945, pp. 267–281.

The Story of Gus, in *Radio's Best Plays,* Joseph Liss, ed. New York: Greenberg, 1947, pp. 303–319.

All My Sons (1947), in *Collected Plays,* New York: Viking, 1957, pp. 57–127.

An Enemy of the People (1950). New York: Viking, 1951. (Adaptation of Henrik Ibsen's play.)

The Crucible (1953), in *Collected Plays,* pp. 223–330

A Memory of Two Mondays (1955), in *Collected Plays,* pp. 331–376.

A View from the Bridge (1955). New York: Viking, 1955.

A View from the Bridge (1956). Revised version; in *Collected Plays,* pp. 377–439.

After the Fall (1964). New York: Viking, 1964.

Incident at Vichy (1964). New York: Viking, 1965.

FICTION AND REPORTAGE

Situation Normal. New York: Reynal and Hitchcock, 1944.
Focus. New York: Reynal and Hitchcock, 1945.
The Misfits. New York: Viking, 1961.
I Don't Need You Any More, Stories by Arthur Miller. New York: Viking, 1967.

ARTICLES

"Arthur Miller on 'The Nature of Tragedy,'" *The New York Herald Tribune,* March 27, 1949, V, pp. 1, 2.
"University of Michigan," *Holiday,* XIV (December 1953), 68–70, 128–143.
"A Modest Proposal for Pacification of the Public Temper," *Nation,* CLXXIX (July 3, 1954), 5–8.
"A Boy Grew in Brooklyn," *Holiday,* XVII (March 1955), 54–55, 117–124.
"On Social Plays," Preface to *A View from the Bridge.* New York: Viking, 1955, pp. 1–15.
Untitled comment, *World Theatre,* IV (Autumn 1955), 40–41.
"The Family in Modern Drama," *The Atlantic Monthly,* CXCVII (April 1956), 35–41.
"The Shadow of the Gods," *Harper's,* CCXVII (August 1958), 35–43.
"Bridge to a Savage World," *Esquire,* L (October 1958), 185–190.
"The Playwright and the Atomic World," *Tulane Drama Review,* V (June 1961), 3–20.
"Lincoln Repertory Theatre—Challenge and Hope," *The New York Times,* January 19, 1964, II, pp. 1, 3.
"Our Guilt for the World's Evil," *The New York Times Magazine,* January 3, 1965, pp. 10–11, 48.
"The Role of P.E.N.," *Saturday Review,* XLIX (June 4, 1966), 16–17.

INTERVIEWS

Schumach, Murray, "Arthur Miller Grew Up in Brooklyn," *The New York Times,* February 6, 1949, II, pp. 1, 3.
Samachson, Dorothy and Joseph, in *Let's Meet the Theatre.* New York: Abelard-Schuman, 1954, pp. 15–20.
United States House of Representatives, Committee on Un-American Activities, Investigation of the Unauthorized Use of United States Passports, Part 4, June 21, 1956. Washington: United States Government Printing Office, November, 1956. ("Interview" is not exactly the word for this item.)

Allsop, Kenneth, "A Conversation with Arthur Miller," *Encounter*, XIII (July 1959), 58–60.

Brandon, Henry, "The State of the Theatre: A Conversation with Arthur Miller," *Harper's*, CCXXI (November 1960), 63–69.

Gelb, Barbara, "Question: 'Am I My Brother's Keeper?' " *The New York Times*, November 29, 1964, II, pp. 1, 3.

Gruen, Joseph, "Portrait of the Playwright at Fifty," *New York*, October 24, 1965, pp. 12–13.

Carlisle, Olga, and Rose Styron, "The Art of the Theatre II: Arthur Miller, an Interview," *Paris Review*, X (Summer 1966), 61–98.

WORKS ABOUT ARTHUR MILLER

The entries here, listed alphabetically, include books, articles, and reviews about *Death of a Salesman* or about Miller in general with some relevance to that play.

Bentley, Eric, *In Search of Theater*. New York: Knopf, 1953.

Bettina, Sister M., S.S.N.D., "Willy Loman's Brother Ben: Tragic Insight in *Death of a Salesman*, *Modern Drama*, IV (February 1962), 409–412.

Broussard, Louis, *American Drama: Contemporary Allegory from Eugene O'Neill to Tennessee Williams*. Norman, Okla.: University of Oklahoma Press, 1962.

Chiari, J., *Landmarks of Contemporary Drama*. London: Herbert Jenkins, 1965.

Couchman, Gordon W., "Arthur Miller's Tragedy of Babbitt," *Educational Theatre Journal*, VII (October 1955), 206–211.

"Death of a Salesman: A Symposium," *Tulane Drama Review*, II (May 1958), 63–69.

Downer, Alan S., *Fifty Years of American Drama, 1900–1950*. Chicago: Regnery, 1951.

Driver, Tom F., "Strength and Weakness in Arthur Miller," *Tulane Drama Review*, IV (May 1960), 105–113.

Dusenbury, Winifred L., *The Theme of Loneliness in Modern American Drama*. Gainesville, Fla.: University of Florida Press, 1960.

Eissenstat, Martha Turnquist, "Arthur Miller: a Bibliography," *Modern Drama*, V (May 1962), 93–106.

Fleming, Peter, "The Theatre," *Spectator*, CLXXXIII (August 5, 1949), 173.

Foster, Richard J., "Confusion and Tragedy: The Failure of Miller's Salesman," in *Two Modern American Tragedies*, John D. Hurrell, ed. New York: Scribners, 1961, pp. 82–88.

Ganz, Arthur, "The Silence of Arthur Miller," *Drama Survey*, III (Fall 1963), 224–237.

Gibbs, Wolcott, "Well Worth Waiting For," *New Yorker*, XXIV (February 19, 1949), 58–60.

Gould, Jean, *Modern American Playwrights*. New York: Dodd, Mead, 1966.

Gross, Barry Edward, "Peddler and Pioneer in *Death of a Salesman*," *Modern Drama*, VII (February 1965), 405–410.

Hagopian, John V., "The *Salesman*'s Two Cases," *Modern Drama*, VI (September 1963), 117–125.

Hewes, Henry, "Opening Up the Open Stage," *Saturday Review*, XLVI (August 24, 1963), 34.

"Higher Call," *New Yorker*, XXV (March 26, 1949), 21. (Interview with Lee J. Cobb.)

Hogan, Robert, *Arthur Miller*. Minneapolis: University of Minnesota Press, 1964. (Pamphlets on American Writers, Number 40.)

Huftel, Sheila, *Arthur Miller: The Burning Glass*. New York: Citadel, 1965.

Hynes, Joseph A., "Arthur Miller and the Impasse of Naturalism," *South Atlantic Quarterly*, LXII (Summer 1963), 327–334.

Jackson, Esther Merle, "*Death of a Salesman*: Tragic Myth in the Modern Theatre," *CLA Journal*, VII (September 1963), 63–76.

Kennedy, Sighle, "Who Killed the Salesman?" *Catholic World*, CLXXI (May 1950), 110–116.

Kitchin, Laurence, *Mid-Century Drama*. London: Faber & Faber, 1960.

Krutch, Joseph Wood, "Drama," *Nation*, CLXVIII (March 5, 1949), 283–284.

Krutch, Joseph Wood, "Modernism" *in Modern Drama*, Ithaca, N.Y.: Cornell University Press, 1953.

Lawrence, Stephen A., "The Right Dream in Miller's *Death of a Salesman*," *College English*, XXV (April 1964), 547–549.

Lewis, Allan, *The Contemporary Theatre*, New York: Crown, 1962.

McAnany, Emile G., S.J., "The Tragic Commitment: Some Notes on Arthur Miller," *Modern Drama*, V (May 1962), 11–20.

McCarthy, Mary, *Sights and Spectacles: Theatre Chronicle, 1937–1956*. New York: Meridian Books, 1957.

Morgan, Frederick, "Notes on the Theatre," *Hudson Review*, II (Summer 1949), 272–273.

Moss, Leonard, "Arthur Miller and the Common Man's Language," *Modern Drama*, VII (May 1964), 52–59.

Nathan, George Jean, *The Theatre Book of 1948–1949*. New York: Knopf, 1949.

New York Theatre Critics' Reviews, X (1949), 358–359.

Newman, William J., "Arthur Miller's Collected Plays," *Twentieth Century*, CLXIV (November 1958), 491–496.

Parker, Brian, "Point of View in Arthur Miller's *Death of a Salesman*," *University of Toronto Quarterly*, XXXV (January 1966), 144–157.

Phelan, Kappo, "Death of a Salesman," *Commonweal*, XLIX (March 4, 1949), 520–521.

Popkin, Henry, "Arthur Miller: The Strange Encounter," *Sewanee Review*, LXVIII (January–March, 1960), 34–60.

Shea, Albert A., "Death of a Salesman," *Canadian Forum*, XXIX (July 1949), 86–87.

Siegel, Paul N., "Willy Loman and King Lear," *College English*, XVII (March 1956), 341–345.

Sievers, W. David, *Freud on Broadway: A History of Psychoanalysis and the American Drama*. New York: Hermitage House, 1955.

Steinberg, M. W., "Arthur Miller and the Idea of Modern Tragedy," *Dalhousie Review*, XL (Fall 1960), 329–340.

Sylvester, Robert, "Brooklyn Boy Makes Good," *Saturday Evening Post*, CCXXII (July 16, 1949), 26–27, 97–100.

Tynan, Kenneth, *Curtains*. New York: Atheneum, 1961.

Warshow, Robert, "The Liberal Conscience in 'The Crucible,'" *Commentary*, XV (March 1953), 265–271.

Weales, Gerald, "Arthur Miller's Shifting Image of Man," *The American Theater Today*, Alan S. Downer, ed. New York: Basic Books, 1967.

———, "Plays and Analysis," *Commonweal*, LXVI (July 12, 1957), 382–383.

Welland, Dennis, *Arthur Miller*. New York: Grove Press, 1961.

West, Paul, "Arthur Miller and the Human Mice," *Hibbert Journal*, LXI (January 1963), 84–86.